A Defect of Character

A Novel

A Defect of Character

A Novel

Pamela Kay Hawkins

ISBN: 1929257112
ISBN 13: 9781929257119
Library of Congress Control Number: 2014922178
Pamela Kay Hawkins Publishing
Broken Arrow, OK

To all the creative people in my life, especially Ed and my sons Addison, Jonathan, and Christopher, for believing in me.

PROLOGUE

NOVEMBER 1924

S ome kind of Great White Hope, at least to his client, was how Jake Witherspoon viewed himself. His former Harvard Law School classmates would have sneered as much as the locals at his defending a Negro of intelligence, much less one called "Slo-Joe"—this last not only because the man shuffled when he walked, but also because Slo-Joe's brain had stalled somewhere in preadolescence. Why he had taken the case mystified even Jake at times, and today, when court ran overlong and he wanted to get back to Hulet before the weather turned foul, he cursed himself for a soft-hearted fool and wished he'd never heard Slo-Joe's name.

Outside the courthouse windows, flakes of snow floated down from the flat, darkening sky, occasionally whirling in mini-tornadoes as the wind spun them around in the light from the building. A freak snowstorm is just what I needed today, Jake thought, as he adjusted the scarf more securely around his neck and turned up the collar of his overcoat. Where was his taxi anyway? Surely Little Rock had more than one cab. Jake reached in his pocket for his gloves and put them on. He heard the sound of footsteps in the hall and looked up to see a scrubwoman pushing a cart laden with cleaning supplies. Where was that damned taxi? Jake picked up his briefcase and opened the courthouse door. A blast of icy wind lifted the brim of his hat; he grabbed it with his free hand just in time. The wind made his eyes water, and he ducked his chin deeper into his collar. He stood at the top of the stairs, braced against the wind, and looked down the street. He breathed a sigh of relief as the lights of a taxicab appeared around a corner. At last. Jake adjusted his grip on the briefcase and began the descent to street level. Halfway down the stairs, another man galloped past him, ran to the door of the cab as it pulled to the curb and got in.

"Wait! That's my taxi!" Jake ran down the stairs, almost slipping on the frosted steps, and reached the curb in time to see his cab disappear down a side street.

"Damn!"

"Mr. Witherspoon?"

Jake turned to see who was calling him. Mary Landower stood waving from the courthouse doorway, her long legs showing beneath her fashionably short coat.

"Mr. Witherspoon!"

Now what? He waved to let her know he'd heard her and wearily climbed the stairs back to where his assistant stood waiting. It was nearly six o'clock: so much for the promise he'd made Laura that he'd be home before dark. By the time he called another cab and checked out of the hotel, he'd be lucky if he arrived home before ten, providing the snow didn't get any worse. At least it was Friday, and the court would be in recess all next week for the Thanksgiving holidays.

"It's too cold out here," Jake said, opening the large door. "Let's go in."

Mary nodded, pulling her wool coat tighter around her and preceding him through the open door: "Gosh! I didn't realize it was snowing! It wasn't even supposed to get cold." Mary shivered and rubbed her bare hands together.

Brown hair framed her face beneath her cloche, and Jake thought fleetingly that bobbed hair suited her, though he wouldn't want Laura to cut hers. Watching Laura unpin her hair at night, seeing the waterfall of black silk pour down her back to her waist, was one of his favorite things. But flapper styles seemed to suit Mary, even to the boyish cut of her dropped waist dresses and rolled down hose, and he had to admit her legs deserved to be shown off.

Jake took off his hat and put his heavy briefcase down on the marble floor: "Somehow, the change in the weather doesn't surprise me at all. Well, what's the matter now?" He'd grown used to things going wrong in this case. He braced himself.

"Oh, nothing's wrong. I just wondered if you needed a ride. I saw you miss your cab."

"Bless you, Miss Landower! Have I told you how wonderful you are?" Jake put his arm around her shoulders and gave her a quick hug.

"Not that I remember," she said. Jake noticed a slight flush in her cheeks.

"Well, tonight, you are a lifesaver!"

"I do what I can," Mary said, looking down and pulling out a pair of gloves from her coat pocket. She put them on and tucked a stray wisp of hair under her hat. "Shall we go? My car's in back."

The snow was falling heavily when they reached the lot. A slick dusting of snow covered the pavement, and Jake took Mary's arm to steady her as they crossed to her car.

Mary slid behind the wheel, while Jake went around to the other side and got in beside her.

"Keep your fingers crossed," Mary said, "it's been acting up lately." (To Jake's relief the car started at once.)

Mary pulled out onto the main street. The car fishtailed slightly as she made her turn—"Gosh, it's slicker than I thought. I'm afraid I'm going to have to make a quick stop before this snow gets too bad and I can't get out again. I hope you don't mind."

Jake looked at his watch: "I am in kind of a hurry. Could you take me to the hotel first? I need to call my wife and tell her I've been delayed."

"Would you mind calling from the drugstore? I have to pick up some medicine for my roommate before they close. It's on the way to your hotel, and I'd hate to have to double back."

"Well, I wouldn't want you to have to do that," Jake said, and silently cursed the man who'd stolen his taxi.

"Thanks. I'll hurry."

Jake looked out the window as they drove on in silence. The snowflakes seemed misnamed as their weight and frequency increased. It was more like driving in the middle of a snowball fight. His hopes of reaching Hulet at all tonight, much less at a reasonable hour, dimmed as it grew more and more difficult to see.

The pharmacist stood on the other side of the door, locking up as they arrived. Mary hopped out and ran to the door. "Please, let us in Mr. Keeney," she yelled through the door. "I need Janie's medicine, and my friend needs to use your phone."

Jake saw the man shake his head, but he opened the door. Mary motioned for Jake to come on, so he followed her into the warmth of the store.

"May I use your telephone?" Jake asked, looking around the store. "It's not local, but I'll pay for the charges."

"Help yourself," the man said without much enthusiasm, while he went behind the counter to get Mary's order. "It's there in the corner."

Jake went to the telephone booth and placed his call. Laura answered after three rings.

"Jake, where are you? I was getting worried."

"I'm still in Little Rock. The judge kept us late, and it's snowing here."

"Snowing? It's cloudy here and cold, but it isn't snowing. Is it bad?"

Jake could hear his son and daughter playing in the background, could see their chubby faces in his mind. "It's not good." Jake paused. "I'm on my way to the hotel now, but if it gets much worse, I might not be able to get home tonight."

"Oh, Jake..." (The disappointment in her voice was palpable.)

"I know. Believe me, I want to be home as much as you want me there."

"It's just that you haven't been home since the trial started—"

"Laura, it isn't as if I'd planned it this way." He tried to take the irritation out of his voice. It wasn't her fault either. He took a deep breath. "Look, I'll try my best to get out tonight—"

"No." Laura paused. "If it's that bad, I wouldn't want you on the road. I'd be worried sick."

"Well, we'll see how it goes. Is everything all right there?"

"We're fine." (Jake could almost see her straightening up and putting a smile on her face as she talked.) "Teddy's been down a bit with a cold today, but he's up and going again. Sarah's playing tea party with him in the parlor right now. She loves the set you sent back with Ben last week." (Laura was trying to sound cheerful, but Jake could hear the strain in her voice and his irritation vanished.) "I just miss you, that's all."

"I miss you, too, honey—more than you know. I promise I'll make up for lost time when I get home. If I can't get out tonight, I'll leave first thing in the morning and be home before you know it. Don't forget, we have all of next week together before I have to come back. This trial won't last forever." He heard her chuckle.

"Promise?"

"I promise. It will be over before you know it, and I'll settle down to a quiet, ordinary practice in Hulet and come home to you every night. You'll get sick of seeing me."

"I can't imagine that ever happening..." Laura's voice trailed off and a pang of guilt ran through him. "Jake, I know I'm being silly, but I do wish you'd let Mike finish that trial. I'm worried about you. That last letter—"

"Laura, I told you, it's just some crank trying to frighten me off. There's really nothing to worry about. I'm fine."

"I know, but things are getting nasty—"

Fear shot through him. "Has something happened?" His stomach felt like a rock had dropped into it.

"No. It's just the talk around town."

"But you're all right?"

"I'm fine. I'm just worried about you."

Jake breathed again. "Look, honey, why don't you call Mother and stay with her tonight? You know how she loves having you and the kids—"

"Oh, I don't know. I just fed the children, and Dan said he might drop by—"

"Well, call him and tell him you're spending the night at my mother's. He can come over tomorrow after I get home. I'd worry less if you and the children were at the farm."

"All right. I suppose I would feel better. This house seems so empty when you're not here...so does the bed."

Jake laughed, relieved. "Keep talking like that and I might be home sooner than you expect. Listen, I've got to go. My ride's ready. Go on over to Mother's, and I'll see you before you know it. I love you."

"I love you, too. Hurry home, honey."

"I'll be there as soon as I can. You can count on it." He waited for her to hang up and replaced the receiver.

Mary was waiting by the front door. Jake left some money with the proprietor to cover the call, and they left.

"Everything all right at home?" Mary asked as they inched toward the hotel.

The roads were getting treacherous; Jake was grateful that he didn't have to drive to Hulet tonight: "Fine."

"Are you going to try to drive home?" Mary's hands gripped the wheel firmly as she negotiated a corner. The car slid a few feet sideways before straightening out.

"Not tonight. It seems pretty slick."

"It's like driving on ice." Her voice shook.

Jake strained to see his hotel's lighted marquee through the blowing snow: "How far away from here do you live?" he asked.

"A few miles. Not far."

"Look, it's almost a blizzard outside, and it's my fault that you're out in this," Jake said. "Why don't you come into the hotel when we get there and wait for this to let up a bit. It's bound to blow over soon, and while we're waiting, I'll spring for dinner."

"I don't know...Janie will wonder what's keeping me."

"You can call her from the hotel. She wouldn't want you to risk your neck in this storm. Consider it an order from your boss."

"Do you really think this will let up?" Mary sounded doubtful.

"There's my hotel!"

"Where?" Mary asked, straining to see through the snow. "I don't see anything."

"There, just ahead on the left," Jake said, pointing. "See? You can just make out the marquee."

"I see it!"

"Better slow down a bit...There's a spot over there. Just pull over into that space. We can walk the rest of the way, and I don't think you'll have any trouble getting out again."

Mary pulled over to the place he indicated and shut off the motor. She was shaking.

Jake reached over and patted her hand: "We made it. Now let's go get you warm and have some dinner."

While Mary called her roommate, Jake checked his messages at the desk. Besides a message to call Laura, there was nothing. He smiled to himself, glad that he'd already called, that for once he'd managed to anticipate her. Mary joined him just as he turned to look for her. He checked their coats and led her to the dining room. It was Friday night, and most of the patrons were dressed in evening clothes. An orchestra played dance music at one end of the room, and several couples were on the dance floor. The maître d'hôtel showed them to a good table, near enough to the dance floor to be convenient, but far enough away from other tables to have privacy.

"This is a nice change," Jake said, looking around the room. "I usually have meals in my room."

"I'm afraid I'm not really dressed for the occasion."

"Don't be silly. You look wonderful."

A waiter brought the menu. Jake gave him their order.

"Would you like to dance while we're waiting?" Jake asked.

"I'm afraid I'm not a very good dancer."

Jake pushed back his chair and went around to help her out of hers. "Well, I am. Come on. It'll warm us up."

He took Mary's hand and led her to the dance floor. The music was a waltz, and he put his arm around her waist and guided her effortlessly around the floor. After the dance, he led her back to the table.

"You lied to me, Mary," he said as he pushed her chair in. "You dance quite well."

Mary barely picked at her food. Her hands shook so she could hardly hold the fork without spilling something. She couldn't believe she was actually here, alone with Jacob Witherspoon, and that he seemed glad. All night long he'd been dropping hints, but until he'd held her on the dance floor, she'd been afraid she'd misinterpreted his advances. Now she was certain he wanted her as much as she wanted him. Ever since that day two months ago when he'd interviewed her, she'd been crazy about him. How could she help it? He was the handsomest man she'd ever seen, tall and strong, with lapis lazuli eyes that looked like they saw through to her very thoughts. Just being in the same room with him set her heart pounding in a way the other boys she'd known never had, but then Jacob Witherspoon wasn't any boy. From what she'd picked up, he'd been a powerful lawyer in Washington, D.C., had even argued cases before the Supreme Court, and had won most of them. Evidently, he'd moved back to Arkansas when his father died to take care of his mother's affairs and had given up a thriving practice to do it. Gossip said he'd taken on Slo-Joe's defense in the murder case pro bono for the publicity it afforded, but she didn't believe it. Most of the lawyers she knew wouldn't want the kind of publicity associated with defending a Negro charged with murdering a white man. No, Jacob Witherspoon seemed genu-inely convinced of Slo-Joe's innocence; he was certainly mounting the best possible defense. That he tried so hard, for someone so unworthy of his at-tention, appealed to her. He was married, of course, and she respected his self-control, so until tonight she'd kept her eyes down and had tried to keep her mind on her work when he was around. But tonight...tonight anything was possible...

"A penny for your thoughts," Jake said, amused at the faraway look on Mary's face. To his surprise, she blushed.

"I was just thinking that I'd like to dance again," Mary said, her voice barely audible over the music.

"Wonderful. I was thinking the same thing," Jake said. Just then, the music stopped and a pretty female joined the orchestra. The opening bars of

"Who's Sorry Now?" filled the air, and the woman began singing in a mournful alto. "Shall we?"

In his arms, Mary seemed different somehow. She seemed more relaxed, softer. She smiled up at him, and he thought once more how pretty she looked in her short haircut, how it seemed to set off her eyes. She had beautiful brown eyes and incredibly long lashes. She faltered, and he drew her closer to steady her as they danced. The soft strains of the music pushed him along as he led her slowly around the dance floor. Mary inched closer, until her head almost rested on his shoulder. As he stepped into a turn, the soft warmth of her thigh brushed against his leg. His head swam with the scent of her perfume, her closeness. His hand pressed gently against her lower back; he felt the warmth of her skin beneath her dress and drew her closer. She did not resist, but moved closer until he could feel the round firmness of her breasts pressed against his chest. A slow fire began in his groin....

The music stopped. Mary slowly separated from him. Her eyes held his. The band began playing "Way Down Yonder in New Orleans," and the spell broke. Relieved, Jake walked her back to their table and flagged a waiter. "More coffee, Mary? Dessert?" Jake asked in a tone he hoped sounded normal.

"No, thank you." Her voice sounded deflated. "I suppose I'd better be getting home....The snow's probably stopped by now."

Jake signed the ticket and handed it to the waiter. "Do you happen to know if it's still snowing?"

"Yes sir, it's snowing all right. It's a regular blizzard. You can't see your hand in front of your face." The waiter glanced at Jake's signature on the check. "Will that be all, Mr. Witherspoon?"

"Yes, that's all." (The waiter bowed and left.) "Well, Mary, you heard him. I really don't think you ought to drive in this."

"What choice do I have? I have to get home." She reached for her bag.

"I'll get you a room—"

"Oh, I couldn't let you do that! You've already bought me dinner... and a room is so expensive. I'll be all right."

Jake reached across the table and patted her hand. "I wouldn't feel right letting you drive two feet in this weather. The firm will pay for the room, so don't worry about that. Call your roommate and tell her the weather's gotten worse, so you've decided to stay here for the night."

"But what will she think?"

"That you're too smart to drive in a blizzard. What else could she think?"

Mary blushed: "That you and I—"

"Nonsense! Believe me, I have no ulterior motives in asking you to stay," Jake said and wondered if it were true. "You'll have your own room—on a different floor from mine, if you wish. Everything will be perfectly respectable, I assure you."

Mary smiled shyly: "But I don't even have a toothbrush."

Jake laughed. "OK, I'll spring for a toothbrush, too."

"If I stay, can we dance a little longer?"

She sounds just like a little girl, Jake thought, and somehow the thought eased his mind. "All right, but just a little longer."

"Then I'll stay."

Jake waved to the waiter and ordered more coffee; then he left her, reminding her to call her roommate, while he arranged for her room. On the way back, he stopped at the hotel shop and purchased a toothbrush and a small tin of toothpowder. He returned to the table with his sack of provisions and waited for her.

When she rejoined him in the dining room, Mary seemed more confident, more self-assured. He wondered at the change in her. He gave her her room key, which she dropped into her bag, and her toiletries sack. They chatted about the trial over coffee and danced to a few of the slower selections. The tension Jake felt vanished as they talked, and he found himself wondering why he'd felt uneasy earlier. She was a sweet kid, and he was glad he didn't have to worry about her driving home in this storm. They ordered dessert to keep their waiter happy while they camped at their table and listened to the music. When the last dance of the evening was announced, Jake asked Mary to dance again. She smiled and led the way to the dance floor. As she walked, the fabric of her dress twisted provocatively, revealing the rounded contours of her buttocks, the slender silhouette of her hips, the bare translucent skin behind her knees as she moved in front of him. He found himself unable to keep from staring and suddenly wished they'd stayed at the table. He waited for her to turn around, and when she did, he held her gingerly as they swayed to the music, held her almost at arm's length, afraid of the urgency her nearness created. He tried to tell himself the attraction was not there, but when Mary tilted her head and looked up into his eyes, he saw his own desire mirrored in her face, and his resolve evaporated along with his fear.

They said nothing as they went up to her floor. Alone in the hall, she turned to him and asked him where his room was in a voice that sounded breathy, as if she were barely breathing.

"Down the hall and around the corner."

"Could I see it?"

He knew he should refuse, take her to her door and leave, but the danger intoxicated him as much as the girl beside him. Nothing will happen, he told himself. I won't let things get out of hand.

Mary trembled beside him while he found his key and opened the door. The room was dark. For a moment, he was blind: "Wait a second. I'll turn on a light." He felt his way across the room and found a lamp, while Mary stood by the closed door. He turned the switch and a soft glow filled a corner of the room: "That's better."

"It's cold in here," she said, her voice husky. "Do you have anything to drink?"

"Water?"

"I was thinking of something stronger, if you have it—something to take the chill off."

Jake nodded and disappeared into the bathroom. He came back with two glasses and a silver flask. She was sitting on the edge of his bed. He poured a shot of amber liquid into both glasses and handed her one. "Hope you like bourbon."

"I've never had it before." Mary took a tentative sip. "It's not bad." She held her breath and emptied her glass. A cozy, giddy feeling spread through her. "Aren't you going to join me?"

Jake heard the invitation in her voice and saw it in her eyes. He downed his drink and put his glass down on the nightstand: "I think it's time you went to your own room."

"Don't send me away…"

"Mary—"

"Just one more drink, then I'll go, I promise."

"One more. But then you'll have to go." He poured them another drink.

"Why don't you sit down beside me?" she said. "Come on. I won't bite."

She reached for his hand, and he joined her on the bed. Her nearness tantalized him. He played with his drink, heard the intake of her breath, felt her staring at him, willing him to touch her. It was a kind of game, a competition for control that enticed and excited him. She wanted him to make love to her—there was no longer any doubt—and his body yearned for her flesh with an intensity he'd not felt in a very long time. It was exhilarating. He sat there on the bed, every nerve taut, aware of her thigh an inch away from his own, knowing she'd win if he let her stay much longer. He looked at her, wondering how much he could take without losing the game.

Jake finished tossing the last of his clothes into his suitcase and buckled the straps, grateful that he had already packed most of his stuff before leaving for court that morning. He checked the closet and the bathroom to make sure he hadn't left anything behind and hurried out to his car. It was still snowing, but at least it was no longer a blizzard. Ice glazed the windows, and he cursed the time wasted scraping it off. He had to get home to Laura and the children. Guilt and fear grappled in the arena of his belly as he pushed the starter and nothing happened. He tried again: nothing. He sat still, waiting to try again, controlling the urge to keep at it. His hands stung with the cold, and he stuffed them in his pockets. His right glove encountered a stiff ball of paper wadded in his coat pocket, and he pulled it out. It was the phone message from Laura the desk clerk had given him earlier that evening. The sight of her name written on the note filled him with self-loathing, and he writhed inwardly. It wasn't that she might find out—the likelihood of that was fairly remote—it was that he knew he had betrayed her. It didn't matter that he hadn't had intercourse; what mattered was that he'd wanted to. What he'd felt was lust: sheer, sexual desire. He couldn't even lie to himself that he cared anything about the girl. He pushed the starter again; the engine fluttered encouragingly and died. Then he noticed the time of Laura's call: she'd called after they'd talked. Jake looked at his watch and tried to make out the time: two o'clock in the morning. Much too late to call her, even if she weren't at his mother's...

"Come on car; I have to get home!" Jake gritted his teeth and pushed the starter again. He held his breath as the motor sputtered, then kicked in. *Thank God! With a little luck, I'll be home before dawn.*

Laura picked up the kitchen telephone and gave the operator Dan's number: "Danny? Laura...No, nothing's wrong. I just wanted to tell you that I'm taking the children to Jake's mother's, so we won't be home tonight.... No, he's been delayed. He called a few minutes ago, and there's a snowstorm in Little Rock, so he won't be home until sometime tomorrow.... Don't be silly! He's not neglecting me! The judge kept them longer than he expected, and he got caught in a snowstorm...." (Laura fidgeted in her chair, wishing she could just hang up.)

"Danny, look, I'm too tired to go into all of that right now. Teddy's been down with a cold, and we've been cooped up in this house all day.... Well, I wish he hadn't taken this case, too, but you know how Jake is, and he's convinced his client isn't guilty.... What did you expect him to do? Turn his back on the poor man? It'd be like turning his back on a child.... Danny, I don't want to argue with you! Jake doesn't take those threats seriously, and neither do I. Jake says whoever's behind this would be stupid to try anything, because it would just reinforce his case that Slo-Joe was framed. Besides, he's found some new evidence, and he's convinced he's going to get an acquittal anyway, so they'd just be tipping their hand.... No, of course I don't know what he's found. He doesn't tell me those things, but he says it proves that Slo-Joe didn't murder Clarence Morgan.... No, I don't want you to come over.... I'm not in any danger. I know how the Klan operates, and they don't scare me. Besides, I told you, I'm going to spend the night at Mrs. Witherspoon's, and Jake will be home in the morning, so you see, I'm perfectly safe....

"You worry too much. Jake takes good care of us, and if he thought we were in any danger, he wouldn't have left us alone.... I don't know why you feel that way about him! He's never done anything to you, and he's the best thing that ever happened to me.... If you're going to keep that up, I'm going to hang up this telephone! You forget, Danny, I love my husband, and he loves me, so I'm not going to listen anymore.... I know you're sorry. You're *always* sorry.... I don't know. I might call you tomorrow after Jake gets home. Good-bye, Danny."

Laura sighed and looked at the receiver in her hand before replacing it on the hook. *Why is he always like that? I'm glad he's not coming over tonight!* She picked up the phone again to call her mother-in-law to ask about coming over, but put it back down. She thought about packing the children's clothes and taking Teddy out in the cold. The thought wore her out. As much as she liked Sarah Witherspoon, she liked sleeping in her own house more. The children would be more comfortable at home, too. She smiled and, instead of calling Jake's mother, told the operator to ring Jake's hotel in Little Rock. The clerk who answered said Jake hadn't arrived yet, but he'd be happy to leave a message that she'd called. Laura smiled as she hung up the phone. She knew her husband, and if there were any way he could be home tonight, he would, and she'd be there, waiting for him.

Laura stood up and walked into the parlor where her children sat on the floor. Five-year-old Sarah was trying to get her baby brother to hold a cup and saucer steady without much success. Teddy squealed as the empty cup tumbled onto the floor.

"Mama, he won't do it right! He always drops it!" Sarah's face was indignant.

"Honey, he's not even two, yet. What do you expect?" Teddy's face was flushed, and she felt his forehead. He was a little warm. She picked him up and went to the Boston rocker in the corner. "I'll tell you what. Let me rock him a little while, until he falls asleep, then I'll play tea party with you. Would you like that?"

Sarah looked at her tea things scattered on the floor and sighed. "No, all the tea's cold now."

Laura stifled a laugh and hugged Teddy's body closer to her own. She looked down at the top of his head and felt his hot breath on her neck. "I think he's almost asleep."

Sarah got up and came over to the rocker and looked at her brother's face. "His eyes are almost shut, but he's still peeping at me."

Laura stopped rocking and got up. "I think I can put him down in his crib, and he'll go right to sleep. Why don't you put up your tea set, and when I come down, I'll read you a story."

"All right, Mama," Sarah said and ran to pick up her things, while Laura took Teddy upstairs to the nursery.

When she returned, Sarah was sitting on the sofa, her feet just hitting the edge of the cushion, holding her favorite book in her lap. Laura's heart melted at the sight of her first born, and she sat down beside her and hugged her close to her side. "Let's see now. Where were we?"

"The wizard told Dorothy she had to kill the wicked witch." Sarah's blond curls brushed against Laura's hand as she opened the book.

"Oh, yes. Here we are." Laura read until she felt Sarah's head drop against her shoulder. She closed the book and tried not to wake her daughter as she put it on the end table. Sarah stirred and opened her eyes.

"Mama?"

"Yes, sweetie?"

"When's Daddy coming home?"

"He'll be home tomorrow when you wake up. Come on, now. It's time to go to bed."

"May I sleep with you tonight? Teddy snores."

Laura laughed and hugged her daughter. "I suppose so. But just for to-night. Come on, let's go upstairs."

Sarah was fast asleep when Laura finished taking her bath. Laura put on her nightgown and tiptoed across the hall to the nursery. Teddy was fast asleep on his tummy, thumb stuck securely in his mouth. Laura covered him with the blanket he'd kicked off in his sleep and felt his forehead once more. His skin felt cool, but she stood beside his crib, listening to his regular breathing. Then she lowered the side of the crib and kissed him on the cheek before raising it again and returning to her room. She slipped into bed beside her sleeping daughter and reached for her book. She read until her eyes no longer focused on the page, then turned out the light. *I wonder why Jake didn't call me back?* she thought, before closing her eyes. Then she smiled and snuggled down into the covers. *Because, silly, he's on the road, trying to get home.*

Just how long he'd been on the road, Jake couldn't tell, but thought he must be close to Hulet by now: things had a familiar feel to them, even though visibility was not much better than before it stopped snowing. All during the long drive, he'd tried to figure out why he'd done what he'd done. Laura. Since the day he'd met her, he'd never desired anyone else; he loved her more than his own life. Jake ran his hand through his hair, wishing he'd wake up and find out it was just a dream, that this entire evening was just a figment of his imagination. He'd come close to destroying everything that mattered to him, and it shook him to his very being. How could he face her, knowing what he'd done? Even now, the memory of Mary's body sent desire racing through him. He wanted out of his skin. Jake shook his head, trying to erase the softness of Mary's lips from his mind, trying to focus on Laura, but just as her face appeared, she blurred, faded, leaving only the night's blackness behind.

He drove on, staring at the patch of road shining in his headlights. She read him so well, how could he keep her from sensing this? *Dear God, please don't let her find out. I swear, whatever you want to do to me is all right, but don't let her know. She means everything to me. Everything.* Desperation tore at him. *Please, God, just let me hold her again!*

The storm had been one step ahead of him all night, and though the snow had stopped, the wind had piled the snow in low drifts along the road. The sky grew lighter ahead of him; dawn would break soon. Finally, Jake saw the road to his parents' farmhouse where his family slept. He turned, but decided to go on to his own house. No sense waking everybody at this hour. No, it would be better for everyone, if he just went home and got some sleep. Maybe things would look different in the morning. At least, he'd have a chance to compose himself before seeing them. He pulled back onto the main road and drove toward his house on the other side of Hulet.

Laura woke suddenly, thinking she'd heard something downstairs. She lay in the dark, waiting for her mind to clear, straining to listen, her heart pounding. Sarah turned in her sleep; her soft, regular breathing seemed loud in the silence. Laura reached for the gun Jake kept in the nightstand drawer and slipped slowly out of bed, trying hard not to disturb her daughter. Sarah didn't stir. She paused at the door, opening it slowly and peering into the dark of the hallway. She moved quietly, her bare feet making no sound on the carpet runner. She stopped at the nursery door and looked in. Teddy lay in his crib, snoring quietly. She breathed easier, telling herself it was probably her imagination. She moved to the staircase, holding the gun in front of her, ready to shoot if she had to, and stood still at the landing, listening to the stillness of the night. She shivered in her nightgown, wishing she'd remembered her robe. Then she saw the light. It seemed to be coming from the direction of the kitchen. She moved quietly down the stairs, hugging the wall and searching the floor below for any sign of movement. At the bottom of the stairs, she saw the smoke. She ran toward the kitchen. Flames were everywhere. She dropped the gun and ran back up the stairs. She ran into the nursery and grabbed Teddy out of his crib. He screamed and started crying while she hurriedly wrapped the blanket around him and ran back toward her bedroom. Smoke was drifting slowly up the stairs behind her.

"Sarah! Sarah, wake up!" She shook her daughter roughly with her free hand.

"Mommy!" Sarah woke up, wide-eyed with fright. "Mommy, what's wrong?"

"Sarah, come on! We've got to get out of the house right now!" Smoke was coming in through the bedroom door. Laura grabbed Sarah's arm and tried to drag her out of the bed.

Sarah started crying. "You're hurting me, Mommy!"

Laura coughed as the smoke grew thicker. "Come on!" she grabbed Sarah's hand and held it tightly in hers as she went back into the hall. The smoke was thick now. Teddy and Sarah were crying, becoming more frightened as they sensed Laura's fear as she moved swiftly to the stairs. Flames shot through the staircase wall. Sarah screamed and tried to pull free of Laura's grasp.

"Sarah! We have to go down. It's the only way out!" She pulled at her daughter's hand, but Sarah pulled free and ran back down the hall, screaming in panic. Laura ran after her, yelling for her to come back, but Sarah ran into the nursery and shut the door. Laura turned the knob and followed her, Teddy wriggling and howling in her arms. Sarah sat on the floor, crying, scooting away from Laura as she approached. Laura stopped and fought the panic that threatened to overtake her. She forced herself to remain calm, and reached out her hand to Sarah:

"Come on, sweetie. Everything's going to be all right, but we have to get out of the house. Hold Mommy's hand. That's a good girl. Don't be afraid. We're going to be all right."

Sarah quieted and stood up. The smoke choked her, and she coughed violently. "I can't breathe!" Laura heard the panic in her voice, and she hugged Sarah to her side.

"I know, sweetie. That's why we have to get out." She walked Sarah out of the nursery and back into the hall. "Just think how nice it will be outside in the fresh air. Besides, you have to help me, Sarah. Teddy's too little to help."

She talked to Sarah all the way to the stairs. The flames were higher now, but they could make it if they stayed next to the railing:

"Sarah, you have to stay right by Mommy. Hold onto my nightgown and don't let go. We'll be outside before you know it. Ready? That's my girl." Teddy coughed violently against her shoulder, and she put her hand on his back and patted him. "Shh, baby. It's going to be all right."

She started down the stairs, watching for any place that seemed like it might give way. The fire spread rapidly in their path and attacked the front door. Laura could hear the sizzle of paint as it bubbled in the heat. She felt Sarah's grip tight against her thigh and stepped down to the next level. They were only a few stairs from the bottom now, and the fire hadn't reached as far as the parlor. If they could just get to the parlor, she could break a window, and they could crawl out.

Suddenly Sarah screamed and let go of her gown, streaking past her down the few remaining steps. "Mommy! Mommy! Help me, Mommy! I'm burning!"

"Don't run, Sarah! Wait!" Laura ran after her, holding Teddy as tightly as possible to her chest. "Go into the parlor!"

But Sarah ran to the front door, screaming as the handle burned her hands, sobbing incoherently, her hair and nightgown on fire. Laura ran after her, shouting, telling her to roll on the floor, trying to grab her, but it was impossible holding the baby.

"Jake! Oh dear God! Jake!"

Dread filled him as he rounded the curve and saw the flames. He floored the car. At a safe distance from the house, he pulled the emergency brake, jumped out of the car, and ran toward the burning structure. *Thank God, Laura and the children are safe!* Then he heard the screams...

CHAPTER ONE

AUGUST 1929

Jake woke abruptly, drenched in sweat, and strained to listen above the drumbeat of his heart. A board creaked in the hallway outside his bedroom, and he froze. He waited in the darkness, hardly daring to breathe. He felt underneath the bed for the baseball bat he kept there and, finding it, crept to his door and listened. He heard only the muffled ticking of the grandfather clock in the parlor. A light breath of air lifted the hem of the window curtain by his bed and fanned the moist hair on the back of his neck, cooling him for the briefest moment. Out in the yard a cricket chirped and leaves rustled softly in the summer breeze. Everything seemed normal. He turned the doorknob and opened the door a crack, then wider, and ventured into the hall. Grasping the bat firmly, Jake tiptoed to his mother's room and peeked in. She slept undisturbed, the soft sounds of her breathing audible in the eerie stillness of the night. He closed her door and went into the kitchen. All was in order; the back door firmly locked. He went back down the hallway and checked the bathroom, the dining room, and the parlor. The front door was locked. Everything was as it should be. Jake lowered his bat, walked back to his room, and sat on the edge of his bed. Someone had screamed; he was sure of it.

In the parlor, the grandfather clock chimed the quarter hour, rousing him. Jake picked up his watch from the nightstand and struck a match: four-fifteen. He shook the match and tossed it into the ashtray. The night was almost over; dawn would come soon. He cursed himself for being a light sleeper and the clock for waking him, though he knew the clock was not to blame. It happened every morning, this strange wakefulness just before dawn, the fear that began in his stomach and clutched at his brain. He told himself that there was nothing to be afraid of, that he was a grown man and much too old to lie in bed like some frightened child who imagines a bogey-man under the bed.

Fear grew in the pit of his stomach and spread upward, squeezing his heart and throat so that he only gulped the air. He pulled the sheet over his head and waited. He could sense the rooster in the barnyard, stretching his neck, getting ready to crow. Sweat trickled down the sides of his face; he squeezed his eyes shut and braced himself. The cock's crow split the air, jarring him like the sound did every morning. The knot in his stomach loosened. He lay there, rag limp, as the last discordant notes of the long, scratchy, doodledoo died, and the first rays of the sun reached over the countryside in long fingers of light.

He could breathe again. Tension melted from his neck and shoulders; he threw the sheet back, relishing the smell of fresh air and the return to normality that daylight brought. He sat up and pulled the blue gingham curtains aside and watched as the day began, watched as darkness blended to dove gray, watched as purple brightened first to lavender then pink and culminated at last in the brilliant gold of the rising sun, looking fresh-washed and scrubbed and ready for the day's business.

"Mother, I've got your breakfast," Jake said, pushing the door open with his foot: a tray occupied his hands.

"Jacob?" Sarah Witherspoon's thin voice made no more impression than a pinprick.

"Now, who else would it be?" Jake set her tray on the round, chintz-draped table by the windows facing her bed, the ones with the southern exposure she was so fond of, and pulled back the heavy drapes. Morning leapt into the room, startling the darkness into corners and behind furniture. Jake turned around and smiled broadly. "Look at that sun!"

"No, thank you. I'm already half blind."

"Too bright?" Jake adjusted the curtains, "Better?"

"Much."

"It's going to be a beautiful day. If you're feeling up to it, maybe Annie and I could move you out on the porch this morning—before it gets too hot. Give you something different to look at for awhile. You'd like that wouldn't you?"

"I might at that. Is Annie here?"

"Not yet, but she'll be here any minute. Here," Jake said, retrieving the tray and walking toward the bed. The mahogany four-poster enveloped his mother, but he tried not to notice how tiny and helpless she seemed. "Let me get these pillows fixed so you can sit up and eat." Jake set the tray down on the bed and helped her sit up, ignoring the lack of weight in his arms as he raised her, then carefully placed the sides of the tray over the small lump made by her quilt-covered legs: "There, that's more like it."

Sarah's milk-blue eyes followed her son's movements as she waited patiently through his ministrations. Sometimes Jacob looked so much like his father it confused her. He was slender and tall like Robert, nearly six feet, and he held himself as straight as any pine tree on the place. His hair, the color of polished jet, and his skin—smooth and clear for all its exposure to the hot Arkansas sun—he inherited from her Irish father. But when she looked into Jacob's eyes, she saw only her husband. Robert's eyes had been deep chestnut, and Jacob's were surprisingly blue, the color of a bluebird's wing; nevertheless, it was Robert she saw behind the blueness of Jacob's eyes—his intelligence, his openness, his kindness, his curiosity and love of life. She saw her son's jaw tighten as he lifted her in the bed, heard the timbre of concern in his conversation. *Jacob's a good boy*, she thought, *but he worries too much*. Her forehead wrinkled with the effort thought took. It would be so much easier on him when she passed on and he didn't have to look after her anymore. Sarah sighed deeply.

"Are you all right, Mother?" Jake asked. It was unlike her to show any discomfort or to complain, although he knew she was eaten up inside, and the doctor said she was in considerable pain.

Sarah smiled and some of the old twinkle returned to her eyes. "I'm fine, Jacob. You worry too much."

"Come by it naturally, I guess," Jake said and returned her smile.

"Well, you certainly didn't get it from me!"

"Must've been Dad, then."

Sarah wagged one bony, crooked finger at him. "Don't you blame——"

The door creaked, and Annie Jackson peered around the corner.

Jake smiled broadly at the huge black woman in the doorway: "Come on in, Annie. You're just in time to save me from one of Mother's lectures. She's in a feisty mood. Watch your step with her today."

Annie chuckled and walked in. "Y'all g'on den, Miztah Jake. If she give me too much trouble, I sit on her."

Sarah looked horrified. "You do, and you'll squash me like a bug."

"Den yuh'd bes' b'have an finish dat brekfuss, Miz Sarah. Doc Livsey say yuh ain't been eatin' enough t' keep a squirrel alive."

"Humph. After all these years, I thought you'd learn some manners, but you're hopeless." Sarah turned toward her son, a hint of mischief in her eyes. "Jacob, can't you find someone else to sit with me? Someone who has some respect for an old lady?"

Jake laughed. "Mother, you know I tried, but no one in this town will come sit with you because you're so mean and ornery. Annie's the only one who'll put up with you."

"Now dat's de trufe, Miztah Jake," Annie said, sitting down in a plank-bottomed chair by the round table and folding her arms. "So, Miz Sarah, I guess yuh'd jus bes' mind what I says an stop tryin' t' git me riled up."

Sarah grinned and obediently took a bite of her breakfast.

"Annie, I was telling Mother that it looks like a good day for her to sit on the porch. What do you think?"

Annie glanced at Sarah. "I tells yuh what, Miztah Jake. If Miz Sarah 'cides she want t' go out, I git Bill t' come an hep me t' move her. Y'all git on now. We be jus fine heah."

"OK, if you're sure you can handle things..."

"If you don't mind, I'm not some thing you 'handle'," Sarah said with something like her old authority. "Now scoot! How do you expect me to eat anything with all this going on? If I need anything, Annie'll get it for me."

Jake leaned over the bed and kissed Sarah's forehead. "All right, then, I'm going. I'll see you both this evening."

Sarah reached for his hand and squeezed it briefly. "You're a good son, Jacob. I love you."

"I love you, too, Mother," Jake said, smiling down at her. He took her hand and brought it to his lips before returning it. "I'll see you tonight."

Early every weekday morning, Jake walked the dirt road from his mother's farm to downtown Hulet and began his rounds. His first stop was Wilson's Farm Supply, a feed-and-seed owned and operated by Elmer Wilson. Jake entered the store and walked past the sacks of grain and seed to the back. Elmer sat at his desk recording invoices.

"Good morning, Elmer," Jake said and flipped the page on Elmer's desk calendar.

"Mornin', Jake," Elmer said, not looking up from his books.

"I'll see you tomorrow," Jake said.

Elmer raised his hand in reply as Jake left.

A few early customers stood outside on the boardwalk in front of the yellow Dutch door of Jenny's Cafe, waiting for it to open. They exchanged brief greetings with Jake, as he opened the closed door and walked in.

Jenny Schumacher heard the cheerful jingle of the bell above the door and quickly untied her apron. She smoothed her auburn hair with her hand and hurried into the dining room.

"Good morning, Jake," Jenny said. "Do you have time for a cup of coffee?" She knew he wouldn't stop, but it gave her something to say each morning. Ever since Will had died two years ago, she'd had her eye on Jake Witherspoon. He was a handsome man, somewhere in his late thirties she figured, but it was hard to tell how old he was, and she was too embarrassed to ask anyone.

"Can't stop right now, Jenny," Jake said, crossing off August 22 on the Wilson's advertising calendar that hung on the wall behind the cash register. He opened the door to leave and the brass bell rung merrily. Jake smiled at her over his shoulder as he crossed the threshold, "I might come by after work this afternoon, though, if that's all right."

"Why, that would be fine," Jenny stammered. He'd never taken her up on the offer before, and she was as flustered as she would've been if he'd failed to show up to mark off the days. She didn't have too much time to dwell on it, however, for her customers were filing in, doffing hats, and finding their seats.

"How about some breakfast, Jenny?" Sam Cross called from across the room. "I could sure use some coffee about now."

"Right away, Sam," Jenny said, walking briskly behind the long counter and getting the coffeepot and some mugs at about the same time Jake opened the door to Doc Livsey's waiting room.

"Morning, Doc," Jake called, as he walked through the empty waiting room back to Livsey's private office. Doc's calendar sat on top of a large oak rolltop. Jake tore off the top page and tossed it into the wastepaper basket beside the desk. Doc came into his office just as Jake turned to leave.

"How's your mother doing?" Doc asked, sitting down in the leather chair in front of his desk.

Jake smiled: "Feisty as ever, thanks. Go on out to the farm and see for yourself."

"I might just do that if I have a chance."

"She'd love the company," Jake said. "Wish I could stay and chat, but—"

"I understand. You go on, now." (Jake smiled and left the office.) Doc watched the door close, then rocked his chair back on its legs, folded his hands over his stomach, closed his eyes, and was immediately asleep.

Doc's office was the last door on the boardwalk. Jake stepped down into the street, crossed it, and climbed the three brick stairs to the boardwalk that marked the second block of his rounds. Wickham's General Store was next.

Silas was sweeping his portion of the boardwalk when he heard Jake's footsteps. He stopped and leaned against the doorway, his hands draped limply across the broom handle.

"Mornin', Jake," Silas said.

"Silas." Jake nodded and walked past him to the back of the store and marked off the date on the calendar. The store smelled of cheddar, crackers and pickles, smoked meats, spices, and candy—friendly smells that made him want to stop and talk the day away with Silas. He never would, of course; too much had happened. He glanced at the clock that hung on the wall as he walked out: "Clock's off, Silas."

"That a fact..." Silas pondered the information as he watched Jake cross the street to the bank. "Fast or slow?" he shouted.

"Slow," Jake hollered without turning around.

Silas pushed his hand through the unruly shock of iron-gray hair and leaned the broom up against the doorframe. He walked around the butcher's block to the clock and took it down. Sure enough, the clock needed rewinding.

Jake finished with the other calendars on his route, then cut through the front lawn of the public library. He climbed the stairs to the front door that opened and closed behind him as if by magic at exactly eight o'clock.

Billy Wiggins watched from the newspaper office across the square from the library, hands stuffed in the pockets of his knickers. Jake Witherspoon didn't come into the newspaper office, because it wasn't on his route. The place didn't have a calendar anyway. There had been some trouble between the editor of the *Hulet Town Chronicle* and Mr. Witherspoon, Billy knew, but what had happened or how it had started, he could never find out. Whatever it was, Dan Johnson had sworn never to have a calendar in the place again. Johnson kept track of the day's date and of coming events in his daybook.

Billy had worked for Mr. Johnson for two years now, ever since he was eleven. His father, Ray Wiggins, had plenty of help on the farm with his two sisters and four older brothers and had sent him to Johnson to learn a trade. Printing or newspapering seemed a logical choice since Billy was always making up stories in his head. What could a boy do if he only knew how to make up stories? It had bothered Ray a lot. It wasn't as if Billy wasn't a pretty good hand around the place, but something about the boy troubled him, and he thought Billy would be better off with Dan Johnson, a sensible, down-to-earth sort. Besides, the money wasn't bad for a boy his age, and Billy helped out with expenses. All in all, Ray felt good about the decision. So did Billy. The hours weren't long. A full week's work was unusual—not much happened in Hulet—which left him plenty of time to write and read. Sometimes Mr. Johnson would close the office altogether and go fishing for a few days. Once in a while, he took Billy with him. Mr. Johnson liked fishing, said it gave him time to think. Billy thought fishing suited Johnson because he liked being alone.

Billy liked watching every morning for Jake to finish his rounds and turn into the library. Jake's responsibility for the town's calendars was a dependable fact in Billy's short life, akin to the coming and going of the seasons. As far as he knew, Jake had never missed one single day on the job. But recently Billy had started wondering why he did it. Perhaps it was Johnson's training that had started him questioning.

"If you're going to be any sort of decent newspaperman," Johnson had said to him after Billy had been on the job a few weeks, "you've got to be alert to what's happening around you. You miss a lot just by not looking closely enough or asking the right questions. And listen, boy. Listening's just about as important as looking in this business. And sometimes it's what you don't see or don't hear that's the most important piece of information you have to work with——" Johnson took the stem of the pipe from his mouth, which let Billy know this conversation was important——"Are you listening to me now, boy?"

"Yes sir, Mr. Johnson," Billy said smartly, thinking he should salute or something. He'd been around Dan Johnson long enough to know he didn't give advice out like penny candy. Billy knew this meant Dan thought he might actually be a newspaperman some day.

It's going to happen, Billy thought, staring through the dusty window of the printing room at the closed library door. *I'm going to be a newspaperman and maybe Mr. Witherspoon's the one to help me.*

"Hey, boy!" Dan Johnson stood in the doorway between his office and the printing room. Billy jumped away from the window, stumbling over a bucket in his hurry to get to his post beside the press. "I don't pay you to daydream. We've got a deadline to meet. I believe I explained about deadlines?"

"Yes, Sir!" Billy stood at attention, but his stomach felt as if it'd been kicked. One missed deadline and he was out.

After two years, Billy still couldn't set the type very fast, and if it wasn't exactly right, Dan would dump all the type out on the floor and make him do it all again. "It'll teach you to pay better attention to what you're doing," Dan had said as Billy scrambled after the scattered lead type he'd worked so hard to set his second month at the paper. "And, you'll learn to be quicker in the bargain."

Fear of dumped type unexpectedly contributed to the betterment of his spelling as well. Billy didn't want to tell Dan, though he wondered if his boss didn't know anyway, but a lot of the mistakes were spelling errors. He hadn't quite mastered Johnson's handwriting, and he'd had to guess at the spelling of some of the words in the copy Dan gave him to set. He'd told Jenny Schumacher his problem when he went to get a lemonade at her cafe after work one day when his type had been tossed twice. He'd come close to missing his deadline, but at the last moment, Dan had pitched in and helped. They made the deadline, but Billy needed a drink.

Jenny's lemonade was almost as good as his mother's. After she took care of the other customers, she came over to his table and sat down. Billy didn't mind. Jenny didn't seem like a mother or a girl; she was just Jenny. They'd been friends since she'd come to Hulet four years ago. Billy liked her because she always listened to him as if he were saying the most important things she'd ever heard. She never made fun of him, not even when he told her he wanted to be a writer instead of a farmer like his dad. Jenny loaned Billy books—books she'd brought all the way from Virginia when she married Will Schumacher and moved to Arkansas. Sometimes she had him read to her and helped him with the hard words. He liked the books, especially the ones by Charles Dickens and Mark Twain, and he liked talking about them to Jenny, who liked them just as much as he did, even though she was a girl. Billy had a suspicion Jenny had given the idea to his father of apprenticing him at the paper. He was pretty sure she'd done some talking on his behalf to Dan Johnson, who was always hanging around her cafe when he wasn't writing something or drinking, though how he got the liquor, Billy had no idea.

The day of the twice-tossed type, Jenny gave him a dictionary bound in cracked red leather, which had belonged to Will before he'd died unexpectedly of scarlet fever. Billy took it gingerly. It meant a lot, that dictionary. Jenny didn't talk about him much, but Billy knew she hadn't parted with something that was Will's easily.

"Gosh, Jenny, thanks. Thanks a lot," Billy said, rubbing his hand over the soft crackly cover. He looked into Jenny's brown eyes. They were moist and looked like Maisy's, gentle and big. (Maisy was his mother's milk cow, really her friend, the one she talked to when she hung out the laundry.) "I've never even seen one before, except in Mr. Johnson's office. Never could use it, though: Mr. Johnson's real funny about his books. If I touched it, he'd prob'ly skin me alive. Can you show me how to use it?"

Jenny smiled, took the dictionary, and started explaining how to look up the words, jumping up occasionally to take an order or refill someone's coffee cup when the place got too busy for Susie Wickham, Silas's youngest daughter, to handle alone. Billy sat at the cafe table, thumbing through the book, his tongue wrestling with new words, until Bertha O'Casey arrived at five o'clock to help with the supper rush.

Since then, in addition to his reading, Billy had tried to memorize five new words out of the dictionary each day. Then he'd try the new words out on Jenny. Some of the words were new, even to Jenny, and she'd look at the definition with him and try to learn the new word herself.

Billy thought about Jake Witherspoon all that morning as he worked. Dan came in and looked over his shoulder as he set the type.

"Not bad," Dan said, and walked back into his office.

'Not bad' was about as much approval as Billy ever got from his employer. He figured Dan was in an especially good mood today, so he might be able to approach Dan later, if the mood held, and ask him about Mr. Witherspoon. He resolved to work particularly hard this morning and try not to make any errors that might change Dan's mood. He set the type and double-, then triple-checked it for mistakes. When he was satisfied that the type was perfect, he went into the storeroom and got the broom and swept the entire printing room floor. Billy even put the broom back in its place. Then he ran a sample copy for Dan to proof. Dan was sitting at his desk, writing, so Billy laid the sample on his desk and went into the print shop to wait for a propitious moment. Thirty minutes later, Dan came into the shop and handed the sample back to Billy.

"No corrections," Johnson said, and, apparently not noticing the swept floor, went back into his office before Billy could say a word. Billy saw the door close behind him and decided he'd better wait a few minutes before going in after him and asking about Witherspoon. He tried to think of the best way to approach his boss, and came up with a dozen, all of which he rejected. In the end, he decided to just ask his questions and see what Johnson did with them. It couldn't hurt anything to ask. He knocked on the door, but there was no answer, so he opened the door quietly and looked in. Dan Johnson sat at his desk, staring at a blank piece of paper in front of him, puffing absent-mindedly on his pipe.

"Are you busy, Mr. Johnson?" Billy couldn't always tell. Sometimes Dan looked like that when he was composing a piece for the paper; other times, he was just daydreaming. There was no reply, so Billy figured he was daydreaming: "Mr. Johnson?"

"What is it, boy?" Dan asked, and turned from the paper to stare at Billy. The boy had light brown hair, a lock of which continually fell over his right eye. Dan was always surprised by Billy's eyes. They weren't an ordinary color like brown or blue, but were a kind of honeyed green, pale and intelligent. He seemed taller somehow.

"Mr. Johnson? Can you tell me why Mr. Witherspoon does what he does around here? I've been thinking, and I don't remember anyone ever telling me why he started changing the dates on calendars."

Johnson sat up straight in his chair and looked hard at Billy, pointing his pipe stem at him. "Look here, boy, I don't want to talk about that fool Witherspoon. I don't know what you're so interested in him for anyway; he's just crazy. Crazy as a loon, that's all. There's nothing else to it."

"But why does everybody let him change their calendars? Do they just feel sorry for him? And what does he do in the library all day?"

"I said I didn't want to discuss it." (Dan's voice told him to keep his mouth shut.) "You through for the moment?"

"Yessir."

"Then I suspect you've got other places to go. Be back here by three, so we can put this edition to bed." Dan turned back to his paper and puffed on his pipe. The smoke curled lazily up beside his ear.

Billy stood there a moment. Johnson said nothing more, so Billy went into the print shop and got his cap. *Well, he didn't kill me or anything*, Billy thought. *Guess it wasn't such a good day to ask him about it after all. I'll just have to wait and try again—or maybe I'll just ask somebody else.*

"See you at three, Mr. Johnson," Billy said, poking his head into Johnson's office. There was no answer, so he shut the door and went out into the blazing sunshine. It was almost eleven.

Billy ran across the square to Wickham's. He wanted to get to the general store before the women started coming in. He had some things to get and he didn't want the whole county knowing about his business. The women usually arrived at Wickham's about eleven-thirty, ostensibly to pick up some necessary they'd run out of at home, but they really wanted to see Silas's wife, Ruth, and each other. Billy had seen them, just standing around the store in little cliques, gabbing the day away about this, that, and the other.

The door was open to let the air circulate a bit in the store, but no one was in sight. The only sound was the steady hum of the ceiling fan. Billy walked to the counter and hit the bell.

"Be right there," Silas called from the backroom, which was set apart from the store by a curtain. A few seconds later, Silas Wickham emerged, clapping his hands together to dust them off.

"Well, hi there, Billy." Wickham smiled. He had a soft spot in his heart for the boy, maybe because he and Ruth had four daughters and no sons, maybe because Billy just was the kind of boy you liked on sight. "Haven't seen you in a coon's age. Been too busy, I guess." (Billy nodded.) "Well, what can I get for you?"

"Two pencils and a writing book, please, Mr. Wickham."

"You want writing paper, or one of those hardcover books you write in?"

"The hardcover kind."

"Some of that printer's ink got into your brain, Billy? You gonna write like Dan Johnson now? Maybe end up workin' for some big time Washington newspaper?" Silas teased, as he put the stiffly bound notebook on the counter beside the pencils.

Billy blushed and stuffed his hand in his pocket: "How much do I owe you, Mr. Wickham?"

"Let me see, now. Comes to twelve cents."

Billy counted out the money and gave it to Silas who punched a register key. The cash drawer slid out, and he dropped the change into the proper slots. Then he cocked his head and looked sideways at Billy: "I s'pose you know about our special today?"

"Special?"

"Yep. Anyone who spends more than ten cents here today gets a free piece of penny candy. So I guess twelve cents makes you entitled to choose what you'd like."

Billy couldn't believe his luck. When he was just a kid, Mr. Wickham used to give him a piece of candy every time he came in the store. But he was too old to ask now, and he couldn't justify spending money on candy. Jenny's lemonade was a different matter: learning was thirsty work, and Jenny was teaching him a lot. That made lemonade a business expense, he figured, but candy was just candy. Billy pointed to the jar in front of him. Mr. Wickham lifted the lid of the candy jar, and Billy picked out a lemon stick with white sugary swirls.

"Thanks, Mr. Wickham."

"You're welcome, Billy. Here's your sack. Come back now, hear? (Billy took the sack and grinned.) "And don't let Johnson work you too hard!" Silas shouted, as Billy walked out the door—paper sack in one hand, candy stick already in his mouth—and headed down the boardwalk to Jenny's cafe.

CHAPTER TWO

A t about ten o'clock weekday mornings, Benjamin Hawley or Michael Townsend would walk up the stairs and enter the quiet world of the Hulet library. This morning it was Ben. Hawley, a tall, gaunt man in his mid-thirties, carried a fat, brown leather briefcase, scarred at the edges. He waved a greeting to the librarian, who returned it with a smile and went back to the book she was reading. Ben walked across the faded carpet runner to Jake's table and sat down, reached for one of the law reviews, and began reading. It was several minutes before Jake noticed his presence. When he did, he grinned broadly, displacing the intense frown of the scholar with the teasing twinkle Ben remembered. For a moment, his stomach tightened with memory, but there was no time to dwell on it: Jake never wasted time, and he didn't like for others to waste it either.

"What can I do for you, Ben?"

"I wanted to talk to you about the Runyon murder."

"Runyon? I don't recall anyone by that name."

"Sure you do—Joe Runyon? Murdered about the first of June? All the details were in the *Chronicle*."

Jake shook his head: "Don't take it. Sorry. Why don't you just fill me in?"

Ben summarized what he knew: Mill Creek's new preacher and his wife were the ones who had discovered Runyon's body. It'd been a fluke, really, that they'd gone out to the Runyon farm that day. They had decided to make calls on the people in the outlying countryside to get acquainted and, perhaps in the process, increase their church rolls, and so had come to the Runyon place. The preacher went up to the door and knocked, but there was no answer. Just as he turned to leave, his wife called to him from the car that she'd seen someone move past a window. He knocked again, and when there still was no answer, he walked along the front porch until he reached the window his wife indicated and peeked in. Fanny Runyon was rocking back and forth in a chair, fully clothed, apparently in some sort of trance. Lying in a pool of blood at her feet was her husband. The Mill Creek authorities called in Hulet's sheriff, ostensibly because Hulet was the closer town.

Though the Runyons lived within ten miles of Hulet, nobody knew much about them. They'd been reclusive, staying out on their farm and not mixing with the townspeople, only coming into town to buy feed for the few animals they kept, supplies for themselves, and occasionally seed for the farm. They were a tight-lipped couple, not exactly unfriendly, but they didn't invite conversation. It was a difficult case. Except for the corpse, the house was as untouched as a museum display—no signs of an intruder, no apparent motive, just Fanny, rocking by her husband's body. Joe Runyon had been stabbed twice and his neck broken, but the sheriff and his men hadn't been able to find a murder weapon. With nothing else to go on, Fanny had been brought in as a material witness. Questioning proved futile: Fanny seemed oblivious to her surroundings.

"She won't say anything?" Jake asked without looking up. He doodled on the legal pad in front of him.

"Nothing. She's under guard at the county hospital."

Jake's pencil paused briefly: "Under guard?"

Ben nodded: "Sheriff says it's for her protection. The theory is that if she didn't murder Joe, someone else did, and the murderer may decide to go after Fanny if he thinks she knows or saw something she shouldn't. Judge Cravens ordered tests to determine her physical and mental state. Then there's always the possibility that she killed her husband and that this trance is all an act."

"So where do you come into all this?"

"The judge appointed the firm to represent her interests for the time being, since she's apparently incompetent." Ben paused, leaned closer to Jake. "I've tried to talk to her, but she just stares off like she doesn't see or hear me…. I don't think she does, either. I'll tell you, Jake, that woman gives me the creeps."

"Do you think she killed her husband?"

"No. Neither does Townsend."

"Then who did?"

"Don't ask me; ask Mrs. Runyon!"—Ben pushed away from the table, exasperated—"I do think she knows what happened, but she won't talk. Talk? Hell, Jake, she doesn't even move unless someone moves her. Maybe she can't talk, or maybe she's just too frightened." Ben pulled a package of cigarettes out of his shirt pocket and lit one: "Want one?" he asked, holding out the pack to Jake.

"No thanks, maybe later."

"Suit yourself." Ben placed the package back in his pocket and took a deep drag on his cigarette. "I wish I knew what that woman was thinking."

Jake shoved a glass ashtray toward Ben, then rocked back in his chair: "Have you talked to the doctors?"

"They don't know any more than we do. They think she's in some sort of shock. But whether it's caused by finding her husband murdered, by seeing him murdered, or by doing it, they can't tell." Ben looked over at Jake. "One thing's for sure, if Fanny Runyon didn't kill her husband and knows who did, the judge's right: she's in a lot of trouble if the murderer thinks she *can* talk."

"Then you think the murderer is still around?"

"Well, I'd be long-gone if I'd killed someone, but the possibility certainly exists."

"The thing that bothers me," Jake mused, resting his elbows on the chair arms and interlacing his fingers, "assuming that Fanny was there at the time…"

"Go on."

"I'm just wondering why the murderer didn't kill her, too."

"Maybe he didn't know she was there, or maybe he didn't think he needed to. If she was like she is now when he left…?"

"I see your point." Jake let his front chair legs hit the floor again. "If she's faking it, I hope she can keep it up forever—if she's not guilty, that is."

"Well, I have to get back. Think about it, will you, and see if anything clicks?" Ben pushed his chair back, got up, and held out his hand.

Jake shook it: "Don't know how I can help."

Ben shrugged: "Well, just keep it in mind. I'll check with you tomorrow."

Jake went back to his journals, but he couldn't concentrate. His head ached, a deceptively gentle pain which augured one of his tortuous migraines. Something lurked on the edge of thought, something vaguely familiar. He massaged his temples, trying to recall … what? He could feel it, a tangible presence that pushed at the invisible wall between him and it, making his head throb with its insistence. Jake's elbow nudged a journal off the table.

Startled, the librarian looked up from her book: "Something wrong, Mr. Witherspoon?"

"Just knocked this off the table, Virginia," Jake said, holding up the retrieved journal. "Sorry I bothered you.

"It must be about time for lunch," he said, pushing his chair back and getting up. "I think I'll leave you in peace for awhile."

"Have a nice time," Virginia said, smiling at him before returning to her reading.

The sun was at its zenith. His eyes stung with the glare from the street. Jake fought their automatic closing as he stumbled his way across the square and the narrow street. At the boardwalk, an awning afforded some relief and his eyes opened warily, becoming narrow slits from which he could see things directly in his path but which blocked all peripheral vision. Jenny's Cafe felt closer than Silas's grocery, so Jake made his way toward the friendly diamond-patterned windows and muslin curtains. The bell above the door rang as he walked into the cooler shadows of the cafe. The buzz of conversation stopped briefly, becoming surprised greetings as he entered.

Jenny heard the bell in the kitchen where she was helping Bertha with the lunchtime orders. She liked this time of day; she liked being busy and the friendly smell of food cooking for her customers. Not many strangers came to Hulet, so the people who showed up for the noon meal were mostly regulars. The overhead fan turned lifting stray wisps of hair off her neck as she worked cutting thick slices of the bread she'd baked that morning. It was a hot day, and most of the men wanted something cool. Still, vegetable soup, its aroma mingling pleasantly with the smells of fresh-baked bread and frying bacon, bubbled in the pot on the huge, cast iron stove, tempting even the hottest patron.

Susie Wickham blew through the kitchen doors, stuck orders on the clothespins in front of Bertha, and bobbed around like a balloon caught in an airy crosscurrent.

"Guess who just came in?" Susie said, not waiting for them to guess. "Jake Witherspoon! There must be something wrong, don't you think?" Susie stopped, out of air.

Bertha turned slightly from in front of the stove where she was dipping out a bowl of soup and frowned. "Susie, I swear...Sure and you'll go on about nothin'—"

"Nothing!" Susie seemed to inflate with indignation. "I'd like to know, Mrs. O'Casey, when the last time is that you remember Mr. Witherspoon coming in here for lunch! You know yourself he's never done this before. Nothing? Why you can set your watch by what that man does." Susie, her point made, checked her orders on the table, arranged three plates carefully on one arm, and picked up another with her free hand.

"Want me to get the door?" Jenny asked, wiping her hands on the dishtowel that hung from her waistband.

"That's OK. I can manage." Susie hit the swinging doors with her hip and disappeared into the dining room.

"And what do you think that means?" Bertha said, throwing several slices of bacon into a large iron skillet.

Jenny smiled. She liked to hear her talk. Bertha's Irish brogue was somehow soothing, calm, no matter what the topic: "What what means?"

"All that blither about Mr. Witherspoon."

"Well, I can't think it's as momentous as Susie makes it out to be. The man's just hungry and didn't want to walk all the way to his farm in this heat…" Jenny paused, her hand resting lightly on the ripe tomato she was about to slice. "Honestly, the way this town goes on about that man…"

A moment of silence followed while she cut the tomato into even slices. She reached for another—"I'll admit it is a little odd about the calendars, but that's the town's fault, don't you think?" (The second tomato dispatched, Jenny began on a third.) "You know, Bertha—" Jenny waved her knife to illustrate her point—"it has to be the town. The way everybody waits for him…" Jenny shook her head and went back to her slicing, suddenly quiet.

Bertha turned a bacon slice with her long, black-handled fork: "Now that you mention it, I don't know why the town waits for him like that"—she turned the flame down and placed an iron press on top of the sizzling strips—"Why do you?"

"Because everyone else does, I suppose…Will always did—I never thought to ask why. When he died I just kept on doing things the way he had. Jake Witherspoon was such a part of the town, I never questioned."

"Well, the man seems harmless enough. I don't think you'll be comin' to any harm with him."

Jenny turned away to wash her knife in the sink and to hide her face: "I hardly think I'll have any occasion to be with Mr. Witherspoon at all, Bertha. I can't imagine what you're thinking."

Bertha smiled to herself but said nothing as she removed the press and set the bacon strips on brown paper to drain.

Jake couldn't have told them why he'd turned toward the cafe instead of walking home like he always did. True, he had a headache, and the sun was blinding and incredibly hot, but that was to be expected. The fact was he just wanted to be with people, other people. Not that his mother wasn't good company, she was, but today he didn't want to look at her and worry about how thin she was getting. He didn't want to think about her dying. Not today. Today, he wanted to sit in the shade of Jenny's Cafe, listen to the soft whir of the ceiling fans and the chatter of conversations, and wait for his headache to abate. He went to the telephone by the cash register and rang the operator.

"Lula? Jake Witherspoon. Get me the farm, please."

"Hi, there, Jake. Just a moment. I'll ring."

Jake waited until he heard Annie's voice on the line: "Annie, I won't be coming home for lunch today."

"Dere be sumpthin' wrong, Miztah Jake?"

"No. Nothing's wrong, Annie. I have a headache, and it's just too hot to walk home today." He paused. "How's Mother?"

"Oh, jus fine! She gone out on de po'ch dis mo'nin'. She stay fo' a good long time jus enjoyin' de heck outa dem roses. She 'sleep now, so she won' even know yuh weren't heah. Jus gets ridda dat headache."

"Thanks, Annie, I will. Tell Mother I'll talk to her later."

"Sho' will, Miztah Jake. Y'all g'on now, an' don' worry 'bout nothin'."

He hung up the phone, relieved, and walked back to his seat. Susie was just putting his food on the table.

"Jake?

Jake turned to see Ben Hawley approaching: "Hello again. Have a seat." Jake pointed to the chair opposite him and sat down to eat his sandwich.

"Don't mind if I do," Ben said. "Susie, just bring me a bacon and tomato sandwich and the largest iced tea you can manage."

Susie jotted the order down on her pad and left, sticking her pencil behind her ear as she went.

"Go ahead and eat," Ben said as Jake put his sandwich back on the plate. "Mine'll be out in a minute."

Jake ate for a minute in silence while Ben read from a newspaper he'd brought with him. "That Runyon murder?"

Ben lowered his paper. "What about it?"

"It seems familiar somehow."

"In what way?" Ben folded the paper, laid it on the table.

"Now that's the crazy thing…I don't know, exactly." Jake lapsed into silence. He scratched his ear absentmindedly before resuming. "Maybe it's just too clean." He stopped again and then said, as if to himself, "Stabbed twice and his neck was broken?"

"So they say. Why?"

Jake squeezed his eyes shut, trying to see the picture in his head: vague shadows. He opened his eyes. "You're going to think I'm crazy, Ben."

"I've known you too long to think that, Jake. What is it?"

"I've got this feeling...like I know the murderer." Jake shook his head. "No, it's not that. It's more like I've seen that kind of murder..." He smiled self-consciously, "I told you. It's crazy."

"Maybe not. Tell me more about this other murder."

"Forget it. I probably read something somewhere, that's all. Here's Susie."

Ben wanted to press Jake for more, but Susie appeared at his elbow.

"Can I get you anything else?" Susie asked, putting Ben's food down in front of him.

"Nothing for me," Ben said. "Jake?"

"No, I'm finished, but I could use some water."

"Sure. Be right back," Susie said and left with Jake's plate.

Jake thought while Ben ate. "You know, I don't think I'd heard of the Runyons before this morning."

"Nobody had—anyway, not until the *Chronicle* article appeared. Elmer and Silas knew them, but only because they sold them supplies. Near as anyone can figure, the Runyons have been living in the area about two years or so. It was about that long ago that they started showing up in town for supplies. Silas says they came in about four times a year and were real close-mouthed. They'd hand him a list, he'd fill it, they'd pay, then he'd help them load it into their truck, and they'd leave."

"What did Elmer say?"

"About the same. Odd, isn't it?"

"Nobody else ever talked to them?"

"No one we know of—at least no one we can find."

"Who'd they buy their place from?"

"Some real estate agent by the name of Snow—Ralph Snow, I think. Lives down in Fort Smith. Works for one of the banks. Near as I can tell, the property was abandoned for years and reverted to the bank for foreclosure."

They ate for a moment in silence.

"But why would they move to that house?" Jake asked as Ben finished. "Could they have had some connections to the place?"

"None so far. No, Mike and I just figure they were strangers looking for something cheap and isolated."

"Did you find out where they came from?"

"No. Like I said, nobody seems to know anything about them except their names and the kinds of things they bought for the farm. The sheriff did turn up something interesting though."

"What's that?"

"Well, they bought the place outright, cash on the barrelhead. Struck us as mighty interesting—two people from nowhere with enough cash to buy a farm outright, not to mention their stock, feed and supplies. Sheriff says they had no cash crop, just grew enough to winter their livestock, which didn't amount to much—a couple of horses, a mule, three dairy cows—nothing that would bring in more money."

"That's odd, all right." Jake thought a moment. "You know, it might be worth hiring someone to trace the Runyons' movements in the last five years, or at least the last three. My dad used to say if you smelled something rotten, follow the money trail. My nose says find out where the Runyons got their money, and you'll find a key to the husband's murder."

"Larry's already investigating it. That's right down his alley." Ben stood up to leave as Susie brought Jake's water.

"So you wait." Jake pulled a headache powder packet from a pocket in his trousers.

"So we wait. Got a headache?"

"Yeah, comes from reading too much. This will take care of it." Jake dumped the headache powder into the water and drank it. He grimaced and shuddered. "If that stuff didn't work so well, I'd never drink another drop." He hunched his shoulders and shook his head. "Ugh!"

"Well," Ben said, "I've got to get back to the office…just in case there's something to do."

"I'll walk out with you," Jake said, getting up. He looked at the table. "Where's my check?"

"I'm paying this time."

"Ben, you don't need to do that. I've got money."

"Just chalk it up to an unaccustomed fit of generosity brought on by having my brain stimulated for a few minutes. You can get it next time."

"All right, thanks."

"Don't mention it. How about tomorrow?" Ben said, as he paid the bill.

"For lunch?"

Ben nodded.

"I usually check on Mother at lunch, but I can call the farm before we go, if you don't mind things being up in the air?"

"Don't mind a bit. Give me a call tomorrow," Ben said as they left the cafe. "By the way, how is your mother these days?"

"She has her good days and her bad days."

Ben smiled: "Don't we all….Well, see you tomorrow."

"I'm looking forward to it," Jake said, realizing as he did that he really was. It had been a long time since he'd sat and talked to a friend.

Jake was back in the library an hour earlier than usual. His headache had dulled, but something persisted, annoying him like a gnat moving in front of his eyes on a summer evening that he couldn't quite see to get. Every once in a while this happened, this feeling that something was there, stuck in some invisible compartment of his brain, something he should know. He'd been sick—some kind of breakdown. Selective amnesia, that's what they called it. What it meant was that approximately ten years of his adult life was missing. Strange what he remembered: Like the party his folks had thrown to celebrate his getting his college degree from the University of Arkansas in 1913. He remembered the music, the lights, and how proud his father had been when he toasted Jake's success. It was ironic, Jake thought, that he remembered that toast but had no memory of his father's death. Robert Witherspoon had died in 1922 of a heart attack, Annie'd said, and he, Jake, had been at the funeral, had "been such a comfort" to his mother, and he remembered nothing. His mother had suggested visiting Robert's grave, but he refused—he just couldn't face the reality of a tombstone, not yet.

There were no problems remembering his childhood—going to school, sunny days fishing, playing ball with his friends. Silas Wickham was his best friend in those days. He remembered one year when his dad took them camping, exploring as far east as the Mississippi. Ben Hawley was a few years younger than they were, but they'd let him tag along on their camping trip, and they'd found they really liked the younger boy.

Ben and Silas had both served in the war, Jake knew, but neither brought it up around him. That no one mentioned the war to him let him know he had not had a part in it. The worst part was he didn't know why. He'd tried to ask his mother about it, but something always stopped him. He was afraid to hear her answer.

There was a woman somehow connected to the black time, but he saw her only occasionally in dreams. The dreams were vivid and frightening, but he could never remember them when awake. Just flashes now and then of flames and a woman. Sometimes Jake shut his eyes and strained to make her face appear, but then his head would pound with a violence that made further thought impossible.

The doctors had told him his memory would come back in its own time, that he was not to force it. But it had been four years since he'd been released from the hospital, and the years were still lost. No one talked about the lost time, and Jake never mentioned it. He was ashamed. He knew he'd been sick, but his was a mental illness. It was not something you talked about, and somehow he felt responsible—like he'd done something to cause it. That his father had died during the lost years seemed to make him responsible for that, too. His mother never seemed to blame him, nor did anyone else treat him with anything but respect, but there was a distance between him and his old friends, and a tacit understanding that the space was not to be crossed—not by them, not by him.

His first morning back in Hulet, he awoke before dawn as usual, got dressed and walked into Wilson's feed store. Without thinking, he turned the page on Elmer's calendar to the day's date, and he had known: he was responsible for starting the day. He looked at Elmer, and Elmer didn't say anything, just smiled, and Jake knew he was right. He moved on to Will's Cafe—now Jenny's—and changed the calendar there, too. When Will Schumacher smiled at him, Jake felt satisfied, like something had been put back into place. He'd always done this. He couldn't remember exactly when he'd started being responsible for starting the town's day, but it didn't matter. He knew it was his job, and he'd been faithfully changing the dates on their calendars ever since.

He'd had the same feeling when he stumbled upon articles about law in the library. He understood their importance without knowing why, and he didn't stop to question it. Legal questions were somehow familiar and gave him an eerie sense of security, as if he were visiting with good friends. Most likely, it was something he'd studied in college sometime. It didn't matter: it was good just to know he understood. He had an uncanny ability to remember everything he read and to understand subtle legal nuances of and connections between cases. He'd been reading law regularly. Finally, he'd been given his own space in the library, not that the Hulet library was normally crowded. Somehow word got around, and the local lawyers started asking him to research cases for them. Some even offered to pay him for his services. He hadn't taken their money, but their offers let him know that they thought he was doing something worthwhile and that there was solid value to his opinions. Somehow it made up for the lost years.

The muscles in his right hand jumped, bringing him back abruptly from the brink of reminiscence. The Runyon case was the cause of this unusual sojourn into the far country of memory. His mind, normally disciplined, wandered back to his conversation with Ben. *I really ought to talk to Ben again.*

Outside, the air was heavy with moisture and the smell of dust. The resultant translucent haze cloaked the town but did nothing to shield Jake's eyes from the glare of the afternoon sun. Jake made his way from the library to the faded red brick, two-story building next to the bank where the law firm of Townsend, Hawley & Branch occupied the north corner office on the first floor.

Billy Wiggins had finally finished setting the new copy Johnson had given him after lunch and was engaged in sweeping the back room of the newspaper office. Broom in one hand, dustpan in the other, he walked past the paned window just in time to see Jake Witherspoon leave the library.

Now what is Mr. Witherspoon doing? Billy thought, stopping to watch as Jake paused outside the library door, shaded his eyes, then walked quickly down the steps and across the square.

"Finished already?"

Billy jumped and whirled around at the sound of Dan Johnson's voice.

"Yessir," Billy said. "I just finished sweeping. The type's all set and ready to go."

"So you thought you'd just look out the window and daydream for a while. It that it?" Johnson's voice was ominously low.

"No sir, I just saw Mr. Witherspoon as I walked past the window. See?"— Billy held up his broom and dustpan for proof—"I was just putting them up."

"What's so dadgum fascinating about Witherspoon? Is he all you have to think about today, boy?" Johnson exploded and crossed the room in three strides to where Billy cowered involuntarily in front of the window. Johnson rubbed the dirt from a pane with his shirtsleeve. "Well, where is he?"

"Uh, I don't know, sir," Billy stammered. "I just happened to see him leave the library. When you came in, he was starting across the square."

"He left the library, you say?" Johnson looked full into Billy's eyes as if to see if he were lying.

Billy straightened a little. He wasn't lying, and he hadn't been daydreaming. "Yessir. That's what got me lookin'. I've never seen Mr. Witherspoon out anywhere this time of day before. He never leaves the library until five or so."

"And how would you know that?"

"Aw, Mr. Johnson, everybody in town knows that..." Billy's voice trailed off. He looked down at his shoes. There was a small spider just to the left of his right shoe, crawling lazily along the floor. Billy wondered whether he should squash it, but it didn't seem to want to hurt anyone, so he just let it crawl on by, heading in the general direction of where Johnson stood. Suddenly, it disappeared into the shadow cast by one of the windowpanes. Billy stood there, watching, waiting for the spider to come out into the light again.

"What *are* you looking at now, boy?"

Johnson's exasperated voice broke Billy's concentration on the spider, and he looked up quickly—"Just a spider. It's on the floor."

"Well, I didn't figure it was hanging from the ceiling," Johnson said. "Let me see the type you set. Then I want you to set one more story and help me run the press."

Billy led Johnson to the type trays, heart pounding, not so much from his narrow escape from Johnson's wrath, but from the knowledge that he was going to get to run the press tonight. Not just a sample page, but run the press. He handed the sample pages to Johnson to proof and watched his face closely as page after page were read and put down without so much as a cough from Johnson.

"Not bad, boy," Johnson said as he dropped the last page onto the floor. "We'll need to reset page one, though. I just finished talking to the sheriff. He said I could run a follow-up on that Runyon murder."

Billy's ears pricked. He remembered the story Johnson wrote the day after the murder—the strange couple, the lady who might've killed her husband, but who couldn't or wouldn't say anything. It was like the start of a novel, and he'd watched each day for more information, but Johnson hadn't written anything more about it, and the murder had happened at the beginning of the summer. He'd wondered why Johnson hadn't done anything more, but his boss didn't always appreciate inquisitiveness from him, so he didn't ask.

"Gosh, I'd almost forgotten about the Runyons. Is she going to trial or something?"

"You'll have time enough to read the story when we've set the type." Johnson rolled up his sleeves, his mouth set in a tight straight line.

Billy got the tray and started to work. He was a bit disappointed in the article. Really no new information at all, just that Mrs. Runyon was being held for observation at some hospital and was being transferred next week to another hospital in Little Rock, this one specializing in mental disorders.

It was well after five o'clock when Billy and Dan Johnson finished printing the last copies of the *Hulet Town Chronicle's* Thursday edition. Billy started folding the sheets and rolling the papers tightly, tucking the end expertly into the bottom of the roll.

Then he and Johnson loaded the papers into the back of Dan's truck. They'd deliver them before dawn the next morning—Dan in the driver's seat stuffing rolled papers into postboxes as he drove past, Billy standing up in the back of the pickup throwing papers onto waiting porches or lawns with an arm worthy of any major league baseball pitcher.

Michael Townsend ran his hand through his thinning gray hair. The gesture, no longer necessary, remained from younger days. Now fifty-five, the senior partner of Townsend, Hawley & Branch sat at the head of a large oak table, distressed with indentations from years of notes taken with too heavy a hand. Seated at either side of the table with him were his partners, Benjamin Hawley and Laurel Branch—this unfortunate moniker bestowed by the man's mother, a romantic steeped in the classics. No one called him Laurel, of course. He was known as "Larry" to the town and his friends, who, if they knew, never brought up the subject of his given name.

"Have you dug up anything more on the Runyon murder?" Townsend asked, opening a folder stuffed with sheets of yellow legal paper.

"You mean besides Joe Runyon?" Larry said, grinning. (Ben cracked a smile, but Mike was clearly not amused.) He cleared his throat and continued: "I have nothing on the Fort Smith connection yet, but I finally got the results of the autopsy we requested."

"Good heavens, man, why didn't you say so? What are you waiting for?" Townsend seemed irritated.

Larry shuffled through the papers in front of him, pulled out copies of the report, and handed one to each of the other men. While they were scanning the report, Larry summarized: "As you can see, we don't have a definite time of death since so much time elapsed between the murder and the autopsy—"

"Any fool should know to perform an autopsy in a suspected homicide!" Mike interrupted, while perusing the page in front of him.

"We've already been over that, Mike," Ben said. "Be grateful that the district attorney was as upset as we were and got Cravens to order the exhumation—"

"Gratitude is not the emotion I'm experiencing at the moment—"

"May I finish?"—Larry looked from one to the other of his colleagues.

"Get on with it." Townsend's fingers drummed impatiently on the table.

"You remember that that Mill Creek sawbones listed the primary cause of death as a broken neck?" (The other men nodded.) "Well, the coroner says that those stab wounds were more important than he thought. He said Joe Runyon was killed by someone coming up from behind, shoving a knife up behind Runyon's diaphragm into his lungs, and then breaking his neck. He said it must've happened pretty fast—two quick knife thrusts, a twist of the neck, and he's dead. Runyon wouldn't have had time to struggle."

"Does he think Mrs. Runyon could've done it?" Townsend asked.

Larry scooted forward in his seat: "In order to kill Runyon, the murderer had to be strong enough to hold him from behind with one arm while stabbing a knife into Runyon's lungs twice with his other hand and then break his neck with one quick twist. According to the coroner, a man has to be the killer. No woman—certainly not one as short as his wife—could get that kind of hold on a man as big as Runyon. Another thing: the doc said the murderer knew exactly what he was doing, said he saw the same method of killing used by some special units in the war."

"So it's premeditated, and our killer probably served in the military," Ben said.

"Sure looks that way."

"Larry," Townsend said, relaxing somewhat, "take that report on over to Judge Cravens and stop Fanny's transfer. There never was enough evidence to hold her, and now with this, Cravens will have to let her out."

"Sorry to differ with you, Michael, but the judge isn't going to release her—not with a murderer on the loose. She still could be a material witness, and even forgetting that, she might be in danger herself."

"That's not our problem now. We've got to get that woman released."

"What about her mental condition?" Larry asked. "Where's she going to go; who's going to take care of her, if we get her released?"

"Are you suggesting we ignore our client's constitutional rights and let her rot in that poor excuse for a hospital or in some jail?" Townsend sounded incredulous. "Get Mrs. Runyon released," he said, stopping after each word. "We'll deal with what should be done with her afterwards."

Ben walked his pencil through the fingers of his right hand before speaking. "What's her condition, Larry? Did you talk to Dr. Riker?"

"She's the same, but—"

"But?"

"Riker thinks she may be faking."

"Faking? You're kidding."

"I wish I were, but Riker thinks she's putting on an act for our benefit."

"Not ours necessarily—" Ben glanced at Townsend who raised his left eyebrow in response—"perhaps, for the murderer's.... If she is faking, then she obviously thinks she's in danger...and that means she definitely knows something."

"All the more reason to get her out and move her somewhere the murderer can't find her," Townsend interjected. "If he's still around, he's certain to hear about the move. He could get to her anywhere between here and Little

Rock. Frankly, I'm surprised he hasn't tried to get to her at the hospital. There's certainly nothing there to stop him."

"He might not agree with Dr. Riker about her faking," Ben said, "or maybe our killer doesn't think Fanny Runyon knows anything that'll hurt him."

"Well, if she doesn't, then why is she faking?" Townsend asked, jotting a brief note on one of the papers in the folder.

"Maybe she's not," Larry said. "That was just Riker's opinion. If you ask me, she's as crazy as a quilt. Who knows? Maybe she's always been nuts, and Runyon knew it, so he kept her out on the farm. Maybe that's the real reason they never mixed with people."

"Great Scot, Larry," Townsend said, closing the folder in front of him. "I hope you don't investigate as haphazardly as you speculate. Have you been reading your mother's dime novels again?"

Before Larry could rise to the bait, the conference room door opened a crack:

"Excuse me, but Mr. Witherspoon's here. He says he needs to talk to Mr. Hawley." Penelope Long, who doubled as both the firm's receptionist and legal secretary, appeared to be disembodied. Only her head with its unruly mass of red curls showed through the space between the door and its frame as she waited for instructions.

Townsend glanced at Ben who shrugged. "Show Mr. Witherspoon in, Miss Long."

"Yes, sir." Miss Long's head disappeared, and the door closed again.

"Do you know why Jake Witherspoon would come here?" Townsend asked Ben.

"No. I saw him at the library this morning. We bumped into each other at Jenny's and briefly discussed the Runyon case——" Ben stopped as the door opened and Jake followed Penelope into the room.

"Mr. Witherspoon to see you," she announced and left, closing the door behind her.

"Jake!" said Townsend, rising from his seat and extending his right hand. "What a pleasant surprise!"

"Mike, it's good to see you," Jake said warmly as he took the offered hand. "Ben. Larry."

The two nodded, and Ben gestured for him to take a seat at his side of the table.

"Thanks, Ben, but I didn't know you were in a meeting."

"Sit down, Jake," Townsend said. It was an order.

Jake smiled and sat—"I wanted to tell you something that occurred to me after we talked, Ben. It may help you with the Runyon case." Jake paused for breath and saw the polite attention in their faces. Suddenly his own face felt hot; his palms began to sweat. He felt ridiculous, like a kid trying to sound important. Who was he to tell them anything?

"Before you continue, Jake, let me bring you up to date," Ben said. "We just got some new information."

Townsend interrupted: "I'm sure Jake wouldn't be interested, Ben. Let's just listen to what he has to say."

Jake felt as if he'd been punched in the stomach. He stood to leave: "No, that's all right. I can see you're busy. Anything I had to say can wait till later. It wasn't all that important."

"Where are you going?" Ben asked.

"Home. I need to check on Mother—she's been ill," he added to the others. "I'll talk to you later, Ben. Please excuse me, gentlemen. Sorry to have bothered you." He smiled awkwardly and turned toward the door.

Ben got up hurriedly and put his hand on Jake's shoulder. "You had something you wanted to tell me. What was it?"

"Just an idea—nothing that makes any difference." He paused, forced a smile as he nodded to the other men in the room—"Larry. Mike. Good to see you again." He opened the door.

"Don't forget: lunch tomorrow," Ben said.

"I'll call you," Jake said and left the office.

Michael Townsend ran his hand across his head and frowned. "Now what was *that* all about?"

"I don't know," Ben said, a frown playing across his brow.

"Good Lord, Michael," Larry said, looking hard at a long scratch on the table, "did you have to be so obvious?"

"What do you mean?"

"Just that Witherspoon would have to be an idiot not to know what you thought of his opinions," Larry said.

"Look," Townsend paused, stood, and went to the window. Jake was almost across the square. Townsend turned around and faced the other men: "Look, Jake's great when it comes to research, but I don't think it's a good idea to bring him into our discussion of cases….I didn't mean to hurt his feelings—hell, he was *my* partner for God's sake—but he's not well. No telling what it would do to him."

"But, Mike," Ben interjected, "he could've remembered something."

Larry tapped the end of his pen on the table: "Didn't you tell me he was working on some murder trial before the accident?"

"Yes," Townsend said, walking back to the window. Jake was well down the road to his farm now. "But I don't think he remembers anything about it. Hell, he doesn't even remember being a lawyer! Such a damned *waste!*" (He looked over his shoulder at Larry.) "I wish you'd known him before. He was the best trial attorney I've ever seen—the best thing that ever happened to this town."

"I don't understand," Larry said. "Why was he so important to the town?"

Mike left the window and took his seat. "Ever wonder why the shop-keepers wait for Jake to do whatever fool thing he does before they open for business?"

"Sure I have. I just assumed they felt sorry for him."

"More like they feel sorry for themselves." Mike paused. "Oh, part of it has to do with his folks: The Witherspoons settled this town, gave a lot of folks their start—hell, they even loaned me the money to set up this office when I first came to town. Good people. Real good people. You don't meet many like them anymore, do you, Ben?"

"Sure don't."

"So they wait for Jake out of respect for his parents?" Larry prodded.

"Like I said, that's part of it, but it's not the whole story. No, it's out of respect for Jake, too. The Witherspoons were like royalty around here, and Jake? The crown prince. He was a prodigy, bright—real bright. You should've been here for the party his dad had when he graduated from college—"

"The whole town showed up for that one," Ben said. "It was some shindig."

"But when he won that full scholarship to Harvard Law School...well—"

"The town went nuts," Ben finished.

"So the town's proud of him? Something like 'hometown boy makes good'?" Larry asked.

"No, it's more like Jake was the town's child," Mike said. "Its hope anyway..."

No one said anything for a few minutes.

"What possible connection could the Morgan murder have with this one?" Mike said in exasperation. "They convicted Slo-Joe and hanged him years ago."

"Who's Slo-Joe?" Larry asked.

Ben answered: "Slo-Joe Freeman. The retarded Negro accused of Clarence Morgan's murder. Jake was his defense attorney. The trial was in recess when the accident happened."

"Did Jake think the Negro did it?"

Townsend's mouth twisted into a near grin: "No, not Jake Witherspoon, defender of the downtrodden and demented. He said he was onto something that would prove the Negro didn't do it. I never found it."

"Who took over when Witherspoon...?"

"I did," Ben said. "I was pretty green back then..."

"Look," Townsend said reaching for his pen, "this isn't getting us any-where. The past is past, and there's nothing we can do about it now. Only Jake knew anything about that case, and he doesn't remember anything about anything."

"So you don't think he could have remembered something that might have a bearing on the Runyon murder?" Larry asked.

Townsend shook his head: "Not anything having to do with five years ago. The doctors said when his memory came back, it would be like a flood, not bits and pieces. No——" Mike sat back in his chair and looked at his partners——"whatever he remembers probably has to do with some case he read about in a newspaper or in one of the law reviews."

Jake took the long way home; he wanted time before he had to face his mother and Annie. He saw himself as those men must have seen him all along: a mental cripple, someone to pity. How could he have ever thought that anyone really *valued* his two cents? What did he know about anything? They were simply humoring him for his mother's sake. Humiliation washed through him. He couldn't live this way anymore, not now, not knowing what they thought of him. The time had come to face his past, and his mother held the key. He had to talk to her. She wouldn't want to tell him——she was protecting him from something. It didn't matter; whatever it was, however horrible, not knowing the truth was more intolerable than any reality he might have to face.

CHAPTER THREE

"Annie...Annie!" The strain of pushing air through her lungs and out of her mouth drained the last bit of energy from Sarah Witherspoon's body. She lay there, under the old wedding ring quilt she'd made for her hope chest long ago, and thought how ridiculously small her voice sounded for such a great effort. Already she felt detached from her body—that pitifully thin, weak frame she'd inhabited for the last few years. Whatever had happened to her other body? The strong one that did everything effortlessly and gracefully? It seemed to her that it had happened overnight, this change from youth to old age. Yes, it was time to leave...

"Miz Sarah! Oh, Miz Sarah, don' go yet—"

Annie's voice sounded far away. She was worried, poor dear: "Annie," Sarah said, her voice barely audible in the stillness of the late afternoon, "Robert's...here." A faint smile passed across her lips; she sighed and was silent.

"Oh Miz Sarah, Miz Sarah..." Annie took the thin white hand on the quilt, kissed it, and pressed it to her own black cheek. Tears stung her eyes and ran down her cheeks unnoticed.

Annie's knees ached from kneeling so long. The bed creaked as she pushed her hands down on the mattress to help herself up. Sarah's body lay small and still under the faded quilt. The eyes were closed, the mouth relaxed, as if in sleep, but Sarah herself was gone.

Annie walked to the phone in the hall and rang the operator: "Miz Lula? Dis is Annie Jackson ovah t' de Witherspoon's farm. I needs yuh t' get me Doctah Livsey, please."

"Is Mrs. Witherspoon all right, Annie?"

"Yes'um."

"Nothing's wrong?"

"No'um. I jus needs to talk to de doctah."

"Well, I'll get Doc for you now, Annie."

"Thank yuh, Miz Lula."

"You're welcome, Annie."

Annie waited. She hadn't lied exactly. Miz Sarah was all right...now.

"Annie?"

"Hello? Doctah Livsey? I needs fo' yuh t' come out t' de Witherspoons' right now, iffen yuh can."

"Is Mrs. Witherspoon worse, Annie?"

"No suh. She crossed ovah."

"She's dead?"

"Yessuh."

"I'll be right out....Annie, is Mr. Jake home?"

"No suh, not yet...But he be home soon, an I jus thought it'd be bettah iffen yuh wuz heah."

"I'm on my way."

"Yessuh. Thank yuh."

The phone clicked; Annie replaced the receiver. The house was so quiet she could hear the steady hum of cicadas in the fields. She stood still, listening to the sounds of the farm—sounds so much a part of her life she seldom heard them as separate: A brief breeze rustled the needles of the old pine tree outside the kitchen window. A pinecone splashed into the creek that snaked behind the house on its way through the land. Below the low hill, where her clothesline stretched between two tall pines, drying sheets flapped lazily, while the clothespins creaked with their weight like miniature swings. Somewhere a crow cawed, its voice harsh, raspy. Annie smiled, remembering a day when she and Miss Sarah made a scarecrow out of straw-stuffed clothes for their small backyard vegetable garden. Master Jake must've been three, maybe four.... While she and Miss Sarah struggled to tie that scarecrow high on a pole in the middle of a patch of waist-high corn, Jake ran full tilt at the crows yelling, "Shoo!" Oh, he was fearless, then! He'd disappear between the corn rows, then dash out into the newly tilled soil, waving his arms and yelling at the top of his lungs——never mind he was trampling seedlings with each step.

"Landsakes that chile wuz a caution," she said, shaking her head at the memory. For a moment she stood there, the memories thick around her. She brushed the air in front of her eyes with one hand, then walked heavily down the hall into the spotless white kitchen. A colander of fresh picked string beans sat on the large kitchen table in the center of the room waiting for her to finish nipping off their ends, stringing them, and breaking them into pieces for cooking. A pot of cold water sat on the large black and white gas range, filled with quartered, peeled potatoes. Pieces of chicken lay submerged in a bowl of cool, salted water, waiting to be dried, then dredged in seasoned flour for frying. Yeast dinner rolls rose under a clean dishcloth on the counter. *More than enough food.*

Shadows crept along the sage green linoleum floor. *Bong, bong, bong, bong!* The grandfather clock in the front room sounded the hour. She had enough time before Doc Livsey got there and Mister Jake came home to put Miz Sarah to rights.

It surprised her somehow to find Miss Sarah's body still lying just as she'd left her. She went into the bathroom and took a washcloth, two towels, and a bar of the castile soap Sarah liked and brought them to the bedside. She filled a basin with water and set it on the table by the bed. Then she carefully undressed her tiny mistress and bathed her.

"How many times I done dis? Oh, Miz Sarah, I *will* miss yuh...Don't fret none 'bout Miztah Jake now, heah? He gonna be fine."

After she'd bathed her, Annie got Sarah's brush and comb from the vanity, walked to the wardrobe, and looked at its contents. She chose a powder blue dress that looked like it had never been worn: "Yes, Miz Sarah, dis'll do jus fine."

The wardrobe stood beside the west window. Annie drew the drapes, and the sun, lower now on the horizon, painted the room with honey. *We're in fo' a fine sunset*, Annie thought, as she paused at the window and looked out.

Past the newly mown lawn streaked with shafts of gold and shadow, the last of Sarah's roses climbed the white pickets of the fence, their blazing red flowers clustered in ready-made bouquets. Beyond them the brown and green fields stretched away to the line of pine trees that at this distance seemed to touch the watercolored sky. Behind their dark green border flowed the river, its silver ribbon glinting through the trees. It occurred to her that nature never cared about the momentous events in human life. Sarah Witherspoon had cared for this farm and this house for the better part of fifty years. Now she was gone, and the sun didn't pause in the sky at her passing; the river continued its journey to the sea; the roses still bloomed gaily in the yard. Only people mourned. And they paused only for a season.

Doc Livsey's knock on the front door intruded on the silence, just as Annie finished arranging Sarah's hair. She put the brush down on the bedside table, smiled reassuringly at Sarah, and went to answer the door.

Annie heard the soft ticking of the clock in the parlor and noticed that her footfalls kept time as she walked. At the front door, she quickly brushed a wiry strand of gray hair from her damp forehead and smoothed the front of her dress before turning the knob. Doc Livsey, his black bag in hand, pulled the screen door open and entered the house.

"She laid out in de bedroom," Annie said, stepping back to let him pass. "I hopes I di'n't do nothing wrong by fixin' her up," she said to his back, as he walked the familiar length of the hall to Sarah's room.

Doc Livsey stopped at Sarah's doorway and turned to face Annie. *She's getting old*, he realized with a start. Annie was heavy—a great pillow of a woman—but she seemed drawn. The round, chocolate face was ringed with small corkscrews of black hair, heavily frosted with gray. The rest of her hair was braided tightly around her head. It sat there like a laurel wreath awarded for some Olympic feat. Her skin glowed with perspiration. Her huge brown eyes were pink-tinged, and the usually smooth brow was furrowed with concern. Doc smiled kindly: "No, Annie, you did just fine."

The crease in Annie's forehead disappeared, and she nodded her appreciation.

"You can come in with me, if you like," Doc Livsey said.

"Thank yuh, no, Doctah Livsey. I jus soon waits out heah, iffen it suits yuh jus de same. I gots things t'do; Miztah Jake be comin' home."

"Well, let me know when he gets here. I'll break the news to him, if you'd like."

"Yessuh. Dat'd be de way Miz Sarah'd want it.... I be in de kitchen iffen yuh want sumpthin'. I gots some cold buttermilk in de ice box."

"That sounds mighty good, Annie."

Annie smiled: "I fix yuh a big, tall glass."

"I'll be out directly," Doc said. He stepped across the threshold of Sarah's room and closed the door.

Annie stood there for a moment, then went down the hall to the kitchen. It was dimmer on that side of the house, so she turned on the light over the kitchen table. In the morning the sun streamed into the room, catching the white of the porcelain sink and enameled pots. But in the evening, it was the first room in shadow. Annie didn't mind; she liked this room better than any in the house. She'd spent countless hours in this place. It was hers even more than the kitchen in the house she and Bill shared. She sat down in the plank-bottomed chair she liked, pulled the colander of beans toward her and set to work.

A bit later the back screen door slammed, and she heard the scuffling sound of shoes being wiped on the doormat in the mudroom outside the kitchen.

"Annie!"

"I'se in heah, Miztah Jake," Annie said, as Jake walked into the kitchen.

"I see Doc Livsey's here. He said he might look in on Mother," Jake said, as he put his arms around Annie's shoulders and gave her a quick hug. He grinned as he saw the floured chicken over her shoulder. "Fried chicken?" He walked over to the stove and lifted the lids on the pots. "Um, um. Mashed potatoes. Green beans. Rolls, too?" He started to lift the towel covering the rising bread.

"Y'all bes leave dem be. Dey's gots t' sit a few mo' minutes."

Jake let the towel fall and walked over to the window above the sink: "How can you stand to cook in this heat? It's about to cool off, though," he said, raising the window. "The wind's kicking up. Looks like we might be in for a storm—" a fresh breeze blew into the kitchen, pushing the heated air out of its way—"Isn't that better?"

"Yessuh, it sho is."

"Well, if Doc's here, I suppose Mother's awake," Jake said. "I'll just go in and say hello."

"But Doctah Livsey's in dere."

"Don't worry, Annie; I'll knock first."

"Bes yuh wait fo' de doctah, Miztah Jake."

There was something in her tone..."Something's wrong. Is Mother worse?" Jake studied Annie's face, and the blood drained out of his own: "I'm going in there."

"Don' go in dere, Miztah Jake. Jus sits down heah wid me and wait fo' de doctah."

Jake stood there, not wanting to voice the thought that sprang to mind: "She's dead...isn't she?" The words stuck in his throat as he said them. He groped for a kitchen chair and sat down across from Annie.

Annie reached across the table and patted his hand: "Yessuh, she is. She passed jus a little bit ago. I knowed yuh'd be comin' home soon...I called Doctah Livsey an he come right ovah."

"But how did it happen?" Jake stared at Annie's face. "She looked so good this morning...She was all right when I called at lunch...How could she be *dead*?"

"It happen dat way sometime, Miztah Jake. It do seem sometime likes dey get a burst a energy, dey coluh come back...sometime, dey makes sense when dey ain't been makin' no sense fo' a long time...," Annie shook her head. "De Bible say de Lawd works in mistirus ways, an dis sho is one...It *sho* is...Maybe it's so's we kin membah dem dat way instead a sick an hurtin' so..."

"Were you with her? Did she say anything?"

"Yessuh, I sho was. She call me, an I comes right in. She was dyin'—I could tell right off she's leavin us—an I calls t' her. Den she smile, like she see me standin dere, an she say my name and 'Robert's heah'. Den she go... real peaceful-like."

"She said Dad was there?" Tears spilled over Jake's eyelids and ran down past his nose. He reached for his handkerchief, wiped his eyes, blew his nose.

"Jake?"

Doc Livsey stood in the kitchen doorway. Jake started to rise—

"Don't get up," Doc said as he approached the kitchen table.

"Can I see her, Doc?"

"Of course you can. I thought you might want me to answer some questions first."

"If you don't mind, Doc, I'd like to see her."

"Sure, Jake. You go on in, and I'll stay here with Annie for awhile."

"You don't need to be any place else?" Jake stood.

"I left a message with Millie and Lula that if anyone needed me, I'd be out here. They know where to find me if they need me. Go on, now. I'm going to sit down and have some buttermilk Annie promised," he said, as he pulled up another chair to the table and sat.

"Why don't you stay for dinner? We've got more than enough—" Jake glanced at Annie; she nodded—"that is, if you don't have other plans...?"

"No plans at all."

"Much obliged, Doc. Thanks.

Doc smiled in response.

Jake walked toward the hallway, paused, and addressed Annie: "Get Doc something stronger than buttermilk, if he wants it, Annie. You know where I keep it."

"Yessuh."

"I'll join you, Doc, after I've seen Mother. Annie?"

"Yessuh?"

"Would you mind calling Bill and asking him if you could stay late tonight? Better yet, ask him if he'd like to have dinner here.... Does he know?"

"Nosuh, I jus call Doctah Livsey. I didn' think t' call Bill."

"Do you think he'd mind?"

"Nosuh. Bill put quite a store by yo' mama. He come. Don' think no mo 'bout it."

"I'll be back," Jake said and left.

Doc waited until he heard the sound of Sarah Witherspoon's bedroom door open and shut: "He seems to be handling this pretty well."

"Yessuh. 'Scuse me a minute." Annie moved to the stove and put the chicken pieces into the big cast iron skillet she used for frying. Hot grease spattered and sizzled. She took a long-handled fork from the counter and turned the pieces. She watched until they'd browned, and then turned the flame down and covered the skillet.

"Now I kin gets yuh dat drink, Doctah Livsey. I jus needs t'get dat chicken on."

"I can get my own drink, Annie. You go and call your husband. Now," Doc said, looking around the kitchen, "where does Jake keep the whiskey?"

Annie frowned. She didn't like the doctor snooping in Miztah Jake's liquor, but there wasn't much she could do: "In dis cabinet heah. Dere's ice in de box. Glasses be ovah by de sink. Yuh sho I can't gets it?"

"I'm fine, Annie; go call your husband."

"Yessuh." Annie frowned again but left the kitchen.

Doc Livsey was surprised to find Jake's liquor cabinet well-stocked. He squatted to have a better look: several bottles of hard-to-come-by Scotch, bourbon—even some decent gin. He reached for a bottle of bourbon, stood up, and unscrewed the top. The rich, sweet scent filled his nostrils: "Ah." His own bootlegger hadn't been able to get good bourbon for several months; Doc wondered how Jake had come by it. He got an old-fashioned glass from the cabinet Annie had indicated and poured himself about two fingers of rich amber liquid. He downed it, neat, before pouring more and adding ice. He twisted the glass in his hand, watching the ice swirl lazily in the bourbon. He put the glass to his lips and sipped slowly. Sometimes death had its compensations.

CHAPTER FOUR

The curtains were drawn, the room dark, except for two small lamps on either side of the bed. In their soft light, Jake saw his mother. She lay on the counterpane dressed in a blue dress. He'd seen her wear it only once before, on Easter, he thought, the year before she became ill. He came closer to the bed, slowly, so as not to disturb her. She looked as if she'd just lain down to rest a bit before going to church. Jake stood over her, looking at her face. Her eyes were closed, as if she were asleep. Her skin was smooth and relaxed; the look of pain, that tightness around her mouth, was gone. Her hair, white and thick, framed her face. Her hands were placed on top of each other at her waist. Her ankles were crossed; her dress arranged in perfect folds. Annie had put Sarah's best shoes on her feet and pinned a small bunch of fabric violets at the collar of her dress. Jake sat down beside the bed.

It occurred to him that for all their closeness, he really knew very little about his mother. He knew she and his father originally came from back East. Connecticut? Her maiden name was...? O'Something. Annie would know. He had no idea whether there was anyone left back there that he should notify. She'd never talked much about the years before she married his father, Robert Caldwell Witherspoon. There'd been a painful rift over religion: Robert's family was Presbyterian; Sarah's family was Irish Catholic. Sarah left Catholicism when she married and had been active in Hulet's tiny Presbyterian Church since its founding, much to the chagrin of the Baptist population. He should notify the minister. What was his name? Bell? Reverend Bell? It sounded right.

A vision popped into his mind: Sarah, kneeling beside his bed, teaching him to pray. He hadn't prayed in a long time. Funny how death made you remember things like prayer, like church. Like God. "Now I lay me down to sleep./ I pray the Lord my soul to keep./ If I should die before I wake,/I pray the Lord my soul to take..." She'd said that every night with him when he was little. Where was his mother's soul now? Had God listened to her? He remembered knocking on her bedroom door one night after he'd been released from the hospital. There was no answer, so he called her. When she didn't respond, he quietly opened the door. There she was, on the floor by her bed, praying. He cleared his throat, but she kept on as if he weren't there, so he listened. She talked to God as if He were in the room instead of invisible and presumably somewhere called Heaven. She talked about her concerns, and her friends' concerns, and the needs of the country and the world. He heard his name and quickly withdrew from the room, silently pulling the door closed after him. He didn't want to know what she said to God about him. But now, when he couldn't ask and she couldn't answer, he desperately wanted to know what she knew, what her prayers for him were about. He had so many questions, so many things he wanted to know, to say—too late. Too late. The words repeated inside his brain like an ancient incantation, hypnotically rhythmic, merging with the beat of his heart. His skin prickled, almost stung, as quick drops of perspiration formed on his forehead and trickled down his back and chest.

Without warning lightning hit nearby and plunged the room into blackness. Thunder crashed, rattling the windows. Another bolt lit the room, a blue-white flash illuminating his mother's face—a white, painted mask like a clown's. Her lips seemed to move. Rain beat at the window-panes. Outside, wind lashed the grass. Lightning flashed. A report like a pistol fired beside his head resounded as a limb fell somewhere close to the house.

"Miztah Jake, come quick! Lightnin' done hit de tree by de back doah!"

The door opened, and Annie's familiar bulk stood framed in the light of an oil lamp. Around her, bright rays streamed into the room. Darkness fled leaving only the familiar behind. Jake glanced at his mother's face; the mask was gone.

"I'm coming." Jake rose and made his way toward the light. "Where's Doc?" he asked, as Annie preceded him down the hallway.

"He bees out back, tryin t' keep dis house from catchin fire."

Fire! Terror gripped him. Blood pulsed against his eardrums. His heart pounded against his ribs, threatened to break through. He stopped, paralyzed, waiting for his heart to burst.

"Lawd, Miztah Jake, is yuh all right?"

The concern in her voice reached him, and he managed to nod.

"Den come *on*! Dat pine tree's too near de house, an Doc Livsey he cain't put out de fire by hisself."

Suddenly, the urgency of the situation checked his fear.

"Get some blankets and bring them outside!" Jake said, pushing past the startled Annie to the kitchen and the back door. He grabbed for the shovel on the mudroom wall and rushed out the back door. Wind caught the screen as he opened it, slamming it into the house and holding it there. Jake didn't bother with it or the driving rain that soaked him through in a matter of seconds. He ran towards Doc who was trying to pull brushwood away from the lightning split pine. A branch, torn like an arm from the trunk, blazed in the dark. Sparks flew and ignited some grass.

"Try to keep it from spreading," Jake called, planting the shovel blade firmly in the newly wet ground. Beneath the muddy surface, the blade hit rock hard ground. Jake stamped on top of the shovel's blade, feeling the ground give slightly under his weight. Muscles straining, he lifted the heavy dirt and threw it on the burning limb. Sparks leapt upward. Annie called something from the house, but the wind caught her words and blew them away. Jake kept digging and throwing dirt on the fire. Little rivulets of flame from the fallen branch flowed toward the house through grass still dry at its roots. On the periphery of his vision, Jake saw them arranged like a fiery spider's web. A gust of wind lifted one fragile tendril from the web and set it down to weave another.

"Doc! Look there!"

Doc, still dragging brush to safer ground, looked and saw the glowing webs. He dropped his load and ran toward the house.

"Annie!" Jake shouted, "Bring those blankets!"

The figure in the doorway lumbered down the back steps to the ground, arms laden. "I'se comin, Miztah Jake!"

Her words reached Jake's ears about the time Doc reached her. Grabbing some blankets from Annie's arms, Doc ran back toward the spreading flames as the rest of the blankets fell to the ground. Annie bent to pick them up, heedless of the wind whipping at her dress and the drenching rain. Blankets clutched in each hand, she moved as quickly as she could toward Jake and the fallen log. Her sodden skirt clung to her legs impeding her progress. The stricken branch hissed menacingly as rain touched charred spots still tender from the recent assault. A soft thud of dirt buried the sound. Her back to Jake and the dying limb, Annie turned her attention to a glowing line, inching slowly forward. She threw one waterlogged blanket at the line and smothered the erstwhile tributary. A bright orange spot off to her right caught her eye. Dragging the other blanket behind her, Annie moved toward her target and buried it. On the other side of the smoldering branch, Doc worked furiously to thwart any further outbreak. Stamping small flickering lines with his feet, he slapped at others with blankets.

"It's out." Jake's voice carried above the rain and wind.

Doc and Annie, their eyes stinging from smoke and strain, straightened slowly, willing their backs to an upright position. The crisis over, they looked at their surroundings bemused. Sensation awakened slowly: muscles protested, backs screamed. Profound fatigue and damp, chilled-to-the-bone cold seeped into them. With tacit agreement, all three moved toward the farmhouse. Gravel crunched in the driveway, and they turned toward the sound. The glare of headlights blinded them briefly. A truck pulled in front of the gate, and the driver turned off his lights.

"Bill!" Annie shouted to the shape emerging from the truck's front seat.

The figure, holding a limp square of newspaper over his head with one hand, waved with the other, and slammed the cab door shut with his hip.

"Whatcha'll standin in de rain fo'? Ain'tchall gots no sense?" Bill said, as he ran toward them in a half-crouch, trying to avoid the storm's fury.

His words acted like the snap of a hypnotist's fingers. Thunder boomed behind them. As if it were some starter's pistol, Annie, Doc, and Jake bolted toward the farmhouse.

The others were already in the kitchen when Bill reached the mudroom a few seconds later. Jake walked over to where Bill stood, soaking wet and holding the limp, dripping paper over his head. Jake took the newspaper out of Bill's hand.

"Doesn't seem to be doing much good, Bill," Jake said, as he dropped the soggy paper into a trash can by the screen door.

"No, suh, Miztah Jake, it sho don't, but den I didn't mean t' be a-standin' in de rain fo' so long, an I sho didn't 'spect t' see y'all standin' round as if yuh didn't have sense....It's not fittin'," he added in a reproachful tone.

"Hush yo' mouth, Bill Jackson!" Annie turned on her husband with protective fury. "Yuh don' knows whut yuh's talkin' bout. Not fittin'! I s'pose yuh'd think it fittin' iffen we lets dis heah house burn t' de groun 'roun po Miz Witherspoon!"

Bill backed up two or three steps as his wife advanced until his back felt the wall. Behind his irate wife, Bill saw Jake and Doc as Sarah's death forced itself back into their minds and extinguished the laughter. He sidestepped his wife and spoke directly to the two men: "I'se sho sorry, Miztah Jake...Doctah Livsey. I didn' know 'bout no fire, an I sho didn' mean no disrespec'." His speech finished, the black man shifted his gaze to the green, linoleum-covered floor. His tall frame seemed to shrink as his dripping denim overalls made slow puddles around his shoes. The two puddles grew, joined amoeba-like, and became one amorphous, shallow lake that moved silently across the green expanse.

"I know you didn't, Bill. I'm just glad you're here." Jake walked over to where Bill stood and put his hand on Bill's shoulder. "I need you....There's a lot to be done. A lot to figure out."

Bill straightened. "Yessuh. Dat's de trufe, fo' sho. I hep anyways I kin."

"I knew you would, Bill. Thanks."

"Yessuh."

Jake took a deep breath and glanced at Doc who stood in his own lake, listening. A broad grin broke across Jake's face: "I think the first thing we ought to do is get dry.

"Doc, I've got some things you can change into. Annie, do you think that food is still fit to eat? I, for one, am starving, and from the looks of everyone else, I bet I'm not the only one."

"It be fine, Miztah Jake. I be sho a dat befo' I comes outside."

"Great! Well, go get some dry things on—Bill, you can borrow some clothes from me, too—"

"I gots some things heah," Annie broke in. "Miz Sarah, she say I kin do some things from home, an dey's still in de washroom."

"Well then, that's all settled. We'll meet back in the kitchen for food in a minute."

Annie shook her head vehemently. "No suh. I'll fix y'all up in de dinin' room. Bill an' me, we eat in de kitchen."

"You really don't have to go to all that trouble, Annie. We'll be fine in here."

"No suh," Annie said, shaking her head emphatically. "Now dat wouldn't be fittin'! Miz Sarah won' stans fo' it." (That was her final word, and there would be no argument.)

"Come on, Bill. I gets yuh dry clothes." Annie grabbed a candle from a nearby shelf, lit it from the kerosene lamp, and walked to the door that led to the basement—"Yuh comin'?"

Bill looked at the other men, shrugged his shoulders, and followed his wife's back through the door and down the stairs.

Jake took two candles from the shelf, lit them, handed one to Doc: "Shall we?"

"Lead on. I'm so clammy I could grow moss."

A cool breeze blew through the window carrying the fresh smell of rain. The candles on the table flickered in the breeze; an oil lamp sat on the counter, its flame steady and bright. The farmhouse kitchen glowed with warm, golden light. It was still raining, but the rain, though steady, was no longer frightening.

Annie reached for the hot pad that hung above the back of the gas stove and opened the oven door. The rolls were nicely brown. She removed them from the baking sheet and transferred them to a bun warmer. She speared the chicken frying in the skillet and put the pieces on brown paper to drain while she set the dining room table and two places for Bill and herself in the kitchen. That finished, she arranged the chicken on a platter and placed it and the rolls in the roomy warming oven above the stove.

"Honey, whut gonna happen t' Miztah Jake, now dat Miz Sarah done passed?" Bill asked, staring into the flames of the candles in front of him.

"What d' ya mean, 'whut gonna happen?'" Annie glanced at Bill, then returned her attention to spooning the green beans, simmered with bacon and onion, into a serving bowl.

Bill watched as she placed the bowl beside the chicken in the warmer and reached for the boiled potatoes.

"Well, I'se jus thinkin'...Miz Sarah, she done took care a de farmin' mattuhs since Miztah Robert passed. How Miztah Jake gonna take care a bidness now she gone?"

"Same way Miz Sarah done it when she gots so sick," Annie said, pouring the potatoes into a colander in the sink. "Dem lawyuhs in town, dey handles it all." She took a potato masher out of the pottery crock she used for utensils, transferred the steaming, drained potatoes to a bowl, and started mashing.

Bill sat watching his wife work and thought, while Annie finished the potatoes and scooped them into a serving dish. Then she took a big chunk of cold butter and plopped it in the middle of the steaming mound. Bill's mouth started to water.

"Suppuh 'bout ready? Hit sho do look good, honey. Um, um, it sho do."

Annie smiled at him over her shoulder—"Miztah Jake say he be wantin' gravy wid his supper. Yuh kin go on an eats iffen yuh's too hungry t' wait a few mo' minutes."

"Cream gravy? I reckin I kin wait." Bill thought some more, while Annie stirred flour into the fried chicken drippings and added milk. "Yuh gonna tell 'im 'bout de lawyuhs, or is dey gonna tell 'im?"

"Miz Sarah done lef all dat in a lettuh for Miztah Jake," she said, pouring the finished gravy into a gravy boat. "I'se sposed t' give it t' him, when I thinks he be ready."

Annie got the food from the warming oven and, after taking some for Bill and herself, arranged the rest in serving dishes on a large tray.

Bill shook his head. "Sho don' seem right, her dyin' like dat, widout tellin' 'im 'bout things."

"Bill! Yuh knows whut dem doctahs tole Miz Sarah!"

"Don' git all riled up now, sugah. Miz Sarah, she 'bout de finest white woman I'se eber knowed, but she sho had a blin' spot 'bout dat boy a hers. Yuh gots t' know dat she protected 'im too much. Doctahs or no doctahs, a growed man gots t' know whut happens 'roun heah, a right t' know 'bouts his own fambly! Don'cha be lookin' at me dat way," Bill said, seeing the anger in Annie's eyes. "Miztah Jake be de man a dis house, an de sooner he fines out 'bout things, de sooner he gonna gits better."

"I gots t' git dis on de table." Annie lifted the tray and left the room.

CHAPTER FIVE

J ake awoke disoriented and wrestling with his sheets. His body shook. His head pounded with excess adrenaline, while unfocused bits of a dream darted across his mind. A rooster's crow shattered the peace of the countryside. Jake lay there, feeling his heartbeat slow to normal, and hoped the throbbing in his head would lessen now that morning had broken. Through the bedroom curtains the sky showed gray—an eerie half-light, sifted through air so heavy with moisture that light drifted in granules to the ground. Jake felt heavy, too—muffled, as if the weight of the morning air were wrapped around his limbs. Moving them seemed impossible. He didn't want to move. He wanted to lie in bed and let the heaviness take over, fill his brain, smother thought.

A bird sang nearby, mocking the grayness of the day. Jake listened as the solitary song became a duet. His headache abated; he stood and made his way to the bathroom.

Bathed, shaved, and dressed, Jake walked down the hall, avoiding his mother's closed door. In the kitchen, he made coffee. When it had finished brewing, Jake poured himself a steaming cup and sat down at the table to wait for Annie. It was uncomfortable to be just sitting. He had caught himself starting to cook his mother's breakfast. He had fixed her breakfast every morning since her illness made her bedfast. Annie could've done it, but he enjoyed it, enjoyed taking her tray and chatting with her about nothing before he left for town. He liked taking care of her: it made him feel more like a man.

There was an awkwardness about being grown and still living in his parents' house. He'd never mentioned it, but he'd felt it keenly. There were times when he longed for a woman, times when desire welled up inside him so that it took all his strength to vanquish it. The force of his emotions scared him. What would he unleash if he gave them free rein? His breakdown and amnesia were caused by something—something so terrible, his own mind wouldn't acknowledge it. He had to keep his self-control or risk being some kind of monster.

"Yuh up already, Miztah Jake?"

"Annie. I didn't hear you come in."

"Now dats de trufe. Yuh's sittin dere like yuh's stone cole deaf." Annie lumbered over to the stove. "I sees yuh done made coffee."

"Why don't you get a cup and sit for a second?" Jake drained his cup and held it up. "Since you're pouring..."

Annie filled his cup before pouring her own. She put the pot on a back burner and took out a small iron skillet.

"Yuh ain't had brekfuss yet." It was a statement rather than a question.

"I'm not hungry." Jake looked at his watch and picked up his cup.

"Yuh hasta eat sumpin. I'se not budgin' till yuh do."

Jake looked over the rim of his coffee cup and drank to keep from laughing. "Maybe an egg and a piece of toast."

"Dat ain't hardly nuff t' keep a mouse alive!" Annie said, emphasizing her point with the skillet. "Y'all's gonna needs lots mo den dat. How bouts I fix yuh some a dat good bacon an some grits on de side?"

"No, really, that's all I want. It's getting late anyway. I've got to get into town."

Annie looked at him as if he'd gone mad. "Now whut yuh gonna do dat fo'?"

"I have a job, Annie. People depend on me."

Annie turned her back to him and took a sip of her coffee before crossing to the icebox and taking out a half-loaf of bread, a wire basket full of eggs, some butter, and returning to the stove.

"I hope you're not fixing all that for me," Jake said, amused and annoyed at the same time.

Annie said nothing, just lit the broiler and the front burner.

Jake watched as she cut two thick slices of bread, buttered them and put them on the broiler rack to toast.

"Annie, did you hear me?"

Annie plopped a hunk of butter in the skillet and was silent until it melted.

"Miztah Jake?" she said, without turning around, "Iffen y'all s'cuse me fo' sayin' so, dere's things t' be done heah dat needs yuh lots mo' den dat town." She cracked two eggs and put their contents into the skillet.

Jake stiffened, took another sip of his coffee. "You can handle things until I get back."

"Yessuh," Annie said, setting Jake's breakfast down in front of him, "I kin, but I still thinks yuh ought t' be heah."

"I'm not going to argue with you, Annie. I'm going to town this morning, and that's all I'm going to say about this subject. Understood?"

She turned away and mumbled something unintelligible.

Jake ate his breakfast in silence then left by the back door to avoid passing Sarah's room. He didn't want to sit in the house waiting for Tom Mooney to come in his hearse and take her body off to the funeral parlor. Annie could handle that. He didn't need to be here. He needed to be alone, to get out of the house, to walk, to work, to do the things he always did.

Jenny waited for Jake to arrive. She'd put on her prettiest work dress, though why she'd bothered she didn't know. Jake hadn't shown up after work yesterday. He hadn't even walked in to tell her something had come up…Of course, it wasn't a formal date or anything, just that he'd said he might drop by for a cup of coffee. As she refilled salt and sugar containers, she glanced again at the clock: eight-fifteen. Well, no matter, she'd just have to open without him.

Faces, disjointed images, half-glimpsed scenes, discordant sounds continued to flash through Jake's brain like some motion picture gone wild. He staggered to the side of the road, sat down, held his head in a vise made of his hands, and tried not to go mad.

Sam Cross came through the yellow Dutch door of the cafe and, after exchanging greetings with the other regulars, headed for his usual booth in the north corner, right next to a front window.

"Any chance of gettin' some coffee this mornin', Jenny?" he called across the room.

"Sure, Sam. I'll get some fresh from the kitchen and be right back." Where was he anyway? She glanced at the clock as she hurried to the kitchen: thirty-five minutes after eight! Jake had never been this late.

Forty minutes later Sam was at the register, waiting for Jenny to ring up his order. There was still no sign of Jake.

"How was your breakfast, Sam?"

"Real good."

"Glad to hear it. That'll be thirty-five cents."

"Here," Sam said, handing over the change. "Say, did ya hear about Sarah Witherspoon?"

Jenny kept her head down, as she deposited the coins in their slots. "Jake's mother?"

"Know any other Witherspoons 'round here?"

Jenny smiled as she looked up. "Now that you mention it, no. What about her?"

"She died."

"Died? I didn't even know she was sick."

"Yep, been sick for over a year. Doc said she died late yesterday afternoon."

"How sad..."

"Yeah. Nice woman, Mrs. Witherspoon..." Sam shuffled his feet, suddenly uncomfortable. "Well, got to git on back to the farm. Got things to do."

"Bye, Sam," Jenny said, but Sam was already out the door.

Ben Hawley opened the office door and tossed a newspaper on top of his desk.

Larry looked up from his reading: "Something wrong?"

"I ran into Doc on the way over here. Jake's mother died last night."

"No kidding? Poor guy. He seemed pretty upset yesterday, and then to go home to that..." Larry sipped his stale coffee, grimaced.

"Yeah, it's a shame. The Witherspoons were a close family once. Old Mr. Witherspoon died while Jake was still living in Washington, then his wife and children died in that freak fire, and now Mrs. Witherspoon's gone...Jake's the only one left." Ben paused for a moment, noticed Larry's coffee cup: "Any coffee left?"

"I hope not, for your sake. This stuff is terrible," Larry said, looking at the liquid in his cup with disgust.

"I'll ask Penny to brew a new pot."

"Good idea...Say, I didn't know Jake lived in Washington—D.C?"

"Where else? He moved there right after law school, long before you came to Hulet. President Wilson was still in office."

"What was he doing? Something to do with the war?"

"No, we hadn't gotten into it yet, though now that I think about it," Ben said, a grin beginning at the corners of his mouth, "I suppose you could say he was involved in a war of sorts: he worked for the Justice Department."

"The Justice Department? I thought he practiced law in some firm before moving back here, although I didn't know it was in D.C. The 'firm' was the Justice Department?"

"No, you're right: Jake *was* a partner in a firm before joining Mike in 1923. He left the Justice Department before Harding took office."

"Of his own accord? Or one of those political things?"

"I don't know. You'll have to ask him."

"What good would that do?"

Ben sat down behind his desk and opened the newspaper: "Not much good at all."

Jenny finished putting the last of the clean dishes in the cupboard. She untied her apron and turned to Bertha, who was sitting down, probably for the first time that day.

"Bertha, could I ask you something?"

Bertha looked up from staring at her swollen ankles: "What is it, love? Sure and somethin's been on your mind all day."

Jenny sat down across the table from her friend, picked up some clean dishtowels, and began to fold them. It gave her something to do with her hands. "It's about Jake Witherspoon."

Bertha sat up in her chair and folded her arms on the table: "I was thinkin' it might be about him."

Jenny was startled. "Why would you think that?"

"No reason at all. It's just me tongue startin' out on its own again. Now, what about him?"

"Well, yesterday morning he mentioned he might come by the cafe on his way home for a cup of coffee"—Bertha raised her eyebrows, but Jenny didn't notice. Her eyes were fixed on the dishtowels in front of her—"He didn't, of course...." Her voice trailed off.

Bertha knew when to keep her mouth shut, so she waited.

Presently, Jenny looked up. "Well, now I know his mother died and..."

"And?"

"And—" Jenny folded a dishtowel in half, carefully smoothing the crease with the palm of her hand—"and I was wondering whether you'd think it was awfully forward of me if I called at his farm sometime and asked if I could do anything." She reached for another towel and waited for Bertha's reaction. When nothing was said, Jenny raised her eyes, and was surprised to see a broad smile on Bertha's face.

"So it's *that* way, is it?" Bertha's smile spread to her voice. (Her delight was so obvious that Jenny felt herself blushing.) "Now, now, none of that, girl! It's nothin' to be ashamed of, your likin' him and all."

"It's not that I'm smitten or anything, you understand—"

"Oh, I understand," Bertha said, her voice returning to a respectful tone. "I understand you wouldn't want to go and do something that might have the whole town thinkin' you're interested in steppin' out again."

"Is that what you think would happen if I called?" Horror filled Jenny's voice. "Oh, Bertha, I'm so *glad* I talked to you before I did something that foolish. I wouldn't ever want to put Mr. Witherspoon—"

"It's *Mister* Witherspoon now is it?" Bertha reached across the table and captured Jenny's hands. "Look at me, love. You are as precious to me as one of my own daughters. I wouldn't tell you anything but what I thought was the best thing for you to hear, and that's always goin' to be God's honest truth... Jenny, it's time." (Bertha nodded slowly while her eyes searched Jenny's.) "You've been actin' the part of Will Schumacher's widow long enough. It's *glad* I am, m'girl—glad you've found someone who makes you feel alive again!"

Jenny flinched, and Bertha hurried to finish. "I know you're not forward, for heaven's sake! I know, too, that Jake Witherspoon hasn't a clue about what you're feelin'. I hoped, of course, but even *I* didn't know for sure, and I'm with you every day! So don't be worryin' about what other people might think. I'm just glad to see you takin' notice of the feelings you've buried all these years." Bertha patted Jenny's hands.

"Oh, *please* don't be nice to me," Jenny said, just before the tears she'd been holding back escaped and ran down her cheeks.

Stricken, Bertha moved to Jenny's side.

Jenny didn't notice; her very bones ached with the pain of Will's death, of years wasted, of loss. Suddenly, Jenny shook her head and gently extricated herself from Bertha's awkward attempt to comfort. She walked to the sink and splashed cold water on her face, while Bertha returned to her chair and waited. When Jenny turned around, her eyes were swollen and red, her face puffy, but she was smiling.

"I haven't done that in years," Jenny said, but there was no apology in her voice. She took a deep breath and smoothed her hair back from her face. "I must look a sight," she said, more to herself than to Bertha. Jenny took another deep breath, straightened her shoulders, and grinned: "Want to join me in a *very* big piece of pie?"

Jake stood up slowly and started walking back toward the farm. He felt like he'd just awakened from a very deep sleep; his brain still stumbled over dreams. His face stung, itched. He reached to touch it, and was surprised when his fingers came away wet. The road ahead blurred for a moment. It didn't matter; he knew this road, could've walked it blind.

The pasture gate creaked noisily as Jake slipped the rusty, wire loop over the post and pushed it open enough to pass through. Old wagon wheel ruts were all but invisible, overgrown now with a mixture of grass, weeds, and what remained of summer's wildflowers. He secured the gate and noted other signs of neglect: the precarious angle of the post, the splits in the weathered boards. For a moment Jake stood motionless looking across the fallow fields, absorbing the sounds, the beauty, the barrenness of disuse. The land here was deceptive, seemingly flat because of the tall grass which distorted the true reach of the horizon. Between here and there lay shallow valleys and sudden mounds of earth. His destination lay just to the north of where he stood, on one such rise overlooking a particularly deep valley.

Jake hesitated below the hill, listening to the wind as it blew through the pines at the top. His shadow stretched like pulled taffy to his right, and he began the short climb to the top, where he knew they would be. As he neared the spot marked by the tall pines, he saw the picket fence had been recently whitewashed, and he was grateful—grateful that someone, probably Bill, perhaps Annie, had not left them untended. A hard lump formed in his throat as he saw the large stone marker at the back proclaiming the family name and the four white crosses. He swallowed, but the lump remained and grew larger as he entered the family cemetery where his wife and children lay buried alongside his father. He knelt beside Laura's grave, gently touched the cross that bore her name, and remembered....

CHAPTER SIX

Jake's shadow, crazily disjointed on the uneven terrain, stretched out beside him as he approached the land he had shared with Laura. The property, several acres, looked as it had when he bought it—unsettled, wild—as it must have looked before settlers came with their axes and plows. He scanned the northern horizon, squinting against the bright rays of the sun lingering at the world's edge, looking for some telltale sign of their presence. Thickets, weeds, and shoulder-high saplings hid the creek Sarah had played in. The pines were taller, denser than he remembered, as were the cottonwoods and elms. Only Laura's apple tree and the blackened chimney remained to mark where their house had stood. His heart felt tight in his chest, as if his ribs had shrunk. Nothing remained of his wife, his children, their lives together but an apple tree, a chimney, and three white crosses in a family plot...and memories. Thank God for the memories—of the night they died, of the horror and helplessness, yes, but that wasn't all. Sometime in the day's quiet solitude he'd found Laura and Sarah and Teddy—their faces, their voices, their love—and even, their forgiveness.

"Billy!"

Dan Johnson's voice startled Billy, made him jump. Johnson stood in his office doorway, frowning. Billy's heart raced, kept pace with his brain, as he tried to remember the morning's events, anything that might account for Johnson's mood.

"Billy!"

"Yessir?"

"Are you deaf, boy?" Without waiting for a reply, Johnson turned away. "Come into my office. I've got something I want you to do."

Billy hurried to the office, and waited. Johnson sat down, filled his pipe, lit it, and leaned back in his swivel chair. Dan puffed on his pipe for a full five minutes before speaking.

"Up to a reporting assignment?"

Billy couldn't believe what he was hearing. "Yes, sir!"

"All right, you've got one." Johnson scooted back from his desk, pulled out a notepad and pencil from the top drawer, and handed them to Billy. "Take these; go out to the Witherspoon place. Interview Witherspoon about his mother. She died Wednesday; the paper needs to acknowledge it."

"I thought you didn't like the Witherspoons—"

"What of it? *Witherspoon* may be a fool, but his parents helped found this town. His mother was as near as they come to a local icon."

"Did you know her?"

Johnson took the pipe out of his mouth, put it down in the battered metal ashtray on his desk. "Look, I don't have all day. Can you get me what I need or not?"

"I can do it—"

"Then get to it. I'll need it by three."

"Yes, sir!"

Johnson turned back to his desk, picked up his pipe—which had gone out—dumped the spent tobacco in the metal trash can he kept on his right, and started to refill it. By the time he'd tamped the tobacco in the bowl, Billy had grabbed his cap and was halfway down Main Street.

Billy ran until he came to Johnson's house where he kept his bicycle—a gift last Christmas from his father and mother, who thought it might help him in his job. They had gotten the used two-wheeler from a neighboring farmer whose boy had outgrown it in exchange for some badly needed cash. The Wigginses were not wealthy, but they owned their farm outright and were frugal. Billy put the pad and pencil into the wicker basket, proud that he could ride to Witherspoon's. After all his daydreaming, he was finally going to meet Jake Witherspoon, and on official newspaper business. As he pedaled down the road toward the Witherspoon farm, his mind formed questions for the interview. That his boss would write the actual article rankled, but if Billy asked intelligent questions, well—well, Johnson might think of him in a different light, as a real reporter, not just as some kid who set type and swept floors. *Perhaps,* Billy thought, *I can find out why Mr. Johnson doesn't like Mr. Witherspoon. Maybe, I can even find out why Mr. Witherspoon does what he does in town, and what he does in the library.* His thoughts ran on, until he remembered that his assignment was to find out about the man's mother, not the man.

A car horn blared behind him, causing him to swerve a little. He stopped at the side of the road, and waited for the car to pass, but it pulled up beside him.

"Hello, Billy! I certainly didn't think I'd see you this morning. Has Mr. Johnson declared Friday a holiday?" Jenny smiled at him from behind the wheel, and he grinned.

"Gosh, no." (Billy blushed.) "I'm on assignment."

"Is that a fact?"

Billy drew himself up: "Mr. Johnson sent me out to the Witherspoon place to interview Mr. Witherspoon about his mother."

"So you're finally going to get a chance to write!" Jenny seemed as excited as he was.

"Well, not exactly. Mr. Johnson's going to write the article." Billy's head drooped a little, but then he looked up. "But I'm going to show him I could've done it, if he'd let me."

"You do that," Jenny said firmly. "It's a start. Mr. Johnson must have some confidence in you, or he wouldn't have sent you on such an important assignment."

"Well, it's not all that important. It's just an obituary for Mrs. Witherspoon."

"That's nothing to sneeze at, Billy Wiggins. Sarah Witherspoon was an important woman in this town. I'm glad to see your editor recognizes it."

Billy stood there, holding the handlebars of his bicycle, one foot on the ground, the other resting on the uppermost pedal. "Where are you going? Did *you* declare a holiday?"

Jenny laughed. "Well, maybe I did. I left Bertha in charge for awhile. As it happens, I'm on my way to the Witherspoon place myself."

Billy tried not to show his disappointment. There went his chance to be alone with Mr. Witherspoon. "You are?"

"I brought some food for him. He's bound to have a lot of company with the funeral tomorrow, and I haven't really had a chance to pay my respects."

Billy thought her voice sounded queer, like she was reciting a speech, but all that really registered was that Mr. Witherspoon was going to have a lot of company. Maybe he wouldn't have time to talk! The thought of going back and facing Dan Johnson without the interview chilled him.

"Is something the matter?"

"I, uh, was just wondering if Mr. Witherspoon will be able to talk to me with all of that company there."

"Why, Billy Wiggins! I'm ashamed of you!"

Billy blinked. What had he done now?

"Any reporter worth his salt would know how to get that interview, company or no company!"

"But, Jenny, I'm not a real reporter—"

Jenny cut him off. "Mr. Johnson seems to think you are, or he wouldn't have sent you."

He thought about that for a minute. "Well, to be honest, I don't think there was anybody else to send."

"He could've gone himself."

"Oh, no, Jenny," Billy said, shaking his head. "Mr. Johnson doesn't like Mr. Witherspoon. Not at all. He won't have a calendar at the paper; won't even talk about him."

"Well, that's the most *ridiculous* thing I've ever heard. Why wouldn't he like Mr. Witherspoon? What's Jake ever done to him, or to anybody else for that matter?" Jenny was indignant.

"I don't know why he doesn't like him—Mr. Johnson won't talk about it—but it's for sure he doesn't like him."

Jenny shrugged her shoulders: "Well, that has nothing to do with sending you instead of going himself."

Billy squinted and tilted his head. "It doesn't?"

"No, it certainly doesn't. Whatever else Mr. Johnson may be, he is a professional journalist. He wouldn't let his personal feelings stand in the way of a good story. If he'd thought going himself would've gotten him a better story, he'd have gone." Jenny looked Billy straight in the eyes. "You can be sure of that."

"Yes, ma'am."

"Jenny," she said firmly. "Now you'd better stop talking to me and get on with your assignment. I'm just glad I'll be there to see you handle this situation." Jenny put the car in gear and fluttered her fingers at him. "Toodle-loo."

Her voice had a lilt to it that Billy heard all the way to the Witherspoon farm.

Jenny hoped Billy hadn't noticed her nervousness. He hadn't said anything about her being dressed up, but then she'd been in the car, so maybe he hadn't seen. She took a deep breath, and let it out slowly. "It's only natural to be a bit nervous," she assured herself, as she drove along. But she was more than a bit nervous: she was positively terrified of going to Jake Witherspoon's. What would people think? What if—

"Oh, *bother* what if! It's not like I'm doing anything wrong. For heaven's sake, I'm taking him some food! Bertha's right. No one's going to think anything about it." Jenny took another deep breath, sat up straighter, and fixed her eyes firmly on the road ahead. "So, Jenny Schumacher, you will march right up to Jake Witherspoon's door, give him the pies, and see what happens."

Annie was on her way back to the kitchen when she heard the front gate creak. She went to the front door and opened it. A small woman with soft brown eyes and a pretty figure was coming up the stairs of the front porch bearing a pie in each hand. Her thick auburn hair was pulled back and held with a large emerald green bow tied at the nape of her neck. She wore no hat to protect her fair skin from the summer sun. Her dress was white, belted at the waist. A small green pin on the collar was her only other adornment. She wore real silk hose and on her feet were smart, white heels with thin straps across the instep.

"Hello. I'm Jenny Schumacher," the woman said, as she crossed the porch to the door. "Is Mr. Witherspoon here? I heard about Mrs. Witherspoon's death, and I just thought I'd bring these by." Jenny smiled, and held out one of the pies, as Annie opened the screen door.

Annie liked the young woman immediately. There was something charmingly direct in her manner—a refreshing change from the others who'd come to visit. She held the door open wider and took the offered pie. "Yessum, Miztah Witherspoon's here. Won'cha come in Miz—"

"Schumacher," Jenny said, stepping inside, "but no one calls me that anymore. Just about everyone in town calls me Jenny."

Annie looked more carefully at the young woman. "How come dey do dat?"

"Well, I suppose it's because of the cafe—" Annie looked blank, so Jenny continued—"I own Jenny's Cafe in town."

"Well," Annie said, as if that explained everything. "Dese pies sho' do look good," she said truthfully, taking the other pie from Jenny. "Yuh kin waits heah, while I fetch Miztah Jake," Annie said, nodding to a chair.

Jenny made herself comfortable and watched the maid walk down the hall. Jake's home was nothing like she'd thought it would be. For one thing, it was much larger than she'd anticipated. For another, a graceful picket fence, painted white, but almost covered with roses, framed the house. Somehow, she'd never pictured Jake in a house bordered by roses. Larger trees dotted the front yard, and flowers lined the walkway leading to the large front porch, complete with swing, that wrapped around the two-story frame house. The house was also painted white, but the shutters were an inviting shade of green.

The interior was even more unexpected. From where she sat, everything was immaculate: she could see herself in the shine on the hardwood floors. Even the carpet runner in the hall, though obviously not a recent addition, looked rich and well taken care of. There was not a trace of dust anywhere. She saw an arched entryway, just a bit down from where she sat, and decided to take a peek, before the maid returned with Jake. Looking around kept her from fidgeting. She got up, looked in at Sarah Witherspoon's parlor, and promptly forgot everything else.

Jake saw her as he came down the hall. She was standing in front of the bookshelves, evidently engrossed in a book. She almost looked unreal, like someone in one of Max's paintings—Jake stopped. It'd been a long time since he'd thought of Maxwell Howe. For a moment he stood there remembering, wondering what had happened to Max in the last five years… But this was not the time.

Jenny still had not noticed him. He hated to disturb her, but felt odd watching her when she was unaware of his presence. "Jenny?" Jake spoke quietly, so as not to startle her. There was no response, so he entered the parlor and tried again. "Jenny?"

Jenny whirled in the direction of his voice and quickly closed the book. She knew she must be blushing, but there was no help for it: "Jake! I didn't hear you come in. I mean—well, you might as well know. I was sitting in the hall where your maid asked me to wait, but as you can see, I started snooping and saw this room. I couldn't resist it, and now you've caught me. I hope you know I don't usually go wandering around someone else's home without being invited—It's just so…"

"It's quite all right," Jake said, smiling. He came closer. "It *is* a nice room, isn't it?"

Jenny nodded, "It's lovely."

"It was my mother's favorite room. She'd be very happy to know someone else feels the way she did about it. I see you've seen the books." Jake waved his hand to indicate the shelves that lined the walls.

"I'm sorry—"

"For what?"

Jenny looked down at the book in her hand and slowly held it up. Jake took it, looked at the title.

"*Jane Eyre*? Mother *would've* liked you. Have you read it?"

"No, I'm afraid I haven't——"

"Well then, you must take it home." Jake held the book out to her.

"I'll just get a copy from the library——"

"Borrow this one. *Jane Eyre* was Mother's favorite novel. She'd never forgive me if I let you walk away without it. You can return it when you've finished." Jake took her hand and pressed the book onto her palm. "I insist."

"Thank you."

Jake still held her hand, and found he was reluctant to let it go. "You're welcome," he said, and released her, turning toward the loveseat as he did. "Won't you sit down?"

"I can only stay for a moment," Jenny said, but sat down on the seat across from him. She could still feel the warmth of where he'd held her hand...

"Yes, of course. Annie said you brought pies. Thank you so much. I was in the cafe for lunch—Wednesday, I think it was. To be honest, with Mother's death, I've lost track of the days——"

"I was so sorry to hear about your mother's passing...."

As she spoke Jake realized that Jenny was not merely being polite; she seemed genuinely affected by his mother's death. He could tell by looking in her eyes...He'd never realized how brown her eyes were...nor how beautiful.

Annie sat in the comfort of her kitchen, inordinately pleased that Miss Jenny had come to visit. "Miz Sarah," Annie whispered to the ceiling as she cut the pies, "I sho' do like dat Miz Jenny. She 'minds me a little a Miz Laura; don'cha think she do? Jus a bit?"

Annie thought some more as she finished cutting the pies. Then she ran her finger along the flat of the knife blade where some of the cherry pie filling had stuck and popped her finger into her mouth.

"Tell yuh one thin', Miz Sarah," Annie said, looking up in the air as she dropped the knife into the sink, "She sho' kin make good pies. Yessum, deys almos' good as mine."

Annie lifted the slices out of the pie plates and arranged them on two different serving plates. Then she washed and dried Jenny's pie plates, so she could take them home with her when she left. As Annie hung the dishtowel on its holder, a thought occurred to her, and her mouth widened into a mischievous grin. She waddled happily over to the kitchen table, picked up the plates, and took them to the dining room.

Jenny felt Jake watching her and suddenly felt self-conscious. How long had she been babbling on? Her cheeks felt warm. She reached for the book, took it in both hands to keep them from betraying her.

"I really must be going," she said, standing. (Jake stood.) "Bertha will have a conniption if I leave her alone too long with Susie."

"Are you certain you can't stay?" Jake asked, sounding genuinely disappointed.

"I'm afraid I do have to go, but thank you for the book. I'll return it just as soon as I finish, and I promise I'll take good care of it."

"I know you will." Jake smiled down at her, aware of how small she seemed this close. Her eyes reminded him of a doe he'd seen once which had wandered into the backyard early one morning. The deer's eyes were large, colored a deep, soft brown. In them he'd seen a mixture of keen awareness and vulnerability. He saw the same qualities mirrored in Jenny's eyes. Perhaps it was this that made him want to reassure her...to protect her. "I'll walk you to the door."

"Doc said the funeral is tomorrow," Jenny said as they left the room. "If there's anything you need, anything I can do, please let me know." She looked up at him and grinned. "I don't think you'll be needing any more food, though. How many pies have you received?"

Jake smiled, grateful to Jenny for the light note; he tried to match it. "One or two, but I'm awfully glad you brought those pies. Rest assured, they will not go to waste. Several people have already been here to pay their respects, and Annie assures me more will be arriving after the funeral tomorrow…Anyway, I'm grateful for your thoughtfulness, and for the chance to enjoy your company, even if it was for much too short a time."

They had reached the front door, but Jake was reluctant to open it. She was so close, he could smell the tantalizing perfume of her skin, feel her warmth. His heart pounded unnaturally in his chest. He wanted to reach out to her, hold her in his arms. He cleared his throat.

"I know this might not be the proper time to say so, Jenny, but I would very much enjoy seeing you again." (His eyes searched hers, but they told him nothing.) "Perhaps, when all of this is over…?" Jake cleared his throat again, tried to avoid her eyes, and adopted a lighter tone.

"Perhaps I could stop by when you've finished the book? We could discuss the novel, if you'd like. It might surprise you to know that *Jane Eyre* happens to be one of *my* favorites as well."

"It does surprise me a little." Her voice sounded strange, and she realized she was holding her breath. She was afraid to say more. She wanted him to keep talking, to keep her with him a little longer. Her eyes searched for his. A little closer and they would touch. Every muscle strained toward him, and yet she couldn't move. The attraction nearly overwhelmed her. She wanted him to pull her to him, hold her in his arms. Her heart beat erratically, and with all the power at her command, she willed him to step closer…

Ring!

They both started at the doorbell's interruption. Jake recovered quickly and opened the door.

A young lad, clad in blue pants and a light yellow shirt, stood staring off into the distance. Jake was not pleased at the boy's timing.

"Yes, what is it?" Jake said, in a voice gruffer than normal.

Jenny stepped from behind Jake, as she recognized the new visitor and heard the irritation in Jake's voice.

"Well, Billy Wiggins!" Jenny exclaimed in a tone that she hoped hid her displeasure at seeing him at this particular moment, "I certainly didn't expect to see you out here." (Billy doffed his cap and looked at her as if she'd lost her mind.) "I didn't know you knew Mr. Witherspoon."

Billy stood there, cap in hand, wondering what in the world Jenny was up to. That she was up to something was plain. He watched as Jenny looked back at Mr. Witherspoon.

"Jake, I had no idea you knew Billy."

Jake opened the screen door. Jenny stepped onto the porch and stood between the boy and him. It was obvious that this boy meant something to her, but what? He coughed, joined them on the porch: "Well, actually, I don't think we *have* met. Have we, son?"

"No sir, Mr. Witherspoon," Billy said. "We haven't met before."

"Well then, let me introduce you," Jenny said, smiling at both of them.

She seemed animated; the sun caught her hair and set it on fire. Billy had never thought of Jenny as pretty before, but in that moment on the porch, he knew she was beautiful. So did Jake.

"Mr. Witherspoon, may I present Mr. William Wiggins, a reporter with the *Hulet Town Chronicle*, and,"—Jenny moved next to Billy and beamed at him—"my very good friend."

Billy blushed, but stepped up to shake Jake's outstretched hand.

"That's quite a recommendation, Mr. Wiggins," Jake said, solemnly shaking the boy's hand. "Any friend of Mrs. Schumacher's is always welcome."

"Well, now that I've introduced you two gentlemen, I really have to be on my way." Jenny descended the porch stairs and waved to the two males by the front door. "Good-bye."

"Bye, Jenny," Billy said, using her first name proudly. She'd told Mr. Witherspoon he was her *very good* friend.

"Thanks for coming," said Jake. "And thanks for the pies!" he shouted, as Jenny started her car and backed onto the road. She waved in acknowledgement, changed gears, and drove off down the road.

The two of them stood there on the porch, until all they could see was a little puff of dust in the distance....

"Miztah Jake?" Annie appeared in the doorway just as Jenny's car disappeared. "Dat Miz Jenny? She done lef her plates."

"What?" Jake asked, reluctantly turning from his view of the road.

"I done washed de pie plates, an Miz Jenny lef dem."

"I doubt that she'll miss them today, Annie." Jake regarded the young man at his elbow. "Perhaps you could take them when you return to town?"

Billy blushed. "Mr. Witherspoon, I rode my bike out here—"

"Of course. Well, I suppose I'll have to return them to her myself sometime." The thought was not entirely unwelcome. He turned to Annie. "Don't worry about the plates. I'll deal with them later.

"In the meantime, young man, what is *your* business with me?"

Billy drew himself up, squared his shoulders. "Mr. Witherspoon, I'm on assignment."

"Oh?"

"Yes, sir. I—that is, we—would like to run a featured article about Mrs. Sarah Witherspoon in the paper. I came here to find out some more information about her—things that wouldn't be in the obituary."

"Ah, you want to run a personal story about my mother."

"Yes, sir. Mr. Johnson said she was an 'icon.'"

"He did, did he? An icon…Well, lad, you've come to the right place. This lady"—Jake put his arm around Annie's shoulder—"probably knows more about her than anyone alive, including me." Jake smiled at Annie fondly.

"Annie, no one else is here at the moment, and frankly, I need some rest. Why don't you take this young man—Mr. Wiggins, I believe—"

"Everyone calls me Billy, but—"

"Then we will, too. Annie, take Billy into the kitchen. Get him some food—Lord knows, we've more than we'll ever need—and tell him all about Mother."

"But Mr. Witherspoon—"

"Glad to help you out, son. Annie knows everything there is to know about Sarah Witherspoon. Ask her anything. You're in very good hands. Nice to have met you, Billy. You'll have to excuse me now, but we'll meet again, I'm certain.

"Annie, take good care of this young man. He's a reporter from the town paper." He winked at her over the boy's head and left.

In his room, the door safely locked, Jake collapsed on his bed. *What is wrong with me? How can I even think of another woman, much less, be this attracted? I don't even know her!*

"Well?" Bertha said, as Jenny entered the kitchen.

"Things must've gone smoothly while I was gone," Jenny said, ignoring the question. "You're smiling, so Susie must've been on time."

"A good thing, too. I'd have skinned her alive if she'd been that late this morning," Bertha said, snapping her fingers. "Had me hands full from break-fast right through lunch, but we managed, thank the good Lord."

Jenny nodded, looking around the immaculate kitchen. "You certainly did. There doesn't seem to be much of anything left to do around here. Why don't we call it a day?"

"You don't mean close before dinner?"

"I mean exactly that. Hulet can get along without us for one night. Besides, it's just too hot to cook, don't you think?"—Bertha looked at Jenny as if she'd lost her mind, but Jenny was oblivious—"It's too late to go to the bank," Jenny continued, almost to herself, "so I'll just put the receipts in the safe and wait till Monday—" Jenny closed her eyes and mas-saged the back of her neck with her hand—"then...I think I'll go upstairs and take off these clothes, maybe soak in the tub, and relax. You ought to do the same, Bertha." Jenny smiled at her friend, waved, and turned to leave—

"Just hold on one minute there, miss!"—Bertha shook a clean soup ladle at Jenny to punctuate her remarks—"Sure and I'm not going *anywhere* till you tell me what happened at Witherspoon's."

Jenny grinned and sat down at the kitchen table. "There's really not that much to tell. His maid took the pies. Billy Wiggins arrived to talk to Jake about his mother for the paper. I left. That's about it." She brushed a stray wisp of hair back from her face, then laughed at her friend's disappointed expression.

"All right. That's not *all* that happened...." Jenny paused for effect. "He loaned me a book." Jenny pulled the novel out from behind her back, and held it up for Bertha's inspection. "See? *Jane Eyre*."

"A *book*? And you're all lit up like a big city street? Saints preserve us! And me sittin' here wonderin' did he say anything about your appointment that he missed." Bertha put her hands on her hips, and waited for Jenny's answer.

"It wasn't like that. The man just said he'd come by after work—nothing formal at all—so of course, he didn't say anything about it. He probably forgot about it two seconds after he left the cafe, and then, with his mother dying that night..." Jenny sighed, then smiled. "But he likes me, I think."

Bertha pulled out a chair and sat down at the table across from Jenny. "Because he loaned you a book? Jenny m'girl..." Bertha shook her head in disbelief.

Jenny grinned. "It was *her* book—his mother's favorite—" Bertha rolled her eyes—"and he wants to see me again when I've finished...." Jenny sat for a moment, turning the book over and over between her hands. "You know, Bertha, I think he might ask me out. I mean, *after* a decent interval."

"And if he doesn't?"

"Well, I *do* have the book—" a mischievous grin tugged at the corners of her mouth—"so we have to see each other sometime, at least once."

A brief frown creased Bertha's brow as an unwelcome thought occurred to her. She reached across the table and patted one of Jenny's hands. "Now don't go getting' your hopes all pinned to one man. You don't really know—"

Jenny withdrew her hand, suddenly affronted: "Weren't you the one telling me it was time—past time, as I recall—for me to stop mourning Will and get on with my life?"

"And it is! I'll not be sayin' it isn't, but—"

"But?"

"But...I'm not wantin' to see you get hurt, 'tis all. Take it a mite slower, 'tis all I'm sayin'—"

"For heaven's sake, Bertha! I'm not a child! You can hardly say I'm rushing into something. There's nothing right now to rush *into*! I've never even been out with the man, and thanks to Billy's timing, that's not likely to change in the near future." Jenny pushed back from the table, stood.

"I'm tired, and I'm sure you are, too. I'll see you Monday morning." Jenny walked toward the door, "I'm going to see to the books and get out of these clothes."

Bertha got up then, untied her apron, and folded it over her arm: "Well, I'll be goin' then," she said, trying to keep the hurt out of her voice, "but you'll not find me restin'. Sure and there'll be laundry to do and the house to clean."

They walked into the dining room. Jenny headed for the cash register. Bertha stopped at the front door: "By any chance, are you thinkin' of goin' to the funeral?"

Jenny looked up from the money she'd started counting: "And why shouldn't I? There will be plenty of other people there. I won't be conspicuous."

"Well...Monday morning then."

"Yes. Monday." Jenny resumed her counting.

Bertha opened the door, but looked back. "Jenny?"

Jenny glanced up from her work, "Yes?"

"It's sorry I am for speakin' out of turn. Lord knows I didn't mean anything—"

"Of *course* you didn't—" Jenny walked quickly from behind the counter to where Bertha stood and put her arms around Bertha's ample waist. "Forgive me, dear. I'm just a bit on edge this afternoon. Too much excitement. You were right about not getting my hopes up and rushing into something."

Jenny released her friend and stood back. "I may not always like what you say, Bertha, but I *always* listen." She patted Bertha's shoulder. "Now, go on home and *don't* worry. I'll see you bright and early Monday."

Bertha gave Jenny a quick peck on the cheek and went off down the boardwalk. Jenny finished counting the money, made out the bank deposit, and put everything in the safe. She went upstairs, took a leisurely bath, and then lay down on the bed with Jake's copy of *Jane Eyre*.

CHAPTER SEVEN

ool air blew across Jake's shoulders. He tugged at his sheet, turned over. Morning's brightness seeped through his eyelids, banishing sleep. Jake opened one eye, and realized morning had broken without him. He fumbled for his watch, found it, and sat bolt upright on the edge of the bed. Past eight! He ran his hand through his hair, trying to understand the lateness of the hour. He couldn't remember the last time he'd slept clear through until morning. He shivered, and realized he was cold. *A cold snap in August?*

Jake shook his head and went to the window. A brisk breeze kicked at the curtain. Autumnal crispness filled the room. Outside the day was shockingly bright, hardly appropriate for his mother's burial. The day had more of football than funeral about it. Precisely the kind of day his mother reveled in. Jake smiled and wondered if she'd ordered it especially for the occasion.

With a few notable exceptions, it seemed the entire town of Hulet had gathered for Sarah Witherspoon's funeral. Jake spotted faces of old friends, faces he hadn't seen in years, some strangers interspersed among the crowd. Dan Johnson was not among them. Jake noticed Jenny seated in a rear pew as he left the church service. He was surprised at how many followed the hearse to the farm, grateful that they stopped a respectful distance away from the family burial site and allowed him to enter the fenced area alone, except for the parson, Doc, Annie, and Bill.

His own grieving done, Jake felt detached while his mother's coffin was lowered into the grave. His mind wandered while the parson prayed. He gazed out over the gathered mourners. Jenny wasn't there, but Ben was... and Mike. He made a mental note to visit them first thing Monday. He spotted Silas and Elmer standing together, their wives and children farther back, apart. Nearly everyone wore black. A few wore black armbands. Women's veils flapped in the crisp breeze. Quiet sniffles came from somewhere in the group. Men kept their eyes fixed on the ground, never met his gaze, and shifted from one leg to the other, trying to get comfortable, and keep their legs from going to sleep. Standing together on the hillside, their black clothes glistening in the bright sunshine, they reminded Jake of so many crows. His mother would have loved it.

The pastor stopped, and Jake realized the service was over. He reached down, picked up a clump of dirt, and threw it into the grave. It hit the wood of the coffin softly, like a sigh. It was over. Jake shook the minister's hand, thanked him, hugged Annie, shook Bill's hand, nodded at Doc, and left the enclosure to talk with those gathered on the hill and invite them back to the house.

At the house, his solemn crows turned into magpies, filling the house with cacophonous chatter, before transforming into locusts and converging on the dining room. *A good thing, too. This must be where "groaning board" originated*, he thought, surveying the dining table laden with enough food to feed all of Hulet: a baked ham, stuck with cloves and sliced for sandwiches; fried chicken and mounds of mashed potatoes; green beans cooked with ham and onions; plump loaves of homemade bread still warm from the oven; fat, steaming, buttermilk biscuits; a large assortment of pickles, relishes, canned fruits put up the summer before; and fresh-churned butter in cut-glass butter dishes sat beside bowls of golden honey. And there were pitchers of lemonade, iced tea, coffee, cold sweet milk, and tangy buttermilk to wash it all down. And for dessert, pies of every description, and perhaps even ice cream. Everyone was eating, talking, laughing....

Jake wandered from room to room, marveling at the noise, and the increasing number of people in the house, on the porch, in the yard, coming up the driveway.... Annie and the other women, black and white alike, filled the kitchen like ants in a hill, busy with coming and going, working and chatting. Jake caught snatches of conversations—housekeeping tips, recipes, childrearing, gossipy tidbits—as they put dishes on the table, took them off as people put them down, and washed them again. Adolescent girls dried dishes, eavesdropped on their elders, or whispered their own secrets among themselves. They seemed oblivious to his presence.

He moved outside and was again aware of the unseasonable coolness of the air. He found an empty space by the front door, leaned against it, and watched his guests.

At the north end of the porch, men gathered and took turns cranking the handle of the ice cream maker—their conversation peppered with crop prices, weather predictions, and increases to their livestock this past season. Teenaged boys stood self-consciously in groups, shuffled around, took joking pokes at each other, and tried not to act like kids. *And tried*, Jake thought, *not to think about the girls inside.* He remembered doing the same.

Laughter came from beyond the porch; he walked to the railing. A group of younger children played at marbles in a ring in the dirt below. The littlest children ran playing hide-and-seek in the front yard, squealing in high-pitched voices, while mothers shouted in tones not much lower to be careful, to watch out for their clothes, and not to step on the flowers. It all reminded him of other days—days when the house rang with music and laughter, days when his parents' parties drew the county to their house, days in Washington with Max...with Laura. Laughter and people. They once were a way of life, here and in Washington; perhaps, they could be again.

"Annie, you've had a long day," Jake said, taking in the gray weariness of her. "You go on home with Bill. I can fend for myself the rest of the weekend."

"Don'cha go sayin' no," Bill said, just as Annie started to open her mouth. "Yuh needs de rest, an' yuh knows it.

"We thank yuh, Miztah Jake. Annie be heah Monday mo'nin' same as always."

Jake nodded and started to leave when a thought occurred. "Annie, before you go..."

Annie and Bill both turned to him expectantly.

"I was wondering if you knew where Mother might have kept her records, pictures, things of that sort. I tried to find pictures of Laura and the children—"

"Oh!" Annie's hand went unbidden to her mouth. Tears sprang to her eyes.

Bill bent his head, shook it. When he looked up, a smile tugged at the corners of his mouth. "I *knowed* dere wuz sumpthin' diff'rent....Now, stop dat wimp'rin', honey," he said, putting his arm around his wife. "Dis be *good* news! Sho' do wish Miz Sarah wuz heah."

"So do I, Bill," Jake said, touched by their response.

For a moment no one spoke. Annie buried her face in her husband's shoulder. Bill patted her back and grinned at Jake over her head. When Annie seemed calm, Bill tilted her chin up so he could see her face.

"Honey, don'cha think Miztah Jake need dat lettuh 'bout now?"

"What letter?" Jake looked at Bill.

"Annie?" Bill prompted.

Annie sniffed, dabbed at the corner of her eyes with her apron, then nodded at Bill. "I gots it heah." She reached into a fold of her skirt, and came out holding an envelope, obviously the worse for wear, and held it out to Jake.

"Miz Sarah tole me t' give it t' yuh when I thinks yuh ready. I reckon Bill's right. It be time."

Jake took the envelope, but hesitated a moment before opening it.

Bill nudged his wife. "Bes we be goin' on home now. 'Night, Miztah Jake."

Jake stared at the envelope, barely hearing Bill and Annie's good-byes, as they left the kitchen by the back door.

Annie looked at her husband on the seat beside her, as he started their truck. Suddenly she did something she hadn't done in years—reached over, turned his face toward hers, kissed him as hard as she could, then released her hold on his neck.

"What's dat fo'?" Bill stared at her as if she'd lost her senses. The truck died.

"Nuttin' much," Annie said, smiling to herself in the dark. "I jus feels like it, dat's all."

"Well den, wha'chall doin' all de way ovah dere?" He patted the seat next to his thigh.

"Stop yo' foolishness, ole man, 'n git t' drivin'," she said, moving closer, as he restarted the engine.

Bill grinned, shifted into gear, put his free arm around her, and drove to their place on the other side of the farm.

CHAPTER EIGHT

J ake slit the envelope with a kitchen knife. Inside were a letter and a key. His hands shook as he unfolded his mother's stationary. He stared at the ornate script, her penmanship steady and firm, as yet unmarred by the trembling that characterized her later hand:

"My Dearest Jacob,

"I am writing this in case something happens, and I am not around to tell you in person. So if you are reading this, my fears and hopes must have been realized. Yes, hopes. I hoped with all my heart that one day you would regain your memory and want to resume living the life God intended for you to live. How I have prayed for this day! Know I am happy for you and be assured of my undying love.

"Enough of this! There are matters of which you need to be made aware.

"I have put an envelope in my safe. It contains items you had on your person the night of the fire. I didn't know what to do with them, so I left them all together. The safe is behind the picture of "Blue Boy" in my bedroom. The combination is: Two complete turns to the right, stopping at 25, one full turn to the left to 45, then back right to 32. It should open. If it doesn't, just do it again. Sometimes it's stubborn, but it eventually comes around. After all, it's _my_ safe.

"The key is to my locked box at the bank. All my important papers, deeds, stocks, etc., are in there. Mr. Townsend has one copy of my will; the other copy is in the box. I also put all the pictures of Laura and the children in an envelope, which is in there, too. I hope I did the right thing by *removing them from the house, but the doctors seemed to think they might upset you.*

"Jacob, I do not want you to dwell on the past. I know Laura would not have wanted that; I certainly do not. Son, life is always unpredictable. A minister told me once that life is a tapestry. The darker threads tragedy and pain provide serve to define the finished picture, not to obscure it. God is still weaving your tapestry, Jacob. Trust Him. Remember, there are bright threads still to be used, and remember, too, how much I love you.

"Mother"

I love you, too, Mother, Jake thought, smiling at her sermonette. He pocketed the key—the bank wouldn't open until Monday—and went to his mother's bedroom. The "Blue Boy," an excellent, though smaller, reproduction of Gainsborough's original, hung over the headboard of her bed. Jake moved the bed. The safe was right where she'd said it was, built into the wall behind the painting. Jake shook his head; he'd never known it was there. Had Annie? He wondered, but doubted she had. He spun the dial and tried the combination. He tried two more times before the tumblers clicked into place.

The safe was larger than he'd expected, filled with papers and assorted small boxes which, when opened, contained jewelry, some of which he recognized from days long since past. He sifted through the papers, and put them back in the safe for later. He was curious about the envelope with his personal effects from the night of the fire. It was near the back, tied with string, more of a small package than an envelope.

Jake replaced the rest of the safe's contents, spun the dial, and rehung the painting. Then he took the package into the kitchen, cut the string with his pocketknife, and dumped the contents out on the table. He winced at the sight of a crumpled piece of paper—Laura's last message, left at the Little Rock hotel where he'd stayed during Slo-Joe's murder trial. Without reading it, he wadded it into a tight ball and tossed it into the kitchen trash. A ring with five keys caught his attention: one was to his briefcase—where was his briefcase? He thought for a moment, and decided to ask Mike, or maybe Ben, if they knew what had happened to it. *They must have needed it to continue the case….*Two looked like…house keys. Keys to a house that no longer existed. Jake stopped, put his head into his hands. This was harder than he'd thought….

He pushed back from the kitchen table, got himself a glass of water and looked out the window for a while. He was tired; his neck ached, and his head hurt. He rolled his head down to his chest and back again, trying to ease the tension in his neck. He heard something pop, but it didn't hurt, or help. He rubbed the back of his neck with one hand and went back to the table.

The letter seemed to jump out at him. He hadn't noticed it before. The handwriting seemed vaguely familiar. He picked it up. The postmark read Nov. 2, 1924; the return address was on the other side. *Max!* Something stirred at the edge of his brain. His hand trembled, as he ran his finger under the flap, and lifted out the contents. *Yes! This is the one!* He skimmed the letter eagerly, pausing at the signature. *Good old Max! He probably thinks I'm dead after all this time. I must call him. He's bound to be in the same place, at least still in Washington….* Jake took the letter, paced rapidly back and forth in the kitchen, turned out the light, and went to his room. He stripped quickly, got into bed, and perused the letter:

"November 2, 1924

"Dear Jake,

"So good to talk to you the other day. Glad to hear Laura and the children are well. How is my godson getting on? He must be toddling around quite well by now. I am making it a point to journey to the West in the near future, so I can see that you and Laura are raising him properly, in a cultured and refined fashion, as befits my namesake.

"So much for the amenities, heartfelt though they are, and on to the rather more somber purpose of my letter. (You will notice I did not trust these facts

to the telephone, but actually put pen to paper, which should attest to the seriousness of what I am about to relate.)

"During our telephone conversation regarding your current legal endeavor, the name of the deceased, one Clarence Morgan, I believe, struck a familiar note. After we concluded, the name kept bothering me, until I finally remembered where I had encountered it before: Clarence Morgan, a banker from Little Rock, Arkansas, was among the names mentioned by the former secretary of none other than our recently mourned Jesse W. Smith. (You may remember some of the rumors surrounding Smith's 'suicide' last year?) On second thought, the whole affair may have taken place after you left. Jesse Smith shot himself in the flat he shared with Harry Daugherty on May 31. You and Laura left sometime in March, I believe, so you may _not_ have heard. (Much of what I am about to relate was kept out of the papers, no doubt by our esteemed former Attorney General, who, quite understandably, had no wish to have his 'relationship' with Jesse come under scrutiny, especially coming on the heels, as it did, of Chas. Cramer's suicide two months earlier. I presume you remember _that_ mess.) At any rate, I must enlighten you regarding some necessary background information. I have no doubt that it will pique your curiosity, as much as it did my own.

"You will have heard about the various scandals of the Harding administration. (There are even some who say the death of Harding himself might be among them, but that is beside the point for my purposes today.) Well, rumors have it that poor Jesse's demise was not suicide at all, but Murder Most Foul. It seems that our natty Mr. Smith evidenced an absolute _abhorrence_ of guns, so why, those 'in the know' ask, would he purchase a gun and use it to shoot himself? It simply is not a 'neat' way to go, and, as we all know, Jesse was nothing, if not immaculately tidy in everything. Which brings me to the other nasty rumor, which keeps popping up for all of Harry's trouble: the Matter of the Money, quite a lot of it at that, if Gaston Means can be believed, which is, as Hamlet said, 'the rub.' Whether or not Means is a scoundrel of the first order is debatable, but in this matter, dear boy, he makes entirely too much sense, particularly since his story, (I shall tell you how I came by it at a later date), neither helps his case, nor makes his living to a ripe old age a likely occurrence.

"According to Means, our dear Jesse, meticulous shopkeeper that he was, kept rather detailed ledgers of all monies which had passed through his hands from the considerable graft of the 'Ohio Gang.' Of course, Harry did not know about Jesse's records initially. When Harry found out, Means says Jesse came to him, terrified for his life. Because of his guilt, and his secret knowledge of the Gang's activities, he apparently told Means he intended to enlist Mrs. Harding's help and turn State's Witness. It then seems our conscientious clerk actually told _Harry_ what he intended to do.

"Daugherty then convinced Jesse that he, too, was frightened by his own complicity, and told Jesse to purchase a pistol (for Daugherty's use) on his next trip to Ohio. Jesse did as he was told and bought the requested gun at an Ohio hardware store. Means says he last saw Jesse Smith alive on May 30 of last year, when Smith arrived at his house on N.W. 16th Street.

"Means says that Jesse said he had not been able to see Mrs. Harding in person, yet, but had spoken with her by telephone, and had determined that Harry was attempting to foil their conference. Jesse then supposedly wrote a letter to his wife, _while at Means' house,_ explaining its purpose was to tell her about his 'new will,' which of course has not been found, although I understand Mal Daugherty, Harry's brother, somehow thought _he,_ not Harry, had been appointed executor of Jesse's will. (This is one of the facts in Means' favor; one which has not been explained to my satisfaction by any of the forthcoming statements concerning the matter.)

"Jesse left Means' house alone that night, and Means says he received a telephone call in the wee hours of that next morning. (He implied, although he did not say specifically, that the call was from Attorney General Daugherty himself.) Means was told Jesse had 'committed suicide.' Means was then instructed to go into the apartment that Smith and Daugherty shared and where Jesse's body lay. He was to search the apartment and bring 'every scrap of paper'—I am quoting Means now—back to the 'Unidentified Personage' waiting in an apartment above.

"I will make quick work of the rest of the story as I received it. Means asked to be 'deputized' for this. His request granted, he went to the apartment, and, from his first moment on the scene, decided Jesse's death had <u>not</u> been by his own hand, but that the so-called suicide had been 'faked,' down to the use of the pistol, supposedly purchased for Daugherty's 'use.' Jesse himself had mentioned 'a little white powder'— again I am quoting Means—which he feared had been used 'to dispose of others' in the Gang's way. (No need to speculate on their names now, except to say that, if Means is right, then these people would not be squeamish about committing <u>another</u> murder to protect themselves from prosecution.)

"Yes, Jake, I <u>am</u> suggesting that your Little Rock murder of Clarence Morgan might, indeed, be one more to lay at the door of the Ohio Gang. Last fall, Montana's Sen. Walsh began an investigation into certain suspicious circumstances surrounding Albert B. Fall, our notorious former Secretary of the Interior. I have a grave suspicion of my own, that what we are discovering about the goings on of the Harding Administration will turn out to be merely the Tip of the Iceberg—mark my words, Jacob—only The Tip.

"But back to the Scene of the Crime: Means did as he was told. On the body, he found an envelope stuffed with papers, strapped on a harness underneath Jesse's clothes. This he removed and delivered to his 'superior officer.' Means returned to his home.

"He received another call about six o'clock that same morning, telling him to return to the Wardman Park Hotel, and 'take charge' with the hotel detective. (Of course, no autopsy was ordered, as Smith's death was deemed a 'suicide.')

"Back at 16th Street by eight, another call came, telling Means to get his car, his chauffeur, his wife and son, and to pick up a man, who would be waiting for him at such-and-such a corner at nine-thirty. Means was to take the man directly to Harper's Ferry.

"*Again, Means did as he was told, deciding to include his boy's nurse in the party. He picked up a man, who was indeed waiting at the designated corner, a man whom Means says he had not met before and has not seen since, and drove him to Harper's Ferry, where the man boarded a <u>west-bound</u> train. (Means clearly implies that this man was involved in Smith's—dare I say it?—murder.)*

"*Of course, Means has not related any of this openly. In fact, the man is quite careful to keep his mouth decidedly shut on this point, and I cannot say I blame him in the least. As I said, should what I have told you fall into the Wrong Hands, Mr. Means, and even I, now that I think about it, might be in Grave Danger. (You see how I trust you!)*

"*I have told you these, admittedly inadmissible, details, only to help you in your relentless Quest for your client's Fair Day In Court. (How ever did he come by such an unfortunate name?)*

"*Since Smith wrote to Clarence Morgan, shortly before his demise, and since, my sources tell me, some of Smith's records are still At Large, so to speak—Harry is reportedly <u>beside</u> himself trying to locate them—it occurred to me that this man, whom Means saw board a west-bound train, might have something to do with Morgan's death as well as Smith's. It occurred to me as well, (and, if to me, then certainly to Harry), that Jesse might have sent a portion of those records to his friend Morgan, or perhaps copies of the records Harry presumably possesses, or a letter informing Morgan of his intentions to seek Mrs. Harding's protection—reasons enough to 'dispose' of Morgan, especially with the recent investigations into the Attorney General's odd reluctance to prosecute central figures involved in the various scandals revolving, I believe, around some very high-ranking officials. (You may have heard that Harry himself was called to testify this past month before the Senate. I truly begin to fear for Sen. Walsh's health, for he pursues these scoundrels, as if he were the very Hound of Heaven!)*

"*Means also suggests that much—'millions'—is missing from Smith's ill-gotten estate. Since your Mr. Morgan is a banker...?*

"I will leave the investigation proper to you, but should you find that this link is more than overactive imaginings on the part of Yrs. Truly, I have other documentation to back these seemingly wild allegations—enough, perhaps, to provide your all-important 'reasonable doubt?'

"But this is enough for now. I dare say my hand begins to cramp with all this writing. Remember me to Laura and the children, especially Theodore Maxwell, and let me know what you think of my 'revelation.'

"Yr. Servant,"

Max had signed the letter with his characteristic flourish. Jake marveled again at his friend's audacity, a characteristic revealed to few. To most, Maxwell Howe was an elegant *bon vivant*, a most eligible, albeit elusive, bachelor, whose thoughts ran more to the intricacies of high society than to the intrigues of government.

Jake folded the letter and slid it back into its envelope. He sat on the edge of the bed slapping the envelope against his palm, while he decided on his next course of action. Finally, his mind made up, he grabbed his robe and padded barefoot in the dark to the kitchen. Forgoing illumination, Jake retrieved the package and its contents from the kitchen table and returned everything, including Max's letter, to the safe. Just as he started to close the door, he thought better of it, reclaimed the key ring and the bank deposit box key, shut the safe, and spun the dial. When everything was back in its proper place, Jake returned to his bed.

CHAPTER NINE

Jake inspected the hand-painted sign on the frosted glass of the mahogany door. In gold lettering, painstakingly outlined in black, it read:

TOWNSEND, HAWLEY & BRANCH

Law Offices

Not for long, Jake thought, making a last minute adjustment of his tie and straightening the lapels of his suit. Satisfied, he turned the doorknob and entered the reception area.

"Why, Mr. Witherspoon!" Penelope Long said, her smile wide and welcoming as she stood to greet him, "I didn't know you were coming by this morning."

Jake smiled back: it was hard to resist Penelope when she chose to be charming, which was most of the time. Knowing her, he wondered at those who branded most redheads with quick tempers and fiery natures.

"To be honest, Miss Long, no one knew I was coming. I'd like to talk with Mr. Townsend, if he's not too busy."

"I'm certain he'll want to see you. Why don't you have a seat?" Penelope indicated some chairs in the waiting area.

Jake turned to find a seat, felt a tug on his sleeve. Penelope stepped in front of him.

"Mr. Witherspoon," she said, not meeting his eyes, "I'd just like to say how very sorry I was to hear about your mother's death. She was a wonderful lady. I'll miss her."

"Thank you. I appreciate your saying that."

"Well, I'll just tell Mr. Townsend you're here."

Jake nodded and sat down as Penelope walked to the end of a short corridor and knocked on an office door. Jake heard Townsend's voice, saw Penelope open the door, and close it behind her. His collar felt too tight; he pulled at it with his index finger, straightened his tie, and checked the time on his pocket watch. A door opened. A moment later Penelope emerged from Townsend's office and walked toward him.

"Won't you come this way, Mr. Witherspoon?"

Jake stood. "No need to show me the way, Miss Long. Go back to what you were doing before I interrupted."

Penelope seemed grateful. "Would you like me to bring you some coffee? I'm getting some for Mr. Townsend..."

"In that case, I'd love some."

"Cream and sugar?"

"No, nothing, thank you, just coffee."

"I'll bring it right in," she said and disappeared around a corner, while Jake walked the short distance to Mike Townsend's office and knocked on the door.

"Come in, Jake," Townsend said, opening the door from the inside. "You're mighty slicked up. What's the occasion?" He extended his hand.

Jake shook it: "Nothing in particular. I have some business with you. Just figured I'd dress the part."

"Of course. I was just going to have my secretary get in touch with you about your mother's will. By the way, I thought Bell did a wonderful job with her funeral....Is something wrong?" Mike asked, noting the stern expression on Jake's face as he ushered him into the large, mahogany-paneled office. "Won't you sit down?"

Jake regarded the two captain's chairs facing the huge mahogany desk which stood in front of the western wall of the office. When Townsend sat at his desk, his back was to several windows. A good plan, Jake reflected, since Townsend received light from the afternoon sun without the glare and the distractions that a view like his afforded.

It also gave him an edge in afternoon interviews. This was morning: Jake had no intention of giving him the advantage today.

However, Mike passed his desk and gestured toward two black leather-upholstered wing chairs at the southern end of the room. The chairs, separated by a butler's table, faced each other in front of a now cold fireplace. Filled bookcases rose to the ceiling on either side.

"Thanks." Jake took the chair to the left.

"Now," Mike said, taking the other, "what can I do for you?"

"I do have some questions about Mother's will and the estate," Jake said sitting back, crossing his legs.

"Of course—"

"But before we get into that, perhaps you'd better tell me about my standing with this firm."

Mike's brow furrowed. "I'm not sure I understand."

"Then let me be plainer: What is the current status of our partnership?"

"Partnership?" Mike raised his right eyebrow.

"If memory serves, and it *does*," Jake paused, letting his words sink in, "you and I were equal partners in this firm—at least in 1924—"

"In 1924?"

"Yes. In 1924. I don't believe we dissolved that partnership,...or did we?" Jake paused again and waited for Mike's answer.

Mike reached into his coat pocket and pulled out a pack of cigarettes. "Cigarette? Or would you prefer a cigar? I have a box of Havanas in my desk—"

"Not now, thanks. Maybe later."

Mike leaned forward, struck a match on the inside wall of the fireplace, and lit his cigarette. He inhaled deeply, dropping the match onto the empty grate: "How much do you remember?"

Jake smiled in spite of himself: "You'd be surprised. What I don't remember is why my name no longer appears on the door. Townsend, Hawley and Branch—no mention of Witherspoon that I could find. Hence the query."

Mike sat further back in his chair, crossed his legs, tapped cigarette ashes into the fireplace: "Well, it seems the good doctors were right about your memory returning—"

"Perhaps you'd rather it hadn't?"

"Why would you think that? I don't know what dastardly deeds you've imagined I've committed, but taking advantage of your condition isn't one of them."

"Former condition, if you don't mind——"

"Mind?" Mike's eyebrows shot up. He took a long drag on his cigarette, exhaled smoke, and grinned: "Hell, Jake, I'm *glad* your mind's back, but even you have to admit it sure as hell hasn't been for the last five years. What did you expect me to do under those conditions?" The grin disappeared. Mike uncrossed his legs and moved to the edge of his chair.

"But before you answer that, perhaps you'd better ask yourself how much you've contributed to this law practice lately, before you start implying that I, or anyone else in this office, have not done the right thing by you."

"You had the partnership dissolved," Jake said, his voice calm. It was not a question.

"No," Mike sounded a bit disgusted, "I did not have the partnership dissolved."

"Then what *did* you do?"

"Suspended it——"

"Suspended?"

The grin reappeared on Townsend's face: "Hell, Jake, you didn't think I'd let you out because of a little amnesia, did you? I froze your portion of the assets and liabilities—why should I keep paying you a share of the profits when you're not producing? I'm a charitable guy, but not *that* charitable"—Mike flicked his cigarette butt into the fireplace—"I put your share in a revocable trust, until we knew for certain how you were going to end up. For your information, I discussed this whole matter with Sarah before I did anything. She agreed it was the best option. But to tell you the truth, I'd just about given up on your ever coming back——"

Before Jake could reply there was a knock on the door.

"Could someone please open the door for me?"

Both men stood as Mike went to Penelope's aid. He opened the door; she entered with a large tray laden with a silver coffeepot, two cups and saucers, a creamer and sugar bowl, spoons, napkins, and two large glazed donuts.

"Sorry to interrupt, but I thought you two might be ready for a coffee break," Penelope said, setting the tray down on a round game table in the southwest corner of the office.

"Miss Long," Mike said, as he watched her arrange the cups and saucers, "after you finish in here, please put in a call to Mr. Pedersen."

Penelope handed Jake his coffee: "The sign painter?"

Mike nodded, glanced over at Jake: "That is, if it's all right with you?"

Penelope added two sugar cubes and some cream to Townsend's cup, filled it with coffee, and handed it to her employer.

Jake sipped his coffee: "Fine with me, Mike. The question is will it be all right with Hawley and Branch?"

Penelope watched the two men: something was going on, but what?

"Ben will be delighted. As for Larry,…well, he's a junior partner and will just have to learn to live with it."

Jake laughed, set his cup and saucer on the table, reached across and clapped Mike's right shoulder.

Penelope was at a loss, then suddenly, everything made sense: "You're back!" She nearly knocked over the coffeepot, as she ran to Jake and threw her arms around him.

"Penny, *really*," Jake said, trying to loosen her stranglehold on his neck, "this is not the kind of display we desire in our offices."

But he and Mike were laughing, so she took absolutely no notice. She hugged him once more for good measure:

"Welcome back, Mr. Witherspoon," she said with a satisfied sigh. "I'll just go now and ring Mr. Pedersen."

"How long do you think it will be before you're up to taking on a case or two?" Mike asked, plopping another lump of sugar into his coffee as Penny closed the door. "Ben's coming along, but he's not the trial attorney you were—"

"Stop talking about me as if I'd died, will you?"

Mike stirred his coffee. "You were as good as dead for almost five years. It's going to take time for you to get back on top of things."

"You forget, Mike. You and Ben kept me pretty busy in that library, reading all those law reviews, working up briefs..." Jake paused while he inspected his fingernails.

"Now that I think about it, this firm owes me a lot of back pay." (Mike's head jerked up, while Jake struggled to keep a straight face.) "Let me see..."— he stared up at the ceiling—"How many years have I been sitting in that library, acting as this firm's...clerk?"

"What's going on in here?" Ben Hawley stood in the doorway. He took in Jake's three-piece suit, the tie, the expression on Mike's rather flushed face, and entered the room.

"Sorry to barge in on you, Mike, but Penny said you wanted to see me as soon as I came in." He nodded in Jake's direction. "Good to see you, too, Jake. What's the matter with the ceiling?"

"Not a thing," Jake answered, rising from his seat.

"Jake's back," Mike said in a flat tone.

"Don't you mean Jake's *here*?" Ben grinned, and pushed the intercom button on Mike's desk. "Could you bring another coffee cup in here, Penny? Thanks."

"Pull up a chair, Ben," Jake said. "We were just talking about you."

"Oh? Thanks, Penny," Ben said, as she entered with his cup and saucer.

"You're welcome," she said, handing him the cup. She flashed a smile in Jake's direction before withdrawing.

Ben stared after her, then looked at the two men across the room. He poured himself some coffee: "So, what's up?"

Jake answered: "Mike was just asking me if I were up to taking on a case or two—"

Ben choked on his coffee. It was a minute or two before he could speak: "Is this some kind of joke?" He looked from Mike to Jake.

"Jake's *back*, Ben. He's coming back to the firm,"—Mike finished his coffee in one gulp—"Though with the nonsense he's been spouting this morning, I don't know if I really want him back."

Jake laughed. "Can't say as I'd blame you if you didn't."

Ben addressed Mike: "Is he ready?"

"Oh, he's ready all right. Just don't ask him how he's managed to stay current."

"Why not?" Ben glanced in Jake's direction.

"Because he might tell you," Mike said, "and, believe me, we can't afford it."

Jake smiled benignly.

Ben regarded the two before saying anything. He set his coffee down on a table, dragged a captain's chair nearby, retrieved his cup, and sat down: "That's all very well and good, Jake," Ben paused. "Just don't expect to get your old office back."

Wednesday was nearly over before Jake worked up enough nerve to enter Dan Johnson's office at the *Chronicle*. He and Dan had never hit it off, even when Laura was alive, but it had to be done. Putting it off wouldn't make it any easier, for either of them.

Dan sat in his office, his back to the door, as Jake approached. Jake watched him for a moment then knocked. Dan turned at the sound, leapt to his feet, and jerked open the door.

"You have some nerve showing your face here, Witherspoon!" Dan yelled, his face flushed, and thick cords stood out in his neck.

"I thought we should talk—"

"Talk? About what?" Dan's eyes flashed, his free hand clenched.

"About Laura. I remember—"

"Remember what? That you killed her?"

Jake stepped back with the force of the accusation: "You must be mad! Killed her? What is the *matter* with you?"

"You may not have struck the match, but you killed her just as surely as if you had—"

Jake's hands shook, his heart pounded, constricted by a band of steel— "I never liked you, Dan, but I *never* thought you were crazy. How could you possibly hold me responsible?"

"You and that damned nigger! They warned you to drop it; they told you to let it alone, but you wouldn't, would you? Not you, not the great Jacob Witherspoon—" Dan's lip curled in a sneer—"Defender of the weak? Killer of the defenseless is more like it!"

"Wait a minute—"

"*You* wait! *You* left Laura and the children to pay for your damnable pride! I'm *glad* you remember! *I've* had to live with it for five long years—images of my sister screaming, as she and the babies burned alive in that deathtrap, while you—" Dan spat the word—"lived on, happily oblivious. Oh, I'm *glad* you remember, Jacob. If there's any justice, you'll live with their screams until the day you die! Now get out!"

"Dan—"

"Get out!" Dan slammed the door; glass shattered. He took no notice, dropped into his chair, and reached for his pipe and a match.

Jake stood there for another moment, turned abruptly, and left.

Billy shrank further into the corner shadows. Neither Mr. Johnson nor Mr. Witherspoon had seen him, but his body still shook uncontrollably. He had no wish for Johnson to discover that he had overheard their quarrel. *So that's it...Mr. Johnson thought Witherspoon had caused his sister's death!* Billy heard Dan's chair squeak and sprinted to the printer. His breath came in gasps as he tried to calm himself, look busy. But Johnson did not appear. Billy finished his work in record time. When it was time to leave, he stopped outside Johnson's office, stared at the glass shards that littered the floor—

"Clean that mess up before you go, boy," Johnson said in a tired voice that Billy didn't recognize.

"Do you want me to get someone to fix the door?" Billy stared at Johnson's back and waited for him to turn around. He didn't.

"No. I'll tend to it later. Just sweep up the glass."

Billy went to get the broom. When he returned, Johnson was gone, but his pipe laid in the ashtray, so Billy knew he hadn't left the building, not for long anyway. He swept the last of the glass into the dustpan, emptied it, and put the cleaning tools back where they belonged.

"I'll be on my way now, Mr. Johnson," Billy shouted. He waited for an answer, but no reply came. "I'll see you tomorrow!" Again, no answer. He paused, wondering what he should do, then he remembered Mr. Johnson's pipe in the ashtray. He left by the front door, closing it firmly behind him.

Jenny noticed Dan Johnson as soon as she came out of the kitchen. He was seated alone in the corner booth, staring at nothing. *He looks exhausted*, she thought, as she grabbed a menu, pad and pencil, and hurried over to wait on him.

"Mr. Johnson?"

His eyes shifted to her and seemed to focus.

"Have you been waiting long?" Jenny asked.

"Not long."

He spoke in a baritone remarkable for its lack of regional accent. Briefly she wondered where he was from. She remembered someone telling her once he'd worked on some big city newspaper, but the name escaped her. "I'm sorry for the wait. I was in the kitchen and didn't realize anyone was here." She paused. "Funny, I didn't hear the bell when you came in."

"It rang."

"I must've had the water running." Jenny handed him the dinner menu, poised her pencil above the notepad. "Can I get you anything while you're deciding?"

"No need for apologies, Mrs. Schumacher—"

"Jenny—everyone calls me Jenny around here." She smiled. "I'm surprised you didn't know that, you being a newspaperman and all."

"Well, I didn't want to sound presumptuous—you've never waited on me before. That other girl—"

"Susie?"

"I suppose so—I never knew her name. She usually takes my order." He stopped for a moment, then grinned. "I'm usually not this...what? Late for lunch? Early for dinner?"

The smile transformed his face, erased the haggard, tired look around his eyes, and lessened the deep creases across his forehead. He was much younger than she'd thought, not bad looking when he smiled. *Dark eyes, chestnut hair...graying a bit at the temples...I suppose it was the gray hair—that and Billy's perspective—that made me think he was older.*

"That depends on what you're hungry for," Jenny replied, returning his smile. "If it's lunch, I'm afraid you're out of luck. I do have some soup and pie, if you don't want to wait for the dinner specials."

"Any coffee?"

"Always coffee."

"What kind of pie?"

"Apple...I might have a piece or two left of rhubarb."

"That sounds good."

"Rhubarb?"—(Dan nodded)— "and coffee." She made a quick note. "Black?"

"Sweet and blond."

It took her a moment to realize he was talking about the coffee. "I'll just be a second."

"I don't suppose you'd have a Little Rock paper around? I get tired of reading my own stuff."

She smiled: "I'll see what I can find. Be right back."

He seems nice enough, Jenny thought, as she poured his coffee. She filled a creamer and a sugar bowl, picked up a napkin and some silverware, and put them all on a tray with the coffee and his piece of pie.

She returned to the dining room. He seems sad somehow, she thought, noticing his slumped shoulders as she crossed the room to his table.

"You're in luck," she announced and noticed the quick straightening of his spine as she approached. "You got the last piece of rhubarb pie, and—" she arranged the items in front of him on the table—"I managed to find a copy of the *Kansas City Star* for you to read."

Dan reached for the paper. "Now how did you come by a copy of the *Star?*" He looked at the date. "And it's only two days old—"

"Well, I wish I could tell you, but I honestly don't know. Someone must've been passing through and left it. Lucky for you, though."

"Yeah, this seems to be my lucky day." A grin flashed across his face, lighting his eyes. "Do you always take this good care of your customers?"

"Hope so. Well, I'll leave you to it. Holler at me if you need anything else. I'll be in the kitchen."

"Thanks."

"Don't mention it."

The problem of Jake's office accommodations was solved by the end of the next week: Townsend, Witherspoon, Hawley & Branch expanded to include the office space next door.

"I hope you're planning to bring in enough business to pay for all of this," Ben said, as he watched the men place Jake's furniture in his new office.

"Eventually. But don't worry; the firm's not paying for this."

"Then who is?"

"I am."

"What did you do—sell the farm?"

"No, just got out of the stock market—"

"What *for?*" Ben asked incredulous. "It's sky-high!"

"Exactly." Jake turned his attention to the movers.

"Careful with that credenza! No, not over there. By the window. That's right. Over there. Look out for the floor lamp!"

Jake shut his eyes, rubbed his temples. "Let's get out of here for awhile so I can think."

Ben picked up a carved owl from an inlaid tabletop: "Decorating *can* be trying, can't it?"

Jake gave him a withering look. "As it happens, I have something I want to discuss."

"Wallpaper patterns? Or are you going to paint?"

"Out!" Jake pushed Ben into the hallway.

"OK, OK!" Ben said, laughing, then catching sight of Jake's face, he quickly sobered. "What's up?"

"Just an idea I had." Jake paused, breathed deeply, then plunged: "Ben, I need to know everything about the night Laura and the children died."

Jake, Mike, and Ben sat around the game table in Mike's office. Legal pads, files, scraps of paper littered the tabletop. No one spoke. A knock on the door startled them.

"Come in," Mike said.

"Sorry to interrupt," Penelope said, "but I wondered if you needed me for anything else? It's a quarter past five."

Mike rose from his chair. "Really?" He glanced at his pocket watch. "I had no idea. By all means, go on home. We won't be far behind."

"I'll see you all Monday morning, then. Have a nice weekend," she said, closing the door behind her as she left.

Mike resumed his seat with a resigned sigh. "I'm ready to call it a day. Are we finished here?"

Jake looked at Mike without commenting, walked to a window, raised the shade. The sun, pulsing with red-orange heat, teetered on the edge of the horizon.

"That's all you can tell me?"

"That's all there is to know," Mike said. "Facts are facts, and the facts, cruel though they are, are simple: Your wife and children died because your house caught on fire, and they were unable to get out fast enough. There is no reason whatsoever to believe that the fire was anything other than an unfortunate accident.

"Clarence Morgan died because someone killed him, and a Little Rock jury found that someone to be Slo-Joe Freeman, who was convicted of murder and hanged for his crime. End of facts; end of story."

"What about the threats?" An eighth of the fiery ball slipped toward the horizon, leaving long, jagged claw marks of blood-spattered light across the land as it fought to stay above the earth's edge.

"What about them? From what I understand, no threats ever were made against your wife and children. In fact, no real threats were made against you—just innuendo really, wasn't it?"

"Not if the fire was set." Jake's even tone belied his rage.

"Are you serious about pursuing this?" Ben asked, looking at his notes again.

"I think it's worth investigating." Jake continued to watch the sun's descent.

"We told you," Mike said, "the matter was looked into at the time, and there was no reason—no *reason*, got it?—to warrant further investigation."

"What's done is done. Look, Jake, I'm as sorry as hell that that poor Negro is dead, but he's dead, and there's nothing anyone can do to bring him back now. What good will it do anyone to reopen the case? It's closed. You have no new evidence; a man has been found guilty and been hanged for it."

"And Laura?"

"Jake, no one knows better than I how much Laura and the children's deaths meant to you—to all of us—" (Ben nodded his agreement)—"But facts are facts, and the facts are that we have no proof that their deaths were anything other than accidental."

"So you're not going to consider what I've told you?"

"What? That you think that Laura's death and that of Clarence Morgan might be linked somehow? OK, I might be able to buy that the fire at your house was deliberately set by someone trying to frighten you off the case. I'd even be willing to bet the Klan was in on it, though they don't usually go after white women and children—you did think about that, didn't you? But Morgan's murder? It doesn't have the Klan's mark. And I seem to remember—Ben, wasn't Morgan a Klan member?"

Ben nodded, reached for a pen. "Yeah, there was a pretty good rumor to that effect—"

"So what? Maybe the Klan wasn't responsible—"

"Come on, Jake. Who else would want to frighten you off the case?"

"The murderer?"

"Now that just doesn't make sense," Mike said, rocking back on two legs of his chair. "Why go after you? If your so-called murderer left things alone, he'd get off scot-free with no one the wiser.

"Face it, Jake—no matter what you did, that Negro was going to be convicted. Everyone knew that."

"Everyone but me. I thought at the time he had been set up. There was something about him that—"

"Why would anyone frame a retarded nigger?"

"Who better? He was an easy target—"

"And in the wrong place at the wrong time," Ben interjected. "Don't forget; his fingerprints were all over the place—"

"Of course they were! He was Morgan's hired man, for God's sake!"

"Now don't get excited," Mike said. "I know how frustrating this must be for you. After all, to you this is as fresh as yesterday. But you've got to remember that to us this is all ancient history. It's not going to help anyone to start stirring sticks after all this time."

Jake glanced over his shoulder at Ben who was doodling on his legal pad: "Do you think I'm wrong?"

Ben looked in his direction, but managed to avoid eye contact: "Not wrong," Ben said, resuming his artwork, "I just think you're understandably preoccupied with this whole subject. Who wouldn't be?

"Look—" Ben crosshatched a blank space—"give yourself some time to readjust, to get your equilibrium back, then look at the facts again—"

"Listen to him, Jake," Mike interrupted.

Jake remained silent.

"Look," Mike continued, "I'll make you a deal: Give yourself a month or so. Then if you still think there's more to Morgan's murder and Laura's death than we've explored up to now, I'll set everything else aside until we find out the truth of what happened—I have something at stake in this, too, don't forget. All I ask is that you take some time to let things get back to normal before you dive off into what may be a very dry, very hard lake bed."

Mike rose, walked to the humidor he kept on top of his desk, removed a cigar, sniffed it, bit off the end, and lit it.

Silence hung in the air like the smoke. Jake returned his gaze to the window. The sun had fallen below the horizon, leaving a darkening sky and purple clouds whose golden edges were fading quickly to gray.

"Well," Jake said, breaking the mood, "I'd better be getting back to the house or Annie will have my hide."

Ben grinned and stood, bunching his papers together so he could pick them up. "Must be nice to have someone who can actually cook fixing dinner for you every night."

Jake walked toward the office door: "It is, but don't let Grace hear you talking that way about her cooking. I understand wives are sensitive about things like that. Who knows? I might take pity on you, sometime when I haven't had my fill of you during the week, and invite you two to dinner." He said it teasingly, but there was an edge to his words. He stopped, his hand on the doorknob, and turned: "By the way, do either of you know what happened to my old briefcase?"

Mike answered: "Your mother gave it to me when—well, she thought it might have something I'd need—"

"And did it?"

"Ask Ben. I never opened it."

Jake looked at Ben who had joined him at the door: "Well?"

"Nope. What *did* you do with your case notes? You know, it would've helped, if I'd had some idea of where you were going—"

"They were right there in a folder marked—" he saw the look on Ben's face—"There wasn't a file?"

Ben shook his head. "Not when I got hold of it—"

"And you didn't think that was strange?" Jake tried to keep the anger out of his voice.

"Of course I did, but the lock was broken—"

"Broken?"

Ben looked at Mike for confirmation, "We figured it got knocked around in the confusion—"

"Was there *anything* in it?"

"Nothing that had anything to do with the case. You can see for yourself what's left. I put everything back in the briefcase and put it in my front closet. It's still there if Grace hasn't moved it. To tell the truth, I'd forgotten I had it—"

"I understand. I'd like to get it back though."

"Sure—" (Ben seemed relieved)—"I'll bring it to you Monday. Unless you need it sooner?"

"No, Monday will be fine. No rush. I just wondered what had happened to it, that's all. It was a gift. Well, see you Monday, Mike."

"Be ready to go to work," Mike moved behind his desk and sat down. "We've got a murder case to work on that's *not* closed, you know."

Jake stood on the threshold: "The Runyon case?"

Ben put a hand on Jake's shoulder: "Don't get him started, or we'll be here all weekend long."

"No chance of that," Jake said, "I have other plans for this weekend—Mike?" (Mike raised his eyebrows in answer.) "On second thought, I think I'll take your advice and take some more time before I jump back into full time practice. I've got Mother's business affairs to absorb, and there are some personal matters to take care of before I feel competent to get actively involved."

"Sounds like a good idea to me, Jake. Frankly, I didn't see how in the world you could just pick back up, as if nothing had happened—"

"Then it's settled." Jake opened the door, started to leave—"I promise, Mike, it won't be too long before I start pulling my weight again."

Mike removed the cigar from his mouth and looked at it appreciatively: "I'll make sure you keep that promise," he grinned. "You can count on me."

Jake laughed: "I never doubted it for a moment."

Ben raised his hand in a farewell gesture. "Good night, Mike. We're going home."

"Right behind you," Mike said, propping his feet on his desk. "Just as soon as I finish this cigar."

"Now, Jake," Ben said, as they went out the door, "why don't you tell me about these 'other plans'?"

CHAPTER TEN

Jenny tugged at the blanket on her shoulders as the first rays of sunlight reached her windowsill. Chilly air crept under the covers. Soft morning light knocked at her eyelids, wanting them to open. She rubbed her frozen feet together, clinging to unconsciousness as it slipped away from her.

"Oh, *please* let me sleep!" she groaned, pulling the blanket over her head as she curled into a tight ball. It was useless: she was awake, awake and—"Cold!" she yelled, dragging the blanket with her as she tip-toed gingerly across the bare hardwood floor to the window and slammed it against the tactless signs of morning.

"It's *September*, for Pete's sake!" she said, heading once more for the brass double bed she shared with no one. The sheets were no longer tucked in at the foot of the bed but were twisted together in the middle. Holding the blanket around her with one hand, Jenny tried to make the bed enough to be comfortable, but the blanket kept slipping. She was freezing in her lightweight nightgown.

"I suppose you know this is *your* fault, Will Schumacher," she said, glancing toward the ceiling while she searched for heavy socks in the cedar chest. "I *never* was this cold when you were here. What am I going to do when winter *really* decides to show up? Aha! Socks!"

Jenny clutched the woolen socks to her breast along with the blanket and ran back to bed. Her feet felt so cold they were nearly numb. She rubbed them until blood returned, then put on the socks. Huddled under the covers, Jenny waited for her feet to get warm. A few minutes later, she threw the covers off in frustration, ran to the closet, grabbed the heaviest robe she owned, stuffed her stockinged feet into slippers, and stomped downstairs to make herself some coffee.

Thirty minutes later life looked a bit better. True, it was six-thirty on Sunday morning, the only morning she got to sleep late, but the warmth from the stove felt wonderful as she sipped her second cup of coffee. Her mind drifted back to the days before Will died when Sunday was their day—no cafe, no customers, and, after church, a day of peaceful pursuits.

Sometimes Will read in his armchair, while she worked at her needlepoint. Or if the weather were fine, she'd sit on a stool in his shop out back and watch him steam a curve into wood for a rocker, or carve designs into a dresser, while they talked about their plans. At night Will would take out his fiddle and play for her. Sometimes she'd accompany him on her mother's dulcimer, playing tunes from back home in Virginia until homesickness overtook her. But Virginia wasn't home anymore. Her folks were getting old, her two brothers were married and settled somewhere in the far Northwest. She hardly knew her sisters: they'd been no more than babies when she'd married Will and left home. Now *they* were married and gone, too. Hulet was home—at first because it was Will's home; now, because it was familiar, she owned the cafe, and she had no place else to go.

"Oh well," Jenny shrugged and pushed back from the table, "I suppose I should be grateful to you. You left me with a lot of wonderful memories. I loved being married to you. You only did two things wrong the whole time I knew you: you left me too soon, and you spoiled me for anyone else." She smiled at the ceiling, poured her third cup of coffee, and went back upstairs.

Jake strode down the hill toward the barn, a place he'd avoided for years without knowing why. The trees were turning. Today marked the autumnal equinox, but fall had been in the air for a while. It had begun with his mother's funeral, insinuating itself into the end of August nearly a month before it was invited. Briefly Jake wondered if its early arrival augured a bitter winter, but at the sight of the barn doors thoughts of weather evaporated. *It has to be there,* he thought, his pace quickening. *Mother would never get rid of it.*

The doors protested as Jake let himself in. The morning sun had not penetrated here yet. He lifted the kerosene lamp from its peg on a post, raised the chimney, and lit the wick. Jake held the lamp aloft and turned slowly. The soft glow of the flame revealed familiar shapes: wheelbarrows, garden tools, buckets, carpentry tools, tack, his father's old buggy, the buckboard he used to ride to town—*That has to be it!* Jake thought, encountering a large tarpaulin engulfed by shadow and nearly hidden by stored farm equipment.

He made his way carefully toward the tarpaulin, stopping to deposit the lamp on a stable surface when he discovered he would have to climb over awkward terrain to reach it. He slipped once, nicked his shin nicely, but he didn't stop. The closer he got, the more certain he was.

He searched for the cover's edge and gingerly tugged, afraid of dislodging some unseen item perched atop the tarp. Nothing fell except dust. He grew bolder and pulled. There it stood after all these years: top dusty, but intact; windshield whole, as far as he could tell. The upholstery and tires remained hidden. He scrambled down, gathering in the cover as he went. He folded it in a makeshift package and left it on the packed dirt of the barn floor and went to work.

An hour later the Model A Duesenberg stood wholly exposed: tires flat, leather upholstery dried and cracked, engine encrusted with five years of gunk, rust spots showing on the once gleaming trim.

"A sad comedown, old girl," Jake murmured as he rubbed a headlamp with his sleeve. "For both of us. But never fear—if I can return, so can you." He patted a fender tenderly, sighed.

Sun filtered into the barn through cracks in the old boards. Jake turned down the wick in the kerosene lamp until the flame died. He hung it back on the nail where he'd found it. His resolve stiffened as he surveyed the once elegant automobile—his one extravagant indulgence before leaving Washington with Laura, pregnant with Teddy, and the almost four-year-old Sarah to return to the quiet life of rural Arkansas. He picked up the discarded tarpaulin and draped it lovingly over the Duesenberg.

"I'll be back soon," he promised and left the barn to search for a qualified mechanic.

Two hours later he'd found the man he was looking for.

"Sure. I can fix it. If I can get the parts I need, and you can pay for 'em," he said when Jake contacted him. "Worked on that automobile in Indianapolis back in twenty-two.

"How'd you find out 'bout me? Not too many 'round these parts know—"

"Your brother," Jake said. "Ralph told me you used to work on cars—"

"Yep. Started with Ford in nineteen, but I was itchin' to work on somethin' else by twenty-one. Heard good things 'bout the Duesenberg plant in Indianapolis. The Duesenberg brothers still owned it then. Hired on and stayed on after Mr. Cord bought 'em out. Then the wife got her back up 'bout comin' back here."

"You sound like the man for the job, all right. When can you start on her?"

"Wait a minute."

There was muffled silence on the other end of the line. Jake could barely make out a garbled conversation before the hand was removed from the receiver.

"How much you say you're payin'?"

"I was thinking room and board while you're in Hulet, two dollars a day—a bonus if you get it done quickly—plus parts."

"How quick you want it? Might be a problem if I gotta order parts—"

"I understand. Why don't you come down and see the car and tell me what you think? I'll give you five dollars just for looking her over—and gas money to get here, of course."

"Give me a minute." He muffled the receiver with his hand for another minute. "I can be t' your place tomorrow afternoon. Might be late."

"That's fine! I'll put you up here overnight."

"No need. I'll stay with Ralph out t' his house. I'll give you my final answer after I see the shape that car of yours is in."

"That seems fair to me, Mr. Scott—"

"Good. See you tomorrow."

The line went dead.

"You're in luck," the mechanic said, scooting out from under the car and standing. Scott was alarmingly thin and tall—taller than Jake by a good two inches when he straightened to his full height. "Engine's in pretty good shape—nothing I can't fix with the tools I got here and some elbow grease. Now the upholstery and trim…"—he ran his hand along his angular jaw—"I figure no amount of saddle soap's gonna keep it from goin' pretty dern quick, and the trim's rusted right through in places. Guess you knew the tires were goners…"

Jake leaned against a post, one of several hayloft supports, and listened to Scott's diagnosis. He'd been impressed with Scott's no-nonsense approach and his obvious expertise. Jake was also relieved to discover that Jules Scott was significantly smarter than his brother Ralph.

"Let me see if I understand you, Mr. Scott," Jake said, relinquishing his comfortable prop and walking toward the car. "You can get the car running as soon as we can find new tires—"

"Well,…I could prob'ly get it runnin' without tires—" a grin began at the edge of Scott's mouth—"you'd just be mighty hard put t' go somewheres."

Jake grinned, too: he was beginning to like this Scott fellow. "I see you like things completely clear, Mr. Scott."

Scott regarded his knuckles, fingernails…turned his hands over, inspected his palms. He pulled a gray rag out of his pocket, and without looking in Jake's direction, began rubbing the oil and grease off his hands. "Well, Mr. Witherspoon, it's like this. If you understand what I can and can't do before I get started doin' anything, things'll go a whole lot smoother. For both of us, I reckon."

"Fair enough. Then, as I understand it, you'll have to order new upholstery—"

"Might have to order new seats with the upholstery on 'em. Don't know many folks 'round here who could do a decent job otherwise."

"Right. OK, new upholstered seats—"

"That's, if I can get 'em, mind."

Jake swallowed. "Of course. New seats, new tires, new trim. Is that all you need from the manufacturer?"

Scott ran his hand over a fender. "Might need new headlamps. Can't rightly tell about 'em till I get her runnin'."

"Fine. A man can't have too many headlamps these days."

Scott looked sideways at him, grinned, nodded, "Always better to have more than not enough, all right."

"Do you want to order the things you need, or would you prefer giving me a list and having me contact the factory?"

"Better leave it to me. I know some guys who might give us a break on prices—that is, if you trust me to handle it."

"I trust you." Jake grinned. "I'm a lawyer, remember?"

"Haw!"—Scott slapped his leg—"Now *that's* a good one."

Jake waited for the connection to go through. He took a sip of his drink to steady his nerves. It had taken him more than a month since the encounter with Dan Johnson to decide to confront another old acquaintance. It was ringing—a good sign: at least the number still worked. Five rings. *I'll give it five more before I hang up*—

"Hello?" A male voice answered.

"Hello. I'm trying to locate Mr. Maxwell Howe."

"Who shall I say is calling?" the voice sounded suspicious.

"Jake—Jacob Witherspoon."

"One moment please, Mr. Witherspoon."

A moment later another man came to the phone, a note of irritation in his tone: "Who is this, please?"

"Max? Is that you?"

There was a pause, then: "Who did you say you were?"

"It's me, Max…Jake Witherspoon. I know it's been a while, but don't you recognize my voice?"

"Jake? Is it really you?"

"In the flesh. I know it must be a shock—"

"I thought you were dead," Max said, his voice hollow.

Jake rubbed his arm, where gooseflesh had appeared, and tried to keep the apprehension out of his voice as he answered: "Still have a taste for the melodramatic I see, but I assure you, I'm very much alive—"

"Then *why*?"

"A small matter of trauma-induced amnesia. You heard about the fire?"

It was a moment before Max replied: "They told me Laura and the children had died in a house fire. They told me you were hospitalized."

"I was, but nothing much was wrong with me physically. Mentally? That's another story." (Jake took a deep breath.) "Max, you didn't hear from me because—because I forgot you existed."

"Forgot? Why was I not informed?"

"I'm afraid it was my mother's misguided attempt to protect me—"

"From what? Me?"

"I suppose from reminders of the past, since I'd done my best to block it out. She didn't know you except by name—"

"Surely she knew I was Teddy's—God, Jake, I am *so* sorry…" Max lapsed into silence.

Jake shook off the memories and tried to sound normal. "Thanks… Listen, the reason I called, besides to let you know I'd returned to the land of the living, is to discuss your last letter to me. The one concerning the Clarence Morgan murder in Little Rock. Do you remember?"

There was another pause.

"Max, I don't mean to rush you, but this *is* a trunk call," Jake said, trying to add a bit of levity to the conversation.

"Of course it is…" (Max sounded preoccupied) "Sorry. I was just trying to remember. It has been a few years, you know. Refresh my memory."

"From what you said, I don't think I should over the telephone."

"Oh, *that* letter…Yes, that subject *is* best discussed in person. But surely that case is closed?"

"I'm thinking I might reopen it."

As if on cue, the grandfather clock in the hall struck the quarter hour. A split second later Jake heard Max's clock chiming in the background.

"Still in synchronization, I see," Max said, sounding more like the Max Jake remembered. He paused for a moment. "I would think twice before doing that, Jake. Let it alone."

"I don't think I can, Max. I think there might be more here than even you suspected—"

"Let's not discuss this anymore, at least not over the telephone."

"In person then. I'm traveling to Washington next week—another matter—is there any way we could meet?"

"I can go you one better: stay with me. I have plenty of room."

"I have no idea how long this will take. I don't want to put you out."

"You won't. You can stay as long as you like."

"Are you sure I won't interfere with your other plans?"

"My 'other plans' consist of the usual tiresome dinner invitations—nothing de rigueur. If you like, I will inform the hostesses of your arrival, and you can join me. Or I can cancel all of them, though if word gets out that an eligible bachelor is on his own in this city—"

"Things haven't changed much, have they?"

"Some things certainly have. Well. We shall discuss all that when you arrive. When shall I expect you?"

"October fourteenth—that's next Sunday, I believe. If all goes well, the train will arrive at Union Station about seven o'clock that evening, your time. No need to pick me up. I'll hire a cab. You're still at the same address?"

"Naturally, but you will do no such thing. I shall send my car. Do you remember my chauffeur, Hudgins?"

"Of course. Well then, I'll see you on the fourteenth."

Jake replaced the receiver on the hook. His stomach growled, reminding him that he hadn't yet had dinner. He started down the hallway to the kitchen to see what Annie had left for him, when he heard a sharp knock at the front door. He sighed, went to answer the summons.

Jules Scott stood with his back to the front door, apparently staring at something in the distance.

"Mr. Scott," Jake said, getting Scott's attention. "I didn't expect to see you today."

Scott approached the house entrance, a broad grin on his gaunt face. "To tell the truth, Mr. Witherspoon, I didn't expect you to see me today either, but circumstances changed."

"Oh?" Jake held the door open wider. "Why don't you come in and tell me about it."

"No need for that. Car's ready."

"But I thought you were waiting on the seats to come in—"

"Was. They came yesterday. Thought you might want t' take a spin."

"You mean the car's ready to *drive*?"

"Didn't think you just wanted t' look at it."

"Give me a second to change and get a sweater."

"Reckon I can wait," Jules said.

The door banged shut behind Jake, as Jules reached into his overalls for cigarettes. He shook one out of the pack and lit it. He went over to the porch railing and waited.

"I'm ready," Jake said, just as Jules finished his smoke.

Jules flicked the spent butt into the flower bed below the railing: "So'm I."

Jake glanced at the driveway, expecting to see the car.

"I left it down t' the barn," Jules said, seeing Jake's perplexity. "Didn't want to spoil the surprise, don'cha know."

"Surprise?"

"You'll see."

CHAPTER ELEVEN

Memories—some of them painful, some not—flooded Jake's mind as he drove through the countryside feeling fully alive for the first time since Laura's death. He'd forgotten how much he loved this car, how well it responded to his lightest touch. Jules had earned every penny of his bonus! He hadn't even minded the extra expense of the new paint job, necessary according to Jules, because of a problem with the right fender he hadn't noticed before. "Desert Sand" they called this color. Well, he felt like Valentino, though they could draw and quarter him before he'd admit it to another living soul. He glanced at his watch. *Plenty of time before the service starts*, he thought, as he turned onto the paved street that ran between Hulet and Little Rock. *Let's see what you've got after five years of sitting still.* He pressed harder on the accelerator, relishing the feel of the wheel in his hands, the surge of power, the sheer addictive thrill of speed.

Jenny drove her year-old Model A Ford into the area reserved for parking behind the First Presbyterian Church of Hulet. She noticed it immediately—a car she'd only seen before in movies back in Virginia. *Whatever is a Duesenberg doing in Hulet, Arkansas?* she thought, as she pulled into a space beside it. She got out of the car and walked over to the automobile. It looked brand new, but she knew the company hadn't made that model in years. They had a fancy new version, the Duesenberg J, that was all the rage with movie stars, or so she'd heard. She'd seen Douglas Fairbanks driving one in a newsreel, and it was something to see! She walked around the car, wondering that anyone in town could've owned a Duesenberg without her—and everyone else— knowing. *It must belong to someone passing through,* she thought, running her gloved hand gently along the smooth curve of the fender. She looked around, but the owner was nowhere to be seen. The church bell rang in the steeple above her and reminded her of her purpose. She pulled her coat tighter around her shoulders against the chill breeze and headed for the church.

She saw him immediately, in the second row from the front, on the right.

At a signal from Pastor Bell, Lula May, who rested from her regular weekday job as telephone operator by moonlighting as church organist on Sundays, struck the keys of the organ. The congregation rose from their seats.

Jenny hurried down the aisle toward the front of the church, anxious to find a seat before the hymn began.

"Jenny?" a voice whispered.

She turned and saw Billy Wiggins, motioning for her to join him and the rest of his family in a pew near the middle of the church. Her heart sank, but she smiled and moved into the space they created for her.

"Please turn to page one hundred three in your hymnals and join us in singing 'Great Is Thy Faithfulness,'" Pastor Bell said in the orotund tones he reserved for Sunday services and funerals. "Lula, if you please."

Billy nudged Jenny and held the hymnal so she could share in the singing. She stopped staring at Jake's back, smiled at Billy, and took her side of the book.

Billy's voice only cracked once during the hymn, but he thought he would die. He had no idea what was going on with him lately, but for this to happen while he was with *Jenny.* To make matters worse—much worse—he knew his face was reddening. He could feel the heat rising in his face. He sneaked a peek at Jenny as he put the hymnal back in the holder, but she didn't seem to have noticed his discomfort. She stared straight ahead, no doubt intent on what the preacher was saying. Billy sat back in the pew, folded his hands, and tried to pretend he was interested, too. It was hard to keep his mind from wandering when Mr. Witherspoon sat five rows in front of him, and Jenny was right there beside him. And then there was that car!

"Stop fidgeting, Billy!" his mother whispered, poking him gently in the ribs. "Remember where you are."

"The sermon was wonderful, Pastor," Jenny said, as Bell greeted her at the door of the church.

"Thank you, Mrs. *Schumacher?*"

Jenny nodded, hoping no one had noticed the surprise in his voice. "It was a lovely service," she said, trying to make her escape.

"It's so good to see you again after such a long time. I *do* hope you'll come again. Your husband—"

"Yes. Thank you, but I must be going."

Jenny managed to free her hand without yanking it out of his grasp, nodded and smiled, and made her way as quickly as she could down the steps.

"Jenny! Just a moment!"

The voice came from behind her. She turned and saw Jake waving with his free hand, the other was being shaken vigorously by Pastor Bell. She couldn't help grinning.

A full five minutes passed before Jake joined her beside her car.

"Sorry. I couldn't seem to get away," Jake said. "I haven't been here in a long time—"

"Believe me, you don't have to explain. I haven't attended in over a year—"

"No wonder Bell's acting like the cat that ate the canary."

"Two apostates at once! We should have warned him," Jenny said, laughing.

Her laughter was impossible to resist. It was the tonic he needed, a missing piece of the life he was reconstructing.

"Perhaps," he said when he could, "we should start attending on a regular basis. Think how encouraging it would be for him." (Jenny peered into his eyes, trying to decide how to respond.) "I think it's a splendid idea, don't you? Unless, of course, you have some objections that I don't know about."

Jenny felt herself blush as she answered, "Of course I have no objections to attending church. I've just been exhausted with having the whole cafe on my shoulders since Will's death—"

Jake held up his hand: "No need to explain. I'm an apostate, too, remember?"

His smile was as tender as it was amused, and Jenny felt herself smiling in return. "Thank you. I am a bit defensive on the subject. Abject guilt, I suppose." The corners of her mouth refused to stop turning upward.

"I can't imagine that you could have anything to feel guilty about."

His earnest tone made her uncomfortable. To her dismay she knew she was blushing again. "Oh, you'd be surprised," she blurted. "The truth is Sunday is my only day off—"

"Of course it is! How stupid of me not to have realized...The wind seems to be picking up a bit." Jake looked around, trying to focus on something else besides her face. "I'm sure you're freezing to death standing here. Allow me," he said, opening her car door for her.

There was nothing to do but get in, so she slid onto the seat.

"Well, I guess I'll see you at the cafe when I'm in town," he said, shutting the door firmly.

"Jake," she said, wanting desperately to regain their earlier ease, "it was good to see you. I think I rather enjoy coming to church. Perhaps I should make it a habit."

He smiled and turned to go, but had second thoughts—"Jenny?"

"Yes?"

"Annie said you left your pie plates at my house. Would you mind if I brought them by sometime?"

"Of course not, but you needn't go to all that trouble. I could come by for them, or send Billy—Oh my heavens!" Jenny's hand went to her face. She colored.

"What?"

"I still have your copy of *Jane Eyre*. I meant to return it weeks ago!"

"I have an idea." (Jenny's eyebrows rose expectantly.) "I have to go out of town for awhile," Jake continued, "but when I get back, why don't you come for Sunday dinner at my place? I could pick you up before church, if you'd like. I could return your plates; you could return the book—I'd like to hear what you thought of it."

"Oh, I'd hate for you to—"

"Annie would love to have someone else to appreciate her cooking. Confidentially, she'd like to show off a bit for you, I think. She said your pies were wonderful—"

"She didn't!"

Jake grinned, "Well, actually, no."

"I thought not."

"Her exact words were: 'Dat Miz Jenny make pies 'most as good as mine.' Coming from Annie that's high praise indeed."

"I expect so," Jenny said. "Well, it all sounds lovely, I must admit. And I would like to see Annie again. She seemed like a rare person—"

"Oh, she is."

"Well, why don't you telephone when you get back in town?"

"I'll do that. Well. Good-bye."

"Good-bye," Jenny said and watched him in her mirror, as he walked around her car and opened the door of the Duesenberg. She leaned over in the seat, tapped on her window to get his attention.

"That's *your* car?" she mouthed.

"I know it's a little out of date, but—"

"It's a beautiful car!" Jenny finished for him, raising her voice so he could hear her through the window.

"Thank you. That's exactly what *I* thought when I bought her." He smiled at her before getting into his car and starting the engine. He raised his hand to her in parting and backed out.

Jenny waited a moment, then pulled out behind him, following his dust until the crossroads, where he turned west, and she turned back to town.

Jenny wiped her eyes with the back of her hand, closed the book firmly, got up off her bed, and made her way to the bathroom to wash her face.

Jane Eyre lay on the counterpane. Jenny plopped down on the edge of the bed and picked up the book.

What made you think his interest was anything more than mere civility? she lectured herself, hugging the book to her breast. *Much less that there was some kind of link between you? So he said he'd call you. He also said he was going out of town. And what do you do? You close the cafe on Saturday nights, just so you'll be free when he calls.*

It's Saturday again and here you sit, rereading his dumb book. And does he call? Not on your tintype! Over two weeks! Two weeks without a single word. And how much money have you lost by closing the cafe?

I don't care! I have to have some time for myself, don't I? And perhaps he *couldn't call,* she thought. *Maybe something happened to him...*

Across her mind's eye flashed the image of Jane Eyre hearing Edward Rochester's call across the miles that separated them, knowing that he needed her, that she must go to him...

"Silly, romantic nonsense!" she said aloud, dropping the book on the bed, as if it were its fault that she hurt so. Acute loneliness overwhelmed her. She flung herself across the bed, and cried herself to sleep.

It was dark when she awoke. Her head ached, her eyes felt puffy, but it was hunger that made her get up. She grimaced as she turned on a lamp and made her way downstairs to the kitchen to forage for leftovers.

At first she didn't recognize the sound, a persistent ringing...*the telephone! At last!* She galloped down the rest of the stairs, stopping at the telephone to gather her wits and catch her breath. She brushed a stray lock of hair out of her eyes. It wouldn't do to let him think she'd been waiting for his call...

"Hello?"

"Mrs. Schumacher, please."

The voice was familiar, a deep baritone, but it didn't sound like Jake.

"Speaking."

"Jenny? You sound different on the telephone—"

"Uh, you do, too...I'm sorry. Who is this?"

"Sorry, I thought I'd already told you. This is Dan Johnson."

"Mr. Johnson! I really didn't recognize your voice—"

"How could you? We've only spoken once, and that wasn't over this contraption."

"That's true, I suppose." She paused expecting him to say something. When he didn't, she continued, "What can I do for you, Mr. Johnson?"

"For one thing, you can call me Dan instead of Mr. Johnson, if I'm to address you as Jenny. For another...well, I guess there's no way to say it other than to say it: I was wondering if you'd like to drive over to Hot Springs with me next weekend."

"Hot Springs? Isn't that a bit far to drive?"

"Not really. We could make a day of it. We could leave early Saturday morning—"

"But the cafe's open—"

"I know," Dan paused. "But I noticed that you'd closed for dinners on Saturdays, and I thought—well, I guess I thought you might want some free time of your own. You know, get away from business for a day...?

"I feel that way sometimes. You know, with the paper and all, and I could use some different scenery myself. I was going to go fishing, but then I thought Hot Springs with you sounded much better than fishing alone. What do you say? Will you go?"

"Well...I suppose Bertha could handle things for one day—"

"Great!"

"Wait a minute; I'll have to ask. I couldn't just leave without her saying she wouldn't mind—"

"Have you ever been to Hot Springs?"

His tone softened as he spoke. He sounded more relaxed, as if they'd known each other since childhood. She loved the sound of his voice. The timbre reminded her of a cello—low, resonant, soothing. She sat down, leaned her elbow on the small table Will had made for her birthday the year he died, and listened to Dan talk of Hot Springs with all the fervor of a poet describing a Parisian spring.

As he spoke, she could see them walking, enjoying the fall foliage, seeing the springs. He wasn't quite as tall as Jake, about five-feet-ten or so she imagined, but he had a powerful build and was much taller than her five-feet-two-inch frame. He'd be nice to walk with, to be seen with.

She remembered his smile: he had a nice smile. The dark brown hair with the gray at the temples gave him the look of a man of the world, and he could write....She'd never known a real writer before, certainly not a newspaperman. He had an air about him, as if he could handle any situation that might come along. She liked that in a man. Will had been like that—strong, capable, but gentle....

"When did you want to leave?" Jenny asked, as Dan paused for a breath.

"Then you'll go?"

She smiled at his incredulity. "Well, I have to make sure it's all right with Bertha, you understand?"

"Of course."

"But if she says she doesn't mind, well—Besides, how could I turn you down after that glorious description?" She laughed.

"I can't tell you how pleased you've made me, Jenny. Well. Assuming your friend will take over the cafe for the day, would seven o'clock be too early to get started?"

"Heavens, no! I'll be ready. Would you like for me to pack a picnic lunch?"

"What a marvelous idea! Do you have a bathing suit to take the springs?"

"A girl from the coast of Virginia? I do, sir, but I imagine it's woefully out of style."

"You, Mrs. Schumacher, may turn a lot of heads in your bathing suit, but, I assure you, it won't be because they're looking at the fashion."

She felt her cheeks warm and was grateful he couldn't see her.

"I'll ask Bertha on Monday, if that's not too late."

"For the chance of having an entire day with you, I'd wait much longer than that."

"Why Mr. Johnson, how you *do* go on," she said, surprising herself as her voice dripped with Virginia honey: she was flirting as if she were a girl again.

Jake returned to Arkansas after a month—much longer than he'd intended—in part, because the research had taken longer than he'd anticipated; in part, because Wall Street securities had plunged six *billion* dollars on Thursday, October 24th, the day before he'd planned to leave.

Overnight many of Max's and his friends and associates were bankrupt, and worse was yet to come. On Monday stocks plummeted into a virtual abyss. Wednesday's *New York Times* called Tuesday the "most disastrous trading day in stock market history." People—not just faceless names, but men they both knew—wandered the streets in shock.

Like Jake, Max had noted certain auguries and had withdrawn his funds from the stock market in late August. Monday night they had sat in Max's living room drinking brandy after a sumptuous meal, waited on by servants, and wondering aloud at the timing that had allowed them to escape with their fortunes intact, while all around them lives were devastated. If Jake had not regained his memory; if he had not investigated his financial condition at the precise time he had; if Max had not paid attention to something he *never* paid attention to; if either of them had taken the advice they usually heeded; if they had waited to act…if, if, if! Why had Max escaped? Why had Jake? Why hadn't others of their acquaintance seen the same things they had? Why had they been spared? *Why hadn't Laura?* Jake sipped his brandy, profoundly shaken at the rapidity with which lives could be changed forever by a simple decision. This time, it seemed, the world had been upended.

After the pandemonium of the nation's capital, the bustle of Little Rock's train depot seemed peaceful. The financial tidal wave had not traveled this far inland…yet. Jake knew they were not immune; it would come. But for now there was relative peace, the deceptive quiet before the cyclone.

No one met him at the station: no one knew he was back. Jake reclaimed his Duesenberg and drove to the courthouse. No one questioned him, as he picked up the copy of the transcript he'd requested of Slo-Joe's trial and sentencing. No one looked familiar. No one remembered him. He put the transcript into his briefcase and drove by Clarence Morgan's old address, the scene of the murder.

The sprawling, two-story frame house needed paint. Unkempt bushes grew in what had been a flowerbed in front of the house. Aside from these minor changes, all seemed as it had been five years earlier. Time suspended eerily, and suddenly it was 1924, but only for a moment, for all was not as unchanged as it appeared. Some things were decidedly different. Jake put his automobile in gear and drove out of town.

Autumn's distinctive radiance brushed the countryside with pale gold. Gone were the distorting heat and the filtering haze of summer. The November air was crisp and smelled of pine and smoke, the sky clear and so brightly blue his eyes ached from the sight. Remnant bronze, gold, orange, and scarlet leaves clung tightly to gray-brown and occasional eggshell-colored branches. Tall pines and sturdy cedars dotted rugged hills with shades of green. Here and there springs and creeks sparkled like liquid silver as he drove past. Perhaps it was the season that brought Jenny to mind: autumn's colors were her own. Whatever the conjurer, her image filled his sight as surely as if she stood before him in the flesh.

A light still shone above the cafe as Jake drove into town and parked. The street seemed deserted except for an occasional light above a store or in the window of a nearby residence. It was not that late, but Wednesday evenings in Hulet were usually spent at church or at home and ended early. Now that he was there, he had no idea what to do next. Perhaps he should have called her from Washington to say he'd been delayed. He knew he should call before arriving at her door this late at night. For all he knew she would not be pleased to see him at all. Perhaps he had only imagined a mutual attraction. After all, it weren't as if they had been "keeping company," as his mother used to say. *And*, he thought, *it isn't as if I'd actually asked her out to the farm on a particular day…. Perhaps she thought nothing more about it. Perhaps, the attraction is completely one-sided. It would be just like me to assume an attraction that wasn't there.*

And even if she were attracted to me at one time, he reasoned, *would she really appreciate my showing up at her door, late at night and unannounced, after hearing nothing from me for weeks? I think not.*

And what would I say? Women rarely understand the insistent call of business. How it sometimes has to take precedence over relationships...And how could I explain the urgency of the financial upheaval on Wall Street? To someone who understands nothing of the stock market?

Jake shook his head. No, Jenny would not understand why he hadn't called, why he had to leave in the first place, and even if she did understand, would it matter to her? No, he was moving too quickly, assuming facts not in evidence.

Myriad reasons to retreat bombarded him, and yet he did not leave but continued to sit in his Duesenberg in front of the cafe.

Jenny saw the automobile when she went to open the window after her bath and knew it at once. She shrank back from the open window, her heart beating in gulps, her hands shaking uncontrollably. *What is he doing here? Now of all times!* Her thoughts were incoherent, a mixture of anger and joy that drained her of sanity. She glimpsed her image in the glass and ran for her robe to put on over her nightgown. Had he seen her at the window? Was he coming up? *What makes him think he can just show up at my door without calling first—or at all? And at this hour!* she thought, pulling her dressing gown from the wardrobe.

Briefly she considered putting on a dress, but that might encourage him to come in. She ran to her vanity, checked her appearance, angry with herself that she still cared what she looked like to him. Dissatisfied, she brushed her hair and hurriedly pinned it into a makeshift chignon and powdered her freshly washed face. *Dear God, now I look ill!*—she pinched her cheeks— *Better!* She scurried to the bookshelf, pulled out *The Mill on the Floss*, arranged herself upon the chaise longue and waited—heart pounding—for his inevitable knock on her door.

A moment later, the sound of an engine starting outside the open window transfixed her. The novel dropped unheeded to the floor, as she heard the sound grow fainter and fainter as it moved into the distance.

Jenny rose earlier than usual after a fretful night to prepare for Thursday's onslaught of breakfast customers. By six o'clock when Bertha arrived, six loaves of bread were cooling on a baker's rack, six more were rising for the second time, and Jenny was in the process of putting four dozen cinnamon rolls into the oven.

Bertha silently surveyed the covered loaves on the baker's rack while she unpinned her hat and took off her coat.

"Good morning!" Jenny said, shutting the oven door with relish. "Help yourself to some coffee." She brushed a wisp of hair from her face with the back of her hand. "You can help me ice the rolls when they come out of the oven."

"Cinnamon buns is it? Sure and it must be the wee folk at work," Bertha said under her breath, as she poured coffee into her cup.

"'Wee folk' indeed! I've been slaving like a field hand, and you're giving credit to wee folk?" Jenny said, peeking under the towel covering a rising loaf of white bread.

"Progressing quite nicely, I think," she said with a sigh of satisfaction, before stepping back to admire the results of her efforts.

Bertha sat at the table and sipped at her coffee.

"'Tis a creature of the mornin' you are, for sure. Are you certain you'll be needin' me at all?" she asked, her eyes as innocent as a spaniel's.

"Oh, I'm sure I can find *something* for you to do," Jenny said in a matter-of-fact tone that betrayed none of her amusement, "if I look hard enough. But for the moment, I think I'll pour myself some coffee and join you. I've been on my feet too long."

"By the looks of things, I'd best put on my apron and get to the dishes before there's nothin' left to cook with."

Bertha pushed herself up and opened the pantry door. Three freshly washed aprons lay folded on top of the spare icebox. She took one and tied it around her ample waist.

"While you're in there, Bertha, bring out some of those dish towels, and I'll dry as you wash."

"Have you talked with Mr. Johnson this week?" Bertha asked, as she filled one side of the double sink with hot soapy water and the other with rinse water.

Jenny grabbed a stack of bread pans, handed them to Bertha: "He asked me to have dinner with him Saturday night in Pine Bluff."

Bertha submerged the pans in the soapy water. "Sure and he's not one for lettin' the grass grow." She wiped her hands on a towel, and let the pans soak. "Are you goin'?"

"I said I would." Jenny plopped some muffin pans into the water.

"Um."

"What's the matter with you?" Jenny chuckled and reached for a clean dishtowel. "Don't you like Dan?"

"Don't know him enough to say whether I do or not." Bertha took a brush and scrubbed at the pans.

"Exactly." Jenny reached for a pan in the rinse water, and began to dry. "You know, Bertha?"—Bertha glanced at her as she worked on another pan—"Dan is a lot of fun to be with. I don't know when I've laughed so hard as I'd did that day we went to Hot Springs..." Jenny stopped, remembering.

"I'll not be denyin' that he seems to make you happy and all—"

"Well then, what?" Jenny picked another pan out of the water, dried it quickly.

"Nothin,' I suppose, since he's makin' you happy."

"He is doing that. I'm really getting quite fond of him. He's intelligent—he knows so much about so many things! I'm never bored when I'm with him, and he always thinks up something new to do. Imagine, concerts in Arkansas!"—Bertha's eyebrows rose—"Well, it was just a band in the park, but it was a concert nonetheless."

"Um."

"He's always a gentleman. Bertha, he makes me feel like a woman again—"

"And what were you thinkin' you were before?"

"Don't be difficult!" Jenny said, grinning. "You know quite well what I mean. Since Will died I haven't had a chance to think about being a woman... I think I was working so hard I didn't have time to miss things like dressing up and having someone notice what I looked like, what I had on—You *know* what I mean!"

Bertha didn't say anything for the time it took her to finish the last of the pans and begin on the utensils. "I suppose I do at that," she said at last, "though to tell the truth, it's been so long ago that I felt like anything but a brood mare—"

"Bertha!" Jenny almost dropped the pan she was drying.

"'Tis the truth, plain or not," she continued, a broad grin spreading over her face. "Course I'm not objectin' to the activity that keeps me one."

Jenny blushed at her friend's frankness and quickly turned to replace the clean pans in their cupboard. She could think of nothing to say.

The two women worked quickly in companionable silence, stopping once to take the rolls out of the oven, glaze them, and put another batch of bread in. The kitchen was put to rights in no time.

"And how's Mr. Witherspoon these days?" Bertha asked, as she stacked the last of the plates on the shelf.

"I'm sure I wouldn't know," Jenny said, pausing only briefly as she put the last of the utensils in the drawer.

Bertha started to tease her but saw Jenny's face out of the corner of her eye and thought better of it.

"I'd better go unlock the front door. It wouldn't do to have all this food and the customers locked out," Jenny said, wiping her hands on a dishtowel as she left the room.

Bertha added some more coffee to her cup, sat down at the table, and thanked God that for once in her life, she'd held her tongue.

CHAPTER TWELVE

I t was Thursday evening before Jake called to explain, and it was too late. "Who did you say this is?" Jenny asked.

"Jake Witherspoon."

"Of course…Jake. It's been so long since I've heard your voice, I didn't recognize it." (Jake smiled at her attempt to make him uncomfortable. She was not going to make this easy for him.) "How can I help you?"

"I called to tell you why I haven't called you. I've been out of town…in Washington, D.C."

"How nice for you. Did you have a good time?"

From her tone he couldn't tell if she were sincere or not, so he assumed the best and answered: "I was there on business, but I did stay with an old friend I hadn't seen in a long time."

"Really?"

"We'd, uh, sort of lost touch in the last few years."

"Well, I'm sure you had a lot of catching up to do—"

"Actually, yes. But it was the market that delayed my return—"

"Were you delayed?"

"For quite a while longer than I had anticipated. You see—"

"Actually, no. What does this have to do with me, exactly?"

Jake found himself looking at the receiver, as if it might tell him what to say and what was going on. "Well, the last time we spoke I indicated that I would call you for dinner at my house some Sunday after church. I thought you might have thought I'd forgotten, since you hadn't heard from me in over a month—"

"I assure you, Mr. Witherspoon—"

"Jake."

"Jake then. I want you to know I haven't given your absence the slightest thought—"

"You haven't?"

"Of course not. Why would I? It isn't as if we'd set a certain date for dinner now was it?"

"No, but—"

"And I do remember your mentioning something about leaving town, but I don't think you said how long you'd be gone. Now that I think about it, the whole thing was really quite unspecified in every respect.

"I thank you for your concern for my interpretation of your intentions, but I can say your concern is unnecessary. I thought your gesture was one of friendship and...what was it? Oh, yes! I have your book, and I believe you have my pie tins. I took your invitation as what it was—an opportunity to exchange property. That *was* what you intended?"

Her voice had an innocence he felt certain was feigned, but what could he say that didn't make him look like a fool?

"Perhaps it was," he said, congratulating himself. "Well, I'm glad you straightened me out on that point. However—"

"However?"

"However, I've thought quite a bit about you while I've been away."

"Have you? How nice."

"Yes. I would like to see you socially. Perhaps you'd care to have dinner with me sometime?"

"Perhaps."

"I know this is short notice, but I did just arrive in town Wednesday evening, and this is the first chance I've had to call—"

"And?"

"Would it be possible for me to take you to dinner Saturday night? Oh, I forgot, the cafe's open for dinner on Saturdays—"

"Actually not. I decided I needed more time for myself, so I close at two on Saturday afternoons now."

"Why, that's wonderful! Then you can come?"

"How nice of you to ask, but I already have an engagement that evening," Jenny said.

Jake bit his tongue to keep from asking—"I see." He paused for a second. Of course she was trying to make him jealous, let him know he couldn't take her for granted. She had a right to do that after the way he'd treated her.

"Well, to tell the truth," he continued, "I *had* feared as much when I called this late in the week. Perhaps we could have dinner next weekend?"

"Oh, I *am* sorry, but you see…well, the truth of it is that my calendar seems to be quite full at the moment. Perhaps, you should look *elsewhere* for a dinner companion."

"Jenny—"

"I'm sorry, I'd like to talk, but I do have things I need to tend to. Thank you for calling. Good-bye, Jake." She hung up.

Jake stared at the receiver in his hand until he heard a voice—"Hello?"

"It's Lula. I heard the line buzzing. Did you get cut off? Do you want me to reconnect you?"

"No, nothing like that, thanks, Lula. I was just woolgathering. Sorry to put you out."

"Well, good night, then." Lula rang off.

Jake replaced the receiver.

Saturday evening passed with glacial speed. Jake paced, his footsteps re-sounding in the empty house. Annie lay at home in bed, down with a cold that had plagued her for more than a week. Bill sat with her, acting as her nurse, cook, and intractable jailer when she threatened, regularly, to resume her usual tasks. Jake approved and encouraged their absence. At Annie's age a simple cold transformed too easily into bronchitis or something worse. Snatches of thought flittered through his mind, too restless to land as ideas. Finding himself in the parlor, the fireplace as cold as the air around it, he wel-comed the opportunity to replenish the store of firewood.

The night air smelled of snow. The mercury hovered just above freezing. He turned up the collar of his heavy coat, stuffed his gloved hands in the pockets, hunched his shoulders, and headed toward the woodpile behind the barn. It occurred to him as he made his way down the slope that he needed to move the firewood closer to the house, to a more convenient location. Gone were the days when other hands hauled, fetched, and carried for his family. *Family?* A sardonic smile twisted his mouth as he reflected on his solitude. He rounded the back corner of the barn. The iron rack stood like a somber skeleton in the cloud-veiled moonlight. A few large splinters of wood, the scant remains of what once was a woodpile, lay beneath and beside the otherwise empty holder. Thwarted in his purpose, he crushed his frustration with renewed determination. He began to explore.

He found large, unwieldy logs farther down the line from the barn. He dragged them, one at a time, nearer to the rack. He would move the firewood closer to the house another time—*When it isn't quite so cold*, he thought as his breath made smoke signals in the night air. *That should be enough for now,* he thought, adding another log to the five already there. *By the time I get it cut and split, I should have about half a rick or more. All I need now is an ax.* He clapped his gloves together, dusted bark particles from his coat and jeans. The pungent scent of pinesap clung to his person. He glanced around, trying to remember. He had seen an ax somewhere. He strode to the large doors of the barn and pushed them open. The kerosene lamp still hung on its nail. He lit the lamp, replaced the chimney, lifted the lantern higher, peered into the gloom. Something glinted as the light caught it. *There!* He smiled, and held the lantern in front, as he grabbed the ax and returned to the cold night and the logs.

He chose a nearby stump as his chopping block, set the lantern at a safe but helpful distance, and went to work with a passion that surprised him. It had been a long time since he'd done this kind of physical labor. His muscles remembered but protested as he swung the ax, made jarring contact with the wood. Chips flew. He chopped the logs into two-foot lengths, up-ended these on the stump, split them into two, sometimes three pieces, tossed them behind him, and began again. Soon he found his rhythm. He stopped briefly to divest himself of his too-warm coat. Before long the rhythm of the work took over, driving him past the pain, the fatigue.

It was sometime after midnight when Jake deposited the armload of firewood in the brass container by the parlor fireplace. His clothes reeked of sweat and sap. His boots were caked with dirt and sawdust. Dark, sticky spots from sap and dirt stained his deerskin gloves. Wood splinters stuck in his clothes, his hair. Annie would kill him if he sat on the furniture. He chuckled at the thought, turned off the lights, and started down the hall to the bathroom and a hot tub to soothe his aching muscles and take away the chill from his bones.

Jenny pulled into the church parking lot, trying not to look to see if Jake's Duesenberg were there. It wasn't. All her soul-searching, her agonizing over her wardrobe, wondering at the wisdom of attending church at all this morning was so much wasted energy. Oh well. She cleared her throat, checked her nose for shine in her mirror—a bit pink, she thought, reaching in her purse for her compact. She powdered her nose, dabbed at the corners of her eyes with her handkerchief, and closed her purse with a reassuring click. She removed her hatpin, repositioning it until her hat seemed more secure. She got out of the car, squared her shoulders, checked the seams of her stockings, and entered the church.

She did not see the Wigginses this morning. It was just as well. She did not feel especially communicative. She walked to the front pews, and took a seat near the aisle on the third row on the left by some people she'd seen occasionally, but whom she did not know. The woman leaned forward across her husband and extended her hand.

"I'm Lottie York," she whispered.

"Jenny Schumacher. Pleased to meet you," she said, shaking the woman's hand and smiling.

"Likewise, I'm sure. This here's my husband Ron—"

The man acknowledged the introduction with a curt nod, his mouth a hard line. Jenny felt a chill, smiled again at Lottie, sat back in the pew.

Pastor Bell entered the front of the church through a side door, faced the congregation, motioned with both hands as he said, "The congregation will please rise and join together in singing hymn number two hundred sixty-eight, 'How Firm a Foundation'. Lula, if you please."

The organ sounded as Jenny found the place in the hymnal. *I love this hymn*, she thought as she sang. *I love singing; I love the words*—"Fear not, I am with thee/O be not dismayed—"

A hand took the other edge of the hymnal as someone slid into the space beside her. *Jake.* He smiled down at her, his voice blending with the others—"I'll strengthen thee, help thee, and cause thee to stand—"

There was no help for it. Might as well make the best out of the situation before he thought that she actually *cared*—"For I will be with thee thy troubles to bless/and sanctify to thee thy deepest distress—"

I'm counting on it, she said to God, as her clear alto joined Jake's rather nice bass.

He smiled approvingly as she sang, prompting her to sing better than she'd sung in years. As she improved, he seemed to as well. By the fifth verse they were harmonizing perfectly, the rest of the congregation catching their fervor.

"Well!" Pastor Bell exclaimed, a broad and amazed smile on his face as the last notes died away, "I think I can safely say that the Spirit of God is with us this morning. Hear then, the Psalmist's words: 'This is the day that the Lord has made; let us rejoice and be glad in it!'"

Jake smiled at her as they resumed their seats. To her surprise she found herself returning his smile: all her irritation with him had gone.

"It's good to see you again, Mrs. Schumacher—and *Jake*! Where have you been? We've missed you lately. Hope this means we'll be seeing more of you in the future," Pastor Bell said, as he shook Jake's hand at the church door.

"I'll certainly try to be here as often as I possibly can—"

"If you don't mind my saying so," he said, nodding cheerily to include Jenny, "you sing beautifully together. Would you consider joining the choir? Or perhaps you could get with Lula and honor us with a duet?" He beamed at both of them, hope fairly leaping from his eyeballs.

Jenny blushed and looked at Jake for help.

"Pastor Bell, I'm sure I speak for Mrs. Schumacher when I tell you how pleased we both are with your compliment, but, to be blunt, she and I sang together for the first time this morning. And although I heartily agree with your assessment of her talents, I hardly think that she would want to be partnered with me—at least at this time."

Bell's countenance fell somewhat, then rallied as he turned to Jenny: "Perhaps so, but I'm not one to give up as you know, Mrs. Schumacher. I ask you both to discuss it, and if the timing is not ripe for the duet, then please do consider joining the choir. I don't know if you realize what a profound effect your singing had on the entire congregation this morning." He leaned closer, his voice low so as not to be overheard: "To tell the truth, until this morning's blessed occurrence, I could only classify our congregation as exhibiting the truest meaning of the phrase 'a joyful *noise*'." His eyes rolled heavenward as he sighed.

Jake chuckled: "I promise, Pastor, I will do my utmost to persuade Mrs. Schumacher to lend her voice—"

"And your own," Pastor Bell's eyebrows went up for emphasis.

"God willing," Jake said.

"Oh, He will be!" Pastor Bell grinned from ear to ear, then turned to greet the Yorks who were next in line.

"May I?" Jake asked, taking Jenny's arm and helping her down the steps to the gravel walk.

"Thank you."

"I hope you didn't mind my joining you this morning. I confess when I saw you, I didn't consider any other seating arrangement. It was thoughtless of me. I should've considered your feelings before I acted."

"My feelings?"

"Yes. I won't pretend I didn't understand that you do not wish to see me again. You have every right, but I still find that I do want to see you, to talk to you—"

"To be friends?" she asked.

"Yes. At least friends."

"I do not consider friendship something to be taken lightly, Mr. Witherspoon--"

"Jake. Nor do I." Jake cleared his throat, changed the weight from his right foot to his left.

"Let me begin again…I would consider it an honor, Jenny, if I could count you among my friends. I will be your friend regardless."

She smiled encouragingly, held out her gloved hand. "Then we shall be friends."

"Good!" he said, clasping her hand heartily. "May I walk you to your car?"

CHAPTER THIRTEEN

"Good morning, Penny," Jake said, as he entered the law office the next day.

"Oh," Penelope said, looking startled, "good morning, Mr. Witherspoon! We weren't expecting you in the office today. Mr. Townsend said you were taking some time off before starting back."

"True, but I just got back from a trip to Washington and had some things I needed to get from here."

"Washington! I've always wanted to visit the capital. How was your trip?"

"Eventful—especially after the market disaster—"

"Are *you* all right about that?" Penelope asked, her voice tentative.

"Fine. I got out right after the peak in September, but a lot of people I know weren't so lucky."

"I know…Maybe I shouldn't say anything, but I don't know who else to tell…" Her voice trailed off, and Jake noticed that she'd aged considerably in the few weeks he'd been gone.

"What's the matter, Penny?" A new thought occurred to him—"*You* weren't caught in this thing, were you?"

"No." Penny shook her head, paused. "My sister and brother-in-law were though. They had invested everything they had—not much by your standards, I'm sure—but everything *they* had, and then some."

"What do you mean 'and then some?'"

Penelope managed a wan smile: "They bought a lot on something called 'margin'—nothing more than credit, if you ask me—but they didn't ask me...Well, when everything fell, they had to come up with the money they owed for the stocks and—and they didn't have it, so..."

"So?"

"So they lost their house, then Jimmy lost his job—his employer didn't want anyone working for him that was a deadbeat—that's what Dot said he called him, a *deadbeat*! And all because he'd taken *his* advice!"

Jake shook his head: "I'm not following you—"

"It was Jimmy's boss who arranged for him to buy those stocks! Told him he was too *cautious*, that he couldn't get *anywhere* if he didn't take risks! Then he goes and fires Jimmy for doin' what *he* told him to do! It's not fair—any of it!" Tears spilled over Penny's lashes and ran down her cheeks. She didn't seem to notice.

"How can I help?"

Penelope raised her head, looked at him through her tears, then she laughed, without humor, and wiped her eyes with the back of her hand: "I guess you could help by making sure I don't lose *my* job. They've moved in with me."

Jake smiled: "I don't think you have to worry about that—"

"Have you talked to Mr. Townsend lately?"

There was something sarcastic in her tone that warned him.

"No, not in the last two weeks anyway."

"Maybe you'd better."

Jake was quiet for a moment, then asked: "And Mr. Hawley, Mr. Branch?"

She shrugged her shoulders.

Jake stood there for a moment longer then reached over and patted her shoulder: "Don't worry, Penny. This firm isn't going to collapse around you. Your job is safe."

Penny looked up at him, her eyes searching his.

"I promise," he said, giving her shoulder a final pat before starting down the corridor to Mike's office. Suddenly he stopped, turned around and walked back to her desk.

"Penny, your brother-in-law, Jack—?"

"Jimmy."

"Jimmy…Where did you say he used to work?"

"Over at Pine Bluff."

"Yes, but what did he do there? What was his job?"

"It doesn't matter, he can't get it back…."

Jake sighed in frustration. "What did he *do*?"

"He worked in a drugstore—"

"He's a pharmacist?"

"No, a sales clerk—well, I guess he really managed the place. The owner was never there, according to Dot anyway."

"Can he keep books?"

"You mean records, accounts—that sort of thing?"

"Yes, accounts. Can he do simple accounting?"

"I think so."

"Find out," Jake said, and started to walk off, but stopped again. "Penny, tell me the truth now: can this Jimmy be trusted—really trusted—with money?"

Hope radiated from her eyes; it almost hurt Jake to see it.

"Yes," she nodded, "he can be trusted." Then she grinned broadly, added: "Just don't ask him for investment advice, OK?"

"Don't worry, I won't—and don't get your hopes up too high, Penny, and don't get his up either. This might not work out. Just find out what he can do."

"Thank you, Mr. Witherspoon."

"It's 'Jake' when it's just us, remember?" Jake shook his finger at her. "And don't thank me yet; nothing may come of this," he said, but he could tell she wasn't listening.

Jake opened Mike's office door without knocking. Mike's back was to him and the blinds were drawn. Mike seemed to be staring at nothing. Jake backed out and knocked loudly on the door and came in without waiting for an answer.

"Well, Michael," he said, assuming his best hail-fellow-well-met manner, "I'm back and ready to get started. What's first on the agenda?"

Jake's words sank into Mike's consciousness like so much fish food sprinkled on the water of an aquarium. One by one they floated by him; some found him; most found their way to the bottom sand and dissolved.

"Mike?"

He heard his name, turned toward the voice: someone was there...a man...he couldn't quite make out the face....

"Mike?" Jake dropped the pretense; Mike looked like hell. "It's Jake."

"Jake?"

Mike had been drinking—a lot by the looks of it. Jake walked to the intercom, told Penny to make some strong coffee and to bring two cups into Mike's office: "Is Ben here?"

"I'm here," Ben said over the intercom, "for all the good it does anyone."

"You sound sober, and that's a start anyway," Jake said. "Why don't you bring the coffee when it's ready? Penelope shouldn't have to deal with this today."

"Right."

"Penny?" Jake pushed the button again.

"Yes?"

"Go home. There's nothing more you can do today." She didn't answer him, so he added, "I'll need you tomorrow, bright and early, and I'll need that information we discussed."

"I'll be here!" (There was a pause.) "Thanks again, Mr. Witherspoon."

"Go home, Penny! I'll see you tomorrow." He heard her nervous giggle as the intercom went dead.

"What's going on?" Mike slurred the words, but Jake knew what he was saying.

The office door opened. Ben stood in the doorway with a tray, coffee, and mugs.

"Where do you want it?"

"Anywhere he's not likely to knock it over."

"So," Ben said, putting the tray down on the game table and pouring three cups of black coffee, "how was D.C?"

"Jenny? I hope I didn't disturb you, but I had an idea and wanted to know what you thought of it." Jake fingered the telephone cord as he spoke.

"No, you didn't disturb me, Jake. What did you want to say?" Jenny sat down on the stool by the telephone and tried to keep her voice steady, her tone nonchalant.

"Well, if you're not doing anything this evening, would you mind if I came by for a few minutes? I still have your pie plates, and to be honest, Annie isn't well—"

"Oh, I'm sorry to hear that! What's the matter?"

"Well, it started out as a cold, but Doc says it's hanging on too long as far as he's concerned. I think he's worried about pneumonia, to tell you the truth."

"Oh, no..."

"I know...I'm worried about her, but there's not much I can do to help right now except get Doc to keep an eye on her and try to give her as little to worry about as possible so she can rest. Which brings me back to my point: Bill says those pie plates of yours are worrying her a lot. She doesn't want you to think badly of her for keeping them so long—"

"Oh, tell her I never gave it a thought! The idea! It's more my fault than hers, surely?"

"I know it's silly, but she's from the old school where you always returned a dish on time, and you always returned it filled with something else. I can't fill them up, I'm sorry to say, but I can return them. I could pick up Mother's book while I'm there. I promise I won't stay. I'll just deliver the pie plates and be on my way."

Jenny tried to think of some witty remark, something that didn't make her sound—*Oh, I don't care how I sound!*

"Fine. When did you want to come over?"

Jake breathed again, looked at his watch. "Let's see, it's seven-thirty now.... Would an hour be convenient?"

Jenny stood up, caught her reflection in the mirror, did some rapid calculations: "That's fine. I'll have the book ready for you to pick up." She paused. How to put this without letting him know she'd seen him parked below her window that night? "Do you need directions to my place?"

"I assumed you lived at the cafe—"

"Above it actually. I have the entire second story. There's a separate entrance in the alley, just south of the cafe. You'll see it. I'm at the top of the stairs. Just knock on the door when you get here."

"I'll see you in an hour then."

"Till then," she said and replaced the receiver.

Jake grinned, hung up the telephone, slapped his thigh—*Yes! Now where did Annie say those pie tins were?*

A brisk, cold wind funneled through the alley beside the cafe. Jake pulled the edges of his coat around the stacked pie plates to keep the red velvet box sitting on top of them from being blown to the ground. Scarlet satin ribbons secured the heart-shaped box. On its top sat five silk rosebuds, so deeply red they were almost black. He found the stairs to her apartment and climbed the short distance to her door.

Jenny heard his footsteps on the stairs, tucked a stray wisp of hair hurriedly into her chignon, and smoothed her dress.

He knocked; she counted to five and opened the door.

The light from the apartment formed a golden halo around her which seemed to set her hair on fire. She resembled paintings he'd seen of avenging angels—powerful, all business, and very, very beautiful. He realized at once that his previous notion of her had about as much substance as a soap bubble. An urgent need to understand her gripped him.

"Would you like to come in?" she said, holding the door a bit wider, allowing him a glimpse of the warm interior she inhabited.

"If you're sure it's no trouble...?"

"No trouble at all. Besides you'll catch your death standing in that draft. I know I will, if I have to stand in this doorway much longer—"

"Of course! I'm sorry." He stepped across her threshold quickly, heard the door closed firmly behind him. He turned in time to see her amusement before she could hide it. He chuckled and held out his offering.

"For you. I'm afraid I'm of the old school as well. You've been so patient with us. I simply could not bring myself to return them empty-handed."

"I've never seen anything so lovely...." She looked up at him, her eyes gold-flecked mahogany. "Wherever did you find something like this?"

The angel vanished, leaving in its vapor a vulnerable woman.

His emotions tumbled over one another. All he could think of was how much he wanted to take her in his arms, hold her, and never let her go. He cleared his throat and told the truth: "In Washington."

"Washington?" She was staring at the roses, hadn't even opened the box. She raised her eyes to his again.

"I bought them for you when I was in Washington. You see, you were on my mind, even if I didn't let you know it."

She said nothing, continued to look into his eyes.

"Max—he's the old friend I told you about, the one I hadn't seen in such a long time?" (She nodded.) "Well, he and I were passing by this confectionery a couple of days before I left, and I saw this in the window. Its beauty reminded me of you—"

"Really." (Her tone said everything. The all-seeing angel reappeared.)

He grinned. "I never was very good at flowery speeches."

"I can see that."

"Without the hearts and flowers then. I passed this window, saw this, and thought I'd get it for you."

"Why?"

"I don't know why,"— *Why do women always ask that?* —"I just wanted to buy it for you. It was pretty. I thought you'd like it—"

"I do. Very much." (She smiled again, and his irritation evaporated.) "Won't you sit down?" She gestured toward the sofa.

"Thank you. But I only mean to stay a moment."

"Well, you can sit down for that moment, can't you? I have to get your book...and, I want to open this and see what wonders lie inside a box this pretty."

"Chocolates——"

"Oh, don't spoil it by telling me! Now the book will have to wait...."

Her lower lip actually pushed out a bit, like a child whose surprise had been spoiled. She reminded him of someone.... She plopped down beside him on the sofa, and for the first time, he noticed that her dress was a dark, rich green. It suited her, set off her hair beautifully. And suddenly, the chameleon beside him changed into a delighted girl, eagerly untying the ribbons that held the box. She stopped to set the ribbons and roses carefully on the table beside her, then lifted the box lid: "Oh, Jake! These aren't just chocolates, they're art!"

Even he was taken aback at the multitude of intricate shapes: hearts decorated with gold (could that be edible?), dark chocolate hearts, oak leaves with acorns, milk chocolate-covered walnuts atop what appeared to be caramel, squares, rectangles—geometrical shapes stamped with crowns and cameos, molded shells of various chocolates, buttercreams, gold-wrapped mysteries, and three large truffles of wondrous promise.

"Well," he said.

"Well, indeed..." She continued to stare. "I've never seen anything like these!"

"Neither had I. They come from Belgium, or so the gentleman who owned the store said. They're from Godiva Chocolatiers." Jake chuckled. "I hope you like chocolates. I never thought that you might not."

"I *adore* chocolates! It's been a long time since I've had any——"

"Perhaps, you should try one. However, I must warn you: my father used to be suspicious of any food that looked too good."

"I'll take my chances! But you must have one, too. I can't possibly eat all of these by myself. How much is there?"

"Two pounds."

"Heavens! That settles it: you have to help me." She held the box toward him so that he could choose.

The intoxicating aroma of the chocolate made his mouth water, but he resisted and smiled: "It's your chocolate. You choose first."

"You don't want any?"

"I didn't say that."

Her shoulders relaxed as she laughed. "Thank God! All right..." She pondered her choices and chose a cocoa-dusted truffle. "Now you."

Jake reached for a dark chocolate heart.

"Oh, this is too pretty to eat!" Jenny exclaimed.

"It's too pretty *not* to eat. I didn't buy it to frame."

She laughed at his seriousness and took a tentative bite. "Ummmmm."

"Good?"

She closed her eyes in apparent ecstasy and nodded.

He took a bite. It was superb—better than that—it was...much too good to waste time trying to analyze it. 'Ummmmm' said it all, he thought, as he took another bite.

They sat there savoring the chocolate in companionable indulgence. Finally, the last morsel of his chocolate heart dissolved, and he turned toward her: "Have you forgiven me yet?"

"Give me one more piece, and I'll let you know," she said, eyes still closed, a slight smile on her lips.

"What would you like?" he asked, gazing not at the box but at her face.

"I don't know. Surprise me."

"On one condition..."

Her eyelids opened a bit—"Which is?"

"That you'll let me take you to dinner—a movie, too, if you'd like."

"When?"

"Next Saturday evening?"

"First choose my chocolate," she said, arching her eyebrows.

"A test?"

"Perhaps."

"Let me see…" He grinned, perused the chocolates, furrowed his brow, reached for the last truffle, stopped, then picked up a gold-covered ball and handed it to her.

"What is it?"

"Your surprise."

"I believe my calendar is clear Saturday evening."

"Then you accept?"

"How could I not?" She unwrapped the gold covering and took a bite.

"How is it?"

"Ummmmm…"

"Last night was wonderful, Jenny," Jake said, when he telephoned the next Sunday night.

"I thought so, too, Jake."

"How would you like to join me again next weekend?"

Jenny hesitated. "Next weekend?"

"How about next Saturday night? I heard 'The Iron Mask' is playing in Little Rock. We could go there early, have dinner, and see the movie. Maybe you'd rather have dinner at some nice place and go dancing afterward? Forgo the movie? I realize John Gilbert didn't exactly seem so red hot—"

"I don't think so—"

"Exactly. Poor old Gilbert. Too bad for him that talkies came in—"

"I wasn't talking about the movie."

"Oh?"

"I…I, uh, don't think we should see each other next Saturday—"

"Too soon?"—her silence alerted him—"Or maybe you didn't have as good a time last night as I did…?"

"It's not that."

"Then what is it?"

"I'm seeing someone else."

Jake didn't say anything.

"I wasn't lying the other day on the telephone, Jake. My calendar really is pretty full."

"What happened last night then? He get called out of town or something?"

"I don't know. You asked me out before he did. I wanted to see you, so I said yes."

"And now you don't want to see me. It that it?"

"I just don't want to make it a regular thing."

"I understand," he said, but he didn't—not at all. He waited for her to say something else. When she remained silent, he continued. "Well, let me know if and when you change your mind, Jenny—" (she still said nothing)— "See you around. Good-bye." He hung up without waiting for her reply.

"You had to take over the senior position, Jake. Let's face it, Mike's not snapping out of this," Ben said, as Jake drove to his house after delivering a not-too-sober and miserable Mike Townsend to his wife. "I for one am grateful you stepped in. You probably stopped the firm from going under. I talked to Larry. He agreed wholeheartedly."

"Mike won't like it when he realizes what's happened."

"The way he's drinking, the word is *if* not 'when'." Ben paused. "Have you ever seen him like this before?"

Jake glanced at Ben, then back at the road. "Mike's always enjoyed his liquor, but no, I've never seen him drink like this. It worries me. I know he was hit hard by the market crash, but he wasn't wiped out, he didn't lose everything like so many men I know—"

"Yeah. You know what saved me?"

"No. What?"

"Grace."

"No kidding."

Ben looked at him, confused—"I don't mean that kind of grace!—I mean Grace Hawley, my wife."

Jake chuckled. "Sorry. I should've known—"

"Why? She's never saved me before...I love her—God knows I love her—but she's not exactly what you would call...smart."

Jake grinned. It was true. Grace Hawley had always been a sweet girl, a good wife to Ben, but she'd never been known for her brain. "So how did she save you from financial ruin?"

"I'm not proud of it, but the truth is she made me mad. I pulled out our money to spite her."

"Oh?"

"Yeah. She kept nagging me to take our money out of the market, telling me she 'had a feeling'—now what kind of nonsense is that to base fiscal responsibility on?"

"What was her feeling?"

"That our money wasn't safe with those big business types on Wall Street—said she could tell by their pictures!"

"Pictures?"

"Yeah, the political cartoons in the Little Rock papers I brought home."

"You're kidding?"

"Nope. And she didn't like them, because she *trusted* Will Rogers, and she didn't think *he* much cared for those big money guys either."

"I hate to say it..."

"Then don't. Do you know what I have to put up with now that she's been proven right?"

Jake laughed. "My mother used to say God protects drunks and—" He stopped abruptly.

"Go ahead and say it—fools. The only problem is I thought *Grace* was the fool. Turns out it was me. Now I'll never hear the end of it."

Jake laughed until he was having trouble seeing the road. When he could talk again, he asked, "Anything else I should know?"

"Not really. I filled you in on Fanny Runyon, didn't I?"

"That she's sequestered at Larry's cabin?"

"Yeah. I don't think anyone's interested in her, but Larry and Mike seemed to think it was a good idea to keep her out of sight and out of mind."

"I agree. She's safer there. You said we'd hired a nurse to look out for her?"

"Yeah. And there's a bodyguard who keeps watch. Larry goes up there once a week to bring them supplies and check on things. Other than that, and the usual estate business, not much is going on.

"Oh, I do have some more news," Ben continued. "Guess who's courting Jenny Schumacher?"

Jake's heart turned over, but he managed to keep it from showing. "I'm sorry. What did you say?"

"Jenny Schumacher—you know, Jenny's Cafe?"

"What about her?"

"Well, last summer there was a rumor that she was seeing someone socially. Do you know I even heard that *you* were seeing her?"

"Really?"

Ben laughed. "Yeah, what some women won't cook up! But it seems she really was seeing someone, and guess who it is? Never mind, you'll never guess. It's Dan Johnson!" Ben hooted and slapped his thigh.

"Yep," he chuckled, "I bet ol' Will is just flippin' around in his grave— Sure wouldn't want any wife of mine steppin' out with Johnson—" Ben glanced over at Jake and immediately sobered up. "Sorry, Jake. I didn't mean anything by that. I forgot he used to be your brother-in-law."

Jake stared at the road ahead for a second, then looked over at Ben. "It's all right. Dan and I never had that much to say to one another—" he focused on the road—"How long have they been...?"

"Not that long that I can see, though Flossie—Flossie Burns, Grace's sister?" (Jake shook his head.) "No matter...Come to think of it, I don't guess you would know them—oh well, forget it. Flossie says that Jenny's been seeing Dan all along, since sometime last summer, and that there never was another man, but Gracie thinks that's not so."

"Oh? Why not?"

"You know how women are..."

Jake smiled. "Not really. I've been out of touch a while, you know."

Ben coughed. "Sure. Grace seems to think Jenny was sweet on this other man, and then he dropped her, or broke her heart, or something. Grace says Jenny's only seeing Dan because she's on the—rebound, I think she calls it—some such nonsense."

"Trying to make the other man jealous?" Jake interjected, hoping for more information.

Ben shook his head: "Not according to Grace. She seems to think Jenny's pretty serious. In fact, she's worried Jenny's going to marry the guy."

Jake hit the brake hard; Ben nearly went through the windshield but caught himself.

"Good Lord, Jake! What's the matter?"

"Sorry. Are you all right?"

"Barely."

"Sorry," he said, driving forward slowly. "My eyes must've been playing tricks or something…I could've sworn some animal jumped in front of the car—"

"Deer maybe?" Ben turned around in his seat and looked back at the road. "I don't see anything now, but it sure could've been a deer." He turned back and sat sideways in the seat. "Gracie's daddy hit a deer last month about this time of night—hadn't turned his lights on yet, didn't figure it was dark enough—and it almost killed him. Sure did a lot of damage to his truck. You wouldn't think anything that small could do so much damage—"

Jake let him drone on, grateful for the change in topic, the chance to think.

CHAPTER FOURTEEN

"I said leave me alone, woman!" Mike swiped at the air behind him with his hand, missing his wife by several inches. He stumbled into the bathroom, slamming the door behind him.

Naomi stood flattened against the hall wall, too frightened to move. Silent tears rolled down her cheeks unchecked. In the thirty years they'd been married, Mike had never raised his voice, much less his hand to her. He hadn't always been kind—no, Mike could be downright cruel when he set his mind and his tongue to it—but he'd never hit her before. Never tried to. His sarcasm usually came on when something reminded him that she'd never given him a child—not that he really blamed her. It was more like he'd get angry with himself and take it out on her, hitting where he knew he'd do the most damage....

Her shoulders and body drooped. She stopped crying. She looked at the closed bathroom door. *Now that I think it through, you've been hitting me for as long as I can remember. You just didn't touch me with your hands....*

"Mike?" she shouted from where she stood. "You need me to get you anything?"

"Leave me the hell alone, I said!" The words shot through the door but missed her.

Naomi walked into their bedroom, threw some things in a suitcase. She looked around the room to see if she'd left anything she'd need...nothing. She closed the bag, took it to the closet, where she put on her coat and gloves, and pinned her hat firmly on her head. She stopped, listening. He was throwing up. She heard bits of curses, but refused to care. She rummaged in his coat pocket for the car keys, picked up the suitcase, and walked out the front door, locking it carefully behind her.

I'll visit with Sis for a couple of days, she told herself, as she started the car and put it into reverse. *I'll call Ben or maybe Jake tomorrow, and tell them what's going on. They'll know what to do. I must remember to get to the bank first thing in the morning. I'll just go visiting....*

"Naomi!" Mike yelled again, yanking the door open with such force the doorknob came off in his hand. He didn't notice at first. Threw it down on the tile when he did.

"Damn you, woman! Where in the hell are you? I cut my blasted hand—Do you hear me, woman? Naomi!" He stumbled down the hallway into the kitchen. The lights were on. Something was burning. He could smell it. "Naomi! The damn dinner's burning! Where in the hell are you?"

He staggered to the counter, managed to find a dishtowel. He wrapped it around his cut hand. Smoke seeped through the oven door seams. He opened the door. Smoke billowed into the room. He waved his hand—"Naomi! Come in here right now and get this mess cleaned up!" She didn't come. It was obvious he was going to have to take whatever inedible mess she'd cooked tonight out of the oven. His hand throbbed. He reached for the pan—"Damn!"—he blew on his fingers where blisters were already forming—"Naomi! You'd better get yourself in here!" He grabbed at a hot pad on the counter, pulled the roasting pan out of the oven, threw the contents into the sink. *Meatloaf! Maybe I should be grateful.* He laughed, a bitter sound without humor. *I swear I'll kill that woman when I get my hands on her....*

"Naomi!" Mike listened, heard nothing. He walked into his office, only tripping once—*over that blasted rug I've been telling her to get rid of for years*—found the gin he kept in his bottom desk drawer, twisted off the top and took a swig. The liquid burned as it ran down his throat, causing a coughing spasm. He wiped his mouth with the back of his hand. He held the bottle by the neck and made his way to their bedroom; she was probably hiding in there.

"If you're in there, gal, you'd better pray I'm in a better mood when I lay my eyes on you than I am now, and you'd better have a hell of a reason why you haven't come when I've been hollerin' my head off for you—" He flung the door open, leaving a dent in the plaster wall where the knob hit. He looked around the room. He strode to the closet, opened the door—gone! He yanked open her drawers; a few items remained, but most were gone. His legs gave way. He sat down—hard—on the floor by their bed.

"Naomi?" He felt lost. Where could she have gone? She'd never run to friends about their problems. If there was one thing he'd always liked about Naomi, it was that she knew how to keep her own counsel. Her sisters lived too far away for her to go to them.

He leapt to his feet, ran to the front of the house, frantically looking in the box where he always dumped his keys—they weren't there. Then he remembered: He hadn't taken them out of his coat when he'd come in tonight. He hadn't felt up to it. He opened the closet door, noticed her coat was absent, reached into his coat pocket—empty. The other pocket? Empty. He ran to the front door, pulled on the handle and nearly pulled his elbow out of joint. She had locked the door from the outside! He turned the bolt, opened the door. Sure enough, the car was gone. "Damn!" Mike slammed the door, started to sit down in his chair in the empty living room, and remembered his bottle.

He took the gin into the kitchen, got a glass and poured himself four fingers before returning to the living room. He had to think. His head hurt; his palm throbbed where he'd cut it. He unwrapped the dishtowel. The bleeding had stopped, but it looked nasty. He was almost out of gin....

It occurred to him as he refilled his glass that his life started going downhill about the same time Jake Witherspoon started getting his back. He tilted the bottle, remembered the alcohol, walked to the sink and poured some over the cut on his hand—"Damnation!" He shook his hand in the air, hoping the sting would quit quickly.

"If I don't quit hurting soon, I'm going to sober up," he said to the bottle, as he set it tenderly on the kitchen counter. He picked up his glass, addressed it: "We can't let that happen now, can we?" He smiled wryly, downed the liquid in the glass, and poured another before making his way back to the living room.

Yep. Things started turning to manure when Jake came back and started messing with things he shouldn't have messed with. Hell, what is he trying to do? Opening up that nigger's case! Showboatin' like he always did without givin' a thought to me or the firm. Never listenin' to anyone's voice but his own...

He drank some more gin, eyed the glass suspiciously. It tasted watered down. *And now he's taken over! Drivin' me home last night, like I couldn't be trusted with my own damn car! And Ben went along! Takin' my car keys when I wasn't lookin' like I was some damned adolescent! It's a conspiracy, that's what it is!*

He lifted his glass: "To Jacob Witherspoon—the prodigal son who's returned to the fold and killed his father in the process!" (He drank the rest in one gulp. Wiped his hand across his mouth.) "Watch your back, son. This old man has no intention of going out quietly."

The bell above the cafe door jingled. Jenny looked up from the ledger and smiled.

"Billy! You're early. I'll be through with this in a minute. Find a seat somewhere. I'll join you right away."

"Are you sure you have time?"

Jenny closed the ledger for emphasis. "Finished right now, as a matter of fact. Your timing is always impeccable."

"Bet you thought you'd trip me up with that one, but I know what it means—'flawless'—right?"

"Correct," Jenny said, putting a pen into the desk drawer and shutting it. She got up and came around the counter. "You're getting too smart for me. I think it's about time you found another tutor—"

"Don't you want to help me anymore?"

Billy seemed stricken. He also seemed taller.

"The question is not whether I'd like to help, but whether I'm capable of taking you any further than you've already come."

Jenny led the way to a quiet corner booth and sat down across from him: "Not only are you catching up to me academically, you seem to be passing me in terms of height. How much have you grown in the past couple of months?"

Billy grinned, blushing furiously. "To hear Ma talk, you'd think I'd grown a foot or more every week, but I think it's closer to a couple or three inches—she can't keep me in trousers that fit—" he stuck out his leg—"See, she just let these down last week, and already they're high-waters. She wants me to go back to knickers, but I told her if I was doing a man's work, I ought to be wearing long pants."

"Well, if that article you wrote for the paper last week is any indication of your proper pant length, I'd have to say you're definitely ready for long pants."

"Aw, you're just saying that—"

"I am *not*. I thought it was quite well written—almost as good as anything Dan—Mr. Johnson writes. You can trust me. I'd tell you if it were otherwise."

Billy sat back in the booth, leaned his head against the tall back, and grinned: "The honest-to-God's-truth? I thought it was pretty good myself. But I still can't figure out why Mr. Johnson let me write at all—"

"Didn't I tell you that article on Mrs. Witherspoon would work for you?"

Billy thought a moment, sat up, and leaned toward her over the table between them. "You know I never did get it talk to Mr. Witherspoon that day—"

"I thought he was going to tell—"

"So did I, but he told me Mrs. Jackson knew more about his mother than he did. Imagine that!"

"Did she?"

"Oh, she knew a bunch about her, that's for sure! But wasn't that a funny thing to say about his own mother?"

Jenny smiled and thought of her own mother: "Not really. How much do you really know about your mother?"

"A lot!"

"Does she have a particular talent you know about?"

"Cooking! She's a terrific cook!"

"Does she enjoy cooking? Did she study it somewhere, or did her ability just develop out of necessity?"

"Who cares? She just cooks great!"

"But you don't know?"

"Well, no."

"Any other talents you can think of? Any talent she might have wanted to develop that she hasn't?"

"OK.   You've made your point. I guess a kid doesn't think about those things when you're talking about a parent..."

"So perhaps Mr. Witherspoon isn't as strange as you thought? Perhaps, he's just more honest."

"Yeah. I guess."

"Would you like something to drink while we talk?"

"That would be swell."

"I'll be right back."

Billy nodded, his excitement about *Moby Dick* fading as he thought about his mother and the secret life she had lived without his ever noticing.

She locked the front door of the cafe after Billy left. It was Wednesday, and she had thought she might try going by the church to see what a choir practice was like. The thought flitted across her mind that Jake might be there. Of course that had nothing to do with her wanting to go. She just liked to sing. He did, too. If they both happened to join the choir, well...*well then we'll just let things take their course. If there's still any course to take...*

He hadn't tried to call since she'd turned down his invitation for Saturday. Of course that was only last Sunday...*I don't know what I expected him to do. But what did he expect of me? We've had one date—one! That's nothing to base anything on. Did he really think I'd sit here waiting for months for him to make his move—if he decided to make one? Or did he just think he had no competition? Well, he does! And if he can't compete, well, then he can just stay out of the race!*

As if on cue, the telephone rang. She picked up the receiver, prepared to hear Jake's voice on the other end of the line. It was Dan. He was calling to confirm their date for Saturday night. The sound of his voice brought her back to reality, reminded her of how genuinely fond she was of the man, of how much fun they had together. Yes. She'd made the right decision to stick with Dan. If they didn't have an actual commitment, at least they were friends, easy with each other. There always seemed to be an undercurrent of tension between Jake and her. That she was attracted to him was certain, but it was disconcerting, difficult to understand. No, she told herself, as Dan outlined their Saturday plans, she'd be better off with Dan. By the time they finished talking, choir practice had begun. Too bad.

Maybe it's just as well. I'm tired. I think I'll take a bath and go to bed early. She turned off the downstairs lights and climbed the stairs to her apartment.

CHAPTER FIFTEEN

Jake checked his watch and waited in the alley until he saw the light come on in her apartment above the cafe. He climbed the stairs, took a deep breath, and knocked. A few seconds later, Jenny opened the door, not wide enough for him to enter.

"Jenny, we have to talk."

"What are *you* doing here? I said all I had to say when you called."

"Jenny, just hear me out——"

"Jake, I don't want to fight. It's been a long day, I'm very tired, and I'm in no mood to hear anything, from anyone. Go home, Jake. Call me tomorrow, if you want, but I'm going to go to bed now." She started to close the door, but Jake held it open. Her eyes flashed——"Stop it, Jake! You're doing yourself no good with this——"

"I'm sorry, Jenny," Jake interrupted, his own blood pressure rising at her obstinacy, "but I have to get this settled tonight. Are you going to let me in?"

A mental picture of what they must look like flashed in her brain——she straining to close the door, he keeping it open with one hand, both of them red in the face. *And, like as not, neither one of us actually wanting to be angry with the other.* The problem was…how could she release the pressure on her side of the door without causing Jake to fall flat? A smile flew across her face, but not fast enough: Jake had seen it.

"Jenny," he said, relinquishing his pressure on her door as he sensed her resistance lessen, "let me in. I have something important to say."

Something in his eyes told her to let him in or bury any hope—*of what?* *'Curiosity killed the cat,'* Jenny sighed, opened the door, stepped back so he could enter, and hoped with all her heart that no one had seen.

"Please," she said, with a touch of sarcasm, "won't you sit down?"

Jake started to bristle, then remembered he was here to make peace, not start another skirmish: "Thanks. Don't mind if I do."

"Well, I do mind, so say what you have to say—I told you, I'm tired." Jenny sat on the loveseat across from him, her shoulders squared, her back a ramrod, her mouth a straight line.

Jake cleared his throat, tried to relax: "This isn't going exactly the way I'd planned—"(silence)—"so," he put his hands on his thighs and leaned forward a bit in the chair, "I'll just get on with it—"

"Please do."

"You're not making this easy—"

"I didn't intend to."

Suddenly, he was fed up: "If you want me to go, say so, and I won't bother you anymore, but if you have feelings for me—the same kind of feelings I have for you—then sit there, be quiet, and let me say my piece." The words tumbled out in a rush: it was not the way he'd rehearsed it, but in for a penny, in for a pound....

His intensity frightened her as much as it intrigued her. She had no idea how to respond, so she did nothing. Something in her peripheral vision attracted her attention: the box of chocolates he'd brought her.

"Well? Do you want me to leave?"

Jenny swallowed: "No."

Neither one of them said anything for a moment, then Jake seemed to relax: "I was hoping you'd say that. I didn't want to go."

Jenny said nothing.

"I came here tonight because I owe you an explanation—"

"No—"

Jake held up his hand and cut her off: "Please, let me finish. If you let me finish, then at least I'll know we're arguing about something I've actually *said*." (He waited for a response; there was none.) "Where was I? Oh, the explanation…" (He sighed, looked into her eyes, which, he noticed, were now fixed on him. He couldn't read her expression.)

"There's a lot you don't know about me, and we don't have time tonight for me to tell you everything, but I do want you to know how I feel about you." He stopped, took a breath—(Jenny held hers)—then continued.

"When I told you I wanted to see you that first day at the church, I meant it. Then I had to go the Washington on business—personal business to do with things that happened a long time ago, things that I thought had nothing to do with us; things I had to resolve before there could be an us—"

"*Us?*"

"Please. Just let me finish. This is hard enough as it is." He stopped, clasped his hands tightly in front of him.

"While I was away my return was complicated by the collapse of the stock exchange. A friend, Max Howe—never mind. That can wait." Jake put his head in his hands and rubbed his eyes. He looked up. Jenny sat, her brown eyes glistening, a line between her eyebrows, for once, silent.

"The important thing is this, Jenny: I *want* there to be an us. I care about you…very much….I know I should have called you from Washington, should've called as soon as I got back, but I guess I thought you'd think I was crazy. I wasn't ready to say what I'm saying now—"

"What *are* you saying now, Jake?" Jenny asked in a voice that was no more than a whisper.

Jake got up from his chair, crossed to the loveseat, and sat beside her. He took her hand: "I'm saying I've had feelings for you since the day you brought the pies to my house, feelings that were so strong they scared me. You woke emotions I thought were dead and buried. Part of me wanted them to stay that way…

"That day at church, all my fears vanished the moment I saw your face. I knew I was leaving town, but I had no idea I would be gone so long. Something unexpected happened to me when I was there: I missed you. I know it sounds silly—we've only been out together once—but it's as if—" Jake struggled to find the right words—"as if we're connected in some strange way, as if I've known you all my life—" he held up his hand to forestall her comments—"I know it sounds crazy! But it's true. I missed you terribly. Buying the candy for you helped. It was a promise that I'd see you again.

"When I returned—I came by that night, sat below your window too scared to come up. When I did call, and you said you weren't interested in seeing me, then when we finally went out and had such a good time with each other…then you broke it off again—" Jake shook his head, looked into her eyes—"I thought I had lost you before I'd had a chance to explain, before I had a chance to say that I think I'm falling in love with you, Jenny…and, I'm asking if you feel the same way about me…."

She didn't answer him right away—a thought crossed her mind that this might be some sort of ploy to keep her from being angry with him, but she knew it wasn't. She knew when she looked into his eyes that he meant it, and she knew what her answer was…

"Yes. I feel the same way."

He kissed her then, for the first time—softly at first, then harder as she warmed to his embrace. They parted reluctantly. Jake touched her cheek with his hand, stood: "I'd better go."

He held out his hand and helped her to her feet. She didn't argue. He put his arm around her as they walked toward the door. "I'll let you get your rest now. Just promise me something?"

"What?"

"Promise me that I heard you right; that when I call tomorrow, you won't tell me you're—" He stopped. "But you already have plans, don't you?"

"I'll cancel them," she said, putting her arm around his waist.

He smiled down at her: "Are you sure? I'll understand if—"

"I'm sure. And I promise, you heard me correctly."

"I'll call you tomorrow then." He leaned down, tilted her chin up, and kissed her.

"You'd better," she said and smiled as she opened the door.

She watched him go down the stairs to the alley, watched him until he disappeared in the dark. Only then did she close the door.

She ran her bath, undressed in a daze, then returned to the bathroom, surprised to find it steamy and water already running in the tub. She turned off the faucet, stepped into the tub. Unsteady, giddy with Jake's disclosure, she eased her body into the heated water, closed her eyes, relaxed, let her arms float…remembered the strength of Jake's arms around her…the faint scent of pine that clung to him…the touch of his lips…. A smile played on her lips; she felt seventeen—young, and very much in love.

A rooster crowed in the distance: Jenny groaned and reached for her robe. The night was over, and she'd missed it—its rest anyway—and it was her own fault. She thought about calling Jake and telling him she couldn't cancel her plans after all, but she was afraid he'd misunderstand and think she hadn't meant what she'd said. The truth was she longed to be with him, but she'd wracked her brain all night, and she couldn't figure out a way to tell Dan she couldn't—wouldn't—be seeing him Saturday, and that it wasn't just their date she was canceling, it was their relationship. She didn't think he'd take it well.

The wind whined outside her window; it rattled the panes, wanting in. She threw back the covers and wished fervently for spring as she shivered in the cold. Shaking, she lit a fire in the grate and tried to warm herself before facing the day and Dan. The problem was she hated to hurt him and knew that she would. *Actually*, she thought, *if it weren't for Jake, I could've been quite content with Dan.*

Jenny allowed her mind to wander. It suddenly struck her that the two men in her life had never married. Odd. Dan wasn't what she would call handsome, but he certainly was not bad looking, a bit rugged, perhaps, but in a pleasing, outdoorsy sort of way. He was not as tall as Jake, few men she'd known were, but he was a nice height to walk with, and he was gentle with her, almost shy…Jenny smiled to herself, remembering their first date. He'd surprised her. In all the time he'd eaten at the cafe, he'd kept to himself and rarely socialized with the other patrons. Jenny had heard so much from Billy that she'd only thought of Dan in his terms, and then while Jake was away…

This is not helping! She jumped up from her cozy spot by the fire and set her mind to do what needed to be done.

Dan appeared at the cafe for breakfast, while Jenny waited tables for the absent Susie—a cold, Mrs. Wickham said, but with a fever. Her heart turned over when she saw him occupying the booth Sam Cross had vacated only moments before. He saw her, raised his hand in greeting, and smiled. Her stomach tightened. She took a deep breath, returned his smile, took another deep breath, and crossed the room to take his order.

"Bet you're surprised to see me this morning," Dan said, taking her hand as she stood beside his table.

"I sure am." Jenny removed her hand from his to get the pencil from behind her ear and pull a notepad from her apron: "What can I get for you?"

Dan glanced at his menu: "Coffee——"

"Cream——"

"And sugar——"

"On the table," Jenny indicated the sugar bowl with a tilt of her head. "Do you want me to get your coffee and give you some time to decide?"

"No, I know what I want…" Dan winked at her before glancing back at the menu.

Jenny felt her face redden. "Dan, I'm glad you came in. I——I'm not going to be able to see you Saturday——" She broke off as she saw his face.

Dan closed the menu, put it down. "Why not?"

Jenny looked over her shoulder; the place was filling up: "I——I can't go into it right now," she said, turning back to him, "I've got too much to take care of this morning. I was going to telephone you when I had a break, but since you're here…" she smiled wanly. "I'm really sorry."

He handed her the menu. "Nothing to be sorry about—you can't make it, that's all—and I can see you're busy.…"

"Just bring me the coffee, a couple of eggs over easy, a thick slice of that ham—you do have some of Cross's ham?" (Jenny nodded.) "Great. Some of those biscuits, gravy, and a side of grits. That should do me," he smiled again, "until lunch anyway."

"Got it." Jenny finished jotting down his order as she turned away.

"Jenny?"

She looked back over her shoulder. "Something more?"

Dan smiled, shook his head: "No, guess not—unless I could get some milk when you bring the food?"

"Sure," she said, making a note. She hurried off, grateful to him for pretending milk was all he'd wanted.

As it turned out she didn't have to see him again—Susie's little sister, Lucy, arrived and took over his table—but her guilt over breaking their date haunted her all day. He really deserved better from her, an explanation at least. But then Jake called, pushing all thoughts of Dan Johnson from her mind.

CHAPTER SIXTEEN

Someone knocked on Jake's office door.

"Am I interrupting?" Penelope said, peering around the door into his office.

Jake closed the file he'd been reading. "Not really. Come in."

"Thank you." She closed the door behind her, walked to his desk, and sat in one of the chairs facing him. "My, this chair is a lot more comfortable than I thought it would be."

Jake ignored the remark. "What's on your mind, Penny?" He glanced at the clock on the mantle over the fireplace behind her. "Aren't you working a bit late tonight?"

"I waited until everybody was gone. I wanted to talk to you alone."

"Why, Miss Long," Jake teased, "you're not trying to compromise me now, are you?"

Penelope blushed nearly as red as her hair and looked so stricken that Jake at once repented his thoughtlessness.

"Don't mind me. I was just kidding around—a hazard of my profession, I'm afraid. Things get too serious around here sometimes, and some foolishness escapes my mouth before I know what I'm saying.

"Now, let's begin again. Tell me what this is all about." Jake sat back in his chair, composed his features into his best father-confessor expression and waited.

Penelope smiled at the desk. Her color faded to light pink; only two bright dots of red remained in her cheeks to betray her emotional state. Her hands, knuckles white, were clasped in her lap.

"Is something wrong?"

She looked up, and he realized she was on the verge of crying.

"What is it, Penny? Tell me. I promise I'll do anything and everything I can to help—"

"But you already have! How can I—we—ever thank you for all you've done for us?" It was then that her dubious control vanished completely. She buried her face in her hands and sobbed.

Jake sat there astonished. He had no idea what she was babbling about. His mind retraced the last month for any hint—but she sniffed, seemed about to speak, so he waited for further revelation before deciding the girl had come unhinged.

"Dottie called me and told me what you'd done for Jimmy and her—oh, Mr. Witherspoon!"

"Now, now. Take hold of yourself. Nothing to get overwrought about. I needed someone of Mr. McWilliams's talents. Your brother-in-law possesses some extraordinary abilities—abilities, I might add, that were being entirely wasted in that store in Pine Bluff. There is nothing remarkable about the situation at all."

"How can you *say* that? Don't you know what you've done?"

Penelope sat upright, all traces of discomfort gone.

"Thanks to you, and that dolt who was foolish enough to let him go, I've found a talented, bright man to fill a position I needed to fill. That's all."

"'That's all.'" She leaned forward. "Let me tell you what this means: This means that Jimmy and Dot can get another house—of their own—pay off their debts, and have a normal life again. But all that can't compare to what having this job has meant for Jimmy's self-esteem and their marriage." She paused for a breath.

"Well, I'm glad I could help," Jake said, taking advantage of the break to end her misdirected doxology. He felt intensely uncomfortable with the fanatical adoration creeping into his secretary's eyes. A disturbing thought slithered across his mind: perhaps his teasing remark had come far closer to the target of her intent than he'd guessed. He stood, hoping she'd take the hint. She did. To his relief she extended her hand for him to shake. He shook it. She grinned across the desk at him.

"Well, thanks again," she said, removing her hand from his. She moved toward the door, stopped, turned toward him again. "You know, I didn't mean to frighten you."

"You didn't fright—"

"Yes...I did." She smiled again—her normal, pleasing, familiar smile. "It's kind of nice to know I can make a man like you a bit uncomfortable." She winked and walked out the door in a close imitation of Mae West.

Jake stared, then burst into laughter.

A few days later Jake had another reason to bless the shortsightedness of James McWilliams's former employer: besides being an able accountant and manager, James demonstrated talents in research and investigation. It seemed he'd run into a gap in the Witherspoon records that left Jake's title to some lands along the Mississippi River—prime bottomland—vulnerable to dispute. On his own initiative and his own time, McWilliams had driven over to see the land in question, had researched old county records until he'd found the original handwritten deed and the record of its transfer to Robert Caldwell Witherspoon, Jake's father, on March 3, 1869. James made certain the Witherspoon deed was duly recorded at the county courthouse, obtained an official copy for Jake's records, and returned to his assigned tasks triumphant.

"So you see, Mr. Witherspoon," McWilliams explained, showing Jake a map of the land in question, "that land is prime farming land. It's just lying there, fallow. Near as I can figure, nobody's worked that land since a year or two before your father passed."

"You said no one works the land now?"

McWilliams nodded, cleared his throat: "I was thinking it's a shame to let that land stay unproductive like it is...."

"Go on."

"Well, I was thinking, I could go on down there, maybe find another tenant farmer for the place—"

"How much of a 'place' is there?"

"There's a three-room shack on the property, but it's pretty well—"

"Uninhabitable? Is that the word you were looking for?"

James grinned. "Well, it's not the exact word I'd use, but it gets the idea across."

"So I'll need to build a house for this tenant…and no doubt some sort of barn?"

"Well, I was thinking, things being the way they are, I bet you could get someone in there who would be happy to build their own place, barn, what have you, and work the place for a share of the proceeds and a decent place to live."

Jake massaged his chin. "So you're saying you think you can find me some decent, responsible farmer who'd supply his labor—I'd supply the materials, of course—in return for land to work, a house to live in, and a percentage of the proceeds from the farm?"

"I'm positive."

"In fact, you've already got such a person in mind, haven't you?"

"Mr. Witherspoon, I swear I haven't done anything—I wouldn't do anything behind your back—"

"Relax. Just tell me who this person—"

"Actually, it's a family, sir. They lost their farm this past year. I heard about them in the town when I was digging through the old records. They've got a real good reputation in those parts—"

"So who are these people? Out with it—the whole plan, if you don't mind…."

James took a deep breath and plunged. "Well, there's more than three hundred acres down there, Mr. Witherspoon, not good land for anything other than farming. The Mississippi floods along most of it, see? Well, I thought you might offer him the chance to own, oh, say, ten of those acres free and clear, after a reasonable trial period of farming the whole property, building his house and outbuildings, and seeing what he could produce from that land. Say five years or so?

"If he turns out to be the kind of farmer I've heard he is, he'll end up owning the house and some land, and you'll have a tenant who's making your land turn a profit again." James sat back. "Well, what do you think?"

"OK."

James nearly fell out of his chair. "What did you say?"

"I said OK, go to it, find this worthy farmer and his family and put them to work." (James began picking up his papers.) "Be back by the end of next week. I've got another assignment for you when you've finished with this."

"Yessir. Anything else for today?"

"That's all I have. Just check with me before you leave—oh, you might let me know what my new tenant's name is...."

"Freeman. Roger's his Christian name. His wife's name is—let me see, it's on the tip of my tongue...Millie? Tillie! Roger and Tillie Freeman. I think they have a passel of kids—"

"That's fine. You can fill me in on the whole family once we're sure this Freeman is going to work out. OK?"

"Yessir. I'll check back with you before I leave."

"I am quite pleased with this, McWilliams. Mighty good work."

James blushed, much to his humiliation, and tried to hide it as he put on his coat. "Thank you. I sure hope it all works out."

"It will. Good evening, James."

Billy hated the thought of going into Wickham's General Store at this time of day, but there was no help for it. He was out of writing supplies.

"Hey there, Billy." Silas Wickham waved.

Billy nodded.

"Ruth will be right with you, ladies," Silas said to the group of ladies waiting for his wife. "You'll have to excuse me. Another customer." He retied his apron, came out from behind the long counter, walked over to the shaded corner where Billy stood, trying to make himself as inconspicuous as possible.

"Mr. Wiggins," Silas said in a tone low enough to escape the women's ears, "you're sure a sight to gladden a man's heart." Silas cocked his head in the direction of the women. "You in a hurry, or could you stand keeping me company for a minute?"

Billy glanced over at the women. "Here?"

Just then Ruth Wickham appeared. The males were forgotten.

"You can't abandon me in my hour of need—"

"Gee, Mr. Wickham, I don't know. I have things I need to do—"

"Tell you what. Stay for fifteen minutes—that'll get their minds off of me and into their gossip. Fifteen minutes'll get me over the hump."

Billy looked dubious.

"Stay fifteen minutes, and I'll give you a piece of penny candy—two pieces!"

"You bribin' me, Mr. Wickham?" Billy tilted his head, looked Silas in the eye.

"Sure as shootin'."

"Deal."

They sealed the bargain with a handshake. Silas checked his pocket watch. "You can leave at eleven-fifty. OK?"

"OK by me. While we're waiting, can you get me some things?"

Silas grinned. "Don't know why Ruth can't go somewhere else to do her gossipin'. Makes me so crazy I forget why I'm here. Sure. I can get something for you. What do you need?'

Billy pulled the crumpled scrap of paper out of his pocket and read from his list.

"Mind if I just take the list?" Silas asked. "Might be simpler that-a-way."

"Here. Can you read it?"

Silas pulled his spectacles out of his shirt pocket and put them on. "I can now. You got real good penmanship. Learn that in school?"

"No. Mrs. Schumacher helped me with it."

"Hum. Well, she did right by you. Yeah. I can read this. Want to wait here while I fill your order?"

"If you don't mind, I'll just look around."

"Don't mind a bit. Anything for a fellow male." Silas looked down at him over the rims of his glasses. "Holler if you need me."

Billy glanced in the direction of the long counter where the women chatted away, apparently taken with the subject of their discourse. Mr. Wickham was right. In another few minutes or so, they wouldn't notice if the roof fell down on their heads. He looked around the store, spied a shelf with magazines, comic books, even one or two hardback books. He was browsing when he heard her name. At first he couldn't believe he'd heard what he thought he heard—Jenny and Jake Witherspoon? He sidled closer to the ladies. Sure enough. He hadn't misheard. They were talking about Jenny—his Jenny—and...Mr. Witherspoon?

"Think that's about got it," Silas said, returning to him with the supplies. "Did you find anything else? Did you see that new Popeye comic strip?"

Billy shook his head. "Nope."

"Oughta take a look. It's real funny. There's this sailor—"

"I don't mean to be rude, Mr. Wickham, but is my time up yet?"

Silas checked his watch. "Just about. Something botherin' you?"

"No. Just wondered."

"Well, guess you can look at comic strips some other day. Let's get you that candy I promised. You earned it."

Silas led the way to the tall glass candy jars on top of the counter and stepped behind it: "Pick any two you want—heck, take three. It's not every day I have a male companion during my"—he lowered his voice—"hour... of...darkness."

"You sure?" Billy asked, awed by the choices in front of him.

"I'm sure."

"Wait a second. How much do I owe you for my stuff?"

"I'll add it up while you choose your candy, OK?"

"OK." Billy walked up and down in front of the jars.

"Comes to twenty-six cents."

Billy stuffed his hand into his pants' pocket, pulled out a silver dollar. "Here."

"Say," Silas said, taking Billy's dollar, "I like those pants. New?" He walked over to the register, punched a few keys, and dropped the dollar into the proper slot when the drawer slid out.

"Nah. Ma shortened a pair that my older brother outgrew."

"They look new."

Billy grinned. "Yeah. Ma's pretty good at sewing. She dyed them for me, too."

"Well, they sure look new. Here's your change." Silas dropped the coins into Billy's palm. "How old are you now, Billy?"

"I'll be fourteen in a couple of months."

"That so? You're growing so fast, I thought maybe you were closin' in on sixteen—"

"Nope, not yet," he said, but he was pleased that he looked older. He felt older now that Mr. Johnson was letting him write—nothing important yet, but whole articles nonetheless. And for the last two months, he'd run the press practically unsupervised.

"Guess you're still writin'?" Silas nodded toward the journals and pens, as he put them in a sack.

"Yessir."

"Figured out what candy you want?"

"I'll take a cherry, a lemon, and a root beer—"

"Good choices. That root beer's new, you know?"

"I thought so."

"It's good. You'll like it."

"Well, if it's all right, Mr. Wickham, I really need to get going...."

Silas glanced over his shoulder. The women had circled tightly and were talking rapidly in hushed tones. "Think I'll be safe for awhile anyway. Don't know who they're gossiping about today, but it must be an earful—"

"Well, I'll be going then." It bothered Billy a lot that Jenny seemed to be their subject. He didn't like it one bit that his friend was being talked about behind her back by that bunch of old biddies. Whatever they were saying would be all over Hulet and into the surrounding countryside by the end of the day.

"Sure. Thanks for keeping me out of their sights."

"Thanks for the candy."

"You bet. Come back soon. Enjoyed seeing you."

"Bye."

"Good-bye, Billy—I really should call you 'Bill' now that you're growin' up so fast."

Billy smiled from ear-to-ear as he opened the door. "Not yet, Mr. Wickham. 'Bill' sounds old, like my dad. Thanks anyway. Bye."

Jake rummaged in the file drawer of his desk, pulled out his copy of the Morgan murder transcript, and began to read. An hour later he looked up from the pages in front of him and smiled.

The telephone rang in the hall. Jake marked his place before getting up.

"Hello?"

"Mr. Witherspoon? It's me. James McWilliams? I've finished that business with the Freemans."

"That was quick. How did it go?"

"I think it's going to work out just fine, Mr. Witherspoon. They seem like real fine folks—kids seem nice enough, too. They all seem like real hard workers."

Jake said nothing for a moment: "James, come by my law office at noon on Monday. I have some information I want you to get for me. And, James, I do not want anyone knowing my business, or what I've asked you to do. Understood?"

"Yessir," he paused. "Mr. Witherspoon?"

"Yes?"

"Could you tell me what this is about?"

"Not at this moment. In fact," Jake glanced at his watch, "I'm going to be late for an appointment, if I don't terminate this conversation right away."

"I'll see you Monday at noon."

"Monday. Good work, James. Thanks for calling." Jake replaced the receiver and went to change for dinner with Jenny.

CHAPTER SEVENTEEN

J ake took Jenny's arm as they went down the stairs to the alley. The steps were slick in places with sleet.

"Are you sure we should go out tonight?" Jenny asked, treading carefully and wishing she'd worn heavier shoes.

"I wouldn't put you in danger. Besides, it's not that bad once you get out of this alley," he said. "The wind's blowing most of it off the roads. But we're not going into Little Rock. I hope you don't mind. I didn't want to press my luck."

They reached the ground. To Jenny's relief, the dirt was packed hard but was not at all slick. Jake released his hold on her arm. She tucked her hand into the crook of his elbow.

"If we're not going to Little Rock, where are we going?"

"A little-known, out-of-the-way place a friend of mine told me about on the road between here and Pine Bluff."

"Oh?"

"Here we are," Jake said, opening the car door for her. "It'll warm up as soon as I turn on the heater."

A cold draft blew into the front seat as Jake slid in beside her. "Sorry." He shut the door, started the engine, and reached for the heater. "It'll take a second to warm up."

Jenny shivered, tried to keep her teeth from chattering. "T-tell... m-me...m-more...about...this...p-place."

Jake grinned as he backed out into Main Street. "I think I'll let it be a surprise. You trust me, don't you?"

Jenny nodded; it was all she could manage.

The heater kicked in a few moments later. By the time they turned onto the road to Pine Bluff, her neck had relaxed, and she no longer had to clench her teeth to keep from sounding like a crazed bumblebee. Before five more minutes passed, she was beginning to get hot.

"You all right now?" Jake asked, glancing in her direction as he drove. "Too warm?"

"A bit."

He turned it down. "OK?"

"I'm fine. You weren't exaggerating about that heater, were you?"

"Nope. I try to tell the truth, whenever possible."

"OK. Tell me where we're going."

"I told you."

"I'd like more detail, if you don't mind."

"I thought you liked surprises."

"Sometimes. Chocolate surprises are always welcome—"

"What kind of surprises don't you like?"

Jenny stared out her window, thought of the suddenness of Will's illness and death, and looked back at Jake—"I'll let you know."

"I'm not sure I want to find out. OK, I'll tell you where we're going, but I doubt if it'll help. We're going to a place—a hole-in-the-wall, according to Ben—that looks like a shack. It's called the 'Chicken Shack' by those who frequent it, but Ben tells me it doesn't really have an official name. Its claim to fame is that it has the best fried chicken in the state—"

"Oh?"

"They probably don't compare it to yours." Jake grinned to himself, continued, "You didn't let me finish. Its other claim to fame is that it has the best piano player—"

"Also in the state?"

Jake shook his head: "Nope. This gal is supposed to be way better than that."

"Does she sing, too?"

"Of course she sings! Then there's a makeshift dance floor, and some-times, or so I hear, some friends of hers come in and join her in her music making. Ben says we might luck out on a Saturday night. Keep your fingers crossed."

"Is this place a *speakeasy*?"

Jake grinned, glanced in her direction. "Of course not! Selling whiskey is against the law."

They passed a section marker, and Jake slowed down a bit. "Keep your eyes peeled. Ben said to look for a sign nailed on a tree, on your side of the road, when we passed that section line. The sign reads: 'Red Man Chewing Tobacco,' then has an arrow pointing—"

"There!" Jenny pointed ahead and to the right.

He leaned toward her so he could see better. "That's it! OK, help me locate a road...."

"Any particular kind?"

"Nope. Just a road in the direction that arrow was pointing...There it is!" Jake made an abrupt right turn.

"*This* is a road?" she asked, holding onto the leather strap for dear life, as they bounced their way slowly along the rutted, washed out, dirt path, doing their best to avoid the deepest ruts and chuckholes.

"Ben left its condition out of his description," Jake said through clenched teeth.

"Maybe we took a wrong turn?"

Jake frowned, wiped off the fogged windshield with his coat, and tried to see something through the sleet. "Aha! There it is! See? There, to the left?"

Jenny strained to see anything beyond the glare of the sleet in the head-lights—"Not really."

"Don't worry. We're here, and it looks like we're not the only ones who were crazy enough to show up tonight."

A few more feet and Jenny saw the yellow lights in the distance forming some kind of strange design.

"That's it, all right," Jake said, jubilance sounding in his voice. He pointed at the lights: "See the chicken?"

"Chicken?"

"Yeah. See those yellow lights? It's the chicken."

"I was wondering what it was..."

The outside of the place was as bad—worse—than Jake had described. But she had to admit, the fried chicken *was* the best she'd ever tasted in her life, and the music...? The music was like nothing she'd ever heard: melodies that sounded sweet and sad at the same time; music that kept her feet tapping long after the last note had been played; music that made her feel that Jake and she had shared something rare and fine and momentous, something that tugged at her soul.

"Did you have a good time?" Jake asked, as they turned back onto the main road back to Hulet sometime after midnight.

Her head rested on the back of the seat. She felt warm all over, and it had nothing to do with the sip she'd had of Jake's whiskey. "Why would anyone call that place the 'Chicken Shack'?"

Jake smiled. "What would you call it?"

"I don't know...But it ought to have a name that tells you what it is inside. 'Chicken Shack' just tells you what it looks like on the outside. It has nothing to do with what goes on in there...nothing at all."

"I'm glad you liked it."

"Can we go there again?"

"Sure. Anytime you say."

"How about tomorrow night?"

"Why don't you come out to my place for Thanksgiving dinner Thursday?"

"OK," she said, drowsily. "But can we come back here soon?"

"Soon. I promise," he said, glancing across at her. She was already asleep.

Jake looked up from his desk, stood to greet James McWilliams as Penny announced him.

"James—" Jake held out his hand; McWilliams switched the hat he was holding to his left hand and shook hands—"Good to see you. Won't you have a seat?"

"Thanks." James sat in one of the two chairs in front of Jake's desk.

"How was your weekend?" Jake said, resuming his seat.

"Fine. Yours?"

"Quite nice. In spite of the sleet."

"I thought we were in for it for a while."

"Don't count your chickens, yet. Winter has a way of striking when you least expect it."

"You're right there, Mr. Witherspoon." James shifted in his chair, crossed his legs, and tried to look relaxed. His collar felt a bit tight, but he didn't want to tug at it in front of Witherspoon—not until he knew what was up anyway.

"I suppose you're wondering why I asked you to come to the office today?"

"You said something about wanting to discuss something?"

"Yes—just a minute—" Jake leaned over, activated the intercom— "Penny, hold my calls until I tell you otherwise. I don't want to be disturbed, by anyone, for the next few minutes."

Penny's voice sounded muffled as she replied through the intercom. "Does that include Mr. Hawley?"

"It includes *everyone*."

"Yes, sir."

Jake turned the intercom switch off and looked at James. "I suppose this all seems quite the cloak-and-dagger stuff, but there is a matter I want you to investigate for me, and I don't want *anyone* knowing what you are doing, or for whom you are doing it. Is that understood?"

"Yessir. Before you tell me what it is that you want to involve me in, I want you to know up front that, although I'm mighty grateful for the opportunity you've given me, I will not be a party to anything illegal or even a bit outside the law."

James's neck flushed as he spoke, but his voice was firm, steady. Jake said nothing, appraised the man in front of him.

"Glad to hear it," Jake said. "For the record, if I thought otherwise, you would not be working for me in any capacity—Penny's brother-in-law or not. I need a man I can trust implicitly; someone on whom I can rely to report facts truthfully, without embellishment, and who I know will keep what he finds out and knows to himself. I think you are that man. Am I right?"

James held the brim of his hat with both hands, revolving it slowly as he thought.

Jake waited.

James looked Jake in the eyes: "Yessir, Mr. Witherspoon. You can trust me to do your work—whatever it is. I won't tell a soul, until you tell me it's all right with you. Not even my wife."

"I believe you. All right. Let's get down to it, shall we?" (James nodded.)

Jake rose. James followed him to a long table, piled at one end with manila folders stuffed with papers. Jake sat down at the table, indicated an adjacent chair for James. Jake reached for the top file, pushed it toward McWilliams.

"Open it," Jake said. "That's all I've been able to put together about a couple named Runyon. You might have read something about the man's murder last summer?"—James shook his head as he stared at the papers in front of him—"No matter. Wasn't much information in it anyway. Here—" Jake shoved the second file toward the other man—"This file contains all I can find out about a man named Clarence Morgan, who was also murdered." (James raised his eyebrows.) "Mr. Morgan was killed in 1924. A Negro named Slo-Joe Freeman—wait a minute. Isn't my new tenant's name Freeman?"

James nodded: "Roger Freeman. I suppose they could be related, Mr. Witherspoon, but I doubt it," James said. "A lot of slaves took that last name when they were freed after the Civil War."

"So my tenants are Negroes?"—James nodded—"No wonder he couldn't keep his farm." Jake paused a moment, then continued, "I suppose you're right about the last names. It just seemed like a strange coincidence—I don't know why that should surprise me; there are a lot of coincidences, strange and otherwise, in what I'm about to tell you. Your job is to tell me what is merely happenstance, and what things merit my attention. To know that, we need more information than I have in these folders."

Jake pushed a third folder to James. "This is all I could find about a man named Jesse W. Smith—"

"That name rings a bell. Didn't someone by that name work for the federal government or something?" James's forehead wrinkled in concentration.

"Good man. Yes. *This* Jesse Smith worked closely with former Attorney General Harry Daugherty—"

"President Harding! The Teapot Dome scandal! Didn't they charge Daugherty with something?"

"He was actually tried regarding his administration of the Alien Property Custodian's Office after President Coolidge forced him to resign in 1924."

"Did he go to prison? I can't remember—"

"No. He was freed after two juries were unable to reach a verdict."

"OK, I remember now, but what did Jesse Smith do? Wasn't he in the Justice Department?"

"Unofficially. He was Daugherty's friend. Some say he collected bribes for Daugherty in exchange for the department's non-prosecution of law violators; others say he arranged for 'settlements.'"

"I remember something about this—wait a minute...Didn't Smith die?"

Jake smiled, nodded. "Suicide, they said. The *New York Times* article is in the folder. Read all about it."

James cocked his head, appraised the older man. "I take it you think something else is involved?"

"Could be. In the copy there of the Congressional hearings, you'll find that Mr. Smith corresponded with a number of people before his demise. One of those was our Mr. Morgan."

"No kidding?"

Jake shrugged his shoulders.

"Anything else?"

"This last folder contains the transcript of the Clarence Morgan murder trial in which Slo-Joe Freeman is found guilty and sentenced to death—"

"He's dead?"

"Hanged, dead, and buried in a pauper's grave in the Negro cemetery on the other side of Little Rock."

"I take it, you don't think they got the right man?"

"I never did think he was guilty, but I wasn't able to prove it. You'll understand more after you read the transcript.

"I can't let these files out of my sight, James. They stay in my safe. I want you to read through this information—take notes if you want. I want you as familiar with the contents of these files as I am."

"OK. Then what?"

"Then I want you to find out everything you can about these five people: the Runyons, Clarence Morgan, Jesse Smith, and Slo-Joe Freeman. See if there's any connection between them. Find out everything you can about how and when they died. Then get back to me."

James glanced through the files, then looked up at Jake. "From just what I can see here, that might mean some traveling. . ."

"You'll have to go to Little Rock and Fort Smith—"

"How about Washington, D. C., and Ohio?"

"Maybe. We'll see. I've already done some digging in D.C., and I have a man there working on getting more. It might lead to Ohio. See what you can put together with what I've given you and what you find out. We'll talk whenever you need to."

James cleared his throat. "Uh, I hate to bring this up, Mr. Witherspoon, but I'm going to need some money. . ."

"Don't worry about that. As for transportation, I'm buying another car for business use. You'll be able to use it as long as you're working for me. My company will pay your expenses—"

"So. . .I'm working for the law firm?" James looked around the office with a new appreciation.

Jake laughed. "Not exactly. You are working directly for me—no one else in the firm. I formed my own business concern a while ago; officially, you'll be an employee of that company. However, since I am the senior partner of Townsend, Witherspoon, Hawley, and Branch while Mr. Townsend is indisposed, your duties will sometimes be of benefit to cases the firm handles.

"James, this point must be quite clear. You work for me. No one— *no one*—must know what I've told you, or what you are working on. Do I have your word on this?"

"Yessir, Mr. Witherspoon. You have my word."

"Good. I'll let you get to work on these files then. Let me know if you need anything. When you've gotten everything you think you'll need, let me know, and we'll put you into the 'field', as a friend of mine says." Jake got up, clapped James on his shoulder as he passed. "Good to have you working with me, McWilliams. You're a good man."

Jenny was busy sorting receipts when she heard the cafe bell ring. It was nearly three o'clock; the lunch crowd was long gone. She looked up, thinking Jake might have dropped by to say hello—

"Jenny, can I talk to you a minute?"

"Billy? What are you doing here? Aren't you supposed to be working at the paper?" She smiled, laid the receipts down in a stack, and wiped her hands on her apron. She got up from her desk and joined him. Once again she was struck by how tall he'd grown.

"Well, that's sort of what I want to talk to you about—"

"Dan—Mr. Johnson didn't fire you, did he?" Her brow furrowed. "How about some cocoa?"

"Sure! If it's not a lot of trouble?"

"Not if you help me. Come on. Let's go into the kitchen and see if we can't scare up some cookies to go with that cocoa—"

Billy hesitated.

"What's the matter? It can't be that you don't want cookies? Come on. Out with it." Jenny stood in front of him, hands on her hips.

Billy looked at the floor: "Won't Mrs. O'Casey be upset?"

"So *that's* it! Bertha has gone on some errands and won't be back till four-thirty or so. It'll be just the two of us."

A smile spread across his face: "Well, then, what are we waiting for?"

"Now then," Jenny said, as she removed the pan of cocoa from the stove and poured two steaming cups, "why don't you tell me what's going on? I haven't seen you in a couple of weeks, you know." She put the pan back, got the cookie jar: "Cookie?"

"Sure!" Billy looked into the jar, chose a large sugar cookie dusted with cinnamon.

"You can have more than one..." Jenny nudged the jar against his hand.

"Don't mind if I do, then," Billy said, taking two more.

Jenny took a cookie and sat down at the table with him. "OK, mister. Start talking."

Billy's mouth was full of cookie, so he washed it down with cocoa before answering. "This is good. I guess I was sorta hungry."

"Never knew a young man who wasn't. Talk." Jenny sat back and sipped her cocoa.

"Well," Billy shifted in his chair, "I'm not fired—nothing like that."

"That's good news anyway. Go on."

"In fact, he's left me in charge of the newspaper while he's out of town—"

"He's left town?"

Billy was disappointed that Jenny only picked up on Johnson's absence. "Yeah. He said he'd be gone for a bit during the holidays. He left me in charge."

"How long is he going to be gone?"

"He didn't exactly say how long he'd be away. Said I could handle things."

"Where did he go?"

"I don't know. He didn't say. I guess—seeing as tomorrow's Thanksgiving and all—he went to visit relatives. He takes off to fish sometime, but it's too cold here to catch anything...Maybe he went down South."

"Maybe. I don't remember hearing him say anything about having a family... Who's going to run the paper, while he's gone?"

"I am! I already told you."

"He left you in charge? Why that's wonderful, Billy! About time, too. You'll do a great job, I'm sure."

"Thanks...Jenny?"

"Um?" She raised her eyelids, took another sip of cocoa.

"We really *are* friends aren't we?"

Jenny put her cocoa down. "Of course we are. Why? Do you need some help with the paper?"

"It's not that."

"Then what?"

"Well, it's—well, if you saw me doing something that you thought might hurt me, *you'd* tell *me*, wouldn't you? I mean, even if you thought I might not like it much—?"

"Billy, what *are* you trying to say? Am I doing something wrong?"—Jenny tried to think of anything he might be upset by, but couldn't come up with a thing.

Billy stalled, and bit into another cookie.

"Billy?"

He stared into his cocoa, afraid to look her in the eye: "Are you really seeing Mr. Witherspoon? I mean are you *seeing* him, uh, like someone you... like a lot, or something?" Blood rushed to his face. He covered by grabbing his cocoa and finishing it off —"Any more cocoa?"

"Sure." She took his cup and tried to figure out what was going on as she walked to the stove. "To answer your question, yes, I *am* seeing Mr. Witherspoon, and, yes, I do like him. Very much." Jenny poured cocoa into his cup, her back to Billy. "Is that what this is all about?" She returned to the table and handed him the cocoa.

"Not exactly..."

"Well, then what, exactly, are we discussing?"

Billy sighed.

Jenny waited.

"Well, I can't believe any of it's true, but—"

"But? I swear, Billy, if you keep this up, friends or not, I'll *strangle* you," she said, pretending her hands were around his neck.

"I heard Mr. Johnson and Mr. Witherspoon fighting the other day—"

Jenny's heart skipped a beat—"When?"

Billy looked at the ceiling, trying to remember.

"Billy!"

"I was trying to think. Let me see...I guess it was about—maybe a month ago? No. It had to be more than that—oh, I know!"—he was triumphant—"It was the week after Mrs. Witherspoon died! Yep, that's it!"

Jenny felt confused; she thought Jake and Dan never talked to each other, and that was long before...but Billy was still talking—"I'm sorry, Billy. What did you say?"

"I said, I heard Mr. Johnson say Mr. Witherspoon had killed his sister—"

"What?"

Billy looked at her accusingly.

"I'm sorry, Billy. It was just so—so unexpected. Please, go on."

"Like I said, I can't believe it's true, but that's what Mr. Johnson said all right—that Mr. Witherspoon had killed his sister—" (Jenny was fidgeting; she wanted to say something.)—"What?" Billy folded his arms and sat back in his chair. "Go on. What do you want to say?"

"Whose sister? Jake's or Dan's?"

"Dan—Mr. Johnson's. That's why he won't have anything to do with Mr. Witherspoon, see?"

Jenny waited, but Billy seemed to be finished dropping bombs. Her mind raced, but all she could come up with was that Billy must have misunderstood something. She breathed deeply.

"All right. I can see now why you were worried, though I don't really think either one of us has anything to fear from Jake—Mr. Witherspoon. There must be some mistake."

Billy shook his head: "I don't think so. Mr. Johnson was pretty mad. He broke the glass in his office door, he slammed it so hard!"

That Billy had heard and seen something was certain, but what?

"OK. Why don't you start from the beginning, when you first knew something was wrong—"

"That day? Or when I first knew there was trouble between Mr. Johnson and Mr. Witherspoon?"

Jenny's curiosity piqued: "What kind of *trouble?*"

"Well, you know that Mr. Johnson never had a calendar at the paper, so Mr. Witherspoon wouldn't think he had to come by?" (Jenny nodded.) "Well, whenever I asked him what he knew about Mr. Witherspoon, he'd call him a fool and crazy, so I guessed he didn't like him much—" Billy grinned, sobered quickly.

"But that day was different. Mr. Witherspoon came into the newspaper office on his own, I guess—I didn't see him come in. I heard Mr. Johnson yelling, so I snuck into the hall, where I could see what was going on. Mr. Johnson was so red in the face, I thought his head was going to blow right off"—Billy's eyes widened with the telling—"His veins stood out in his neck, and he was yelling. I'd never heard him yell like that before. He was so loud that at first I couldn't make out the words. Then I heard it—"

"Heard what?" Jenny asked, riveted.

"Heard him say something about Mr. Witherspoon being a *killer*—something like that—and then he said Mr. Witherspoon had killed Laura—that was her name, his sister's name, Laura—as surely as if he'd struck the match! I guess she was killed in a fire or something, 'cause Mr. Johnson said he'd had to live with her screams—oh, I almost forgot..."

"What?" *What else could there be?*

"I guess she must've had some kids..." Billy looked up.

"And?"

"Well, I think they died in the fire with his sister...." Billy's voice trailed off. He didn't like remembering that part; he didn't like remembering any of it, but he didn't want Jenny getting hurt.

"Billy?"—(he looked at her)—"Why did you tell me this today?"

Billy tilted his chair on its back legs. "I heard somebody say something about you and Mr. Witherspoon the other day—"

"Where?"

"Wickham's store."

Oh, my Lord.

"Then I saw you in his car, driving out of town..."

"Oh." *That must've been the night we went to the Chicken Shack.*

They sat for a while, both caught up in their own thoughts, not speaking, until something else popped into her mind.

"Billy, you never said why you aren't working today."

"Oh, that...Mr. Johnson closed the office. He told me to open up after this weekend."

Jenny nodded. "Are you going to live in his house while he's gone?"

Billy shook his head: "No, I'm heading out to the farm when I leave here. I'll stay with my folks until he gets back."

"When did you say he's coming back?"

"He didn't say exactly, just a week or two. He said he'd get word to me—"

"When did he decide to leave town? Do you know?"

Billy shook his head. "No. Must've been one of those things you just decide to do." He bit into a cookie.

"Jenny, you're not mad at me, are you?" (Jenny seemed puzzled.) "You're not mad about what I said about Mr. Witherspoon?"

Jenny smiled, got up from the table: "Of course I'm not angry with you. You're a good friend." She thought a moment. "I *am* going to talk to Mr. Witherspoon about this, though. There *has* to be something we don't understand, because I do know one thing—"

"What's that?" Billy pushed in his chair; it was time to go.

"Jake Witherspoon is no killer. I don't care what anybody says—Shh! I hear Bertha. We'll just keep this matter to ourselves?"

Billy nodded conspiratorially, whispered: "You won't tell Mr. Witherspoon I told you?"

"Of course not. Friends don't tell on each other, do they?"

Bertha O'Casey appeared in the kitchen doorway and stopped in her tracks, hatpin three-quarters out of her hat: "Billy Wiggins is it now?" She glanced at the kitchen table, finished removing her hatpin. "Cocoa and cookies…I should've known you'd be in me cookies the minute my back was turned."

Jenny grinned at Billy who wasn't sure if Mrs. O'Casey was put out or not.

"Now Bertha, don't blame Billy. It was my idea. Besides, we left plenty for you—" she winked at Billy—"The cocoa's on the stove, and it's still hot."

"Well, then it's all right," Bertha said, still straight-faced, as she took off her coat and hung it on a peg. She stuck the hatpin in her hat, and placed it on top.

"I'm going to walk Billy to the door. I'll be back to help."

"Good-bye, Mrs. O'Casey," Billy said.

"Get along with you then, you young rascal, and don't be such a stranger around here," she added, as she tied the apron around her waist. "I might find a cookie or two for you should you drop in."

"Thanks, Mrs. O'Casey!" He smiled broadly, and followed Jenny out the kitchen door.

CHAPTER EIGHTEEN

"It was a lovely dinner, Annie," Jenny said.

"Yes, it was," Jake said, helping Jenny with her chair. "I think you out-did yourself this time."

"I'se glad y'all liked it," Annie said and began clearing the table. "I be in wid yo pie jus soon's I clean up dis mess."

Jenny gave Jake a pleading look.

"No need to hurry on our account, Annie. We're pretty full—"

"Full?" Jenny groaned, "I couldn't eat another thing—"

"At least," Jake chimed in, "not for thirty minutes or so—you haven't tasted Annie's pumpkin pie, yet."

He addressed Annie: "Why don't you and Bill finish your dinner, then check with us? We might be ready for some pie and coffee by then. Mrs. Schumacher and I will be in the other room."

Jake took Jenny's arm and ushered her into the parlor. Jenny arranged herself on the sofa; Jake sat at the other end.

"Everything was wonderful, Jake. Thank you so much for asking me. I dreaded the thought of spending Thanksgiving alone."

"The thought of spending the holidays by myself did not appeal to me either. When I was a boy, this house was filled with people from Thanksgiving until New Year's Day. Mother loved holidays.

"Do you mind if I smoke?"—(Jenny shook her head)—"I don't indulge that often, but I do enjoy a cigarette after dinner, a carry-over I suppose from my father's habit of having a cigar after dinner with his friends." He reached for the cigarette box on the table, opened it. "Would you care to join me?"

"No, thank you. I never acquired the taste."

"Good for you," Jake said, removing a cigarette from the box and lighting it. "I took to it right away myself." He grinned, blew a few smoke rings, and relaxed against the arm of the sofa.

"Now, why don't you tell me what's been on your mind all evening?"

A lie formed in her mind, but when her eyes met his…"Who's Laura?"

"Where did you hear that name?"

Flustered, Jenny mumbled something incoherent, remembering her promise to Billy just in time.

Jake realized he'd frightened her, belatedly attempted to regain control of his emotions. He smoked his cigarette, inhaling deliberately before expelling the smoke from his lungs. He reached over, tapped his ash into a ceramic ashtray on the coffee table.

"I'm sorry. As you've probably guessed, I wasn't expecting that particular question." He avoided her eyes as he spoke, focusing instead on the tranquil seascape above the mantle behind her.

"I meant to tell you about Laura someday…How *did* you—" he glanced at her before refocusing on the painting—"Never mind. It's not important. I suppose the miracle is that you've never asked before this. I keep forgetting how small Hulet is, and how readily people gossip."

He looked so stricken, Jenny repented her question, tried to take it back: "Jake, you don't have to tell me anything—"

"Yes, I think I do. How much do you know?" This time he met her gaze.

She lowered hers to her hands, noticed the faint indentation, still perceptible to her, where she'd once worn Will's wedding ring. She covered it with her other hand, squared her shoulders: "Nothing really. Jake, you must not ask me *where* I got my information. I made a promise. I *can* tell you that the revelation was made to me, not from a desire to carry tales, but from a genuine concern for my welfare—"

"Your welfare?" Jake shook his head, bewildered, "What could Laura possibly have to do with your welfare?"

"My source—you *must* not ask me who—said they'd overheard someone accuse you of...of murdering her—" she stopped abruptly. Jake's face had gone white.

"I think I can understand your source's concern now"—Jake's tone was controlled, icy—"The only remaining question that occurs is: believing that I am capable of murdering my wife—"

Jenny's hand went to her mouth in shock: "Your *wife*?"

"You truly did not know?"

Jenny shook her head; her eyes watered. She swallowed, tried to speak—"I swear...Oh, Jake, I'm so sorry!" Her shoulders shook.

Suddenly she was in his arms, sobbing into his shoulder, while he patted her, kissed the top of her head, murmured soothingly, held her, until her crying subsided, and she lay quiet against his chest.

"Then it *wasn't* Dan who told you?"

"Dan?"—Jenny raised up her head in surprise—"Whatever made you think it was *Dan*?"

"You and he were going out, and he blames me for Laura's death—of course. Mr. Wiggins." The look on Jenny's face told him he'd guessed correctly.

"You won't say anything?" Jenny pleaded.

Jake reached over, brushed a stray wisp of hair back from her face. "Of course not. He must've heard us that day I went to see Dan." Jake shook his head, smiled.

"I don't understand you at all."

"Few people do. Sometimes I don't understand myself."

"Are you going to tell me what happened?"

Was he? It was a bigger question than she realized. What about her warranted this depth of trust? In all the years since Laura's death, he'd never told another living soul about that night, had tried not to let the whole truth surface even in his own mind. Why should he tell her—this virtual stranger—something he'd barely acknowledged to God?

But silence meant the communion he desired, even needed, would remain withheld: There would always be a part of him she could not touch. He feared losing her, and feared her rejection, as she saw his weakness, failure, ugliness exposed.

"Jake?"

He felt her hand caress his cheek. He shut his eyes, let his head rest lightly in her palm. Then he shifted and drew her to him so that her back rested against his chest. How to tell her about the night he failed and they died...? He cleared his throat:

"I met Laura shortly after I moved to Washington, D.C. I had just graduated from Harvard Law School—"

"I didn't know you'd gone to law school." She tried to see his face. His arms held her, gently, but securely enough that she couldn't turn...

He chuckled, but without mirth. "Did you think my name was put on Townsend's firm out of pity?" He didn't wait for her answer—"Trust me. It isn't important to the story. Rest assured you'll learn all you want to know about me in time." He smoothed her hair, and wondered as he did, whether she'd want to know anything about him after she found out the truth.

"Jake?"

"Sorry. Daydreaming. The important part is that Laura and I met. I married her the following year. My friend, Max Howe—the one I went to see in Washington?"—(Jenny nodded)—"Max was my best man. That was in 1917. We lived in Washington. I worked for the Solicitor General's office. I moved up quickly and was a partner in a firm after Wilson left office. I even argued before the Supreme Court once or twice." He paused, remembering.

Jenny waited, lulled by the rhythm of his heartbeat, so near it seemed to come from within her own chest.

"We moved to Arkansas in 1923. My father had died unexpectedly of a heart attack. Mother was left to handle things on her own. I was their only child. I thought everyone would be better off here. I was wrong.

"Mother and Laura got along beautifully—it wasn't anything like that. We already had a daughter, Sarah—"

"Oh!" Jenny's hand went to her mouth as she realized his daughter must've died in the same fire that killed Laura.

Jake didn't notice: he was in the Duesenberg, with Sarah on his lap, pretending to let her drive. He felt her arms around his neck, her breath on his cheek. He rubbed his eyes and continued: "Laura was pregnant with Teddy when we made the trek. Sarah was four, going on five. We lived here until our own house was completed...I'll take you over there if you'd like one of these days. Of course there's not much left to see....

"Mike Townsend offered me an equal partnership in his law firm before I left D.C. We got along well. He'd handled a lot of Dad's business for him before Dad died. His practice was varied. He needed a good trial attorney. It seemed like a good idea at the time." (Jenny felt him shrug his shoulders.)

"There was this murder in 1924, in Little Rock. A man, a banker actually, was stabbed in his home and his neck broken. His name was Clarence Morgan. Normally, I wouldn't have been involved, but there was something about this case: A retarded Negro man was arrested the same day the body was found. Slo-Joe Freeman his name was. No money of course. The case against him was based largely on fear—Slo-Joe was a big, muscular man—and a lot on pure hatred. Not many facts."

"Why did they arrest him then?"

"Slo-Joe worked for Morgan as his hired man. He'd been seen at Morgan's house that day, the last day anyone saw Morgan alive. Morgan had complained from time to time to various people in the community that Slo-Joe was not only dumb, but dangerously so. Local hearsay backed up that impression with stories. I remember one—something about hugging a stray dog so hard he'd broken its neck—"

"How awful!"

"Don't believe it. I never found *anyone* who'd actually seen Slo-Joe hurt anything—intentionally or otherwise."

"So how did you get involved?"

"I read about the case. No one wanted to defend a Negro charged with murdering a prominent—and well liked, I might add—white man. The judge didn't want to appoint one of his friends—good way to lose a friendship in these parts." Jake gave a hollow laugh. "So I volunteered."

"Good for you!"

"Exactly what *I* thought. Actually, I don't know what I thought. Hubris. Pride. Pride, as the proverb goes, most certainly precedes a fall, and, boy, I fell."

Jake's voice trailed to a whisper. He sat very still behind her. Jenny barely breathed.

"There had been threats, veiled and otherwise. The gist of them was that I should drop the case, leave Slo-Joe to twist in the breeze, so to speak. I didn't take them seriously. I didn't really think there was any danger. I was gone a lot. Laura had the kids to take care of; I had a client to defend. I suppose I thought the case would solidify my reputation in the state. My prominence in Washington circles didn't count for much in Arkansas.

"I told myself I was doing this for my family and for this poor, God-forsaken Negro. For the record, I never believed Slo-Joe was guilty of anything more than being retarded and in the wrong place."

"Did you win the case then?"

"I wasn't around to see it through."

"What happened?"

"Court had recessed for the Thanksgiving weekend. It was snowing—a freak blizzard, and I was stranded in Little Rock. I talked to Laura. She was supposed to spend the night at my mother's until I could get home the next day...." Jake stared at the seascape, cleared his throat.

"Jake?"

"I'd been wrong about those threats. Sometime in the middle of the night, the snow abated, and I decided to drive home—to be with Laura and the kids. I can't tell you how much I missed seeing them....

"I drove all night. When I arrived in Hulet, I decided to go on to our house, instead of driving to Mother's and waking everyone up."

Jake's arms tightened around Jenny's shoulders. His fingers dug into her arms. She could feel his heart pounding.

"Jake, maybe you shouldn't—"

"No. It's good to be able to tell someone. To talk about it. Flames were coming out of our house when I drove up the road. All I could think was, 'Thank God, they aren't in that inferno!' But I was wrong about that, too. The last thing I remember was Laura's voice screaming my name—"

"Oh my God, Jake. How horrible!"—Nothing had prepared her for this. Will's death had almost killed her with its suddenness. How had he managed? —"I don't know what to say."

"There's nothing to say. You're wondering how I got through it?"—(she nodded)—"I blocked it out. I was in a sanitarium for months after it happened. I came back here and went on with my life, as if they had never existed. I never asked what happened to me. I never wanted to know. I blocked out everything that had to do with Laura, with law...with living. I stayed in my own little protective cocoon with my own safe routine—changing calendars, living in law journals."

His heartbeat was returning to normal; his hold on her arms lessened. She heard him breathing behind her.

"Is that what the calendars were about—safety?"

"I suppose it was my feeble attempt to control the start of the day: if I started it, maybe it wouldn't get away from me—I don't know. Maybe I'll never know..."

"But you're not there now? I don't understand—"

"Something happened—don't ask me what, or why, or why not years ago rather than now—I don't have those answers. All I know is that suddenly memories poured into me so fast I almost drowned in them.."

They sat still for a moment. Jenny pulled away, sat so she could see his face. His eyes were red, the skin around them white and swollen. She reached for his hand, took it in hers, and kissed the back of his hand. That he still grieved was all too visible. Her mind balked at the thought of his children's screams. She shivered.

"It *was* my fault that they died. I should have been there."

"Don't say that!" She moved toward him, drew his mouth to hers, and kissed him. When they parted, she gazed earnestly into his eyes: "I know you, Jacob Witherspoon. I know you loved them. I can see it even now. I'm sure Laura knew you'd have been there if you could have been.

"Hindsight is always better than the vision we have at the time. You made decisions based on the information you had then, not—what is it now—five years later? Don't torture yourself anymore. You did all that you could, all that you knew to do at the time to protect your family—"

"Dan blames me for her death. Laura was his only sister, the only family he had left—"

"Dan blames you, because he has no one else to blame. He blames you, because he wasn't there to save her either."

Jake looked at her briefly, looked away. Jenny reached over and put her hand on his face, turned it towards her.

"Jake, I believe with everything in me that you loved your family and that you never would have done anything to hurt them. What happened—" her hand shielded her eyes for a moment as if to block out vision—"What happened was terrible. I can only guess at what you've been through. But there is nothing you can do to bring them back or change what happened. You were spared, and through some miracle, you've been given a chance to begin living again. I'm glad your memory came back, for your sake and for mine, but you can't live in the past any more than you can change it. You've got to let it go."

"I can't."

He said it so matter-of-factly, that he surprised her.

"Why not?"

"I don't think that fire was an accident. I think it was deliberately set—"

"You think someone murdered your family? Who would want to kill a defenseless woman and two innocent children?"

"My family wasn't the target. They were after me, or at least trying to scare me off the case—"

"You're thinking about the threats you mentioned?"

"Yes. Someone wanted Slo-Joe found guilty, and they wanted it badly enough to burn down my house. I'm sure that if no one had been killed in the fire, if I hadn't lost my memory and been off the case, that they would not have left it at that. The people who killed my family by mistake are quite capable of intentional homicide."

"You said 'are.' Do you think the person responsible for the fire is still around?"

Jake nodded. He reached for her hands, held them in his. "I think the people responsible for killing Clarence Morgan killed Laura and Sarah and Teddy." He paused to let that sink in. His grip on her hands tightened. "I also think the same people killed a man named Joe Runyon this past summer—"

"Who's Joe Runyon?" Her mind was beginning to reel. The thought occurred that Jake might not be completely recovered from his ordeal. "What does he have to do with all this?"

"That's what I'm trying to find out." Jake dropped her hands. He leaned back on the sofa, suddenly drained. He rubbed his eyes. "Do me one favor, Jenny?"

"What's that?" Jenny moved away to the opposite end of the sofa, crossed her legs, and turned toward him.

"Don't think I'm crazy. I know what I sound like. I know this seems far-fetched and unbelievable—"

"A bit."

"Give me a chance to prove it, or, if I am, to find out I'm completely wrong."

Jenny shrugged: "I don't know what I can do in either case."

"Just believe in me. I need someone I can trust. Someone I can talk to who won't prejudge me. Someone who'll listen, at least until I can find out the truth."

"And if you can't? What then, Jake?"

Jake sat up, sighed. He shrugged and a faint grin appeared: "Well then, I'll have to let it go. I promise you, Jenny. I *want* to get on with my life. I lost nearly five years. I have no intention of losing any more, if I have anything to say about it. What do you say? Will you give me a chance or not?"

Too many thoughts collided in her mind, making it impossible for her to speak. What did he want from her? A friend? A confidante? Someone to listen when he wanted to talk about his dead wife and how much he had loved her? Did he really want to put the past to rest? Once done, did he want her in his future—as his wife? She was startled as someone coughed in the hallway outside the parlor.

"'Scuse me, Miztah Jake."

"Bill. I'm sorry. I didn't realize you were standing there. Have you been waiting long?"

Bill shook his head. "No suh. Annie jus sent me t' ast iffen y'all ready fo dat pie yet."

Jake looked at Jenny who smiled and shook her head.

"Not yet, thanks—"

"Den yo mine iffen we went on home? Annie, she feelin' a mite po'ly, say she finish cleanin' up in de mo'nin'."

Jake stood. "Annie's ill?"

"No suh, she jus be a mite po'ly. She be all right; she jus tired. She be plum wore out aftah dat cole, an' Thanksgibing sho do wear a body out—"

"I should have known this would be too much for her. Of course you can go home, Bill. Tell her to take tomorrow, the weekend too, if she needs it. I don't require her for anything urgent. Tell her I said to get some rest. That's what I need most from her right now. We can wait on ourselves if we need something. Anything else I can do?"

"No suh, dat's mighty gen'rus. I be takin' Annie home now den—Oh, she say t' tell ya dat de pie be in de icebox, iffen y'all 'cides ya wants it. Well, guess I be on m'way. Y'all hab a nice evenin'."

"Mr. Jackson?" Jenny stopped him just as he was leaving.

"Yessum?"

"Please tell Annie again how much I enjoyed the dinner, and tell her not to worry about leaving Mr. Witherspoon alone with company; I was just about to leave myself."

"Yessum, I tell her jus that."

After Bill left the room, Jake turned to Jenny: "Was that just for propriety's sake, or are you really ready to go?"

Jenny rose from the sofa. Jake tried to read her expression but couldn't.

"I think I need to leave."

"Afraid to be alone with me?" Jake said, in what he hoped sounded like a light tone.

"No. It's not that. I just need to be by myself right now."

"I understand. I'll be back in a minute with your coat and drive you home." Jake stood and went on his errand.

"Jake?" she said, when he returned with her coat.

"Yes?" He held her coat for her, helped her put it on.

"I've decided. You're worth taking a chance on."

He turned her around: "Jenny." He drew her to him.

CHAPTER NINETEEN

"Excuse me."

James McWilliams looked up from his reading. Standing beside him was a tall, leggy brunette. A beauty, but from the looks of her, someone Dottie would not like him talking to: "Yes?"

"The librarian told me you were researching an old murder case. The Clarence Morgan murder. Is that right?"

"Why are you interested in what I'm researching, Miss...?"

"Landower. Mary Landower." She held out her hand.

James rose from his chair. "McWilliams is the name, Miss Landower." He shook her hand but did not smile.

"Please take your seat Mr. McWilliams. I didn't mean to disturb your reading. It's just that I thought I might be of some help to you."

"Oh?"—James sat—"How is that?"

"I was an assistant to the defense attorneys in that case."

"Really?"

"Yes. Perhaps I could answer some questions for you."

"Perhaps. Won't you have a seat? My neck's getting stiff from looking up at you, and I'm not used to being seated while a woman's standing."

"Thank you. If you're certain I won't be disturbing you?" she asked, but made her way to the chair across the table from him without waiting for his reply.

"I'm curious, Miss Landower. How did you happen to find out about me?"

Mary smiled disarmingly. "I am no longer a legal assistant, Mr. McWilliams. Frankly, I didn't enjoy the courtroom environment anymore. Things were a bit too stuffy for my tastes, if you know what I mean?" She winked. "I am employed as a secretary here at the library now."

"I see. And the library is *less* constraining?"

"Not in the library, but when five o'clock comes, I'm on my own. It's not like working for a law firm, when you're at their beck and call almost all the time, and when you're expected to maintain—"(she tilted her nose up in the air, and affected a cultured accent)—"a certain element of dignity, don't you know?" She grinned.

"I see," James said, and he did.

"When you asked about material on the Morgan murder, well, everyone here knows I assisted in the Morgan case. It was all anyone talked about for a long time in this town. A long time."

"Why was that?"

"The usual thing, isn't it, when a Negro kills a white man?"

"I suppose—"

"But that wasn't all—"

"It wasn't?"

"No." Mary Landower scooted her chair closer to the table, and lowered her voice to just above a whisper: "Did you hear what happened to the defense attorney's family?"

James's ears pricked up. He leaned closer. "No. What happened?"

"Well—"(her voice took on the same tone as his wife's when she had some particularly juicy piece of gossip to impart)—"the Klan—"

"The *Klan*?"

"You know…the Ku Klux Klan?"—(James nodded)—"Well, I told you I worked for the defense? Well, my boss had received all sorts of threats trying to get him to drop the case so they could hang the guy. But Mr. Witherspoon wouldn't hear of it.

"Say, you don't happen to know a Mr. Jacob Witherspoon, do you? I kind of lost track of him after it happened."

"What happened?"

"A fire." Mary nodded, seeing his disbelief. "It's true. I was right here the night it happened. A shame. There was a snowstorm. He couldn't get home. I guess when he did, it was too late to save them."

"Them?"

"His wife and two kids…I guess you don't know him, huh?"

James ignored the question: "What happened then?"

Mary shook her head. "I don't really know. The other attorney, Mr. Hawley—do you know him?"

"Not really. I've heard the name."

"Well, Mr. Hawley took over for Mr. Witherspoon after the fire. He said Mr. Witherspoon did not feel like continuing with the case. I can't say that I blamed him, but after he left the case, it was all she wrote for Slo-Joe Freeman—that was the murderer's name."

"You thought he was guilty then?"

Mary shrugged her shoulders. "I didn't care one way or the other. I will tell you, though, that Mr. Witherspoon didn't think he was guilty."

"Oh? Why was that?"

"I don't know. You could just tell he thought the guy was innocent. Why else would a man like Witherspoon defend a Negro?"

"I see your point."

"My daddy sure never did. He was real happy when I quit associating with that firm. He called them 'nigger-lovers'. My daddy's not a Klansman, but he sure sympathizes with their cause. So. *Is* there anything I can help you with?"

James thought a moment. "You might tell me anything you can think of that might not show up in a transcript or the newspaper accounts. But, maybe there isn't any more to know."

"First, I need to know why you're so interested." (Mary's voice sounded sly and knowing.)

"I'm writing a book on interesting murders—"

"You're a writer?"

James nodded, smiled.

"Have I read anything of yours?"

"Probably not. I don't write fiction. I'm a fact-man all the way."

"Well, I probably haven't read anything of yours, then. I like novels."

"I thought so. Do you know anything I might be able to use?"

"Sure. Can't see as how it'd hurt anything to tell you. Well,"—her tone lowered to 'confidential' again—"I have this friend who worked in the bank that Mr. Morgan was president of before he was killed. After they hanged Slo-Joe for the murder, these G-men showed up at the bank with a court order to open this safety deposit box that Morgan had."

"You're sure they were from the government?"

"I'm not positive. I didn't see them. But Louise—she's the friend in the bank—swore they were. That was weird enough, but Louise said that Morgan's family and the police had already collected all of Morgan's things from his office safe and the lock boxes his wife knew about."

"You're saying the court order given your friend was for a box his family didn't know existed?"

She nodded her head, looked around the room, and lowered her voice even more: "Know what's really strange about this whole thing?" (James was listening with every fiber of his being.) "The G-men told Louise not to tell Morgan's family anything. That the government would contact his family, when their investigation was finished."

"Investigation? Into what?"

Mary shrugged her shoulders. "Darned if I know. Louise was really scared when she told me about it and swore me to secrecy. Oh!"

"What?"

"If you use this in your book, you won't tell anyone where you got your information will you? I'd hate to get Louise into trouble, and that was years ago—"

"I probably won't use it in my book, Miss Landower—"

"Oh? Why not?"

"When you write nonfiction, you have to have corroborating evidence for facts as unusual as these—"

"You don't believe me?"

James smiled. "Of course I believe you, Miss Landower; I just can't use the information. But thank you for telling me. It is an interesting story. If I ever write fiction, I'll use it—changing names of course, to protect you and Louise."

"Well, I'm sorry I couldn't be of help...."

"That's all right. Thanks for trying."

Mary scooted her chair back and got up. Disappointment showed in her expression, though for the life of him, James couldn't understand why. "Well, when you run into Mr. Witherspoon, tell him hello for me."

"I'll do that. Thanks. I'd better get back to my research." James looked back down at the article he'd been reading before she interrupted him, so he missed the glint of triumph in her eyes as she turned away.

Jake heard the grandfather clock strike the half-hour as he answered the telephone. "Hello."

"Mr. Witherspoon? James McWilliams."

"James?"

"I know it's late. I hope I didn't wake you."

"No. I'm usually up until midnight these days. What's up?"

"Just thought I'd report in before I'm back on the road again."

"Just a minute, James. Let me find something to write with.... Ready."

"I think I've found a link between Joe Runyon and Clarence Morgan—"

"You're sure?"

"Not absolutely, but I'm fairly confident I'm going to find something soon to back up my suspicions."

"What do you know?" Jake heard the rustling of paper over the line.

"I'm pretty sure Morgan met with Runyon—only his name was Andersen, Joe Andersen, at the time."

"Anderson?"

"No, Andersen: A-N-D-E-R-S-E-N. I think that's his real name, but it may be an alias. That's one of the things I'm trying to find out. I'm going from here to Kansas City. I'm pretty sure Andersen was living in Kansas City before he visited Morgan."

"Have you been to Fort Smith?"

"Yes, I went there first. That's what led me to this Andersen. Joseph and Fanny Runyon showed up in Fort Smith with a bundle of money. Cash."

"How do you know this?"

"I tracked down the person who sold them the Arkansas place. Just a second while I find that...Here it is.

"Ralph Snow is the man's name. He remembered them right off because they paid for everything with cash out of a carpetbag. It was the carpetbag as much as the cash that made him remember them. Said he knew they were Northerners right off because of that bag and the way they threw their money around—"

"Doesn't sound much like the Runyons we knew around here. They never said two words to anyone."

"He didn't mean they were showing off. He meant that they'd just take cash out of that bag whenever it was called for." James chuckled. "I'm telling you, Mr. Witherspoon, Mr. Snow hasn't thrown away any Confederate money he might have stashed away. He's ready for the South to rise! He thoroughly resents this 'steady influx of carpetbaggin' Northerners.'"

"But he took their money?"

"You bet he did. Told me he'd fleeced them for five hundred more than the price of the property. He told me this in the strictest confidence, of course, over some moonshine he just happened to have."

"He pocketed five hundred dollars over the price the owners were asking?"

"Faster than you can blink. Old Mr. Snow is a mighty bitter man, especially when he deals with anyone suspected of being from up North."

Jake smiled. He'd known a few of that breed himself: "So what led you to suspect a connection with Morgan?"

"Oddly enough, the carpetbag."

"How's that?"

"When I went to Little Rock, I talked to Morgan's former secretary, a Maxine Hershey?"

"I remember the name. What about her?"

"I asked her if she could remember anything that had happened prior to Morgan's death that had seemed suspicious or odd. At first she said 'no,' that all that had happened so long ago—you know the kinds of things people say when they don't want to remember something—"

"I do."

"Then, suddenly, she stops in mid-sentence and remembers this man who'd come to visit Morgan—let's see…here it is—Mrs. Hershey said ten days or so before he was murdered. She remembered how odd it was to see a man carrying a carpetbag into a bank. She said when she first saw him come in the door, she thought he might be there to rob them, but then it turned out he had an appointment with Mr. Morgan. That was the other thing she thought was odd: Mr. Morgan was expecting him, but she had no record of the appointment on her calendar. I asked her if she remembered the man's name. She couldn't, but we were able to find Morgan's old appointment book—"

"Where in the world?"

"Confiscated by the police in the original investigation. They still had it. Piece of luck, huh?"

"I'll say. And the man in question was…?"

"Joseph Andersen, from Kansas City, Missouri."

"Ah. I see why you're not certain that Runyon and Andersen are the same—"

"Well, there's a bit more to go on. Once Mrs. Hershey remembered that carpetbag, she also remembered it seemed a lot fuller when Mr. Andersen left than when he arrived."

"He robbed the bank?"

"No. Apparently not. At least Morgan never said anything, and the bank's assets were never tampered with."

"What about Morgan's personal assets?"

"That was my thought, especially after I heard a rumor that he had a safety deposit box that his family wasn't aware of—"

"Oh? How did you find out about that one?"

"I talked to a girl named Louise Booker, who works at the bank, and who worked in the vault right after the trial. She swears two men from the government came in with a federal court order to open this safety deposit box registered to a J. Smith. Morgan was the only authorized signer on the account."

"No signature card for this J. Smith?"

"None. Miss Booker and her supervisor were told to keep this information confidential. Mr. Morgan's family was supposed to receive the contents of the box, if their investigation proved the contents actually belonged to Morgan."

"Who did they think this J. Smith was? Had anyone ever seen him?"

"Miss Booker, and everyone involved at the time, thought it stood for John Smith, the usual alias. You know."

"Did the Morgan family ever receive the contents?"

"No one knows. They weren't supposed to tell the family anything about it. Shortly after the trial, what was left of Morgan's family left town."

"Is that all you have?"

"Well, I've got some suspicions, but nothing I want to talk about, until I find out about the Kansas City connection."

"I'm impressed, James. You're better than a lot of professional detectives I've dealt with."

"Thanks, Mr. Witherspoon."

"How are you fixed for money?"

"I could probably use some."

"Stop by the Western Union office in the morning before you leave. There will be some money waiting for you."

"I appreciate it."

"James?"

"Yes?"

"If you run into anything more on that J. Smith, let me know."

"You think it might be a real person?"

"I don't know. That's what I want you to find out."

"I'll check on it. I'll call you again when I have something to report."

"Call me when you get to Kansas City. I'd like to know where you're staying, so I can reach you if anything comes up here."

"Mr. Witherspoon, would you give Dottie a call for me and tell her I'm all right? With this Kansas City thing, I don't know when I'm going to get home——"

"Call her yourself. Put the charge on my bill. It's the least I can do after taking you away from your family. I'll look in on her as well and make sure your family is taken care of while you're gone."

"Thanks. It means a lot to me, Mr. Witherspoon. You've already done so much for us——"

"Hogwash! You're doing more for me than you'll ever know. We won't speak of this again. Agreed?"

"Yessir."

"Good. Now call your wife and get some rest. You've got a long drive ahead of you tomorrow."

Jake replaced the receiver, picked up the pad of paper, and reviewed his notes. He tried to keep from speculating on the importance of the apparent Smith-Morgan-Andersen-Runyon connection, but his heart was beating so hard his hand shook as he held the pad. Why hadn't they seen this connection before? Because Runyon/Andersen—if they were one and the same—was the missing piece, the piece that made everything else fit together. But what business could Runyon have had with Morgan? And assuming Morgan had given him enough money to fill that carpetbag...? *What we have is a lot of speculation, a lot of nothing, without a lot more information. What if Runyon isn't Andersen? What if Andersen is some creditor, some old crony Morgan owed money to? What if J. Smith is John Smith—real or imaginary—and not Jesse Smith? Ahhh! I'll go crazy if I keep this up!*

He rose abruptly, pad in hand, went to his study, unlocked the middle drawer of his desk, tore off his notes and tossed them into it, locking the drawer afterwards. He paced back and forth for awhile. His hands felt clammy; his heartbeat seemed abnormal. He went into the kitchen for a glass, poured three fingers of bourbon into it, thought better of it and added some water.

His mind was working overtime. He couldn't get it to shut up.

Bits and pieces of information, all unbidden, vied for his attention. He strode into the parlor, glass in hand, straight to the bookcases. There had to be something he hadn't read, something that would calm the pandemonium in his head and take his mind off things he couldn't do anything about, at least not at the moment. *War and Peace* might do the trick, he thought, removing the thick book from its place on the shelf. He stood there, staring at the title, which suddenly seemed to describe his entire life. He backed into a chair and sat down. He couldn't remember a time in his life that wasn't one or the other. The only middle ground that might have existed was during the time that amnesia had left him stranded in between. But always, in some part of his brain just out of reach, he had known he was just waiting for the time when he would once again be thrust into frontline combat. *And there was a time when I loved being in the thick of things, loved nothing better than a good fight.*

He looked down at the hand that held his glass. Steady. Adrenaline. Preparation for the battle. That's all it was. It wasn't fear at all. He downed the rest of his bourbon, walked back into the kitchen for a refill. Tomorrow he'd call Jenny. They'd go back to the Chicken Shack, listen to jazz, and he'd ask her to spend Christmas with him, and Christmas morning, he'd ask her to be his wife.

Sally Reynolds finished pounding out a mesmerizing and heavily syncopated piece of ragtime to deafening applause and shouts of approval:

"Dat be by Mistah Scott Joplin, de 'Maple Leaf Rag'! I heared dat man play in m'younger days, ina place y'all sho *nuff* doan wanna know 'bouts!" The black woman laughed heartily at her own joke, then motioned for some men in the crowd to come join her.

"We're in luck," Jake whispered to Jenny. "These are the fellows Ben's always talking about. See the one with the cornet? He's supposed to be great. Yep. There's the banjo—Ben says he's something to watch as well as someone to hear. A trombone, clarinet, and...the man with the bass." He scooted his chair back an inch—all the space he had because of the crowd, packed solid like a fat woman's corset.

They tuned their instruments. Sally beamed: "Y'all's 'bout t' get some kinda treat! One and two and three—"

The whole place was standing, singing along—in and off key, but loudly—to "Alexander's Ragtime Band." It was infectious, Jenny decided. Who could sit quietly when music like that was being played? And by such musicians!

Two encores later, Sally called a momentary halt, while she and her friends took a break.

Jenny slumped happily back into her chair. "I could listen to them all night! Aren't they great?"

"I have to admit, Ben wasn't exaggerating one bit when he told me how good these people were....I'm hungry. Would you like something to eat?"

"Yes. How about some fried chicken?"

"I think that might just be on the menu."

Jake motioned for Sally's granddaughter, a precocious adolescent—cute, sassy, and not one bit impressed by the audience who came to hear her grandmother and her friends play. She'd seen lots better folks than these at her grandmother's feet, begging to hear her play.

"What can I bring y'all?" she asked in an accent that was hard to place.

"Two specials."

"'Nuther drink?"

Jake looked at Jenny who nodded—"Two more, thanks."

"That it?" (They smiled, nodded.) "I'll be back," she assured them.

"What is it about that girl?" Jenny asked in admiration as the young woman disappeared into the back.

"Brains, good looks, and confidence, I'd say." Jake drained the contents of his glass. "Probably inherited them from her grandmother."

"Heredity is a funny thing, isn't it?" Jenny said, sipping her drink, which was mostly water by now.

"What do you mean?"

"Nothing. Every once in a while I think about who I look like, where I got my love for reading and music—"

"Do you play an instrument?"

"Just the dulcimer. I've always wished I knew more. Do you play?"

"The piano—a little. I haven't played in years. My piano burned in the fire." He picked up his empty glass, looked into it.

Jenny reached across the table, covered his hand with hers for a moment before withdrawing it. "I've been meaning to ask you—" she stopped abruptly.

Jake looked up. Put his glass back down on the table: "Ask me what?"

"Nothing."

"It's obviously not *nothing*. What's on your mind?"

"I was wondering if you still wanted to pursue what happened the night of the fire? You probably don't want to talk about that tonight, though. I shouldn't have said anything."

"No. That's fine. As a matter of fact, I *have* found out some interesting information lately."

"Really? What?"

"You remember my theory that the Morgan murder and the Runyon murder might be tied together in some way? That they might have something to do with what happened to my family that night?" (Jenny nodded, said nothing) "Well, I've a lead that might just tie them together—at least the Morgan and Runyon murders.

"I have reason to think Joe Runyon—if that was his real name—not only knew Morgan, but also went to see him a few days before Morgan was murdered. Runyon might have been blackmailing him. There's some evidence that on the day Morgan met with him, Runyon suddenly came into a great deal of money. Cash. The same cash, perhaps, which enabled him to buy the property outside of Hulet and continue to live for the last few years without any visible means of support.

"I also have reason to believe that Runyon and his wife were from back East somewhere—the Northeast, perhaps."

"Why don't you just ask his wife? Didn't you say she was still alive? Only the husband was killed?"

"That's right. But Fanny Runyon is not talking to anyone. There's substantial evidence that she's incapable of communicating—"

"Shock?"

"No one seems to know. Some doctors who've seen her think she might be faking—"

"Faking? Why would she do that?"

"Because she might have seen her husband's murderer—"

"Then she'd be able to identi—Oh!"—Jenny's hand went to her mouth—"Then *she'd* be in danger, too, if the murderer *knew* she could."

"Exactly."

"Is she all right? I mean is she being protected? Is she safe?"

Jake smiled at her concern: "She's fine."

"Then *you're* taking care of her?"

"Not I. Our firm. When she was released from protective custody at the hospital, we decided—actually I had nothing to do with the decision. It was before I regained my memory. At any rate, Fanny is safely secreted somewhere in the Ozarks—"

"Somewhere?"

"I couldn't tell you where she is, if I wanted to. I've never been to Larry's cabin."

"Larry?"

"Mr. Branch, our junior partner."

"She's at his cabin?"

"But not with Larry. He's keeping an eye on her, of course, but we've hired some people to watch over her, and make sure she's well taken care of."

"So she's safe?"

"As safe as we can make her."

"Then you think she might be able to identify Runyon's killer?"

Jake shrugged: "Who knows what she knows, or what she may, or may not, have seen? I'm going along with this because I think there's a good chance that Runyon's murderer is still out there. Why he didn't kill her at the time is beyond me, if she was there to see the murder—"

"Then you don't think she saw anything?"

"I don't know. But she's our client, and as long as the possibility of danger to her exists, I feel it's our duty to see that she's taken care of—at least until she can take care of herself."

"And if that day doesn't come?"

"We'll deal with that when the time comes—Ah!" he said, as their orders were placed on the table by the comely granddaughter. "Trudy, you have saved us from expiring!"

"That'll be a dollar and a half, Mr. Witherspoon."

"And worth every penny. Here's a little something extra for you." Jake handed her a quarter in addition to the cost of their meals.

"Thank you," Trudy dropped the quarter in her left apron pocket and made change for Jake from her right: "Y'all enjoy yourselves," she said, as she turned toward another customer who was trying to wave her down.

Sally Reynolds and her friends were making their way back to the area where her studio piano stood. It would be a while yet, Jake decided, as he saw well-wishers and fans accosting the musicians at every step.

"While we're talking about things that occurred to us since we last spoke..."

Jenny wiped her fingers on her napkin, swallowed the bite in her mouth: "What?"

"Any good?"

"Great. But that isn't what you wanted to talk about. You might as well say it, because I hate it when someone starts to say something and then stops right in the middle. It drives me crazy, until I know what it is."

"Umhum. This *is* good." Jake finished his bite, smiled as he wiped his mouth. "Don't tell Annie how much I eat of this stuff—"

"I will, if you don't finish your earlier thought..."

"OK. Here goes. How would you like to come to my house for dinner on Christmas Eve and help me open gifts the next morning?"

"I'd love to spend Christmas with you!" (A sudden frown took the light from her face.) "But Christmas Eve and Christmas morning? What will people say?"

Jake's eyebrows lifted: "Exactly which people are we discussing?"

"Be serious! There are certain rules in society——"

"That would be *Hulet, Arkansas,* society..." He nodded sagely.

"We *live* in Hulet, Arkansas. I'll grant you, it's quite small—a fact which makes my point all the more applicable."

"All right. I'll concede the gossip mill runs twenty-four hours a day in our corner of the country. But explain to me the impropriety of my invitation."

Jenny blushed—a particular Jake thought both amusing and charming—"Perhaps, I misunderstood," she said, "but I thought you asked me to spend Christmas Eve at your place and celebrate Christmas with you the next morning."

"Yes. I see no misunderstanding."

Jenny's blush deepened. "Then you did expect me to stay overnight?"

"Of course. Oh. I see. You thought——"

"Well, what else was I supposed to think!"

"You were supposed to *know* I wouldn't compromise you, or your honor, in any way. I thought I'd made my feelings clear?"

Jenny was looking intently at him as he spoke. He seemed sincere. "Then?"

"Annie and Bill will also spend Christmas Eve and morning with us to attest—if that becomes necessary, which I very much doubt—that we were properly chaperoned, and that we behaved with the utmost decorum. And, if that isn't enough for you, I've given serious thought to inviting the Hawleys and their brood to join us. Do you have anyone you'd like to invite? We could have one of those Christmases replete with friends, where there is no opportunity to do anything outside the rigorous bounds of propriety."

"Oh Jake, how fun! I haven't had a festive Christmas since leaving Virginia! But you'll have to let me help Annie with the preparations. It's too much for her to do alone. Remember Thanksgiving?"

Jake held up his hands—"I'll leave this entirely up to you, if you'd like——"

"Could we have a real Christmas Eve party? Invite the Hawleys, of course. How about Billy Wiggins and his family? I'm sure they never get to go anywhere, and Bertha—Bertha *slaves* every day, not only at the cafe, but when she goes home. What about the Townsends?"

"Mike hasn't been feeling well of late—"

"Well, perhaps he'll feel better by then—"

"Perhaps. Why don't you leave Mike to me?"

"And your other partner—Mr. Branch? Is he married? I don't even know—Oh, Jake! This is going to be such fun! Thank you for thinking of this...."

"I'm glad you like the idea. Why don't we continue this later? The band's back."

Jenny didn't know which made her happier: that he'd remembered to bring her back to this wonderful place, or that he'd given her this marvelous celebration to look forward to.

He reached for her hand across the table. She put her hand in his and squeezed. She leaned over, whispered into his ear: "When can I get started on the planning?"

"Soon," he whispered back. "I'll let you know, as soon as I've discussed it with Annie and Bill. Do you want to dance?"

"Yes!"

"What did you find out, James? *Are* the Runyons the Andersens out of Kansas City?"

"Yessir, they are, but they're not from Kansas City."

"No?"

"No sir. They arrived here in 1923, sometime in the fall. No one can remember for certain. The man who rented a room to them when they arrived said he thought they came from St. Louis."

"St. Louis?"

"I'm going there next, if that's all right. I've got a pretty strong trail to follow—"

"Go, by all means. Is this all you want to tell me now?"

"No sir. I found out a bundle."

"Shoot."

"Well, it seems that Mr. Andersen worked as a chauffeur when he first arrived in Kansas City. Frances—that's what Mrs. Runyon called herself here—took in sewing to help make ends meet. She was getting quite a reputation as a seamstress when they up and took off—"

"They *took off*?"

"I'm getting a bit ahead of myself. Seems that Andersen quit his chauffeur's job about six months after they settled in Kansas City. He took a job in a haberdashery as a clerk. Did well, too, by all accounts."

"What name was he using?"

"Joe Andersen."

"So Joe is his real name?"

"I don't know yet. But it makes sense. Whenever I hear James or Jimmy, I turn around. I think it'd be easy to forget and do the same thing, if I'd decided to use another name. Makes it easier to get caught, anyway."

"I suppose you're right. What happened?"

"Two things made me suspicious: the first job he had he just quit one day. The man who hired him is still scratching his head over it. Everything seemed to be going along just fine, then he shows up for work, turns in his uniform at the end of the day—no reason given—and never shows up again. They moved from their rented room the same day—no forwarding address. Andersen showed up two weeks later and picked up the few pieces of mail—"

"Mail?"

"I thought the same thing, but the landlord said he didn't know why Andersen bothered checking. All their mail was local, a couple of bills. That's all. Nothing from out of state or personal."

"Odd."

"I thought so."

"What else?"

"Joe works long hours at the haberdashery. Never takes a day off. A 'real hard worker,' 'dependable,' is what the owner said Andersen was. Then one day he asks for a whole week off on a Tuesday—"

"What dates?"

"You're ahead of me, but you're right. The dates match. The day Andersen met with Morgan was three days after he left on his week off."

"And?" Excitement filtered into Jake's voice as he spoke.

"There's something else."

"What?"

"The Monday before his week off, he bought a large carpetbag from the shop before closing time. The owner remembers because he'd been trying to unload this particular bag for a long time. He told me he couldn't imagine what possible use Andersen could have had for it, but he seemed real eager to buy it. Didn't even ask for the employee's discount."

"No?"

James chuckled. "The proprietor didn't remind him either."

"I don't imagine he did."

"No. And when Andersen disappeared, without so much as a good-bye, his boss was glad he hadn't."

"When did he disappear, as you put it?"

"The week after Morgan's murder. Something must've happened, 'cause the Andersens just vanished. Mrs. Andersen left half-altered dresses hanging in the closet. One was still in the machine, half-stitched."

"It sure sounds as if she were in a hurry."

"Both of them. He showed up for work that day, went out for his lunch break, and never came back. He had money coming to him—a week's pay. He never tried to collect it."

"And you're sure these Andersens are the Runyons?"

"Pretty sure. Everyone I talked to recognized Mrs. Runyon's picture—"

"How did you get her *picture*? I didn't know one existed!"

James cleared his throat before answering. "I hope you don't mind, Mr. Witherspoon. I *swear* I didn't say anything about you, or working for you or anything..."

"Out with it. Where did you get the picture?" A knot had formed in Jake's stomach. He braced himself for James's answer.

"Sheriff's office in Hulet."

"What?"

"I'm real sorry, but I thought I might need it, and it was worth taking a chance they'd have one in their files. They did. They took one the day the murder was reported, when they brought her in. They have one of her husband, too, but I thought it might make people clam up if they saw a picture of a dead body."

Jake shook his head, tried to think: "Why would they give it to you?"

"They didn't. The deputy is sweet on Dottie's girlfriend. He gave *her* the picture—"

"He *what*? What did you tell *her*?"

"Nothing. I told Dottie I needed to see if they had pictures of the Runyons, and I couldn't figure out how to find out without somebody asking questions. She said Lucy knew the deputy *real* well. Dottie told Lucy she wanted to see what that crazy Runyon woman looked like, and wouldn't it be fun to see if she could wheedle one out of her deputy? Lucy said, 'If he's got one, I'll have it by sunset,' and she did. I told Dottie I was sure glad Lucy wasn't after *me*. A woman like that is dangerous to know"— he laughed—"if she's not on your side, that is."

"He gave it over without—"

"Just handed it to her, without so much as a peep. She wanted it; he had what she wanted; she got it. Something, isn't it?"

"I'll say. What about getting it back?"

"She never said anything about that. As far as Lucy knows, Dottie has it. Dottie mailed it here the day I arrived. I'm taking *real* good care of this picture."

"Good. Whatever you do, don't let *anything* happen to it. And you say the Kansas City people you've mentioned recognize Fanny Runyon as this Frances Andersen?"

"The ones that saw her anyhow."

"Now what?"

"Now, I go to St. Louis and see where the trail leads from there. I'll go back to Fort Smith and show Mr. Snow Mrs. Runyon's picture, just to make sure we're still talking about the same people—"

"How long before you'll be back in Hulet?"

"As soon as I have the information, I'll be heading back. You can count on it."

"Missing your family?"

"Yessir. I didn't know I'd miss them so much, but I do...Thanks for checking on Dot for me. She said you've been real nice to her while I've been gone."

"Nothing to it. It's the least I can do. Don't forget to call your wife when we're through here."

"Well, that's all I have for now."

Jake grinned. "Call me when you get a room in St. Louis. How's the money holding out?"

"I'll let you know what I need when I get to St. Louis."

"Fine. Good work as usual, James."

"Thank you, Mr. Witherspoon. Good night."

"Good night." Jake hung up the receiver, sat quietly for a moment, thinking, before returning to his bed.

CHAPTER TWENTY

Jenny was turning out the downstairs lights for the evening when the telephone rang.

"Hello?"

"Jenny. It's me. Dan."

"Dan! What a surprise. Did you just get back in town?"

"I've been back for a couple of days, I guess. Sorry I haven't called you until now, but I had to straighten some things out at the paper. I left Billy in charge and..."

"I know. How did he do?"

"Pretty well for a kid. But you know how it is. The paper gets out because that's the fun part of the job. But the filing and the record-keeping sit there waiting for me."

Jenny tried not to let her amusement show in her voice: "I take it you don't like record-keeping and filing either."

Dan chuckled. "It shows, huh?"

"Not at all. It was just a good guess."

"Sure it was. Say, did you miss me while I was gone?"

The question took her by complete surprise. Had he not understood?

"Silence. I guess that means you didn't, huh?"

"No. I mean it's not that. Of course I missed you, but..."

"But? This isn't sounding very good, Jenny."

"I'm sorry, Dan. I thought you understood."

"I guess I didn't. Understood what?"

"I might as well tell you straight out. I'm going out with Jake Witherspoon——"

"Witherspoon!"

"I know how you feel about him, Dan, and I want you to know you're truly mistaken about him. Please don't be angry. You mean a great deal to me. I treasure your friendship, and I don't want to lose it. Please. Try to understand..." Jenny waited for the explosion she knew was forthcoming. There was none. After a few seconds of silence, she wondered if he were still on the line. "Dan?"

"I'm here. I'm trying to figure this all out. Were you going out with him while we were seeing each other?"

"Not really. We'd known each other for several months——ever since Mrs. Witherspoon died. He had asked me to dinner before you called the first time, but then he was called out of town and had to cancel——"

"And I called, and you weren't doing anything better, since he was out of town, so you went out with me. Is that it?"

"No! That is most certainly *not* it! I went out with you, because I wanted to go out with you. Jake and I had no understanding of any kind then——"

"But you do now. Is that it?"

"That's it." (She sighed.) "Dan, I really meant what I said before: You meant——still do mean——a great deal to me. I don't want to lose you."

"OK. Sorry I got upset earlier. You have a right to like anyone you want to like, I suppose"——Dan laughed humorlessly——"I guess I'd just fooled myself into thinking I could be the one. Tell Witherspoon I said he was one lucky... Never mind."

"Maybe one day we could all get together...?"

"Jenny..."——Dan sighed audibly——"Sure. One day."

"We *are* still friends, aren't we, Dan?"

"Sure. Give me a call anytime if you need me. Well,"——Dan's tone of voice changed——"back to filing and record-keeping. No rest for the wicked, you know."

"Bye, Dan. Thanks for calling."

"Good-bye, Jenny. Take care of yourself."

Dan locked the newspaper office door, dropped the key and his empty pipe into the pocket of his coat. He stumbled over a frozen rut as he made his way through the alley to Main Street where he'd parked his automobile. A man lurched into his path from behind some stacked barrels—"Whoa there!" Dan said, grabbing the man's arm before he fell.

"Leggo!" The man tried to jerk his arm away from Dan's grasp, failed.

"Townsend?" Dan lowered his head to get a better look at the man's face. "Townsend? Is that you?"

"Who're ya?" the man said.

His words were so slurred that Dan had trouble deciphering them. It was Townsend all right. Dan shook his head. If he'd not known him for so many years, he wouldn't have recognized the man at all. Mike looked eighty if he looked a day—a rough eighty. A week's growth of beard hid his face. His hair hadn't been combed in that long at least, and by the smell of him, he'd not been anywhere near a bath in even longer. He put his arm around Townsend, supported him to the car.

"Where're y' takin' me? Who're ya?"

"Mike, it's me. Dan Johnson. It's freezing out here. I'm going to take you home—"

"Doan have a home..."

"Fine. We'll go to my place then. I'm not going to leave you out here on the street to freeze to death. Come on. Get in."

He managed to shove Townsend into the front seat of his car before the man slumped over. Dan went around to the driver's side, reached across him and locked the door so Mike wouldn't hit the latch and fall out. He shoved Mike's unconscious form against the door and backed out.

"Better?" Dan asked, after Mike had eaten and downed his fifth cup of strong coffee.

Mike looked at him across the table through eyes that felt as if they had been sanded. The light stung as badly as iodine. He nodded.

"Good. Now tell me. What in hell has gotten into you?" (Mike's eyes were slits of suspicion and something else, something he recognized all too well.)

"Rotgut. What'd ya think it was?" Mike clasped the mug with both hands. It kept them from shaking, and it was warm. He felt like he hadn't ever been warm....

"What's happened to you? How did you get in such a sorry state?"

"Question of the day, isn't it?" His tongue felt like an old sock. He took a drink of the hot coffee, drained the cup.

Dan stood up, got the pot, and refilled Mike's mug. He replaced the pot, turned his chair backwards and straddled it, resting his chin on the chair back. "Drink it."

"In a minute. Gotta go—" Mike looked around the room.

Dan pointed, watched as Mike staggered to the bathroom and closed the door. He returned in five minutes. He'd washed his face.

"You OK?" Dan asked, as Mike resumed his seat.

"What d' *you* think?"

"You cleaned up a bit. It must have helped."

"Give me some more of that stew, will you?"

"Sure." Dan got the pan from the stove, ladled some stew into Mike's bowl—"Enough?" he asked, as he set it down in front of him.

"Yeah. Thanks."

"Don't mention it."

"I'm sorry you had to see me in this shape. I look pretty bad..."

Dan nodded but said nothing, waited.

"Naomi left me," Mike continued. "It's all that damned Witherspoon's fault!"—he hit the table with his fist, slopping coffee onto the table—"I'll *kill* him. I swear. One of these days I'm going to kill that S.O.B!"

"You'll have to get in line, buddy," Dan said, mopping up the spilled coffee with a dishrag.

Mike looked up at Dan's face and remembered. A lopsided grimace distorted his face. "Oh yeah..."

"What did he do to *you*?"

"Forced me out of my own law firm for starters."

"How did he do that? What about Hawley and what's-his-name?"

"Branch. Traitors. Told me not to show up at the office anymore. Took my dadgum car keys from me!"

Dan hid his smile. "How did they do that?"

"Never mind. They took 'em. Naomi left me the next day."

"I can't see how Witherspoon could just waltz into your partnership and get you out without some cause—"

"Cause? I'll give you cause! That damned fool is reopening that old murder case—"

"What old murder case?"

"The one—you know—the nigger killed that white guy in Little Rock? Hell, that case is dead, buried—dust!"

Dan got up, twirled the chair around to its normal position, and sat down. "Then why all the fuss? Let him dig all he wants." Dan drank the last of his coffee. "I don't think I remember the murder you're talking about..."

"Sure you do! Hell, it made big headlines—'Bank President Stabbed!'"—Mike drew his hand across the air in front of him as he said it, shook his head—"Slo-Joe Freeman: convicted, hanged, and buried six feet under five years ago...open and shut." Mike eyed Dan, "Tell me again you don't remember that case..."

Dan dropped the pretense. "I know the case all right. It's the one he was working on when my sister and the kids died.... I know why *I'd* be upset. Why are you?"

"I don't like it, that's all! Can't a man just want some peace in his life? What good's it gonna do anyone, diggin' up all that?"

"Maybe he's trying to atone—"

"Atone my foot! He's got some fool notion that that murder and the Runyon murder—"

"The Runyon murder? You've got to be pulling my leg!"

Mike pushed himself back from the table, held up both hands: "I swear"—he lowered his hands, rubbed his eyes—"And as if that weren't enough, he's got some idea that both murders are somehow linked to Washington!"

Dan laughed, got up to pour himself some more coffee. "Now, I *know* you're nuts. What gave him that idea?"

"Damned if I know! I'm more concerned about Runyon's murderer going after his wife than I am about some fool government conspiracy!"

"Want some more?" Dan proffered the coffeepot.

"No! I'm practically floating as it is…Say, you don't happen to have any whiskey do you? I'm feeling mighty rough."

"I'd say you've had plenty."

"Just one. You know what they say about the hair of the dog…?"

The whine in his voice made Dan's skin crawl: "One. Then I'm taking you home."

"I don't want to go back there."

Dan pulled a bottle from the top shelf of a cabinet: "Well, that's where I'm taking you. After this, you're on your own." He poured two fingers into a jelly glass and handed it to Mike. Mike looked at him out of the corner of his eye— *Like a rat caught with some garbage,* Dan thought, as he watched Mike down the liquor in one gulp and wipe his hand across his mouth.

"Much obliged, Dan."

"Come on. Here's your coat. Let's get going."

Dan got in the car and started the engine while Mike hauled himself into the seat. The tires spun uselessly on a patch of ice for a minute before hitting dry dirt and taking hold. The car shot backwards. Dan hit the brake, shifted gears, and sped off.

Mike decided it was safe to sit up again. "You all right?"

"Fine."

"OK. Just thought you might be mad about something."

"Nope. I'm just ready to get back and get some shuteye. Talk to me. I'm about ready to fall asleep at this wheel."

"After all that coffee?"—(no response)—" What do you want to know?"

"Tell me more about Witherspoon's cockeyed theory."

"Which one?"

"You can start with the Runyons. I did a story about that murder a while back. Remember?"—Mike nodded, looked out the window—"At least I can relate to some of the details in that one."

"Not much to tell." Mike continued to stare out of the window.

"What ever happened to Mrs. Runyon? I seem to remember something about her being transferred to a county hospital for observation?" Dan watched the play of light on the road. He drove carefully now. Ice was everywhere.

"That's old news," Mike said.

"Oh?"

"We couldn't let that happen. Violation of her rights to be held anywhere without being charged with something—"

"I thought it was because she was in some sort of trance...?"

"That was the excuse. There was some thought that she was pretending to be ill; the doctors couldn't agree. Other than that she appeared to be fine."

"So what happened to her?"

"Larry's got her stashed at his fishing cabin in the Ozark river country." (Mike's eyelids felt leaden. He could barely keep them open.)

"Alone?"

"Course not...there's a nurse..."

"Branch stays with her of course?" Dan asked. There was no answer. Dan glanced at the man beside him: Mike was out cold.

Max Howe's letter arrived with a large, brown-paper-wrapped package on Friday, eleven days before Christmas. Jake smiled as he broke the wax seal and thought how glad he was that Max was back in his life. He had planned to call him on Christmas day, tender greetings of the season, and casually slip into the conversation that he was getting married again. Max had to act as his best man. Jenny would probably want a spring wedding when the dogwoods were in bloom. He smiled at the thought. He'd decided to have gemstones taken out of two of his mother's rings and placed in a new setting for Jenny's engagement ring. Christmas was just around the corner. *I'd better get going on that ring, if I'm going to give it to her Christmas,* Jake thought, scanning Max's letter as he walked to his study—

"... thought it odd to see your brother-in-law here so soon after your own visit. No word from any of your family in all these years, then first you arrive, and then a few weeks later, Laura's brother—"

Jake stopped scanning, turned on his reading light and began again at the beginning:

"My Dear Fellow,

"Terribly sorry not to have communicated sooner, but this market mess has caused me no end of grief. Close friends commit suicide at an alarming rate. My social calendar seems to be filled with a preponderance of funereal obligations, many of which occasioned my absence from Washington and the shameful state of my correspondence. (I do hope I am not giving you the impression that I take these deaths lightly, or that they have affected me only as unhappy inconveniences that interfere with my many more trivial pursuits. Such is far from the actual case. In truth, I am distraught by the spate of misery, which has drowned so many of my acquaintances and friends. I stand, as it were, on a dry bank—an unfortunate word choice, but a telling one—unable to give succor to those who are most in distress. I can but try to encourage those, who are left abandoned, to survive as best they can, and to provide what little comfort I may to others, while I give grateful thanks to Almighty God that He has allowed me to escape intact.)

"But to the reason for this letter...

"Imagine my surprise when I stepped onto the platform at Union Station and encountered another Ghost from Times Past, none other than that beastly cad, whose name most thankfully slips my memory, your former brother-in-law! I assure you, it was he; I may not remember the man's name, but I never forget a face. I confess, I thought it odd to see your brother-in-law here so soon after your own visit. No word from any of your family in all these years, then first you arrive, and then a few weeks later, Laura's brother comes to Washington. He seemed in a fearful rush,

and took no notice of me (of that I am quite certain) and after his ghastly display the day of your wedding reception, I had no wish, believe me, to renew our acquaintance.

"(I seem to remember his working, albeit briefly, as a writer for one of the papers here. Didn't you tell me he'd joined the Brits, or some such? I remember he left the country for awhile, before resurfacing at your reception, and, then, thankfully, disappearing once more. Horrible lout! How Laura and he ever could have been related still astounds me!)

"Regarding our earlier conversation about That Matter and That Man, it is my understanding, that <u>he</u> was released from the Atlanta Penitentiary in July of last year. A friend in New York hinted that a manuscript of 'immense importance' was offered to several in the publishing community. The friend seemed to believe our Man had some connection with it. From what my friend intimated, Murder in High Places seems probable. Perhaps my friend's information would aid you in your 'investigations.' Should you wish to contact her, I can arrange a meeting, but you must come here to avoid suspicions. Telephone and say when you can visit again.

"I do wish you could come for Christmas, but I know this is probably out of the question so soon after your last absence. Do write and tell me about the mad, social whirl of Hulet, Arkansas. I am sending you a package, a token of my genuine affection at this joyous season of the year. Its execution was an outgrowth of an acute necessity to focus on something other than the dreariness and sorrow that surround me.

"In all of this, I wish you a Merry Christmas Season and a Very Happy New Year, and, as always, I remain,

"Yr. Devoted Friend & Servant,
"Maxwell Theodore Howe"

Max had written the letter the week after Thanksgiving. What was Dan Johnson doing in Washington, D.C.? Max could have been mistaken—it had been several years since he'd seen Dan, and only that one time. Then again, Jake thought, it was not all that far-fetched: Johnson *had* lived there at one time. Perhaps he was in town seeing old friends, or trying to see if he could return to the bigger journalistic pond of the nation's capital. Not that his career there had been all that impressive. In fact, if memory served, Dan had left his job at the newspaper there because the editors wouldn't give him a byline and had him writing obituaries all week. Then again, it might have been that his own confrontation with Dan had been more upsetting than he realized. Hulet could be too small at times.

Jake returned to Max's information about Gaston Means and his theory about a Washington connection between the Morgan murder and the Harding administration. So, Means had been released from jail? Jake rubbed his jaw, remembered Max saying that Means had been sentenced to the federal penitentiary for violation of the liquor laws, but the scuttlebutt around D.C. intimated punishment for a far worse crime—testifying about Harding's Attorney General to the Senate Investigating Committee. If the rumors about publication of a possible Means manuscript were true...

He put the thought out of his mind for the moment as he spied Max's package. He felt like a kid at the sight. Part of him wanted to wait for Christmas to open it so that Jenny could see whatever it was. Part of him wanted to tear off the wrapping immediately. It seemed years had passed since last Christmas. He stood looking down at the package. *What the heck?* He picked it up again. He'd known immediately, from the weight and the shape of the package, that it was a painting. He tore through the paper, tossing it carelessly onto the floor. *Yes!* It was an original Maxwell Howe, reminiscent of Winslow Homer, but, to his mind, better, much better. It depicted the Mall in spring. He could almost smell the blossoms. He stood looking at the painting for a long time while memories cascaded.... He put down the painting and walked to the telephone.

"Max? It's Jake. If it's all right, I'm leaving for your place tomorrow—"

"Tomorrow?"

"No later than the day after. Is the invitation still open for Christmas?"

"Always!"

"Good. Arrange the other matter for me. I'll telephone you as soon as I arrive."

Bertha knew something was wrong the moment she saw Jenny's face. Her eyes and nose were red. It was obvious she'd been crying. Her instincts were to comfort, but her instincts had been wrong before.

"Bertha, have you seen those aprons I needed to wash? I swear I don't know where my mind is today..."

Bertha stared intently at the chicken she was boning and kept her back to Jenny:

"Aprons? Seems to me you had them when you left to answer the telephone—"

"Of course! I left them on the landing...the *landing*, of all places..." Turning abruptly she left the kitchen.

There they sat, exactly where she'd left them, her dirty laundry in full view of anyone passing by. Her nose stung as she bent down to retrieve the pile of soiled aprons and sodden dishcloths. The lump reformed in her throat. She swallowed hard as she gathered the items close to her chest, turned the knob on the basement door, bumped it open with her hip, and descended into the cool damp of the winter laundry room.

The water was just boiling. Steam hung like cobwebs in the air. She dumped her burden on the ground beside the tub, poured in the water and soap, and added the laundry, stirring and poking it into the water with a broken broom handle until every piece was submerged. While they soaked, and the water cooled enough for her to use the washboard, she removed a previous load from the rinse water, carefully feeding each item through the wringer. She watched for items that tended to curl around the wringer, instead of dropping nicely into the wicker basket beneath. This done, she drained the used water from the rinse tub, and refilled it with cold water and bluing for the load of whites, which were now soaking.

She reached into the basket and procured a damp dress. She hung the clothespin bag onto the taut line that stretched the length of the basement and began the tedious chore of hanging the cleaned clothes. A sharp pain poked under her right shoulder blade as she held one end of the heavy dress and clipped it to the line with a wooden pin. In a way, she was grateful: she could identify and deal with the pain in her back. The pain in her heart was more difficult.

She put the last clothespin on the dress, fixing it to the line, and reached for the next item. A brief hour earlier she'd been as happy as she was miserable now. An hour ago she'd been planning the Christmas party at Jake's, going over the guest list in her head, as she scrubbed laundry, rinsed it, and hung it up to dry. Now the task was the same, but the joy had gone out of it with the telephone call. How *could* he do this? *What could be so important in Washington that he'd leave without giving me any more notice than this?* His words kept repeating in her head—'I don't know when I'll be back home. It'll be after Christmas, though, I'm afraid'—*After Christmas!* After all their planning, after all her excitement—*After building up my hopes for a real Christmas,* she thought. *It's not just missing the chance to have a party, or to celebrate with friends after all these years…it's…being abandoned. Again. It's too much!* The lump in her throat became a boulder too big to swallow. She slumped against the damp laundry and sobbed.

CHAPTER

TWENTY-ONE

Maxwell Howe's Georgian-style townhouse felt like home after the past week's sojourn in New York City. The imposing front entrance, framed with cedar and fir greenery, its double doors adorned with matching wreaths sporting pinecones and fruit, was elegantly festive. In perfect accord with its owner and the season, Jake thought, as he paid the cab driver at the curb and picked up his bag. The door opened before he reached the top of the stairs:

"It is about time you arrived," Max said, "I was about to begin without you." He turned to address the butler:

"Smithers, take Mr. Witherspoon's things to his room and unpack for him, please." (Smithers inclined his head, took Jake's bag, and left for the central staircase and the largest guest room, while Max led the way to the living room.)

"How *dare* you leave me hanging on Christmas!"—Max scowled at Jake in partial jest as they walked across the black and white tile squares of the entrance hall—"Do you *realize* the dinner party I have planned to celebrate? Another hour and you would have had no time to dress for the occasion, certainly no time to open your gifts—"

"Gifts?" Jake raised one eyebrow. "I thought we discussed this before I left."

"You discussed. I merely listened." Max gestured toward the huge, noble fir tree dominating the living room. "What do you think of my tree?"

"It's wonderful. When did you have time to do all this?" Jake asked, his admiration obvious.

"I *always* put up my tree the night before Christmas Eve. I had hoped you would help, but…" Max shrugged his shoulders, took a silver shaker from the top of the bar counter, shook it, and poured the contents into two martini glasses. "Here."

"You know why I wasn't here," Jake said, accepting the cocktail Max held out to him—"Thanks."

"Well, sit down, and tell me all the details." Max sat down in his favorite chair and looked at his gold pocket watch. "I think we should leave the gifts until later this evening, after the dinner guests leave. Does that meet with your approval?"

"Anything you say, Max." Jake sipped his drink. "How much time do I have before this party begins?"

"Two hours. I never have dinner served earlier than eight o'clock. You know that."

"How many are coming?"

"Six others. You know them all. They should arrive for drinks at seven. I should think that gives you ample time to relate what Gaston Means had to say."

Jake settled back into the cushions of the sofa. A fire crackled on the hearth, greenery ornamented the occasional brass sconces, their candles lending a soft, golden glow to the wood paneled room. A plush wool carpet covered the floor in warm, deep red. From where he sat, it was difficult to believe that three feet of snow buried the ground outside and even more clogged the streets of New York. The truth was that he was exhausted, not only physically, but emotionally as well. Yet Max's question and its answer filled him with excitement. He was beginning to make some sense of this puzzle.

"I am waiting," Max reminded him. "Of course, if you would rather not confide…?"

"Max!" Jake said in utter disgust. "Do me the courtesy, and *very* great favor, of dropping the dilettante persona while we are alone. I don't mind when others are present, I understand the need, but please, *not* when we're alone. Agreed?"

A huge grin spread across Max's face, obliterating the mask. "Agreed. It becomes a habit you know, and I have to admit, I have acquired a soft spot for the old boy."

They both laughed, as Max got up from his overstuffed chair and made his way back to the wet bar, hidden at opportune times by a faux bookcase which closed like a cabinet over the offending supplies. "How about another?"

"One more. But that's it." Jake rose reluctantly from the sofa, crossed to Max—"You don't want me to make an ass of myself in front of your company."

"Of course not." Max filled Jake's glass, his own, garnished each with two stuffed olives, and handed Jake his replenished glass. "You *are* going to fill me in?"

"Of course I am. Do you want the blow-by-blow or the important highlights version?" Jake resumed his seat on the sofa. Max sat in the chair adjacent.

"We do not have time for the blow-by-blow, you have to get cleaned up for dinner, just give me the highlights. I assume they warranted a mid-winter trip to New York?"

"I think so. I spoke to your publishing contact, as you know. She arranged for the meeting with Gaston Means.

"I must confess, if I were not familiar with my side of the facts, his story, though fascinating, would not have the truthful ring that it does."

"Means *is* a character," Max agreed. "There never was any doubt about that. But in this, when he has little to gain and much to lose, I tend to believe him. And I, too, am coming from corroborating facts, as you know."

Jake nodded, took the cocktail pick out of his martini and slid an olive into his mouth. "These are Means's intriguing pieces. Whether or not they'll fit into my puzzle remains to be seen..."

"Go on. I am, as they say, all ears."

Jake set his drink on a coaster on the table between them. "The first thing that intrigued me was his chauffeur—"

"His chauffeur?"

"Evidently one of the perquisites Means enjoyed in the Justice Department's employ was the use of a chauffeured limousine. The driver was one Josef Andersen, a taciturn Scandinavian immigrant—"

"Not a citizen?"

"Naturalized while he was in Means's employ as a matter of fact."

"So what makes this man so interesting?"

"Remember our conversation about the Runyon murder?"—(Max nodded)—"My investigator has uncovered evidence that Runyon was perhaps an alias. He used another name in Kansas City—Joseph Andersen."

"Aha."

"Means also told me the same things you mentioned when I was involved in the Morgan murder case—"

"The one you were trying when Laura…?"

"Exactly. He was adamant that Jesse Smith's death had been a murder, *not* a suicide. He mentioned Smith's meticulous and detailed records of supposedly illegal transactions authorized and encouraged, if not ordered, by Daugherty. Millions are still unaccounted for, according to Means, not only from Smith's own ill-gotten estate, but also from monies he—Means—collected at the express instruction of President Harding's Attorney General. The will Smith told Means about the night before he died has never been found either."

"So?"

"One thing at a time. This is not exactly a straight line of investigation."

"So it seems."

"When Means was told to clean up the scene of Smith's death—"

"I remember. Go on."

"Do you also remember that Means was told to pick up a man at such-and-such a corner in Washington and drive him to Harper's Ferry?"

"Vaguely."

"Well, he did pick up this man—Means gave me a detailed description—and he picked him up in—"

"Of course. The limousine. The chauffeur was driving, I assume?"

"Exactly."

"So Andersen, who is Runyon, actually saw the man—"

"Who Means thinks was the former Attorney General's hit man for Jesse Smith, and who knows who else...?"

Max sat back in his chair, twirled his glass slowly by the stem and thought. "It certainly gives one a reason to do away with the unfortunate chauffeur, if...?"

"That was my thought. Why bother, if all he knows is that you are a passenger in his employer's car?"

"So Andersen must have found something to link the passenger to the murder of Jesse Smith—"

"Or to something equally as threatening."

Max sat up, leaned closer. "What would that be?"

Jake shook his head, shrugged. "I'm not sure I know yet, but I'm fairly certain that this reaches far beyond Smith's murder and graft—"

"What else have you discovered?"

"Just that the victim in the Little Rock murder, Clarence Morgan, was the only person on the signature card for a safety deposit box registered to a J. Smith. That our man Andersen showed up with an apparently empty carpetbag for an unscheduled appointment with Morgan just before his murder occurred—Morgan's former secretary swears that Andersen's carpetbag seemed full when he left her boss's office."

Max whistled softly. "What else?"

"I don't have all the pieces yet. But it looks like Andersen then changed his name to Runyon, and he and his wife traveled for a while before showing up in Fort Smith, Arkansas, where they purchased the property outside Hulet. With cash. The man who handled the transaction remembers that Runyon kept the cash in a carpetbag. Coincidence?"—Jake shrugged, ate his last olive—"They moved to the place near Hulet shortly afterwards. Runyon was murdered there last summer."

"Six years. It took Smith's murderer *six years* to track the chauffeur?"

"Not necessarily. He may have known Runyon's whereabouts all the time but—"

"But until the financial transaction, the contact with Morgan—"

"That's what I think."

"All right. My curiosity is piqued—"

"Excuse me, Mr. Howe." Smithers stood in the archway separating the entry and the living room.

"Yes. What is it?"

"You asked me to call you an hour before the guests are to arrive."

Max and Jake both stood: "Thank you, Smithers. Is Mr. Witherspoon unpacked?"

(Jake finished the rest of his drink.)

"Yes, sir. I took the liberty of laying out Mr. Witherspoon's evening clothes. Your baths are drawn and ready."

"Very good. Thank you, Smithers," Max said, watching as Smithers left the room. "Now I regret planning this infernal party..."

Jake clapped his friend on the back as they walked toward the entrance hall: "Well, don't. I'm in a convivial mood, and I'm starving. Frankly, I'm tired of thinking about this whole mess. It's all I've done for weeks. I could stand a break for an evening."

"I suppose so," Max said, as they climbed the central staircase to the second floor. He stopped abruptly—"Aha!"

"What?"

"I *will* hear the end of your story! You will tell me the rest after the guests leave—Christmas, you know. We still have not opened our gifts! Now, I can be a congenial host without wishing my guests were engaged elsewhere. See you downstairs," he said, turning left at the top of the landing.

Jake shook his head in amusement as he watched his friend disappear into his rooms. Then he turned in the other direction, grateful for Smithers's efficiency and the hot bath that waited.

CHAPTER
TWENTY-TWO

J enny put her book down and listened. It sounded like someone knocking
on the cafe door. *Can't they read?* she thought. *We're closed.* The knocking
persisted. Sighing heavily, Jenny checked her face in the mirror, resigned
herself, and went downstairs to see who needed to see her so badly that they'd
come to her door. The thought occurred that it might be Jake, but her heart
didn't even so much as flutter. He hadn't telephoned since he'd left town; she
no longer leapt at the sound of it ringing.

She peeked over the banister as she descended the staircase, trying to see
who was bothering her. It looked like a woman. As Jenny drew closer to the
door, the woman stepped to the window, cupped her hands around her face
and peered in, then drew back at once. The woman's face was unfamiliar.

Jenny unlocked the Dutch door, but only opened the top section: "I'm
sorry. We're not open. The cafe's closed for the holidays."

"Please. I've driven all the way from Little Rock to surprise a friend of
mine. I can't find his house, and I haven't found so much as a cup of coffee all
day. Could I just come in for a moment and get warm? If you have anything...
I'd pay a lot for a cup of coffee about now."

Jenny's inclination was to shut the door in her face. In the first place the
cafe was closed: What nerve to ask her to open just because *she* was lost! In the
second place, there was something about her Jenny just didn't like. From the
bright red lipstick and heavily applied eye makeup, to the closely bobbed hair,

rolled down hose, and the shortest skirt and coat that Jenny had ever seen, everything screamed "flapper," in the worst sense of the word. She was beautiful, but in a hard sort of way. Jenny moved to close the door: "I'm sorry. I can't help you—"

"Then could you tell me how to find Jake Witherspoon's house?"

Jenny stopped: "Just a moment." She secured the top of the door, opened the whole thing, and stood back. "Come in."

The woman smiled—it was not warm—and strode confidently past Jenny into the cafe's waiting area. "I see Jake's name still opens doors," she said, looking around as if appraising her surroundings. She found them wanting. "Where may I put my coat?"

Jenny wanted to tell her to keep it on, she'd be leaving immediately, but she had to find out what business this woman had with Jake. "I'll take it."

"Thanks." She removed her hat, gloves, coat, and handed them all to Jenny. While Jenny hung up her coat, the woman walked into the dining room, surveyed the tables, chose a booth by the window, and sat down.

Jenny walked over to the booth, sat down opposite her, and reached her hand across the table. "I'm Jenny Schumacher. I own this cafe."

"My name's Mary Landower," she said, squeezing Jenny's hand briefly. "Do you know Jake?"

Jenny squirmed uncomfortably at the obvious familiarity. "Oh, yes. I know Mr. Witherspoon quite well. We're old friends."

"Really?" Mary's eyes raised and lowered. "Funny. I don't remember Jake's mentioning a Jenny Shoe—I'm sorry. I've forgotten your last name."

In a pig's eye you have —"Schumacher. It's a German name."

"How nice. You don't sound German...?"

"It's my married name—"

"Oh!"—Mary's demeanor changed dramatically—"You're married!"

Jenny started to correct her, then thought better of it. "I really don't have much to offer you, Mrs...."

"*Miss.* Not all of us are as fortunate as you are, Mrs. Schumacher. Sometimes I think all the really good men are already taken—"

"Really?" Jenny forced a smile. "As I was saying, Miss Landower, I'm not prepared for company. The cafe's been closed since Christmas Eve and won't reopen until January second."

"If you could just fix me a cup of coffee? A sandwich would be heaven! Anything at all..."

Her smile is positively Machiavellian, Jenny thought, wondering that Will's interest in that man could finally be put to use in describing a woman, much less a woman sitting in one of her cafe booths! What could she have to do with Jake? *Well, I'm not going to find out unless I ask:* "I'll make some coffee. Why don't you come with me, and we'll see what I can find for you to eat?"

"You're *too* kind!"

That remains to be seen. "This way," Jenny said, leading the way to the kitchen.

She turned on the light and got a coffeepot out of a cupboard. (Mary had already made herself at home.)

Jenny found the coffee beans in the pantry, measured some into the grinder, and ground it to her liking.

"How is it that you know Jake Witherspoon?" Jenny asked, as she put the ground coffee into the pot.

"We used to work together." Mary lit a cigarette, looked around the room. "Could I have an ashtray?"

"I'll have to get one from the other room."

"Don't bother. Here," Mary picked up a saucer, tapped her ashes into it, "I'll just use this."

Jenny filled the coffeepot with water and put it on the stove. "Coffee will be ready in just a minute...You were telling me how you and Jake met?"

"Was I?" Mary grinned knowingly, took a drag on her cigarette, blew the smoke out in little rings. "I really shouldn't tell you about Jake and me...but, just between us girls, it was *hot* stuff. *Hot.* You know what I mean?"

"I'm not sure I do." Jenny busied herself getting two cups and saucers from the cabinet.

"I was his legal assistant in Little Rock during a very important case. He represented the defendant. As you can imagine, we were together a lot, and one thing led to another..." she let her voice trail off suggestively.

"And?"

Mary laughed. "Details, huh? I don't blame you. It must get pretty boring in this burg. I bet *nothing* happens around here. I'd go nuts if I had to stay here very long. How do you do it?"

"I manage. And it's not as dull as you think. Sometimes it's quite interesting—"

"Well, that sure describes Jake. Maybe this town fits him more than I thought it did."

"What do you mean?"

"Just that Jake's like that, too—all upright and gentlemanly on the surface, but underneath, he's all wolf."

"When did you say you worked with Mr. Witherspoon?"

"Five years ago—oh, I get it! You're thinking about his wife, aren't you? Were you friends with her or something?"

"I never met the woman."

"Whew! That's a relief! I mean it'd be just like me to be talking about my sexy fling with Jake and be telling his wife's best friend or something... My mouth is always getting me into trouble like that."

"Surely not."—Jenny opened the icebox—"Cream?"

"Why not?" Mary stood up, put her right foot up on the chair and adjusted her hose before doing the same with her left.

"Sometimes fashion can be a downright pain, don't you think?" She stretched her arms over her head, rolled her neck from side to side before sitting down again. "The one thing I like about it now is that I don't have to wear all that restricting underwear anymore. Didn't you just *hate* that stuff?"

"Here's your coffee and cream. Do you take sugar?"

"Not really. I do if the coffee's not any good. The office coffee when I worked with Jake was just like *tar*. I piled in the sugar back then, but a girl's got to watch things like that. You could get fat, lose your figure. Men don't like fat on women. Jake liked me because he said I was soft without being fat—"

"Did he?"

"Oh, yes. I think his wife had let herself go. Don't you think it's usually the wife's fault when the husband starts fooling around with other women? I do. I know if I ever marry again—"

"Again?"

Mary stared right at her. "I was married once."

"You're a widow?" Jenny found that hard to believe, but she was beginning to think anything was possible.

Mary put out her cigarette in the saucer. "Not exactly. Divorced."

Jenny drank her coffee, made no comment.

"I know what you're thinking..."

"Oh?"

"You're thinking it was because I had that affair, but you're wrong. I was single when Jake and I were hot and heavy. And *I* divorced *him*. He had it coming, too....Say, are you going to fix me a sandwich?"

"I don't seem to have anything, Miss Landower. I'm awfully sorry."

Mary shrugged, lit another cigarette. "It's all right. Hey, you didn't know anyone would be showing up today, so don't feel bad. You saved my life with this stuff, though. Good coffee."

"Thanks."

"So...can you tell me how to get to Jake's place?"

"I could, but I'm afraid it won't be of much help. He's out of town."

"Out of town! Well, do you know when he's coming back?"

"I haven't the faintest idea. I don't believe he knew when he'd return."

"Where'd he go?"

"I'm afraid I can't help you there, either."

"Well,"—she reached into her bag, pulled out a memo pad and a pen, started writing—"I'll just leave this with you, if that's all right. If you'd see that he gets it when he returns?"—she held the note out to Jenny who took it—"I know he'll want to see me. It's my address and telephone exchange.

Tell him I still live in Little Rock, and I'd love to hear from him...*any* time. Be sure to tell him I was here, won't you?"

"I promise. I will tell him all about our visit as soon as I hear from him."

"Great! Thanks so much." She stood. "Well. I guess I'd better head back to Little Rock. It was nice to meet you, Mrs. Schumacher. You're a real nice lady. If you ever get sick of living in this one-horse town, look me up. I think we'd get along great! Oh. I guess you're stuck here, huh, what with your husband and all? Oh, well. Who knows what the future will bring? Thanks for the coffee. I'll just get my coat and be on my way."

Jenny watched, her forehead pressed against the cafe window, until Mary's car disappeared from view. *She's worse than a tornado*, Jenny thought. *In one short afternoon she's managed to destroy all my illusions about Jake. What a fool I was to believe he cared...about anything.*

She straightened up, made her way back to the kitchen. The telephone rang. She walked past it without so much as glancing in its direction. The last thing she wanted to do at that moment was talk. She'd had enough talk to last her for a while.

Automatically, she ran the water in the sink, added soap, and cleaned the kitchen. The floor looked dirty, even though she'd mopped it the night before. *What it needs is a good scrubbing.* She rolled up her sleeves, got a bucket and a brush. She moved all the furniture she could manage out of the kitchen, swept the floor thoroughly. She filled the bucket with soapy water and got down on her hands and knees on the floor and started scrubbing. The pain in her back numbed the ache in her heart; the circular motions kept her mind occupied.

A full hour had passed and the floor was waxed and shining when her defenses began cracking, letting the doubts, the questions, the pain, the disillusionment out in a torrent of rage at the depth of his deception and betrayal, not only of her, but of his tragic family, which he had so poignantly claimed to have loved! All the while, behind their backs and hers, he was an adulterer and a liar. *And I have been a fool to think otherwise. I should have known. He cares for no one but himself. How could I have missed the signs? The unexplained absences, the trips to God-knows-where without any thought as to how he might be upsetting any-one else's plans. He's a liar! Billy tried to warn me. Dan tried to—Oh, Lord, what must he think of me?* She slumped onto a kitchen chair, rested her elbows on the table, and held her head in her hands.

Oh, my God, what if Dan is right and Jake is responsible for his family's death? Everything rebelled against the thought...but he *was* capable of violence. She'd seen it that night he forced himself into her apartment. Billy had wit-nessed that awful fight between him and Dan...Then there was that busi-ness about the calendars; the man had been out of touch with reality for years! How could she have ignored the evidence that this man was highly unstable, maybe even crazy? Hadn't he admitted he'd been in a mental hos-pital of some kind? *O God.*

CHAPTER
TWENTY-THREE

Jake returned to Max's living room, a puzzled expression on his face.

"What is the matter?" Max asked, looking up from the society section of the Saturday paper. "Do not tell me the future Mrs. Witherspoon has succeeded in perplexing you?"

Jake responded to his friend's teasing by lifting his eyebrows: "Why, Maxwell, if I didn't know better, I'd say you sounded a bit jealous."

"Not at all, thank you. I have all the female company I want. There are advantages to being the most eligible bachelor in Washington society, you know. A wife would definitely limit my options. I am surprised at how quickly you have forgotten. Sorry. That was not meant unkindly."

Jake laughed—"I know you better than that, Max, and I've never known you to have an *unintentional* slip of the tongue."

Max started to protest, but Jake stopped him mid-mutter: "I took no offense," Jake said, as he reclined on his favorite sofa. "There's no need to explain anything to me."

"Well then, explain it to *me*. What happened just now?"

A frown line formed above the bridge of Jake's nose. "Nothing really. It's just unusual for her to be out this time of day."

"She was not at *home*? *This* is what the look was for?"

"What look?"

Max sighed: "Never mind. The more I find out about this *affaire du coeur* of yours, the more confirmed I am about remaining permanently unattached. Call her again in an hour or two. She may be playing bridge—"

"Jenny doesn't play bridge." Jake bent over to pick up the business section of the paper that lay on the floor beside Max's chair.

"Pity. But I suppose you will remedy that deficiency in time...By the way, you never told me the rest of Gaston Means's information."

Jake opened the paper, scanned the articles— "I think I told you everything Christmas night, while we opened the gifts. By the way, I want you to know how much I appreciate the painting you sent to Hulet. You really are *quite* good, Max. I wish you'd own up to it and start signing your real name to your art. When I looked at the painting, I swear I could almost smell the cherry blossoms and feel the breeze coming off the Potomac!"

"Bushwa! I appreciate the praise, dear boy, undeserved though it may be, but I ask you...how would it look? There are those in this town who have made it their mission in life to question my masculinity. That I am a dabbler in paint would only give them far more tinder than I am willing to give. In my position, I must have the respect of the men with whom I deal. A dilettante is amusing—everyone has dreams of grandeur—but a man, seriously devoted to art, is quite another matter in the circles in which I move. As you know.

"And *you're* wrong, you know,"—Jake raised his head from his paper— "You *never* told me what this mysterious man looks like. For all we know, I may have seen him in my travels."

Jake glanced at the bottom of the page, closed the paper. "That would be more luck than anyone's entitled to, don't you think?"

"I *do* get around. Nothing is impossible in this business, so tell me what you know. Who knows? I may be able to trace his identity for you."

"All right, although the description Means gave me could fit just about anyone. Then there's the fact that six years have passed. Disguises. He could have dyed his hair, grown a mustache, a beard...?"

"He could be dead?" Max added, rolling his eyes in disgust.

"I don't think so," Jake said, missing Max's sarcasm. "I think he's alive, well, and still in the murder and mayhem business."

"All the more reason to give me his description..."

"I hate to disappoint you, Max, but this man is about five-feet-ten inches tall—give or take an inch, according to Means, who thought he might have been wearing some kind of boot because of the weather that night—"

"Go on."

"The usual: brown hair, brown eyes, stocky build..." Jake's voice trailed off.

"No distinguishing marks, scars, tattoos?"

"None that he saw. Remember Means only saw this man at night, fully clothed. They didn't exactly trade war stories over drinks."

"Good idea!" Max reached behind the chair and pulled the bell rope. "The sun crossed over the yardarm hours ago."

Smithers appeared in the archway. "You rang, sir?"

"Yes. Mr. Witherspoon and I would like—What *would* you like, Jake? A martini?"

"No. Not tonight. A bourbon and water, please, Smithers."

"I'll have Scotch over ice, Smithers—I believe we're out of ice at the bar."

"I'll see to it right away, Mr. Howe. Is there anything else you would like?"

"Cheese and crackers sound good—" he looked at Jake who nodded agreement—"Fine. Bring us the drinks and have Cook fix us an assortment of cheeses, anything she thinks might hold us until dinnertime."

"Yes, sir." Smithers inclined his head and left to perform his tasks.

"I'm getting spoiled with all of this attention, Max. You're making it very difficult to leave."

"Then don't. New Year's Eve is barely two days away. Why not stay and ring in the New Year with me?"

"I couldn't, Max. Jenny would kill me if I missed spending Christmas with her, and then left her alone on New Year's Eve."

"Then you're set on leaving tomorrow?"

"Dead set." Jake glanced at his pocket watch. "I think I'll try to ring her up again before dinner."

"Go right ahead. You interrupted me just as I was starting Winchell's column." (Jake got up and started out the door.) "You know, Jake, something funny just occurred to me."

Jake stopped in the doorway——"What?"

"That description *does* fit a lot of men."

"So?"

"It could fit a lot of people I know or am acquainted with. It even fits your former brother-in-law, now that I think about it——"

"I'm calling Jenny." Jake turned to leave, but thought better of it: "Whatever else Dan Johnson may be, Max, I *don't* think he's capable of murder. Besides, when Jesse Smith was murdered, he was still overseas. He moved from there to Arkansas——a few months after we moved to Hulet, remember?" He smiled, "Tell Smithers I'll be back before my ice melts."

Jake was starting to replace the receiver when he heard her voice on the line: "Hello, honey! Surprised?" He sat down at Max's desk, leaned back in the well-padded leather chair, and prepared to enjoy the conversation. "I phoned earlier, but I suppose you were out——"

"I was here."

"Why didn't you answer?"

"I wasn't in the mood to talk."

"Is something wrong, honey? Are you tired? Sick?"

"Actually, Jake, it's all three: Something is most definitely wrong. It's made me sick at my stomach, and I am very, *very* tired...and, another thing: don't call me honey."

Jenny's tone took him completely off guard. He had been prepared to eat some humble pie for not calling until now; he had expected her to be irritated with his absence, but this didn't sound like irritation. Something like fear began in the pit of his stomach.

"Jenny, I'm sorry I didn't call sooner. I missed you terribly on Christmas Day. I was in New York City on business, and when I returned to Max's, he'd planned a dinner party. I had to clean up and help Max entertain the guests. Afterwards, it was too late to telephone." (He could hear her breathing. She was still on the line at least.) "I know you're disappointed about the Christmas party—"

"Is *that* what you think I'm talking about? You're wrong. I *was* disappointed after all the plans we had made for Christmas—I don't like being told five minutes before you leave that you're leaving. I don't think I'm strange in that. I think what you did was rude, uncaring, and selfish. But that's not why I'm upset, now. Believe me, in comparison to what I know now, your behavior over Christmas seems trivial—"

"What *are* you talking about? What else could I have possibly done? I can't imagine what has upset you so—"

"Imagine a woman named Mary Landower."

The name knocked the wind out of him with the force of a physical blow. His mind reeled. He couldn't think.

"Nothing to say? Smart. There's nothing *to* say, is there, Jake? Unless you'd like to explain how you could say the things you did on Thanksgiving—how you loved Laura and your children *so* much, how you were *wracked* with guilt! You should be, but I doubt it somehow.

"What I want to know is *why*? Why would you want someone like that? She's pretty all right, even beautiful, but she's nothing but a tramp! And don't try to deny the affair. Miss Landower was only too happy to fill me in on all the hot—her word—details of your sordid little fling.

"Want to know the funniest part? For one second she was afraid she'd said too much. She thought I might have been your wife's friend'"—she struggled not to cry—"Know what? I wish I *had* known Laura. Her life with you must've been horribly lonely. She probably needed a friend—"

"That's enough!"—Jake fought to speak through the anger—"I've listened to you berate me, call me things I don't deserve—"

"Don't you? Don't you deserve *anything* you get?"

Suddenly all his anger vanished. He felt drained and overwhelmingly sad: "Don't do this, Jenny. I love you."

"I guess that's too bad for you then. You *lied* to me, Jake, and not about something unimportant. When I think of how wretched I felt when I heard your *tragic* story. How *heroic* I thought you were to search for the truth, to avenge their deaths with it!

"What a *fool* I was to believe in you, so incredibly gullible. I thought we were *close*. I just found out: I don't even know who you *are*." Her hands shook as she slammed the receiver back in its hook. She couldn't stop shaking. *God, please don't let me have to talk to him again.*

The telephone rang, jarring her. *I won't answer it. There's nothing more to say.* The bell kept ringing until she thought she'd lose her mind if it rang one more time. Anger welled up, forced her to answer—"I'm *telling* you—"

"Jenny? It's me. It's Dan. Are you all right?"

"Dan? Thank *God*."

"I'm coming over." He didn't wait for her answer. It had not been a question.

Max's laughter at Winchell's sardonic wit died as soon as Jake walked into the room. He rose from his chair and went to his friend who looked like he might collapse at any second. "My *God*, Jake! What has happened? Is it Jenny?"

Jake managed a wan smile. "It most definitely *is* Jenny. *She's* fine. It's the relationship that's dead."

"Probably nothing more than a lover's spat. Here," Max brought Jake his drink, "you look as if you need it. Calm yourself and think a minute. Women are emotional creatures. Who *knows* what goes on in their minds? In my experience these things have a habit of blowing over eventually. I cannot imagine this being anything truly serious."

Jake sat, downed his bourbon, and looked at the ice: "No, Max. This is serious. It's over, and there's absolutely nothing I can do about it."

The color had drained from Jake's face. He seemed to age almost as he spoke. *No,* Max thought, whatever happened between them, *this was not the usual lover's quarrel.*

Max pulled the bell rope to summon Smithers. When he appeared he asked him to bring in some ice, the bourbon and Scotch and leave them. After Smithers had left to comply, Max tried once more: "Would it help you to tell me about it?"

"I don't know. Part of me wants to tell *someone*——"

"Jake, for heaven's sake! I have been your friend for nearly thirteen years. Surely by now you know I can keep a confidence?"

"It's not that. I'd trust you with my life, Max. You know that——"

"Then what is it?"

"I don't want to lose your friendship."

"I do not think, after everything we have been through, that that is bloody likely, do you?" Max smiled, trying to make him see the fallacy in his reasoning.

Smithers entered bearing a tray.

"Cook fixed these appetizers for you instead of the cheese and crackers, Mr. Howe. She said she had not realized our supply was so low. She apologized and hoped these would do——boiled shrimp and stuffed mushrooms. Shall I freshen your drinks, gentlemen?"

"We will fix our own drinks for now, Smithers. Tell Cook these will do nicely. I trust dinner will be at eight?"

"Yes, sir. I'll just leave these things with you then." Smithers set the things in order on the bar and left the room.

"What do you think of me, Max?" Jake asked, as he poured bourbon into his glass, added a splash of water from a silver pitcher.

"What do you want to know?" Max smiled and stirred his Scotch and ice with a swizzle stick.

"Do you think I'm a liar?"

"Good Lord, no! Is that what Miss Schumacher thinks? That you are a liar?" Max drank from his drink——"She must be raving mad."

"No, Max. She's right."—(Max choked on his Scotch)—"Are you all right?"—(Max coughed, nodded, tried to regain his breath)—"You're sure?"

Max coughed again, cleared his throat: "Ah. Do not ever do that again… All right. Start at the beginning. Have you always been a liar? Or is this a recent development?" Max said it lightly, but Jake's expression froze the smile on his face.

"I don't know. Perhaps you can tell me."

"What *are* you talking about?"

"The night Laura and the children died in the fire, there was a freak snowstorm in Little Rock. I told myself it was dangerous to drive home in a virtual blizzard. I had missed a taxi, and my legal assistant offered me a ride to my hotel. I called Laura and told her I couldn't get home that night. She was upset, but you remember Laura…? She never complained, just made the best of everything. She had a knack for overlooking anything wrong that I did." Jake paused a moment.

"Do you know, that in all the time we were married, she never *once* said I was selfish, uncaring, insensitive—"

"Were you?"

"Jenny said so. Tonight—"

"Well, she was upset—"

"True. Rightly so, I'm afraid. I'm also afraid her words rang too true for me to ignore."

Neither one said anything for a moment. Then Max ventured a question: "May I ask what upset Jenny so?"

"The night that Laura died, I could have driven home earlier. The truth is I didn't want to leave right away."

"Oh?"

"My assistant, the one who offered to drive me to the hotel…?" (Max nodded) "I neglected to mention a salient point…"

"Which is?"

"Her name is Mary Landower, and five years ago, she was a very attractive, very…*willing* young woman." Jake dropped his head into his hands, avoiding Max's eyes. "Technically—as a lawyer I often rely upon these help-ful technicalities—I did not engage in intercourse with the young woman—"

"My God, Jake..."

"Don't interrupt me, Max. I don't think I'm capable of repeating this." Jake lifted his head, picked up his glass.

"Believe me, I've gone over this a million times in my head, asking my-self the same question over and over again: Why? I didn't love the girl. The thought of messing around with her had never occurred to me before that evening. Even that evening the attraction seemed almost... hidden...until it was too late.

"That's also a lie. It wasn't too late even then to stop it. I could've sent her to her room before anything happened."

"Then what is the truth? Why didn't you?"

Jake lifted his eyes, looked into Max's—"God help me, I don't know."

Max sipped his drink. "Am I to assume that Jenny found out about this... slip...of yours?"

Jake nodded. "I don't know how. I didn't think anyone knew. It only happened that one night, and that was five years ago..." He shook his head: "I don't suppose it matters now. The only thing is that Jenny seemed to think that we'd had some kind of ongoing affair, and, Max, I *swear* that was not the case."

"So she thinks you betrayed Laura, and if Laura, what would keep you from doing the same to her...? I see."

"That's not all." (Max's eyes looked weary as he returned Jake's gaze.) "She holds me responsible for Laura and the children's deaths—"

"Bushwa! How could she make that kind of leap? I think you have estab-lished your whereabouts at the time of the accident." Max downed his drink, got up abruptly, and went to fix himself another.

"The thing is," Jake continued, "I think the same thing. I think that's why I couldn't remember anything for so long. I didn't want to face—" Jake stood and joined Max at the bar. This time he didn't bother adding water to the bourbon.

Max returned to his seat, stirring his drink absentmindedly, "OK, I think I can speak rationally about this now.

"To answer your original question—what do I think of you? Granted, this information does not fit my original conception or description of you. However…, I have never known *one* perfect mortal in my life, and I am fast approaching the venerable age of sixty. What you did was wrong. What makes it worse—for you—is that you truly loved your wife. I know that. And I am convinced that Laura knew that, too. It must have been agony….

"The other thing I know about you is that you have always been in control—"

"What do you mean? Me? In control?"

Max nodded: "As long as I have known you, Jake, you have had to be on top of things, be the leader, the one in the know, the one in charge. In short, the one controlling the strings. From what you say, five years ago, you were no longer in control—"

"Are you saying I have no guilt, because I couldn't control my *sexual* urges?"

"Heavens no! Do not be absurd! I am not a priest. I am not here to absolve you, or to preach to you about your sinful behavior!" Max rose, began pacing—"Perhaps I should ask you what you think of me? I would be surprised if you came *close* to knowing who I really am….

"All of us have a shadow man dogging our steps that we cannot shake, no matter how hard we try. He reminds us at our best that we are not as good as we appear to be; he bites at our heels with guilt when we find ourselves behaving far beneath our own expectations. That is the human condition. That is why we yearn so for redemption." Max paused and looked directly at Jake.

"I cannot provide for your redemption, Jake, as much as I would like to. I cannot provide my own. I can only tell you this: that you will never be able to live with your shadow man until you tell yourself the truth, the whole truth…and, yes, nothing *but* the truth—I think you are familiar with the words. You need to understand their meaning…and practice it."

Max stopped pacing, walked to the bar, and picked up the appetizer tray. "I think we need to eat these. Cook apparently went to a lot of trouble."—He bent down, proffered the tray to Jake—"By the way, while you are deciding on your next move, may I make a suggestion?"

Jake took some shrimp, a mushroom, and avoided looking at his friend: "Why not?"

"Stay here for awhile. Cancel your train reservations for tomorrow. I trust your New Year's Eve plans have been revised...?"

"Are you certain you still want me to stay?"

"If I am one thing, Jake, it is that I am *not* a fair-weather friend. Your weather seems pretty foul at the moment. Besides, what are friends for?

"And, if you are wondering, I am fresh out of sermons for the duration. You will have to go to church to hear another."

"Thank you...Max?"—(Max was setting the tray back on the bar, and reviewing his choices)—"Are you sure you didn't miss your calling?"

CHAPTER
TWENTY-FOUR

The emotional toll of the last two hours left Jenny devoid of strength and grateful for Dan's presence. She had cried, yelled, poured out her anger, walked across five miles of kitchen floor, and had acted like a woman on the verge of nervous exhaustion. *I've been reduced to behaving like one of those inane women in dime novels. How can he sit there quietly listening, while I rant and rave like a demented idiot?* However he managed it, she was profoundly grateful. His calm reserve soothed the raw places on her heart like an ointment. He let her talk without interruption, and now there was no need to say more.

"Where's your tea kettle?" Dan's voice was like a bow drawing across a cello's middle register.

"Tea. What a good idea." She started to rise—

"No. Sit where you are. I'll fix the tea. I'm quite capable of boiling water...when I have something to put the water in. Just tell me where you keep your kettle." He smiled.

He looks so different when he smiles. "It's underneath that far cabinet, to the left of the stockpots—"

"Got it." He pulled the kettle out of its cupboard, filled it with water, lit the gas burner on the stove, and put the kettle on. "Now, if you'll just point out where you hide your tea?"

Jenny managed an amused chuckle, pointed to the canisters arranged on the northernmost counter. "There. The second one from the right."

Dan lifted the heavy wire spring that sealed the jar, sniffed: "Smells OK." He busied himself opening cabinets until he found a suitable teapot.

"I'm no connoisseur of tea, but I've drunk my share. The English swear by it, even regulate their days by it." (He measured tea into the pot as he spoke)—"I knew blokes during the war that stopped *fighting* at tea time. For a time like this, tea is mandatory."

"You were in the war?" Jenny asked, watching as he took charge of the tea preparation.

"I wasn't the only one, you know," he said, turning to grin at her briefly before he began searching for cups and saucers. "I don't suppose you have any cream?"

"A restaurant without cream? It's in the icebox. Where it should be."

She was beginning to feel better, more like herself. Her eyes still burned, but her headache was abating since she'd managed to calm down: "What did you do in the war?"

"What everyone else did—fought and tried to stay alive."

"You don't want to talk about it, do you?"

The kettle whistled softly. Dan waited until it screamed shrilly before removing it from the flame. He slid a metal spoon into the ceramic teapot, poured the boiling water onto the spoon—"The metal absorbs the heat just enough to keep the pot from cracking," he explained, as he saw her brow furrow. He removed the spoon, replaced the lid.

"The war wasn't what I thought it would be. It wasn't pretty." He paused. "No, I don't suppose I like talking about it. To be honest, I never think about it. It was the tea that made me remember England. I liked England."

"When were you there?"

Dan looked at her as he waited for the tea to steep: "During, and a bit after the war was over. I thought I might settle down there but ..."

"But?"

"I missed my sister."

"Laura?"

Dan nodded. "She was the only family I had left. Our folks died when Laura was still pretty young."

"You took care of her?"

"Yeah." Dan lifted the teapot lid, looked in: "It's ready. How do you take your tea?"

"I've never had tea in the English style before. Why don't you make mine like you like yours?"

"I like mine with sugar and cream."

"I usually have mine plain, but I'll try it your way."

"If you don't like it, say so. My ego isn't fragile."

Jenny grinned and took the cup and saucer he'd prepared. She took a tentative sip—"It's different, but I like it."

Dan pulled out the chair across the table from her and sat down. He tasted his own tea: "Not bad. It's hot anyway."

"It's quite good—really. And very much appreciated. It's just what I needed."

"Good."

"Dan, may I ask you something?"

"Ask away." He looked at her over the rim of the cup as he drank.

"I don't mean to pry, but…"

"But?"

"I don't think I can put this all behind me without understanding what you think of Jake—"

Dan set his cup down in the saucer; his voice changed tone, became harsh: "You don't want to hear what I think of him ."

"I wouldn't ask you—I know how painful it must be for you to talk about your sister—but I really do feel I need to understand."

"All right. Just remember, *you* asked me—" Dan got up, retrieved the teapot, refilled his cup, and refreshed Jenny's. "What do you want to know?"

"I suppose I want to know why you hold him responsible for Laura's death—"

"Who told you I did?" Dan's eyes narrowed. His face seemed to close up.

"Jake," she said, barely catching herself before betraying Billy.

"He would. Did he also tell you that he'd been receiving all kinds of threats warning him to drop that case he was working on? That he left Laura and the kids alone for weeks at a time? That she'd begged him to drop the case, because she was worried for their safety?"

"You mean his *family* had been threatened?"

"Surely you don't think *that* would've deterred him? He had a name to make, and that case had headlines written all over it. Can you imagine a better career-maker? It was a win for him either way. If his client—did you know he was defending a *nigger*—" he stopped at the look on Jenny's face— "Sorry. It's just that I get so angry...when I think of the consequences of his infernal pride!"

"Maybe you shouldn't talk about this. I didn't know how much it still upset you—"

"No. It's all right. Besides you need to understand some things..." he took a deep breath. "Where was I?"

"You were saying he had nothing to lose by defending...his client."

"Right. If Jake loses, then he can claim that he had no chance to get a just verdict for a...Negro man accused of killing a white man in the South. If he wins, he's a hero, who against all odds and with only altruistic motives—ha! Well, you get the general idea"—Dan leaned his chair back from the table— "The only thing he hadn't figured into his calculations was what it might cost his family. As it turned out..." Dan shrugged.

"You're telling me that Laura had *asked* him to quit the case and that he *knew* they might be in danger?"

"I'll try to be fair. It's not easy, you know. I don't think it ever penetrated his thick skull that a situation could arise that he couldn't handle. No. I don't think he took the threats seriously. As far as neglecting Laura and the children...?"

"He neglected them?"

Dan nodded, took another sip of his tea. "All the time. But I don't think he realized the seriousness of that either. I think he probably thought he'd make it up to them later. As it turned out, they didn't have the time."

Jenny let him alone with his thoughts, but then she remembered something: "Jake thinks they were murdered, that the fire was deliberately set. From what you say, so do you."

"Of *course* I think it was set!"

"Then why was there no further investigation? Why do Jake's partners think it was an accident?"

"Because they're stupid, and because they didn't *want* to find out who did it—"

"Why not?"

"How long have you been in the South?"

"I'm a Virginian. All my life."

"And I suppose you've never heard of the Ku Klux Klan?"

"I didn't think they were still active…"

Dan tipped his chair forward: "Trust me, Jenny. The Klan is still alive and well in Arkansas. I'd be willing to bet it's going strong in Virginia, too."

"So when a white woman and two children are murdered here, and the Klan is suspected, people just shut their eyes to it? That's not the Klan I've heard about—"

"Don't get me wrong! No one thinks the Klan wanted to murder Jake's family! They think it's just a horrible case of misinformation—"

"You think it was just a *mistake?*"

Dan stood abruptly—"It was a mistake all right, and Jake's the one who made it. None of this would've happened if he'd just done what he was told and dropped the whole damned mess!"

Jenny started to say something, but she didn't want to distress him any more. He was obviously upset. She could tell he was having difficulty controlling himself. She wanted to go to him, to comfort him. Something told her to stay right where she was and say nothing. She drank the rest of her tea. It was cold. She drank it anyway. Dan stood at the sink, his back to her.

I was right. This confirms everything I thought; Jake is, and always has been, concerned only with himself. Poor Dan! He's suffered so much! He's lost everyone in his family. And he's right about Jake: He could've done something to prevent their deaths. He could've been with them, protected them in some way! I've seen how he just blazes ahead, with no thought for the destruction it causes in other people's lives. I'm not going to pay for his ego with my life. He's going to have to live with the havoc he's wreaked, the agony he's caused in his own life through his own stupidity and arrogance, and he's going to have to do it without me!

"Did you say Jake thinks the fire was set?" Dan asked, without turning around.

Jenny sighed, rose, and walked toward him: "That's what he said, but it doesn't matter what he thinks——"

"What do you mean?" Dan turned to look at her.

"I mean I really don't care what that man thinks about anything."

"So you've seen the light?"

"I'm not sure that *light* is the word I'd choose ."

Dan shrugged, "Granted. Still, I'd like to hear what cock-and-bull theory he's put together to explain away what happened. But he probably doesn't have one. He's just speculating, trying to wriggle off the hook he's put himself on. I imagine it's getting downright uncomfortable about now, now that his memory has so *conveniently* returned." Dan stared out the back window to the shed behind the cafe and the barren winter landscape beyond.

"You're right about his theory being pretty far-fetched," Jenny said, looking out at the same landscape as she stood beside him. "He not only thinks someone murdered his family, but he also seems to think that the same person, or persons, murdered that man in Little Rock *and* that farmer who was killed sometime last summer. I can't remember his name, but I think his wife went crazy or something. Jake said they'd moved her out to his partner's place for her protection." (Jenny's lips pursed involuntarily as she remembered her concern when Jake had confided these things to her.)

"What?" Dan asked.

"Huh? Oh, nothing. It's just that he even tried to get me to believe that all these murders might be tied to some kind of government conspiracy"—she shook her head—"I can't believe what a fool I've been!"

Dan put his arm around her shoulders. "Don't feel alone. Jake Witherspoon fooled a lot of people for a long time. I'm just afraid it isn't over yet."

"No?"

"Government conspiracy? Who's he going to try to make his scapegoat now? The governor of Arkansas?"

Jenny grinned in spite of herself—"It's worse than that. He mentioned *Washington*."

"You *are* kidding?" Dan released her in his astonishment.

"I'm afraid I'm not."

Dan shook his head. "Maybe I shouldn't be angry with Jake anymore. He's crazy. He's gone completely off his rocker. I'm just glad you're no longer involved, Jenny. The way he's acting, I'd be worried about you," Dan looked into her eyes. "Maybe I'd better stick pretty close, keep an eye on you..."

"I think I'd like that."

He put his arm around her again. She let her head rest against his shoulder and felt the turmoil of the past weeks leave her. She was safe.

The new year was officially underway, and things were returning to a semblance of normality after the subdued holiday season. Though their friends feigned optimism, no one actually believed economic recovery was in sight. On the contrary, the Wall Street Crash of 1929 seemed to have repercussions that continued to ripple throughout the country. No one knew what the final toll would be. Privately, Jake mused on the enormous tidal wave that seemed to be crashing around his own head. Though his finances were intact, his plans—of love, marriage, enduring happiness with Jenny—were wiped out. Gone. If comparisons between the two events could be drawn, he thought, then the entire country soon would be inundated, overwhelmed by the flood of consequences about to rain down on it from October's Crash. After all, who could've imagined that his own misstep, a relatively minor one at that, could gain such momentum and hit with such force that it annihilated everything, *everyone*, he held dear?

"Mr. Witherspoon?"

Jake looked up to see Smithers standing beside him. He hadn't heard him enter the study—"Yes?"

"There's a telephone call for you, sir."

"For me?" *Jenny?* Jake looked around the room for the telephone. "Where do you want me to take the call, Smithers?"

"You can take the call in Mr. Howe's room, sir. He said you might require privacy."

That sounds hopeful...Good old Max, he thought, as he followed the butler to Max's suite.

Smithers withdrew, closing the door behind him, as Jake picked up the extension.

"Hello?"

"Jake, it's Ben. I need you to come back here right away." (Ben's voice sounded strained, ominous.)

"What's going on? Trouble?"

"You could say that. Someone made an attempt on Fanny Runyon's life last night—"

"Good God! Is she all right?"

"We really don't know—"

"What do you mean you don't *know*? Was anyone *hurt*?"

"She ran away. Her bodyguard was hit—"

"She *what*?"

"You heard me. Larry happened to arrive shortly after the attack. She was gone. He'll fill you in when you get here. How soon can you get back?"

"As soon as I can get a train out—"

"How about flying?"

"*Flying*? Did I hear you correctly?"

"Jake, I'm not kidding. I need you back, and I need you back now. Flying's the fastest way to get here—"

"Not if the fool thing crashes, it isn't—"

"It's not going to crash. You know what I'm up against here, Jake. It's not like Mike's any use."

"I'll see what I can do. I'll telephone you later."

"I'm at the office, but I'm shutting down early. Call me at home after six, OK?"

"OK."

Two hours later, thanks to Max's connections, Jake had managed to find and hire a Lockheed Vega with an experienced pilot to fly him to Arkansas the next day. They would leave from Washington, D.C., early in the morning and fly to Little Rock, with an hour's stop at Nashville, Tennessee, along the way to refuel. Jake arranged for Ben to pick him up at the airfield and drive him back to Hulet. To his relief his preparations for departure left no time to reflect on the dangers of flying cross-country in January, which Max assured him were grossly exaggerated.

His plane landed safely at the Little Rock airport early the next afternoon. The flight had been uncomfortable to say the least. The heater on board had done nothing to dispel the bone-chilling cold where he sat, and every inch of his body felt frozen solid. The flight itself put him in mind of a runaway buckboard he'd been on as a child. It was not an experience he wanted to repeat, but he was alive, relatively well, and safely back on terra firma.

"So how did you like flying?" Ben asked, as they drove away from the airfield.

Jake glared at him and put his hands closer to the heater: "I didn't fly back here to chat about the dubious benefits of aviation. I came back because you told me I was needed. Urgently. I assume that means you have something *urgent* to tell me. Talk."

"I don't know where to begin—"

"How about giving me the basics? You know. What happened? When, to whom, and, if you can, venture an opinion as to how and why this attack— that's what you said it was, I believe?"— (Ben nodded)—"why this attack occurred. I'd also like to know how they/he/she/it, or whoever found out where Mrs. Runyon was living—"

"So would I." Ben glanced across at Jake. "Strange, don't you think, that she's been there for months now and nothing? All of a sudden—*boom!*"

"Define boom." Jake's hands were beginning to thaw, but his toes remained frozen inside his shoes.

"According to what Larry told me, there were actual shots fired—"

"Good Lord! At whom? How many people did we have up there?"

"There is the nurse we hired to look after her——"

"How *is* Fanny's mental health these days?" Jake caught the look on Ben's face: "Sorry. Go on. But somewhere in the telling answer this one for me, all right?"

"If I can…As far as we know, Fanny seems to have been jolted out of her—whatever she was in—enough to scream something as she ran out of the cabin, anyway. Larry says the nurse swears she yelled, 'He's going to kill me,' or something to that effect. You can ask Larry her exact words when we get to the office."

"Well," Jake said, stretching his feet toward the warm air near the floorboard, "it sounds as if she's cognizant. She at least realized someone was after her."

"Exactly, and it sounds like she might have recognized the man." Ben looked over at Jake who whistled softly in response.

"What makes you think that?"

"Larry said the nurse and bodyguard both said she went nuts as soon as she saw the guy——"

"He was in the place?"

Ben shook his head. "No. Neither of the others in the house got a clear look at him. In fact, it was Fanny's screams that scared him off with only the guard being wounded."

"OK. Tell me again. Who was there at the time?"

"The evening bodyguard and the nurse, and Fanny, of course. Larry arrived about ten minutes after it happened. The bodyguard had been shot, Fanny was gone, and the nurse was shaken but trying to keep the guard from bleeding to death. Larry called an ambulance and the local police——"

"How much do they know?"

"Not much. They bought Larry's cover story—you'll love this Jake. He told them Fanny was his aunt, that she had had a nervous breakdown, and that he'd hired the nurse and the bodyguard to look after her, since he worked out of town. He told them he thought the water, the peaceful setting, might help her regain her mental balance. He said someone had tried to break in and had attacked them in the cabin and had caused a relapse. She'd run into the woods during the confusion. Could the police help him find her? He was concerned for her safety."

"They bought this?"

Ben grinned. "Hook, line, and sinker. Most of it's true, of course. The guard and the nurse corroborated his story. They had been told much the same thing when we hired them. As far as they were concerned, Fanny Runyon *was* Larry's aunt. Her precarious mental state was undeniable.

"When they questioned the guard, he said he'd glimpsed the intruder just as he realized he'd been shot. The nurse didn't see a thing. She heard the shots, heard Fanny screaming something about someone trying to kill her, and then everything went black—"

"She was hit?"

"It looks like Fanny might have knocked her into something in her panic to get out."

Jake leaned forward: "The guard saw the attacker?"

"Not enough to identify him. But he's sure it was a man in hunting gear."

"That could be anyone."

"Not if the nurse is right about Fanny—"

"What do you mean?"

"The nurse swears Fanny seemed to know who it was and that he was only after *her.*"

"Have they found Fanny yet?"

"No."

"Let's hope her would-be attacker hasn't either."

CHAPTER
TWENTY-FIVE

Jake swiveled his desk chair, gazed out his office window at the falling
snow, and wondered how Fanny Runyon was faring. In the past two days
the temperature had dropped well below freezing. As well as anyone could
ascertain, she hadn't even grabbed a coat before running into the woods.
Larry's cabin was located in a valley, deep in the Ozarks. It was a good place
to hide, if you knew what you were doing. It was an easy place to get lost, if
you didn't. With all he knew of Fanny Runyon's resourcefulness, his hopes
of finding her alive were getting dimmer with every snowflake. If she died,
his hopes of making sense out of this mess died, too. If he were right—but
without her testimony, how would he ever know? To his knowledge, she was
the only person who could identify the man at the cabin.

He was willing to bet the man at the cabin was the same person who had
murdered Fanny's husband, Joe. She also could confirm James's information
that they were indeed the Josef Andersens, the same Andersens employed
by Gaston Means at the time of Jesse Smith's mysterious demise. He had so
many questions! Why did she and Josef leave Washington, D.C., so soon after Means's strange passenger was dropped off at Harper's Ferry? Were they
frightened? If so, of what? And why didn't they change their names to Fanny
and Joe Runyon immediately? What business did Josef have with Clarence
Morgan? Why did they leave Kansas City so soon after her husband's trip to
Little Rock? Where had they gone in the interim? Why did they decide to

settle in Arkansas? Had she witnessed her husband's murder...? His head ached with the questions he had for her. Would he ever find the answers without her?

Something told him that the man who had tried to kill Fanny at the cabin was the same person who had murdered both her husband and Morgan, and was the man whom Means and Andersen had taken to Harper's Ferry the day after Jesse Smith's supposed suicide. And if he had killed Morgan, then it was highly likely he also knew who set the fire that killed Laura, Sarah and Teddy, if he hadn't set it himself.

If Fanny could link the man with Means, then he was most likely involved in Jesse Smith's death, even if he hadn't actually pulled the trigger. And if linked to Smith, then, according to Means, to the former Attorney General of the United States! And if Means could be believed, the responsibility for many more high level deaths might be laid at Harry Daugherty's doorstep. If he could just connect this man with Means! Fanny might be his missing link... *And at this point, Witherspoon, she's just as hypothetical as the one that supposedly links us with the apes.*

He turned around to face the pile of briefs that awaited his review. Besides the mess with Fanny and her disappearance, there were these messes that Mike had left for him to clean up.

The intercom on his desk buzzed.

"Yes, Penny?"

"There's a Mr. Maxwell Howe on the line for you."

"Put him through....Max! That was fast. I assume you have something for me?"

"You will have to decide whether I do or not," Max said, his voice scratchy and interrupted by static.

"Tell me what you found out, and I'll let you know."

"No one, from the *federal* government anyhow, knows anything about a court order for the contents of that safety deposit box."

"You're sure?"

"As sure as my sources here can make me."

Max's sources were *always* impeccable: "So what's your explanation? Are forgeries of federal court orders that easy to come by?"

"I have discovered over my years in this business that nearly anything is available, if you have enough money and can find the right people."

"So it isn't out of the realm of possibility?"

Jake meant the question as rhetorical. Max took it as such: "I assume you are wondering about the importance of that box? You asked for my explanation?"

"Do you have one?"

"Shall we call it a best-guess scenario?"

"Call it what you want," Jake said. "Guesses are fine with me."

"What if you were right and that box belonged to Jesse Smith, not some anonymous J. Smith? What if Jesse got his banker friend, Morgan, to stash some of those missing millions in graft in the box?

"You said Means told you that Smith had written a new will, which not only cut out Harry Daugherty, but also removed him as the executor of Smith's estate. The one that Smith never had a chance to give to anyone? The one Smith told his wife about? Perhaps Daugherty feared Smith's will was also in the box."

"So you think Daugherty sent the fake court order?" Jake asked, interested. The same thought had occurred to him.

"Someone connected with this mess did. But I am not convinced it was Harry. Although, the box easily could have contained the missing account books—those accounts Smith so meticulously kept? The ones detailing the Justice Department's illegal transactions? If the box held those…?"

Jake rocked back in his chair. "I see what you mean. There may be a lot more than money at stake if that's the case."

"Millions in cash is enough motive for murder," Max said. "But millions *and* evidence of illegal activities, in very high places? That could make Teapot Dome look like a tea party. Wars have been waged over less."

Jake swiveled his chair, turned to face the window. The snow still fell with no sign of letting up. It tempered his excitement: "You realize all of this is speculation? We have no proof, no hard evidence?"

"Not yet," Max agreed, "but if you can tie the murders of Morgan and Runyon to this man whom Means took to Harper's Ferry, then Means can make a pretty good case that the fellow was hired by Daugherty. From what you say, Means is willing to testify to his involvement in sanitizing Smith's death so that it appeared to be a suicide."

"*Willing* isn't the word. He's already written it in black and white for publication——"

"You are serious?"

"That's what he said. Means's book is due out sometime this year."

"Does he realize he is putting his neck in a noose?"

"Means is a character all right"——Jake chuckled remembering the man he'd talked to in New York——"He went through all those hearings, went to prison as Daugherty's sacrificial lamb——"

"Why *did* he go along with it?"

"I asked him the same thing when I was in New York," Jake said. "It seems there was an agreement——"

"Which was?"

"Means was supposed to keep certain critical material from the Grand Jury, while making it appear that a thorough investigation was proceeding. In fact, he was leading Congressional investigators only to enough information to warrant his own indictment. As Daugherty's decoy, he was to draw the legal fire while the big game got away.

"Means went along with the indictment and pled guilty to charges of accepting bribes while working with the Justice Department. Members of the press were encouraged to cover a staged review of these crimes.

"Means's sentencing was deliberately delayed to give the newspapers ample time to beat the story to death. After being saturated with facts, the public was bored with the subject."

"Let me interrupt you a second, Jake. Did Means think he would spend time in jail?"

"No. When the time came for sentencing, there was to be some dramatic judicial reprimand, after which his sentence was supposed to be suspended, and he was to be put on probation. The rationale was that Means could be useful in helping further Congressional investigations into the matters before the Senate Investigating Committee."

"I see," Max said. "So what happened?"

"Means displeased Daugherty by not uncovering certain incriminating documents Harry thought the investigators had——"

"What documents?" Max asked. "Daugherty was tried in twenty-six on malfeasance charges pertaining to his administration of the Allied Property Custodian's Office. He hung two juries and was released——"

"Don't you see? That makes Means's story even more convincing," Jake said. "He told Daugherty the committee had no documentary evidence against him. Daugherty insisted they had. Means was obviously correct——"

"Jesse's missing accounts!" Max's excitement reached through the static on the telephone line.

"Makes sense to me," Jake agreed, "since Daugherty was never indicted for anything even approaching the seriousness of murder charges. If we can prove his complicity in these murders..."

"There is no statute of limitations on murder is there?" Max asked.

"No. There isn't. Reason enough to silence anyone who might be able to involve you in a capital crime, wouldn't you say?"

"All right. So why did Means just get out of the federal penitentiary? He seems to have kept his side of the agreement."

"When Daugherty did not believe his report about the nonexistence of incriminating evidence, he apparently criticized Means's investigative abilities——"

"Means went to jail—is writing this book—out of wounded pride?" Max sounded incredulous.

"I don't think Means thought it would come to time in jail. Evidently, when Daugherty impugned his reputation as an investigator, Means called Senator Wheeler——"

"Wheeler was in charge of the investigation as I remember."

"That's right. Anyway, Means told Wheeler to subpoena him and he would testify against the former Attorney General."

"So what happened?"

"He told me he hadn't counted the cost of going up against Harry Daugherty."

"So after serving two years in prison, he decides to publish his accusations? That sounds a bit like sour grapes...?"

"I think the thing that convinced him to do it was fear," Jake said. "Just before Means's release he heard from Thomas B. Felder, his lawyer and the former legal advisor for Harding's circle. Felder was convicted with Means on bribery charges. Felder told Means, and it is a matter of public record—"

"I think I do remember reading something about Felder in the *Times*."

"Most likely his obituary—"

"He died?"

"*Suddenly* is Means's word for it. It does seem convenient that Felder dropped dead just after announcing his intentions to take his case before the Supreme Court to clear his name—"

Max picked up Jake's train of thought—"Which would, of course, bring Daugherty's name into things..."

"You see Means's point?" Jake asked. "He feared for his life once he was released—"

"Why would Daugherty bother?"

"Means thinks Daugherty's still afraid someone will spill the beans about certain deaths surrounding the Harding administration."

"But?"

"Max, *we're* getting pretty close to doing just that! By my count, only two witnesses remain who can connect Harry Daugherty to anything other than what he's already been tried for."

"*Two* witnesses?" Max pondered a moment. "Means and that man he took to Harper's Ferry—that is, *if* we can ever find out his identity."

"OK, three witnesses then."

"And the third is?"

"Fanny Runyon."

"Ah, the silent witness."

"Apparently not—well, I take that back. For all I know, as things stand now, she may be silenced permanently."

Jake filled Max in on Fanny's disappearance before they hung up.

The sky was nearly dark outside his office window. He got up from his chair, made a fire to keep from freezing. *Lord, please let Fanny Runyon be alive. Lead her to someplace safe, where she can find the help she needs.* He stirred the fire for good measure, sighed, and returned to the job of sorting through the untouched files on his desk.

The sound of the telephone's insistent ringing woke Jake. He turned on the light beside his bed: four o'clock in the morning! He waited a moment, allowed his head to clear a bit, and hoped fervently that whoever was calling would stop and let him go back to bed. After a few more rings, it was clear the caller wasn't giving up. He grabbed his robe on his way to the telephone in the hall.

Ben Hawley didn't wait for his greeting, just started talking: "Jake, sorry about this, but there's no time to waste. Have you got something to write with?"

"Ben?"

"Write this down. I don't know how much time we have—"

"Slow down! Time for what?"

"I just got a call from Larry who just talked to Fanny Runyon—"

"Good God! Go on. You've got my attention."

"Have a pencil? Paper?"

"Yes. Shoot."

"She's in a place called Blue Mountain—"

"Where is that? I've never heard of it."

"Write this down. Larry gave me directions for you—"

"Wait a minute. Why didn't Larry just go and get her? She knows him. She and I have never laid eyes on one another—"

"She wants protection, someone who can guarantee she'll be safe. She's pretty scared from what Larry says, and I guess she wasn't too impressed with his place. Can't say as I blame her after what happened—"

"Why me?"

"Larry said you had connections who could help her——"

"What made him think *that*?" Jake asked.

"I suppose I did, but what difference does it make now?"

"You're right, Ben. Give me those directions..."

Jake had been driving for nearly three hours along roads that barely deserved the name when he saw what he'd been looking for. A weathered board, crudely shaped like an arrow, pointed down a muddy, ice-packed strip of land, deeply rutted, with a large mound of snow-covered earth in its center. Scratched on the board was PORTER. Jake shook his head, parked his car near the split-rail fence that lined the north side of the dirt road which intersected with the wagon path, and hoped he didn't have a long walk ahead of him. There was no help for it though; his car wouldn't clear the center of the wagon trail. He sure didn't want to get stranded this far from help in this weather. He pulled his collar up, stuffed his hands into his pockets, and started walking down the path.

Fifteen minutes down the road, he saw the dark boards of the shack. Smoke rose lazily from a central stone chimney. *It might be called picturesque in different circumstances*, he thought. The dogs in the yard took something away from its rustic charm. As soon as he got within shouting distance, dogs leapt toward him, teeth bared, snarling and barking. Fear froze him in his steps, until he realized they were chained. *There must be more than six of those mongrels in the yard*, Jake thought, trying to figure a way to approach the house without getting torn to pieces. Jake stood, not moving a muscle, and wondered that no one had mentioned this minor obstacle. A movement at the dwelling caught his eye. What appeared to be a man stepped out onto the downward sloping porch that ran along the front of the shack. A rifle was in his hand.

"Shut yer yaps, dogs! Cain't hear m'se'f think wi' yer carryin' on!"

The dogs dropped to the ground, quiet as death.

"Say yer piece, mister, 'fore I take it in mind to shoot yuh where yuh stand."

"I was told Fanny Runyon might be staying here. I'm Jake Witherspoon." Jake took a step toward the shack, stopped as the man raised his rifle, cocked it, and pointed it in his direction.

"Jes stay put 'n yuh'll live a mite longer, hear?"

Jake nodded. The man said something to someone standing in the shadows behind him. Jake couldn't quite make out what it was. If Fanny were here, he thought, why would she want to leave? No one could get past those dogs if they tried. The man with the rifle looked like he could take care of himself and a few more as well. Something was happening up at the shack. Two women appeared beside the man. If his life had depended on it, Jake couldn't have picked out which one was Fanny Runyon. Even at this distance Jake could tell both of them had led hard lives. Both were slender to the point of being gaunt. Both were angular, no traces of femininity anywhere. Their hair, which might have lent some softness to their features, was pulled back tightly from their faces, presumably captured into buns. *Put them in men's clothes*, he thought, *and you'd have a hard time telling they weren't men themselves.* The two women embraced briefly. Then the man said something to one of them, who stepped directly behind him and followed him into the yard. Jake heard the dogs begin to growl. One sat up on its haunches, as the two made their way toward the place where Jake stood. Suddenly the dog was on its feet, teeth bared—there was a sharp yelp, as the man kicked the dog and sent him sprawling.

"I said shut yer yap!" the man said.

Jake caught a glimpse of the woman's face: as gray as the winter sky. Black circles rimmed her eyes, their color lost in the distance between them. She had a haunted look. Jake watched her as they came toward him. This woman was Fanny Runyon. He had no doubt.

CHAPTER TWENTY-SIX

Fanny looked back over her shoulder as they began the trek back to Jake's car. He followed her gaze. The man and his wife stood side by side on their porch, watching them, as they walked down the frozen dirt road. Fanny stopped, raised her hand in silent farewell. The couple nodded, turned away, and disappeared into the blackness of the shack's doorway. Fanny began walking again, head down, purposeful.

"How did you come to be at the Porters' place?" Jake asked, his voice sounding too loud in his ears.

Fanny glanced sideways at him but said nothing.

"Their name was Porter, wasn't it? I assumed so because of the sign…"

Fanny walked on in silence beside him. The coat she wore over her dress didn't fit, seemed too thin in this cold. He remembered that her own coat had been left behind in Larry's fishing cabin when she fled. The one she had on must belong to the Porter woman. He glanced back at the shack, wondering that a woman that poor had an extra coat. The thought entered his mind that the one Fanny wore had not been a spare coat at all.

"They seem like a nice couple," Jake said, trying once more to establish contact. Nothing.

They trudged on a few more yards, their eyes trained on the difficult path ahead.

"Real nice."

The sound of her voice startled him. Minutes had passed since he'd said anything. *At least she makes sense and can talk.* For a moment there, he'd wondered if she'd reverted into her trancelike existence. He made no immediate reply. It was like coaxing a wild deer to eat from your hand: Any sudden movement or sound and it might bolt in fear. He glimpsed his car in the distance and pointed—"My car's over there. On the other side of that fence."

Fanny raised her head, followed his finger with her eyes, nodded, and went back to studying the ground before her feet.

"It has a heater. You must be freezing with nothing on heavier than that coat."

Fanny pulled the coat around her. "I'm all right."

They reached the main road. Jake led her to the passenger side of the car, opened the door for her, and held it while she got in. It was only then he noticed she was shaking. He said nothing, closed the door.

He started the engine, turned on the heater, and sat there for a moment, letting the car warm up. Then he pulled out onto the road, turned around, and headed back the way he had come. Ten minutes later Fanny stopped shaking, turned her face to her window.

"I don't suppose I'll ever see those folks again," she said, as if they'd been carrying on an extended conversation all this time. "They were real nice to me. I suppose I would've died if they hadn't come along when they did..."

"When *did* they come along, Mrs. Runyon?" The formality of the title sounded strange to him. For months now, she'd been "Fanny" not "Mrs. Runyon" in his mind.

"I don't know exactly when it was....I just ran for the longest time, didn't even feel the cold until I fell over a tree limb. I had no idea where I was or what direction I was running in...I just ran. I kept on running until my legs just wouldn't work anymore."

"What happened then?"

"I sat down."

"Where?"

"I didn't know then, and I don't know now. I just sat down. I couldn't go another step....Then the Porters came along and took me to this store and gave me money so I could use the telephone. I got a real nice operator. She found Mr. Branch for me" —Fanny turned to face him, a look of bewilderment in her eyes—"Not one of those people knew me...they treated me real nice…She made me take this coat. I didn't want to. It was the only one she had."

Her eyes seemed to bore into him, seeking something from him he couldn't identify.

She clutched the coat tighter around her, turned back to her window.

Jake couldn't explain the effect she had on him. After all the stories he'd heard about her, he had expected something different from the woman who sat beside him, and yet he'd known her on sight.

He was driving east toward Hulet when he realized he couldn't take her there. In the rush to find her, he hadn't thought what he'd do with her afterwards. He needed to talk to her, find out what she knew, what she could tell him. But *then* what? Where would she be safe now?

He drove around a curve and passed a small country store with a gas pump in front of it. A sign said OPEN in the window. He drove on down the narrow, winding road until he found a place to turn around.

Fanny looked at him as they headed back in the other direction.

"I'm hungry," Jake said in answer to her unasked questions. "It's nearly noon, and I haven't had a bite since early last night. I thought you might want something to eat, too. I saw a store a way back. We can make a rest stop there and get some gasoline. If they have a telephone I can use, I'll put in a call to a friend who can help me get you somewhere where you'll be safe for the time being." (She said nothing, just stared at him.) "Is there another place you can go?"

She looked down at her hands, shook her head, and returned to staring out her window. He couldn't remember seeing anyone so completely alone before.

Jake watched her out of the corner of his eye as he finalized the details of the makeshift plan with Max. She stood holding the cup of hot coffee, warming her hands instead of drinking. She seemed so lost…vulnerable—"I'm sorry, Max. My mind wandered for a second. What was that?" Jake listened carefully, while Max repeated his instructions and clarified the timing. "Got it. I'll meet you there." Jake hung up.

He walked over to where Fanny stood holding her coffee. "Did you find anything for us to eat?" Jake asked, casting a cursory glance around the store for edibles.

"He has some beef jerky. I couldn't find anything else."

Jake nodded and walked over to converse with the storekeeper. A few minutes later, he thanked the man, gave him some money to cover the coffee, a few pieces of the dried beef, the gas, and the cost of the phone call.

They got back into the car. Jake turned toward Fanny Runyon and smiled.

"He told me there's a decent cafe about twenty minutes down this road. We'll stop there and have a good lunch. How does that sound?" He started the engine, pulled back onto the road, and headed southeast toward Little Rock.

"Fine."

"Mrs. Runyon, I can't imagine what you're feeling and thinking right now. I know you have to be exhausted, and you're probably still frightened..." (Fanny looked over at him, but said nothing.) "You have every right to be scared, but I want you to know that I'm doing everything I know to do to make sure you'll be safe from now on."

Fanny just kept staring.

Jake drove on awhile in silence, until he spied the cafe and pulled alongside it.

"Thank you for your kindness, Mr. Witherspoon," Fanny said, replacing her napkin in her lap. "I hadn't guessed I was that hungry. The Porters fed me what little they could...."

"I don't mean to rattle on so. It just seems so long since I talked to any living soul..."

Her eyes seemed to plead for understanding. To his surprise Jake found himself responding to something kindred in the woman across from him:

"Believe me, Mrs. Runyon, I understand…My wife and two children died in a fire, five years ago. I…uh…I arrived too late to do anything. They died in front of me.

"There is an entire section of my own life that I managed to ignore for a long time."—Fanny's eyes flickered with something; he looked away—"I'm discovering, a bit late I'm afraid, that ignoring things, however painful and distressing, doesn't make them disappear. In fact, I'm finding quite the opposite."

Fanny stared at her lap, twisted the napkin in her hands: "That evening I was milking our cow…in the shed out back…when it happened…."—Jake waited, afraid to interrupt—"I saw the man leave the house. I was pretty sure he didn't see me. I'd never seen him before, but Joe had warned me….

"Mr. Witherspoon, I *swear* I didn't know what was going on. There wasn't any noise…no sound at all to let me know…." Her voice broke. She smoothed the napkin back out in her lap, picked it up, folded it, laid it on the table between them, focused on it as she continued:

"Joe was on the floor in front of my rocker when I got in the house—" she met his eyes briefly, lowered her gaze to the napkin—"I didn't think he was dead at first…Then I knew…. I guess I just sat down." (Her voice sounded like someone dreaming, talking in her sleep.) "I remember I was scared, real scared…I just shut down. You know?"

Jake nodded. He knew.

A few minutes later, the only waitress in the small cafe brought their check to their table. He paid the bill.

"You said you saw the man who killed your husband?" Jake asked, after they were back on the road to Little Rock.

"I saw him all right."

"Was it the same man who shot at you at the lake cabin?"—(Fanny stared straight ahead, nodded)—"Would you recognize him if you saw him again?"

"I'll never forget what that man looked like."

"What *did* he look like?"

"He's dark—dark hair, dark eyes—"

"When you say dark do you mean he had black hair, eyes…?"

"No. Not black...more of a dark brown. Yes, that's it. Dark brown hair and eyes about the same color."

"A white man?"

"He was white all right, but his skin was browned, like he'd been out in the sun a lot over the years."

"How tall was he? What about his build? Was he a big man, slender, stocky...?"

Fanny looked at Jake, then let her head rest on the seat back: "He's not as tall as you are, maybe two-, three inches shorter. I guess you'd call him stocky. He's probably about your age, though maybe a bit older. I noticed he had some gray in his hair when I saw him out the window...

"I thought I was safe there...thought he'd never find out I'd seen him that night...thought if I'd just keep real quiet and never say a word about what I knew to anyone..."

Fanny opened her eyes, turned her head toward Jake: "It's just like you said, though. Seems like the more I tried to pretend I didn't know what he looked like—the more I tried to block out his face from my memory—the bigger his face became in my mind. And then that morning...I saw him out the cabin window...

"You know the funny thing? At first I thought I'd made him up, that it was just my mind making pictures in my head again...I saw that gun.... Something seemed to rip in me, and the next thing I knew I was running and running and running till I tripped over that log.... When I called Mr. Branch, I guess I'd decided I just couldn't run any more."

Jake reached over, took her hand, and squeezed it. She smiled, left her hand in his, turned her head back toward the window: "It's snowing again. I always liked snow. I grew up with snow all around. It always seemed so pretty." Fanny turned back, looked at Jake's profile as he drove:

"Do you want to know something funny?" (Jake smiled.) "I never liked it when winter ended. Most people like it when the sun comes out and things begin to warm up. I used to hate it. The snow melted and turned dirty in the mud that stirred up from underneath. The smell! Damp, rotting vegetation...everything slimy, smelling of rot and decay. I used to think it would go on forever...."

"And did it?" Jake prompted, not wanting her to stop. In some strange way he did not fully comprehend, she soothed him with her conversation.

"Oh, yes. In time. When the sun stayed out, longer and longer each day. I used to think when I was a girl that the sun fought a kind of battle with the snow, melting its beauty, stripping its sparkling white covering from the land, exposing all the decay that lay underneath, and the snow had no chance, because the sun knew something the snow did not."

"What was that?" Jake asked, smiling at the story and the new tone in her voice.

"Why that he would win in the end."

Jake laughed. "How did the sun do that?"

"He turned up the heat, dried up the dampness and the rot. He made them food for the new life that he called up out of the ground with his light, and then..."

"And then?" (Fanny laughed, and the sound was so unexpected Jake started)—"What's so funny?"

"Nothing. I was just remembering how happy I was in the summer."

They drove on in silence for awhile. Jake wondered how to broach the subject again. There were so many unanswered questions still to be asked, and something about her description ate at him. It was not just that it matched the one Gaston Means had given him.... They had so little time before Max arrived at the airfield in Little Rock to take her to a place where she would be safe from whatever forces sought to harm her. Strange how things conspired. It wouldn't have occurred to him to put her on an airplane even as recently as one week ago. Now it seemed the most obvious solution.

"I suppose you have things you want to ask me," she said, reading his mind. "I don't know how much time we have together, but you should ask me what you want to know. I will tell you what I know as truthfully as I am able."

He felt as if she'd given him a great gift, not just access to information.... It was more than that somehow.

"Go on. Ask." She smiled encouragement.

"Thank you."

Jake stood in the cold and watched until he could no longer see the plane. He wondered how long it would be until they met again. Max had told no one but the pilot their next destination, and the pilot had no idea who his female passenger was. There would be no contact with Fanny Runyon, until the time came when she was needed to testify against the man she'd seen at the cabin, the same one she'd seen leave her home the day her husband was murdered.

He left the airfield and stopped for a quick dinner before getting back on the road to Hulet. He'd considered stopping for the night in Little Rock, but he decided against it. He had things to think about, things to figure out, things he'd put off too long as it was.

Fanny had given him a lot of the answers. Yes, she and Joe had changed their names from Andersen to Runyon. Josef had worked for Gaston Means, and had chauffeured him and the man who she believed eventually killed Joe to Harper's Ferry. Her husband had not been a stupid man. He knew things were not aboveboard at Means's house on Sixteenth Street. When Jesse Smith was killed—he'd asked her why she'd said "killed" instead of "died" or "committed suicide," and she'd said that was what Josef had told her—Josef Andersen decided to leave Means's employ. He was an honest man and did not want to get drawn into something illegal. He had not counted on being followed. Followed? he'd asked. Yes, she'd said, at least to Kansas City.

Josef had heard about Clarence Morgan from a former friend in Washington. Fanny didn't know why her husband had gone to Little Rock to meet with him, but when he came home, yes, he had had a bag full of money. She didn't ask where or why he'd gotten it. She'd learned it was much better not to know some things by that time.

One day—the day they'd left Kansas City—Josef came home in a panic. The man he'd taken to Harper's Ferry had followed them to Kansas City. He was very afraid. They left town the next day. They'd moved around, never staying more than three days in one place, until her husband felt that they would be safe in Arkansas. That's when he'd purchased the property that had brought them to the farmhouse outside of Hulet. Then one day they'd gone into town to buy seed and supplies...

Jake drove, hearing Fanny's voice in his ear: *I was sitting in the wagon when Josef gets in and drives out of town like the devil was after us. He told me he'd just seen the man we'd been running from all this time. I asked him if the man had seen him, and he shook his head—perspiration was just pouring down his face and it wasn't even March yet.... He said he didn't think so. I looked back, to see if I could see anyone following us, and he jerked my arm so hard I thought it had come out of its socket. He said, didn't I know what happened to that woman in the Bible who turned back to look at Sodom and Gomorrah? I said, 'Well where did you see him?' He said, 'He was coming out of the newspaper office and walking right toward us...'*

That's what she'd said...out of the newspaper office. The description fit. Even Max had noticed.

But it doesn't make any sense, Jake thought. Dan never knew Harry Daugherty. Sure he'd worked at that newspaper in Washington, D.C., but he'd left, gone to fight in the war, was in Europe until just before he moved here. Besides, he lived in Hulet long before the Andersens moved to Arkansas. The coincidence was just too much, even if Andersen *had* seen Dan, and Dan *had* killed Jesse Smith, even Clarence Morgan, he would *never* have killed Laura, Sarah and Teddy. Not his own flesh and blood. *No.* There must be some other explanation. Dan just looked like this other man. Fanny never knew the man's name. She didn't know her description fit Dan Johnson. Only two things made it look like Dan might be the one she'd seen: the description happened to fit—but then it also fit a lot of average-looking men; and the fact that her husband had seen this man coming out of the Hulet newspaper office. A lot of people who fit that description could have had business at the newspaper office. The man they'd seen didn't have to be the owner of the newspaper. In fact, the murderer might very well have visited the newspaper in hopes of obtaining information, finding out if anyone like the Andersens lived around there. *I did it again...jumped to conclusions, just assumed...No.* No matter how much he disliked his former brother-in-law, Jake couldn't believe Dan was capable of murdering his own sister.

The night closed in on him as he drove toward Hulet and the farm. As the lights of Little Rock disappeared, the snow that had stopped while he ate dinner began again in earnest. The wind picked up. Blowing snow stretched across the road in vertical sheets of impenetrable white. Their glare as his headlamps caught them rendered normal speed impossible. He slowed the Duesenberg to a crawl as he strained to see the road through the torrent of snow on the windshield. Falling snow blended with blowing and accumulated snow so that the roadbed blurred into its surroundings. All he could do was creep ahead and try to stay on the road without ending up in a ditch. His hands clenched the wheel as the storm continued to worsen. His nose nearly touched the windshield in the effort to see. *I don't remember driving in weather this bad*, he thought, cursing under his breath as the car fishtailed sharply, began a sideways slide. Jake turned the wheel into the slide, barely gaining control before hitting a large drift.

It was the slide that triggered the memory of that November night in Little Rock. The snow had been as thick and as bad as this when Mary Landower drove him from the courthouse to his hotel. Jake's brain tried to turn off the movie that began inside his head, but it seemed the projectionist had fallen asleep, leaving the reels to run as they would.

Jake sat trapped behind the wheel of his car, mesmerized by the film that materialized on the sheets of snow in front of him. Strangely detached, he viewed himself as if from a theatre seat, while an actor playing Jake Witherspoon strutted about on the screen. He saw himself dining with Mary, dancing. Watched as arrogant assurance grew into lust. The director called for close-ups of the young woman's physical allure, focused on her heavily made-up eyes, the lashes that batted with invitation, of the male lead's smarmy Lothario. The next scene showed the cowering and fallen hero driving frantically through the blizzard to save his True Love and his tattered self-respect.

Jake cringed in shame as the poorly written farce played itself out as high drama in his deluded character's eyes: Charlie Chaplin plays Oedipus, the clown who would be king. *A self-blinded one at that*, he thought, without the slightest twinge of sympathy as the welcome *slap, slap, slap* of the film's last frame told him the movie was at last at an end. He could go home.

The storm subsided as he turned off the main road and began the last leg of the journey. It had taken much longer than he'd thought, and he was anxious to get some rest. Then there it was. As clearly as if she were sitting beside him, he heard Laura telling him why she couldn't spend that night with his mother: "I just fed the children, and Dan said he might drop by..." He heard his own voice telling her to call her brother and tell him not to come, that she'd be at her mother-in-law's house. He thought he'd talked her into going to his mother's, thought she was safe. She hadn't gone; she wasn't safe. Had she called Dan? *Had* Dan come by?

Jake remembered snatches of other conversations: Of Laura's surprise at Dan's sudden move to Hulet, when she'd thought he was so happily settled in England. Of her bewilderment when she learned Dan had bought the Hulet newspaper, when he'd told her in a letter only months before how much he'd hated journalism and had only done it because of their father's prodding in that direction...

Jake remembered his own surprise that Dan would leave his life of "high adventure"—Dan's phrase for his war exploits and their aftermath—for the anonymity of small town existence. It had bothered him as well that Dan would want to join them in Arkansas, in a small town where they were bound to run into one another, after making it quite plain that he was thoroughly opposed to Laura's choice of husbands.

The timing of Dan's move to Hulet had been unusual, too, now that he thought of it: Laura had received Dan's letter explaining his intention about two weeks before Jesse Smith died. The postmark on his letter was from England. But had Dan still been overseas when they received his letter? Could he have been in Washington, D.C., at the time of Smith's murder—if in fact it was murder?

Dan had moved to Arkansas about one week *after* Smith's death. But what possible connection could there be between Dan Johnson and Harry Daugherty?

Now that Jake thought about it, there were several questions that had no adequate explanations regarding Dan Johnson's activities. For instance: where had the money come from to buy the newspaper? Laura had told him that Dan had used up his inheritance long ago. In fact, lack of funds had been Dan's reason for taking the position at the Washington paper and the impetus for leaving to seek his fortune in the battle arena of Europe.

But do I really think Dan is capable of murder? Outside the necessities of war? Jake thought, as he turned onto the road that led to the farm. He remembered Dan's disruption of their wedding day and Dan's explosion at the newspaper office when he'd tried to reconcile with Dan last summer. Then there was Laura's dismay at Dan's target practice in the field in back of their house. *Dan is good with a gun*, he thought. Jesse Smith was killed was a gun. Dan could have been in Washington when Jesse died, and was within two hours driving distance of Clarence Morgan's house when the banker was murdered…But Morgan and Runyon were stabbed and their necks broken. *It's one thing to shoot a man, quite another to stab a man and break his neck.*

Jake pulled in front of his house but remained seated in the Duesenberg thinking. There was still the question of motive: why? What possible reason would Dan have had for killing any of them? Unless there *was* a connection with Harry Daugherty…

Jake got out of the car and started toward the house. He could believe Dan murdered all three men, but there was still no way he could credit Dan's responsibility in Laura's and the children's deaths. It was a wall he could not penetrate. He opened the door to his house: *Maybe Dan knows who set the fire?* That would explain a lot. *Perhaps*, Jake thought, *Dan was there and was as powerless to prevent their deaths as I. If he is involved in some other way in these other murders, perhaps he is guilty of complicity in Laura's death. Laura, Teddy, Sarah—all dead.*

Only after he lay down to sleep did Jake remember Dan's rage, his words: Now Jake would have to live with their screams as well.…

CHAPTER
TWENTY-SEVEN

J ake stared out of his office window and waited for James McWilliams. Ben was due to arrive for the meeting in fifteen minutes. A lot depended on what they had been able to discover. If what he suspected were true, nothing would be too far-fetched. He didn't want to consider it, but even Jenny's life might be at stake. *And what will I do if it is? Anything I say she'll think is born out of jealousy at having lost her to Dan.* He stuffed his hands in his coat pockets, contemplated the flat, gray sky. *Perhaps I'm wrong about everything. There's still that hope.* He turned as someone knocked on his door and entered.

"Come in," he said, glad for the opportunity to see Ben before James joined them.

"No sense in standing on ceremony is there?" Ben said, crossing the room and taking a seat at the table where he could set his papers. A tray with coffee cups, glasses, and a pitcher of water sat in the center.

"None," Jake answered, joining him at the table.

"Where's McWilliams?" Ben asked. "And where's the coffee? You know I can't think straight this early in the morning without coffee."

"Penny's making it. You're early, you know."

"I know all right. Jake, you know something?" The springs in Ben's chair squeaked as he leaned back and regarded Jake with an expression that fell

somewhere between disgust and amusement. "Things were a *lot* less complicated when Mike was at the helm of this firm."

"Are you complaining?"

"Don't get me wrong. You've done a heck of a job getting this office back
on track. You've managed to sweet-talk the old clients into staying. After
Mike let things go to hell in a handbasket, that couldn't've been easy. My
hat's off——"

"But?"

"No buts. Thanks to you and our clients' word of mouth, we've even
signed some new clients..."

"Is this where the but comes in?" Jake asked, his eyebrows arching.

"*But* spending all this money and time on a case that's settled——"

"Settled? You mean because Slo-Joe Freeman was hanged for a crime he
didn't commit? Is that your idea of settled?"——(Ben shifted uncomfortably in
his chair, avoided Jake's eyes)——"Perhaps you meant my family's murder? The
six-year-old multiple homicide that was called an *accident,* because nobody
wanted to stir up anything? Or perhaps, you're talking about last *year's* homicide? The Runyon case that no one's done anything about since last summer?
Or perhaps you've some *other* case in mind?"

Ben sighed, held up his hands in a gesture of surrender: "You win."

"You had *something* to say."

"All right, Jake. I'll level with you. All this makes me *real* uncomfortable. Do you know what you're dragging us into by investigating this stuff?"

"You want out, Ben? I won't hinder you, if you don't want anything more
to do with this. You're right. What I'm investigating *is* potentially dangerous.

"Tell you what? I'll go you one better, Ben. If you like, I'll leave the firm.
You and Larry can go on as if I'd never regained my memory. No hard feelings. Just say the word..."

Ben said nothing. Jake got up to answer the buzzing of his intercom. "Yes?"

"Jim—uh, Mr. McWilliams is here."

"Thanks. Send him on back, will you, Penny? How's that coffee coming?"

"Almost done."

"Fine." Jake returned to the table. "McWilliams will be here any second. If you want to back out, Ben, now's the time."

"I'll see it through. On one condition…"

"Which is?"

"Promise me you won't pursue this if you can't *prove* your case. Circumstantial evidence is one thing; proof is quite another."

"Believe me, Ben, I'm not in this for some kind of personal vendetta. I just want to know the truth, and if I can, I want to see the person or persons responsible for these deaths brought to trial.

"I'm no fool, Ben, at least not anymore. I'm not going to bring murder charges against anyone without proof, and I'm not going to scream conspiracy in high places without a lot more than I have right now."

"What *do* you have now?"

"That's what we're here to find out, isn't it? But as of this moment? I have strong suspicions, a fair amount of circumstantial evidence, and an eye-witness who can't identify anyone until we get our hands on the right suspect."

"Fanny Runyon?"

Jake nodded, and stood up to greet James McWilliams who was opening the door.

"James," Jake said, shaking his hand, and showing him to the table, "it's good to see you. Have you met my partner, Ben Hawley?"

"A pleasure, Mr. McWilliams." Ben stood and held out his hand for James to shake.

"For me, too," James said, shaking his hand. "Penny's told me a lot about you, Mr. Hawley."

"Call me Ben," Ben said, resuming his seat. "I have a strong impression— from Jake here—that we're going to be doing a *lot* of business together from here on out."

"Have a seat, James," Jake said, sitting down at the table, "and tell us what you've found out."

Jake sat in the dark after everyone else had left the office for the day. It was as bad as he'd feared it might be. Among them they'd managed a circumstantial tie-in between Clarence Morgan and Jesse Smith. They could prove Morgan and Smith had known each other and had corresponded near the time of Smith's "suicide". They had a witness to certain so-called government agents who had produced a federal court order allowing them to confiscate the contents of a safety deposit box registered to a J. Smith, but whose only signatory was Clarence Morgan. They could prove no such court order was ever issued. They could prove no such agents were authorized to act for any federal agency.

They also had proof concerning Slo-Joe Freeman's innocence in the murder of Clarence Morgan. The only fingerprints at the crime scene were Freeman's, but that argued against Slo-Joe's guilt, since the house belonged to Morgan, yet his fingerprints were nowhere to be found—as if the place had been sterilized. The trial transcript showed that Freeman had access to the Morgan home and that he'd found Morgan's body, which made Slo-Joe's prints at the home not only reasonable, but also argued strongly that his presence at the crime scene had occurred *after* the real murderer had destroyed all other prints and had left the scene. All these things raised more than the required reasonable doubt to acquit Slo-Joe of murder.

With Fanny's information, they were able to link Joe Runyon with Morgan via the money and the timing of Joe's absence from Kansas City. Morgan's former secretary's testimony, and Morgan's own appointment book, corroborated her story. And since they could prove that Joe Runyon was also Josef Andersen, Gaston Means's former chauffeur, they could link Runyon to Washington, D.C., and to the man who Means was convinced was the former Attorney General's hitman, the one who killed Jesse Smith. Fanny confirmed that Joe Runyon had seen this man, that the same man had followed them to Kansas City, and that Joe Runyon had seen him again in Hulet, Arkansas, shortly before Runyon was murdered in his home. Fanny had seen this man with her own eyes that night and again when he attempted to attack her at Larry Branch's fishing cabin. Runyon's description, Fanny's description, and Means's description of this mystery man all matched. Fanny could recognize the man, but she did not know his name and neither did Gaston Means.

It all makes sense, Jake thought, *if I'm right, and Dan Johnson is our mystery man. Dan kills Jesse Smith on Daugherty's orders and boards a westbound train at Harper's Ferry. No one knows him. He's been in Europe for years. He's a trained soldier and presumably has killed before. He has no money, but he does have a sister who lives in Hulet, Arkansas. Not only does he have a safe place to go after killing Jesse Smith, but also is close enough to Little Rock to keep an eye on Clarence Morgan, a man whom Daugherty might suspect of keeping Jesse Smith's all-important account books. Not to mention the missing millions in graft money. He had the means, the opportunity, and, if hired by Daugherty, the motive to kill Smith and Morgan.*

Runyon posed a threat on two fronts: Joe could identify Dan as his passenger the night after Jesse Smith's death and tie him to Means, and if to Means, then to Daugherty, who would fiercely oppose the connection. That Runyon apparently had discovered the Smith-Morgan link made him dangerous to Daugherty as a rival for the money and accounts *and* as a potential blackmailer.

Fanny could link Dan to Runyon, but anything else was speculation. Means could link him with Washington and identify him as the man Daugherty ordered him to pick up and take to Harper's Ferry, but there was no evidence to prove he murdered Jesse Smith.

And what about the threats *he* had received, warning him away from the Morgan trial? The fire that had killed his family? Jake put on his coat and grabbed his briefcase. It made sense if Dan was Morgan's killer that he would want Freeman convicted. A conviction meant no one would look for anyone else. Case closed. It made sense that Dan would not want anyone from his family circle involved. It also made sense for Dan to want Slo-Joe to have the poorest defense possible, and the one with the least publicity. *My involvement guaranteed headlines and guaranteed the case would get my best effort: I'm beginning to see why he always held me responsible for Laura's death...What did he do to foster the threats? I suppose he could've stirred up the Klan without too much trouble. What if Laura did call him that night and tell him she and the children would be at Mother's?*

What if the Klan arrived at my house to set the fire as a warning which somehow got out of control?

It all made far too much sense for Jake to ignore. Something visceral told him it was all true. The only problem was he couldn't prove it, unless Dan Johnson himself provided the proof he needed....

Jenny's given me no choice, Jake thought, as he watched for Bertha to leave the cafe for the day. *She won't talk to me on the telephone, so she'll have to talk to me in person.* The problem was how to get her to do it. He was afraid that if he went up to her door and knocked, she'd simply lock him out. He'd decided against joining the regular cafe customers for two reasons: one, what he had to say to her required privacy; two, it would be too easy for her to stay in the kitchen and send Susie out to wait on him. He could not cause a scene for several reasons, not the least of which was the potential indignity of being tossed out of the cafe by her other customers. Hulet was a very small town at times. The best plan he could come up with was this one. *If it just doesn't backfire.* He offered up a silent prayer as Bertha opened the back door of the restaurant and stepped out. He pulled back into the shadows under the stairs that led to Jenny's apartment, waited for Bertha to pass by and turn the corner onto Main Street. *So far so good.* Jake stepped into the alley and proceeded with stealth to the back door of the cafe, praying as he went that it would not be locked. Hardly anyone locked their doors in Hulet, but lately things had not been going his way. A quick glance into the kitchen window revealed that today was no exception. Billy Wiggins sat at the kitchen table with Jenny. Jake withdrew quickly. *Now what?*

It had been good seeing Jenny again, Billy thought, as he rounded the corner onto Main Street. With his new responsibilities at the paper, he hadn't had much time for socializing. Mr. Johnson seemed to turn more and more of the daily writing and business details over to him. It pleased him that Dan trusted him to handle things when he wasn't around. He liked newsgathering, and he liked writing articles. By now, running the printing press was second nature. What bothered Billy was that even when Dan was in his office, he seemed preoccupied.

"Mr. Wiggins, I presume."

Billy followed the sound of the voice. Mr. Witherspoon sat in his Duesenberg in front of Doc Livsey's office.

"Hey, Mr. Witherspoon," Billy said, coming over to the car. "I didn't know you were in town today."

"I felt like getting out. With all this snow and cold weather lately, when I saw actual sunshine, I decided to take a ride into town."

Billy put his hand on the hood of the car. "Boy, if I had a car like this, I'd drive it every chance I got."

"Want to go for a spin?"

"You mean it?"

"Did I look like I was kidding?" Jake asked. He patted the passenger seat beside him. "Come on. Unless you have something better to do?"

"On Saturday? Gosh no!" Billy hurried around the car and got in.

"Where to, Mr. Wiggins?"

Billy grinned. "Anywhere you say, Mr. Witherspoon!"

Jenny walked toward Jake's car. The expression on her face told him this was not going to be easy. Billy stood at the corner of the alley. Behind her back, he held up crossed fingers as a signal to Jake.

"Well, I'm here. You have one hour."

Jake opened the passenger side door. She got in. She could have been a store mannequin for all the warmth she exuded. She stared straight ahead, said nothing.

Jake followed her example until they were safely on the road heading out of town.

"I thought we needed some time to talk without any interruptions," he said.

"Well, this certainly fits the bill. Are we going somewhere specific, or am I just being held captive in a moving vehicle?"

Jake grinned, "No one will ever accuse you of being slow, Jenny."

"So I'm a captive." (She did not sound amused.) "You'd better say what you have to say, then, Jake. An hour is what you bargained for, and from what I know about you—including, I might add, your underhanded tactic of enlisting *Billy* in your cause—an hour is all the time you're ever going to get."

"Fair enough. For the record, I was honest with Billy. He decided to help convince you to talk to me of his own volition. Regardless of what you think of my tactics, I'm glad they worked. I had to talk to you...explain things... clear the air between us—"

"If you think I'm going to change my mind...?"

"I hope you will, of course. Why else would I go to all this trouble?" Jake glanced at her; she still stared ahead. "I do know that, if after what I have to say, you still feel and think the way you do now, then there is nothing more I can, or will, do. All I'm asking from you now, Jenny, is that you listen."

She turned her head toward him, "I'm listening."

Jake smiled slightly. "Now that you are, I don't know where to start—"

"How about starting with Mary Landower?" Bitterness laced her voice.

Jake drew a deep breath. "OK. Why not? What do you want to know?"

"I don't know that I want to know anything..."

"Well, then why don't I just start and tell you everything *I* know about her? If you don't mind, I'm going to pull over and stop, so I don't get a crick in my neck trying to talk to you while staying on the road."

"Suit yourself. It's your time." Jenny looked out her window.

It wasn't just because she was looking out the window, it was something in her attitude that reminded Jake of Fanny Runyon and the overwhelming sadness that seemed to emanate from her being. Suddenly he realized that Jenny's anger stemmed from being deeply hurt...by him. It made him even more determined to withhold nothing from her, to tell her everything.

"I met Mary when I handled the Slo-Joe Freeman defense in the Clarence Morgan murder trial. I told you about the case at Thanksgiving—"

"You told me a lot of things at Thanksgiving."

"What I told you then was true. My sin was not telling you the *whole* truth, not that I lied about the things I did say."

"We'll talk about that *after* you've finished with Miss Landower. She was rather a large omission, don't you think?"

"Yes. I deliberately left her out of the discussion—"

"Really?" Jenny's tone dripped with sarcasm.

"I had two reasons for leaving her out: I didn't want you to think badly of me, and I didn't want to remember what happened that evening. As long as I live I don't think I'll ever be able to completely forgive myself—"

"Don't tell me you're trying to say it only happened *that* evening?"

"I don't know what Mary told you, but...Why don't I go back to the beginning and tell you what I know?"—(Jenny turned away, looked out the window)—"Thank you. Not having to look at you while I tell this helps."

Jenny looked over her shoulder at him, glared, returned to her window view.

"As I said, I met Mary when I took the case in Little Rock. That would've made it sometime during the summer of 1924. My firm hired her, because we needed a secretary and someone to help with various details in the courtroom. She acted as a general assistant. Ben Hawley actually had more contact with her than I—"

"*Please.*" Jenny turned, her tone and expression deprecatory.

"This is not amusing for me," Jake said, an edge creeping into his own voice. "Please don't crucify me for every unintentional pun. I'll never get through this, if you do."

Jenny returned to her window.

"*Nothing* passed between Mary and me until the night court broke for Thanksgiving recess—"

"You're asking me to believe that you spent *months* working with this girl and nothing happened until that *one* night?" Jenny fixed her attention on him.

Jake didn't flinch from her gaze, looked directly into her eyes: "I'm not asking you to *believe* anything, Jenny. I'm merely asking you to *listen* to what I *know*.

"I'd left my car at the hotel that day—I don't remember exactly why I decided to take a taxicab to court, but I did. When court recessed, a snowstorm had blown in. I called for a taxi. It took longer to arrive than I expected—I suppose I was daydreaming or something. At any rate by the time I saw the taxi, a man was running past me down the courthouse steps and was into the cab and around the corner before I knew what happened. Mary was still at the courthouse. She offered to give me a ride to my hotel."

"How convenient."

Jake ignored her comment, continued: "The storm was getting worse. I've gone back over this a hundred times in the last few weeks, Jenny. It was nearly a blizzard outside, but if I'd really wanted to get home that night, I could have. As it was, I did make the effort to get home that night, but not until much later, and not until I'd managed to betray Laura and everything I thought I stood for.

"Just to let you know, I did not have intercourse with Miss Landower... not technically, anyway—"

"I don't know that I want to hear the details of your sordid little affair—"

"Sordid it was, certainly. I would not classify it as an affair. To this day I don't know what came over me...lust, of course. Mary was very attractive—"

"And willing, I suppose..."

"You know, I honestly had no idea *how* willing she was until things progressed to a point where it was obvious even to me."

"Next you'll try to convince me *she* seduced *you*."

"Nothing of the kind! I'm not trying to weasel out of anything here! I'm trying to tell you I found out I wasn't the kind of man I thought I was. I'm trying to tell you I not only failed Laura—by the way, Jenny, I *loved* my wife with all I had to give. I never even *looked* at another woman after I met her. I think that's what surprised me most about everything that happened...that I was surprised. I didn't care one whit about Mary Landower! I suppose I was flattered by her attention, by her obvious desire to go to bed with me. I suppose

I was excited by the adventure, the challenge of seeing how much I could get away with without actually committing adultery, as much as I was by her physical allure." Jake paused, as he realized the import of what he'd just said.

"Technicalities...I'd always hidden behind technicalities, I suppose. Suddenly the *technical* distinction I'd made between adultery and what was actually going on in that hotel room disappeared. It was as if someone had trained this glaring light on the two of us, exposing everything for what it was—what you said, sordid—and what I knew it was: a betrayal of Laura... sin. What I did that night *was* adulterous.

"I have no idea what Mary thought about the rest of my time with her. I jumped off the bed, pulled on what clothes I'd taken off, threw my few unpacked things into my bag, and I ran—don't laugh; I'm not kidding—I ran out of that room and that hotel and went straight to the car and drove home as fast as I could.

"All I could think of was getting home to Laura and praying that she'd never, *never* find out what I'd done. Of course, *that* part of my prayer was answered, wasn't it? She never did find out what I'd done.

"Did I ever tell you about my mother? She was one of the finest women I've ever known. Both of my parents were very special people. You would've liked them. They would've liked you, too.

"Anyway, Mother raised me to believe in God. She read the Bible every morning of her life. At the end, Annie read it to her. Every night when I was a boy, she would kneel with me beside my bed and listen while I said my prayers. When I was grown, she still knelt beside her bed every night and said her prayers. For my mother and my father, being a Christian didn't mean going to church on Sundays and holidays. For them, being a Christian was *life*.

"I tell you this to let you know I knew better. I wasn't raised to be this... adulterer...that I became that night. I always thought I was better than that. Better than other people who behaved that way. I guess I just always thought I was better...period.

"I told a friend recently that I'd discovered something, something I hadn't realized before: I can't ignore the things I've done anymore and pretend—either that I didn't do them, because I didn't want to be the kind of person that did things I was ashamed of doing, or that the things never happened.

"Do you know anything about Freud?" (Jenny shook her head) "It doesn't matter. He'd be wrong about me anyway, because he'd try to say I lost my memory of that night and everything associated with it because I didn't want to face my own sexuality or some such rot. The truth is much simpler: I didn't want to face the fact that I was guilty, and that my guilt had consequences that went far beyond my own circumstances.

"'An eye for an eye, a tooth for a tooth'—now *that* seems fair. But I sinned *one* night—oh, it was the logical result of a lot of sinning over several years, just not in that area, a result of my stupid pride, my lethal arrogance—no matter. The consequence of *my* sins took the lives of my wife, my daughter, my son, and even, as it turned out, the life of an innocent, defenseless—another pun—Negro, because I wasn't around to help him. That's not arrogance or pride: I could have proven reasonable doubt.

"So I didn't tell you about Mary Landower, because if I told you, I'd have to look at my face mirrored in your eyes, and I would have to see a sinful man whose failures caused—directly or indirectly doesn't really make damn bit of difference here—I'd have to admit that I *was* responsible for their deaths.

"You see, Jenny, I did tell you the truth on Thanksgiving: I did love my family. I just didn't love them enough to put them before myself. Perhaps I wasn't capable of truly loving them. But as much as I knew how, I *did* love them. I also told you I felt responsible for their deaths. I suppose I wanted your sympathy. The truth is I was responsible: because of my failures, they died. I just didn't tell you *how* I was responsible. I didn't want you to look at me the way you're looking at me now. . . .

"My hour is just about up, so I only have one more thing to say, and then you can ask me anything you want to ask. I promise I'll tell you the whole truth, at least as I am capable of knowing it."

Jake looked down at his hands; to his surprise they were clasped so tightly together that his knuckles were white. He unclasped them, wiped his palms on his pants. He turned back towards Jenny, who sat like a sphinx against the passenger door.

"The last thing I have to say is this: I love you. Until I spoke to you that last time from Washington and you told me we were through, I suppose I didn't realize how much you truly meant to me. I felt like my heart had been ripped apart. I tried to toss it off, bury my feelings for you like I'd buried my guilt in the past. I threw myself into my work"—Jake grinned sardonically—"It was my retreat of preference and habit, I suppose. It *used* to work. It didn't this time.

"Whatever happens, Jenny, I'll always be grateful to you for showing me what love really feels like, and for making me face the truth of who I really am.

"All that stuff Mother told me about God and sin and forgiveness when I was growing up? Because of you, I finally found out what it all meant." Jake sighed.

"I love you, Jenny. I want you to marry me and be my wife more than I have ever wanted anything. That may sound ludicrous to you at this moment, but I've found I've wasted a great deal of my life up to this point, and as you've pointed out, I have only been allowed this one hour—" Jake pulled his watch out of his pocket—"and I've taken more than that already, I see. Jenny, I don't want to waste any more of my life than I already have. That's all I have to say."

The day seemed grayer than when they'd arrived, he realized, as he waited for her reaction. Clouds had moved in while he'd been speaking and obscured the sun. Without the sun, the interior of the car grew cold. Jenny huddled against the far door, not moving. Her expression showed nothing but profound sadness. The cold began to seep through Jake's coat, robbing him of warmth. He started the engine, turned on the heater.

"I'll take you back home," he said smiling at her. There was nothing more to say that he hadn't said. There was nothing more he could do, but hope... and pray.

Jenny watched him as he drove, his jaw set, his eyes straight ahead. Silence prevailed, broken only by the sound of the tires on the road. She was glad for the silence; she needed to be still.

She gazed out her window and watched the countryside as it passed, eloquent in its simplicity. Autumn's winds and winter's cold had stripped away the lush drapery of summertime, leaving only essential landscape visible through the stark latticework of grass and undergrowth and trunks. Adversity affected people in much the same way, she thought, as she considered the trees, so individual in their treeness: Some stood straight and strong, branches outstretched, welcoming. Others twisted into incongruous shapes or hugged themselves protectively, hiding their main trunk. Still others jutted jagged, broken limbs threateningly, as if daring passersby to come within their reach. Some huddled close to the ground, stunted, or too twiggy-young to disclose their bent as yet to the casual observer. All trees seemed unremarkable, similar, when cloaked in summer's foliage. But nature gave itself no choice: Once every year it exposed itself for what it was with neither frills, nor gaudy covering, nor skin, nor smiles, nor attitude, nor pose, nor inflection beneath which it could hide its soul. *How different from us...so afraid of nakedness, so afraid of seeming vulnerable, of being vulnerable, of being who we are and letting someone else see.*

How brave he is! she thought, marveling at the prodigious courage it had taken for him to say what he'd said. Comprehension blew through her mind, scattered trivia out of its way, as if some window had been opened.

She reached across the seat, touched his forearm: "Jake, could you stop the car for a moment?"

"Is something wrong?" he asked, slowing the car. He pulled into a turn-out and stopped.

"Now I have something to say. I want your undivided attention."

"You certainly have it." He turned toward her in the seat. "What is it?"

Now that she had his full attention, her tongue refused to function properly. She knew why. It was one of those rare, defining moments—a moment when all the pieces suddenly fly together out of nowhere and form a picture so true, so recognizable, that it radiates, fairly trembles with meaning. It was one of those moments she knew held a message that mattered, as if a telegram from God had unaccountably arrived at her door without so much as a knock or the ring of a doorbell. But she didn't need to open the envelope to know what it said—

"Jenny?" Jake's forehead creased with concern.

She smiled, and her smile said everything he'd hoped to hear her say. He opened his arms, and she was there.

Chapter
Twenty-Eight

J ake released her reluctantly. There was one more thing to settle before he could trust their relationship to endure.

"Jenny, can you listen to me for one more minute?"

"What could be left to say?" she teased. "You sound so *serious*."

"Just bear with me…I don't know how I could've left this out. I suppose I was trying so hard to explain my past errors that I neglected to deal with my more recent ones—"

"Jake, don't tell me there's *another* woman—"

"No! I swear there's been no one in my life but you in the past six years—"

"Then what?" Jenny braced herself.

"I want you to understand how sorry I am for the way I've acted toward *you*"—He raised his hand to forestall her interruption—"This is important to me, Jenny. Let me finish."

"I don't know why I behaved so badly, leaving you that first time, while I went to Washington. I suppose I thought it wasn't important at the time. But to remain away, after leaving you with the impression I had given you, and to do so without calling at once to let you know what was happening…and then, to repeat the performance at Christmas," Jake paused, shook his head, looked up at her face: "I have no excuses. I simply ignored your feelings, treated you as if your feelings, and *you*, didn't matter to me. It wasn't that you didn't matter, you did. It's just that other things took precedence—a lot of those things involved my own feelings. When I'm brutally honest with myself and with you, I have to admit that everything—everyone—has taken a backseat to my own list of priorities for as long as I can remember. Until recently it never occurred to me that there was anything wrong with that: I believed that if I did what I felt was right for me, then it would benefit everyone I cared about. I see now how self-centered, how selfish I have been, and how...wrong.

"So before we can go on together—and I do want us to—I need to apologize for all I've done to hurt you in the past. Jenny, I'm sorry. Will you, can you...forgive me?"

Until he reminded her, she'd forgotten the balled fist of hurt and distrust at the center of her being. As he spoke, she felt it unclench and release the small, but healthy, root of bitterness that had survived in its protective grip. She searched her heart for remaining splinters of pain that might fester and infect their love, but there was nothing left. Tears of relief and gratitude welled up, she reached across the space between them, took his hand. "Yes, Jake. I forgive you. Can you forgive me?"

"For *what?*" he asked, genuinely surprised.

"For acting like a fool, for believing the worst about you when I knew—I really *did* know—better. For acting like an emotional weathervane and switching my allegiance with every contrary wind that blew"—Jenny found herself laughing, almost to herself—"You know what? It's true: no one is perfect, not you and not I—and I'm so *glad* you forced me to listen to you. It's made me take a look at my behavior as well. We *are* a pair, aren't we, Jake? You're right. We do belong together. So, are you going to forgive me?"

Jake grinned, the smile so wide the corners of his mouth hurt. "Yes. I have to if we're going to spend the rest of our lives together."

"Is that a proposal?"

"I'll have to get out of the car if you want me to repeat it on my knees..."

"OK."

"Is that a yes?"

Jenny nodded her head, her smile matching his own.

"Good. I'm glad that's *finally* settled." Jake started the engine and pulled back onto the road. He glanced in Jenny's direction. Her expression told him she was waiting for his punch line.

"You don't want one of those big, fancy weddings do you? I ask because I was really serious about not wasting any more time. I thought if you weren't doing anything better, and Pastor Bell can work us into his schedule, we might get married as soon as possible. How does next weekend sound?"

Jenny sat back against the seat, folded her hands in her lap. "Fine."

"I'll pick you up for church in the morning, and we'll ask Bell about it afterwards."

"Good," Jenny said, matching his matter-of-fact tone, "I'm glad that's settled."

Jake reached over, took her hand in his and held it the rest of the way into town.

Jenny rang the operator, and asked for Dan's exchange. Her heart pounded against her breastbone in anticipation of the last unpleasant task left to perform. She had to release Dan before she could feel free to enjoy her engagement to Jake. She didn't know what she could say to him, how she could explain—

"Dan Johnson."

"Dan? It's Jenny. I'm sorry to bother you at home, but I have something to tell you, and it can't wait."

"You're not bothering me, Jenny. What's up?"

She cleared her throat, steeled herself—"I don't know how to tell you this, Dan, but I won't be seeing you socially anymore. I'm engaged—"

"Witherspoon, right?" Dan asked, his voice steady.

"Yes. I know it's a shock after what I said—"

"Not at all. Somehow I always knew it would work out this way."

"You're not *angry?*"

"Of course not. The best man won and all that," Dan paused, "Convey my congratulations to Jake."

"Thank you, Dan."

"Don't mention it. I hope everything works out. I don't mean to cut this short, Jenny, but you caught me in the middle of something—"

"I'm sorry! Of course. Well, thanks again, Dan. Good-bye."

"Good-bye."

He was hurt, she could tell, but he was trying to make it easier for her, and he had. Now she could get on with her plans for the wedding. One week! They must be crazy!

Dan replaced the receiver, leaned back in his chair, and reached for his pipe. He took the tobacco pouch out of his sweater pocket, unfolded it, removed some tobacco, and placed it in the bowl, tamping it down carefully. He reached for a box of matches, struck one, and held it over the tobacco, drawing on his pipe until it lit. He shook the flame out, stuck the pipe in his mouth, and contemplated his options.

It was too bad about Jenny; he'd really enjoyed her company. But something had to be done. And done soon. If what Jenny had told him was right, Jake was getting entirely too close. *And I'll be damned before I'll let Witherspoon take something away from me again. Before that happens, I'll destroy it.* Dan drew deeply on his pipe, savored the taste of smoke in his mouth, used the ball of his foot to rock his chair slowly back and forth. The motion helped him think. He had to think: too much depended on what he did next.

"Happy?" Jake asked, as they drove to the farm.

"Very." She squeezed his arm and snuggled closer in the front seat.

"You're not upset that we're getting married so soon? That it won't be a grand occasion?"

"It will be grand enough for me. Who are you going to have as best man?"

"Ben. He's been a good friend to me."

"What about Max? I thought he'd want to stand up with you."

Jake put his free arm around her shoulders and pulled her nearer: "I asked him to come down, but he's very involved with some things in Washington and isn't available on such short notice."

Jenny cocked her head and looked up at his face. "We could wait, if you want him to be here for you."

Jake smiled down at her. "I don't want to wait until next weekend, now that I know what I want. We'll see Max on our wedding trip."

"We're taking a wedding trip?"

"Didn't I mention it?"—(Jenny shook her head)—"Well, consider it mentioned"—Jenny poked his side with her finger—"And," Jake continued, laughing, "it will take a lot more than that to get me to say anything more about it, so you might as well behave."

Jenny laughed: "You are impossible!"

"Thoroughly. Tell me. Who are you going to have as your maid of honor?"

"Matron. I'm going to ask Bertha. No one's been better, or closer, to me since I moved here." (Jake nodded in agreement) "Jake, can we have someone else at the wedding?"

"I suppose so. But let's keep it small, OK?"

"I was thinking of asking Billy to give me away," Jenny tried to see his reaction. "What do you think?"

"I think it's a splendid idea! I owe a *lot* to that young man. Of course, invite him—and his family, too, if he'd like.

"As long as we're opening this up a bit, I'd like to have Annie and Bill. They practically raised me, you know. What about your folks? I never thought about the wedding being too soon for them to attend. Jenny, I'm sorry—"

"They wouldn't come. They're getting too old to traipse around the country, but since we're visiting Max on this mystery wedding trip...?"

"Done. I'd like to meet your family. You said they were scattered all over the place once. Maybe we should take the time and visit them all."

She smiled. "Not all at once. And not on our wedding trip. I want *some* time alone with you!"

"All right, if you insist," he kissed the top of her head. "So we have the Hawleys, the O'Caseys, Billy and his family—"

"Between Bertha's brood and Billy's crew, the church will be full!"

"Perhaps no one will come," Jake said.

"We can always hope," Jenny said. "I almost asked Dan yesterday, when I told him we were engaged—"

"You told Dan Johnson we were getting married?" Jake's stomach contracted.

"Of *course* I did," Jenny said, pulling away to see Jake's face better. "Why not? He had a right to know. I couldn't very well continue dating him, when I'm engaged to you, could I?"

"No, of course not. I was just surprised, that's all. I have a hard time remembering he was part of your life."

"If you hadn't come to your senses, he might have had your role," Jenny grinned, teasing him.

"How'd he take it?"

"Well, I think. He told me to convey his congratulations to you. He said he hoped things worked out for us. Should I invite him?"

"No. No, I think it would be kinder not to. It could only hurt seeing us together."

"That's what I thought. Maybe later we might be able to be friends with him. It's so silly, when you and he were once related, and now you're marrying me and—"

"Maybe we can. But, honey, don't pin your hopes on that idea. There are a lot of things between Dan and me. Things that won't just vanish because we'd like them to."

"I know. I just think it's a shame, that's all."

Jake drove into the driveway at his house and smiled as Annie and Bill ran out of the kitchen door to greet them. They'd been almost as happy as he was when he told them he was marrying Jenny. He watched, smiling, as Annie gathered Jenny to her, while Bill stood by fairly twitching to get his turn. But it was all Jake could do not to grab Jenny, put her back in the car, and drive until he knew she was not in any danger. The only ace he still held was that Jenny had not told Dan *when* they were getting married. He would have felt better if she'd said Dan had been angry about her news. Dan's calm scared him far more than his rage. *What am I going to do now? How am I going to protect her?* The thought froze his heart: somehow he knew that Dan's hatred of him ran deep, deep enough to make certain that Jake never enjoyed anything, or *anyone* again—not if there was a way he could ruin it for him. No, Dan would not wish him well, no matter what he'd said to Jenny. Dan's blessing felt more like a curse and the chill of it reached to the marrow of Jake's bones.

Billy listened intently as Mr. Witherspoon finished explaining, and nodded solemnly.

"Do you really think Mr. Johnson would hurt Jenny?" he asked.

"I hope not, Billy. But, yes, I do think it's possible."

"You know something, Mr. Witherspoon?"

"What?"

"I'd have thought you were off your rocker if you'd told me this last week, but…well, Mr. Johnson's been acting pretty strange lately."

"Strange how?" Jake focused to hear every word Billy had to say.

"It's not just one thing. It's a lot of things put together—"

"Like?"

"Well, for instance, Mr. Johnson hardly ever talks on the telephone at the office. At times I used to wonder why we even had one. The only time he used it was to call people he couldn't go see in person. Most of the time, it was off the hook—"

"Off the hook?"

Billy nodded, "Yeah, off the hook. He told me he didn't want people bothering him while he was writing. Most of the time, he forgot to put it back, like he didn't care whether anyone could call or not.

"But lately, it's like he's been *watching* the telephone, waiting for it to ring. Tuesday, I was on my way back to the press when I heard it ring. He was on that phone like a rooster on a June bug. He glanced around and when he saw me, he jerked his thumb at me like he was angry, telling me to go on. I heard him close his door. Whoever was calling, he sure didn't want me overhearing their conversation." Billy shook his head at the memory.

"Anything else?" Jake asked.

"Yessir. I saw him take a gun out of his desk drawer——"

"Did he see you?"

"No. I've been keeping out of his sight as much as possible lately."

"Good idea. What about the gun?"

"Well, sir, he checked it to make sure it was loaded, I think. Then he put it back in the drawer and locked it."

"He might keep a gun there for protection——"

"From what?" Billy asked, his mouth twisting with incredulity. "Who's going to hurt him in *Hulet*? Everybody knows everybody around here. *You* know nothing ever happens around here."

"Things happen, Billy. We just don't always hear about them."

"Oh *no*? Well, you can hear everything that ever happens anywhere near here every morning of the week at Wickham's general store! Those ladies know everything, I'm telling you, and if you don't, they'll be more than happy to fill you in on *all* the details. If you don't believe me, ask Mr. Wickham. He'll tell you. *Nothing* gets by those ladies.

"One day I was in the store when those ladies came to see Mrs. Wickham like they do, and Mr. Wickham begged me to stay so those ladies wouldn't start in on him." Billy shook his head. "Know what, Mr. Witherspoon?"

"What?"

"After hearing them go on that day, I wondered why Hulet needed a newspaper. Those ladies knew more than Mr. Johnson and I did, and they got their information from farther away than we did, too. If I wanted to advertise something, I wouldn't call the newspaper. Heck, I'd just tell it to Ruth Wickham. Before the end of the day, it would be all over the country.

"Want to know something else?" Billy continued, "Mr. Johnson knows about those ladies. When he's short of news for the paper?" (Jake nodded, listening) "Well, let's just say, he's been seen over at Wickham's a time or two, eavesdropping on the gossip. I know he does it. That afternoon he'll have the whole paper filled with what he heard over there. The only difference is Mr. Johnson writes it like it's an article." Billy grinned, "Pretty slick, huh?"

Jake smiled, "No flies on Dan Johnson, I guess."

"No sir," Billy's smile faded. "You really think he's going to hurt Jenny? I know he was pretty mad and all about her not seeing him——"

"Did he tell you that?"

"Gosh, *no*. He wouldn't tell me anything like that."

"Then how do you know he's angry?"

"Well, he likes to draw things…you know, like when he's thinking? He's pretty good. I see his stuff all wadded up when I take out the trash. When he started seeing Jenny, he'd draw pictures of her sometimes. Want to see one?" Billy reached for his journal, opened it and took out a wrinkled sheet of typing paper.

Jake straightened and leaned forward, "Sure."

Billy smoothed out the wrinkles and handed the paper to Jake.

It was a startlingly accurate likeness of Jenny.

"Pretty good, huh?" Billy asked, looking over Jake's shoulder.

"Not bad at all," Jake said, returning Jenny's portrait, "I never knew Dan could draw. He's a man of many hidden talents, I guess," he said, trying to keep the acid out of his voice. "So how did you know Dan was angry with her?"

"You said she told Mr. Johnson she wouldn't see him anymore last Saturday night?"—Jake nodded—"Well, when I got here Monday morning, Mr. Johnson passed me on his way out. He looked angry, but all he said was for me to get the articles on top of his desk and get busy. I saw his wastepaper basket was full when I picked up the articles, and I took it out to empty it. There was another picture of Jenny in the trash. It didn't show her so pretty. It had this big black X right through her face, just like he'd kept making it over and over. I didn't keep that one. It kinda scared me, if you want to know. Then Jenny told me you two were getting married and how she wanted me in the wedding and all and…well, I just figured Mr. Johnson was mad because she'd chosen you over him."

"I see," Jake said.

"Mr. Witherspoon? I don't want to think things like this, but...well, if I were you, I'd watch out for Mr. Johnson, too. He never has liked you very much, you know, and now that you've taken away his girl...well. Be careful, OK?"

"I will, Billy. You, too. Thanks for helping me with this."

"Hey, I'm not letting *anything* happen to Jenny. Don't worry, Mr. Witherspoon. I'll do like you said and keep my eyes and ears wide open. If I find out anything suspicious, I'll let you know first thing."

"Fine. Thanks, Billy," Jake stood up, stretched. "By the way, is your family coming to the wedding Saturday?"

"Are you kidding?" Billy grinned. "It's the only thing Ma talks about these days."

Jake watched the guests file into the church from the doorway behind the organ as Lula played the music Jenny had asked her to play. Jenny was right: the bride's side of the church was half full between the Wigginses and the O'Caseys. His side had fewer representatives. Annie and Bill Jackson seemed happy, but self-conscious, in the front pew he'd reserved for them. Grace Hawley sat beside Annie. Larry Branch sat on Grace's other side. Bill wore one of Jake's old suits. Annie looked wonderful in the new green dress he and Jenny had picked out for her when they went to buy Jenny's trousseau in Little Rock.

Jake smiled at the memory of Jenny's excitement that day. He'd enjoyed the day immensely himself, partially because he'd known she was safe. If everything worked out, she would soon be out of harm's way...at least from this source. His reverie was interrupted by the welcome arrival of Silas and Ruth Wickham, along with their daughters. Susie Wickham chose to sit on Jenny's side of the aisle, but to his surprise, the rest of the Wickhams chose to sit on the groom's side of the aisle. Elmer Wilson sat behind them. He wasn't alone for long; Doc Livsey arrived and sat next to Elmer.

A hand on his shoulder caused him to turn around. Ben Hawley's grin stretched across his entire face.

"Don't you know, you're not supposed to be out here, yet?" Ben asked. "What are you doing? Planning an escape route?"

"No, nothing like that." Jake closed the door so the guests wouldn't see them. "If you want the truth, I was looking at our guests."

"Surprised?"

"Amazed is more like it. I'm truly touched that so many people cared enough to come...Doc Livsey, Silas, even Elmer. With the way I've been for so many years...well, I didn't think it would matter one way or the other to anyone—"

"You're kidding of course?" Ben asked.

"No. I'm really *amazed* that anyone still cares. Of course, there's not much else to do in the winter around here..."

Ben laughed, clapped Jake on the back. "It's good to know that with all the new leaves you've been turning over lately, your basic stupidity is still intact. I don't know which is worse, the old, obnoxiously confident Jake, or the new, obnoxiously self-effacing one—"

"Am I to notice that the common thread between the old and the new is obnoxious?"

"Nah. If you weren't obnoxious, I wouldn't know you anymore."

"And I picked *you* as my best man?"

"Hey, did you have another choice?" Ben grinned again, "Besides, I've always liked Jenny. I wanted to make sure you didn't run out on her."

"I won't. I know what I have in her."

"You'd better," Ben said. "There are a lot of folks around here who are quite fond of you, Jake, for all sorts of ridiculous reasons—there's just no accounting for some people's taste. But Jenny's a different story. Jenny's... Well, since Will's death, the town's sort of thought of Jenny like a sister or a daughter, somebody special. Your life wouldn't be worth a plug nickel if you ever did anything to hurt her."

Jake clapped his friend on his shoulder. "Then I have *nothing* to fear. Say, I didn't see Mike out there. Is he coming?"

"No. He won't be here. But that's not all bad news…"

Jake lifted his eyebrows, "Oh?"

"Naomi said to tell you Mike's agreed to get some help. She wanted to know if we'd take him back in the firm, if he got sober."

"What did you tell her?"

"What do you think?" Ben smiled.

"Good. It'll be great to have the old grouch back."

Pastor Bell came up behind them. "Are you two going to stand here gabbing, or are we going to have a wedding? That's our cue."

The opening strains of the wedding march floated through the door, as the men entered the sanctuary and took their places at the front of the church.

Jake leaned over to Ben and whispered, "You *do* have the ring?"

Ben patted his pocket, and as Lula began again, all eyes turned to the back of the church as Bertha began her way down the aisle, followed a bit later by Jenny, escorted by Billy Wiggins. At first, Jake's attention was captured by the realization that Billy stood almost a head taller than Jenny, but as they drew nearer he could not take his eyes off this beautiful creature who would soon be his wife.

CHAPTER
TWENTY-NINE

Billy managed to slip away from the newspaper office shortly after eleven Monday morning. It was easier that he'd thought it would be. Mr. Johnson had asked him to go to Wickham's and buy some more pencils. When Dan told him to go ahead and take his lunch break at the same time, Billy wondered if Dan knew about his conversation with Mr. Witherspoon. But that wasn't it at *all*. Dan wanted Billy out of the office so he could make a telephone call. Billy heard him ringing the operator when he ducked back in for his forgotten cap. To his relief, Dan didn't see him. Billy grabbed his cap, left the office, and headed for Wickham's.

Silas waved as he walked in. The women were gathered at the far end of the counter sounding like a gaggle of geese.

"Billy," Silas said. "Good to see you. Ears burnin' were they?"

"What're you talking about, Mr. Wickham?"

Silas cocked his head in the ladies' direction: "Can't you hear?"

Billy glanced down the long counter, straining to hear what they were saying. He looked back at Mr. Wickham, shook his head.

Silas leaned over the counter, motioned for Billy to come closer. He lowered his voice to a whisper: "They're talkin' about the wedding. You shoulda heard them talkin' you up, sayin' how handsome you looked in your suit and all, how you looked all grown up. You'd be proud to hear them go on! And, for once in my life, I agree with them. You did yourself proud, Billy."

Billy felt himself flush, "Thanks, Mr. Wickham. Uh, is that what they're talking about today, the wedding?"

"Sure. But the *big* news is Jenny's wedding trip."

"Oh? Jenny didn't say anything to me about a wedding trip."

"From what I got from Ruth, Jenny doesn't know much about it herself. Jake told Ruth and me all about it after the wedding. We were eating cake, and he came right up to us and thanked us for coming and all, and then asks if we'll keep an eye on Jenny for him."

"Oh? Is Mr. Witherspoon going somewhere? I thought this was about a *wedding* trip? A groom can't go by himself, can he?" Billy asked.

"Course he can't! But it seems Jake has something real important to tend to before he can take off. He's going to have to leave Jenny alone here for a couple of days before they can get started on their honeymoon trip. They've been at the Witherspoon farm since the wedding. But Jake said Jenny wanted to stay at her place over the restaurant while he was out of town to finish packing for the move to their house. I guess she feels more comfortable being alone there. Jake told me he'd told the Jacksons to take some time off, too.

"I thought that was real nice of him. You know those folks've been takin' care of his family for as long as I can remember. Don't know as if I've ever heard of them gettin' a vacation. Yessir, I thought that was real nice of Jake. It's real good to see him back again, like he was before the accident."

"When's Mr. Witherspoon leaving? Did he say? I'd like to keep an eye on Jenny myself while he's gone. She's a real good friend."

Silas straightened up, looked smug, "I guessed that, seein' as how she asked you to give her away and all."

"Aw, she was just being nice."

"Well. I bet she'd appreciate you lookin' in on her though. Jake said he'd have to leave Thursday morning. He'll be gone until Sunday evening."

"That long, huh?"

"Yep. But he's planned a real nice wedding trip to make it up to Jenny."

"Where are they going?"

"Oh, all over, from what I understand. He said they'd stop in Eureka Springs first, then to St. Louis for awhile. I know he's got stops planned in Washington, D.C., and at her folks' place in Virginia, but that's just the *start*."

"Oh?"

"It's supposed to be a secret, but—" Silas thumbed in the women's direction—"it's not anymore. He's taking her to Europe for a Grand Tour!"

"No! He didn't say *anything* like that to me."

"Like I said, it was *supposed* to be a secret, a surprise for Jenny. I guess it's his wedding gift to her."

"I guess! Wow, she's really going to like that!"

They talked for a few more minutes while Silas got Dan's pencils, then Billy left, hopped on his bike, and peddled out of town.

When he got to the Witherspoon place, he hopped off his bicycle and ran up the porch steps. The door opened before he had a chance to knock.

"Right on time!" Jake said, clapping him on his shoulder. "Come in and have some cocoa and tell me what you know."

"Is Jenny, uh, Mrs. Witherspoon in there?"

"Of course. You wouldn't think I'd let her go back and open the cafe two days after the wedding?"

Billy grinned. "No. But I wanted to ask you something while she's not around."

"What's that?"

Billy lowered his voice, looked behind Jake's back to make sure Jenny wasn't standing there. "Are you really taking her to Europe on a Grand Tour?"

Jake laughed. "I guess that answers my questions. So the gossip telegraph is in prime working order?"

"Like I told you, I heard more at that store than even *I* knew." Billy grinned broadly. "So, is it true about Europe?"

"It's true, and it's all right. I told Jenny all about it."

"Does she know the plan?"

"She *had* to, don't you think? I couldn't pull this off without her cooperation, could I?"

"Guess not. Does anyone else know?"

Jake shook his head. "Nope. Just the three of us—you, Jenny, and I. I think it's safer that way, don't you?"

Billy nodded. "Do you think it's going to happen?"

"I hope I'm wrong. I hope *nothing* happens, and that Monday morning Jenny and I can leave town and just enjoy ourselves on our trip as planned." Jake paused, shook off the melancholy that threatened to mar his mood.

"How about that cocoa, Billy? You've certainly earned it." Jake put his arm around Billy's shoulder and ushered him into the house.

Billy was back at the newspaper office by one o'clock. Dan sat in his office making notes on a scratch pad. His office door was closed. Billy knocked on the glass and remembered the fight he'd witnessed between Jake and his boss last summer. A chill went down his spine. *I sure hope Mr. Witherspoon's wrong about all this,* he thought, as he saw Dan swivel his chair to see who had knocked.

Dan motioned for Billy to come in. Billy turned the knob and entered his office.

"Here are your pencils, Mr. Johnson," Billy said, handing the sack to Dan.

"Took you long enough," Dan said, looking in the sack. "What were you doing all this time?"

Billy clasped his hands behind his back and smiled, "I went out to the farm for lunch after I went to Wickham's. I thought you said for me to go on and eat afterwards?"

"That's right. I did. I forgot. That's OK, then."

Billy turned to leave—

"Wiggins," Dan said, stopping him, "anything interesting going on over at the store?"

Billy nodded, grinned, "Mrs. Wickham's bursting with all her news about the wedding—"

"Wedding? Who got married?"

Billy looked crestfallen. "Gosh, Mr. Johnson, I'm real sorry I didn't tell you before, but I thought it'd just upset you."

"Why would a wedding upset…? Are you telling me Jenny actually *married* that fool?"

Billy nodded, looked concerned.

"When? She just told me about the engagement a *week* ago."

"They got married at the First Presbyterian Church last Saturday morning. I guess Mr. Witherspoon didn't want a long engagement—"

"I guess not. Well. Am I to take it that you attended this event?"

Billy grinned, "Yessir. Jenny asked me to give her away!"

"Sold her down the river is more like it, as far as I'm concerned, young man…Well, get back to work." Dan turned back to his desk.

"They sure were excited about all of Jenny's plans over at Wickham's," Billy said.

"I'm sure they were," Dan said, picking up his pipe and lighting it. "Not much happens in this town. Talk about this ought to last for months," Dan looked over his shoulder at Billy. "Something else on your mind, Wiggins?"

"No, sir."

"Then get back to work."

"Yessir." Billy left the room, stopped at the doorway, "Do you want me to shut your door?"

Dan didn't turn around; the smoke from his pipe curled up beside his ear. "No. Just leave it. I have to go out in a minute anyway."

Billy crossed his fingers as he made his way back to the printing room.

Dan waited until Saturday night to make his move, until he was certain Jake was out town and Jenny was settled in her rooms above the cafe. He watched from the alley across the street as her lights went out and waited.

After this is over and Jake's taken care of, I have half a mind to pay Daugherty a last visit…if he'd done his part right, there wouldn't be any loose ends…There are too damn many loose ends to suit me.

The Smith job was perfect. No one could prove anything, and even that Means fellow, who might have caused a few problems for us, is pretty much finished. He sounds like a lunatic with all his cries of conspiracy, especially after Harry hung those juries. Hah! People sure are stupid.

I'll have to say Means did a good job for us, throwing those Senate dogs off our scent. Just for that, I'll let him live a while longer. Too bad his chauffeur had to go and get greedy on us.

Seems that just as I get one thread taken care of, Harry finds another sticking out somewhere that he thinks I need to cut off. If it weren't for his stupidity in trusting the Smith fellow—Dan shivered with the thought that came to him—*I never could stand fags! That guy was one, if ever I saw one. I would've done him for free...almost.*

That's another beef I need to take up with old Harry. When I signed on, I sure didn't figure on bumping off Morgan, or Andersen, or that Felder guy Harry got worried about down in Savannah. Not for the measly amount he gave me the last time for protecting his miserable hide. No, it's about time Harry and I parted company—permanently. After tonight there's only Jake and that Andersen woman who can trace anything to me.

Dan lit a match, shielding it from sight in the pitch-black alley, and looked at his watch: *Twelve-thirty. Too bad Jake is out of town for this one. I'd have liked him to see what I'm going to do to his precious wife. Too bad he won't hear her screaming like Laura...Killing Jake will be pure pleasure. I think she's been asleep long enough by now.*

Dan crossed the street to the cafe and blocked the cafe's front exit. He made no sound as he crept up the stairs beside Jenny's apartment and jammed the lock on her door. He went back down, pulled a trash barrel underneath the stairs, soaked some rags in kerosene and threw them into the barrel, along with a lit match. Flames shot upwards. He waited to make sure the stairway caught fire before going to the only other exit to the building, the back door that led to the kitchen.

I'll be long gone by the time they get this put out and find her body. And if something goes wrong and she wakes up, I'll just shoot her. It'll sound like an explosion from the fire.

He picked the lock quickly and entered the dark kitchen of the cafe. He could feel the familiar hard steel of his gun as he moved quietly through the kitchen to the stove. Only Jake suspected anything intentional about the fire; only Jake suspected the other murders were connected, and if he had anything to tie him to them, Jake would've moved on it. But Jake wasn't going to live long enough to tell anyone about his suspicions. *Just long enough to know how Jenny died, how she screamed in agony as she burned. I want to see his face. Then I'll kill him and find that pesky Andersen woman. They can't hide her forever,* Dan thought as he worked. *I'll collect from Harry. Give him the business. Bang! No more loose ends.*

He finished pouring a trail of kerosene through the restaurant and splashing some on the stairs that led up to Jenny's apartment. He walked back into the kitchen and picked up a kerosene lamp of Jenny's and lit it—

"Blow it out, Dan, or I'll drop you right here!"

Dan jumped, whipped around to see Jake standing at the door, holding a gun pointed directly at him. Dan held the lamp up, as if to see better.

"I wouldn't do that if I were you, Jake. I might drop this. And, well, you see my point?" Dan nodded toward the floor and the kerosene that snaked throughout the room and formed a puddle where Jake stood.

"I'm not interested in killing you, Dan. I want to see you stand trial—"

"For what? You can't prove anything, Jake, or you would've done it by now."

"I may not have enough to prove everything, like your tie-in with Daugherty..."—Dan's eyes flashed—"I see I've been on the right track... Let's just say I have enough to see you hang."

"Is that so?" Dan snarled. "For what?"

"For the murder of Joe Runyon, also known as Josef Andersen. I have his wife in protective custody. She saw you, Dan. She's an eye witness—"

"She's also out of her mind—"

"Was. *Was* out of her mind. That little trick you pulled at the cabin snapped her right out of it. She remembers everything."

"You'll never prove it. It's her word against mine, and I have this whole town to testify to what an upstanding citizen I am and—"

"Look. It's late. I just want to know one thing."

"What's that?" Dan's arm was getting tired holding the lamp. He had to figure out a way to drop the lamp without getting shot in the process. He wasn't willing to bet Jake would miss just yet. He backed up.

"I *said* don't move," Jake said.

Dan stopped, his back against the stove. "I'm not going anywhere."

"You have that right anyway," Jake said, moving closer and stepping out of the kerosene puddle. "Tell me. Did you really kill Laura, Sarah, and Teddy? Did you really murder your own flesh and blood to get at me?"

"God!"—Dan exploded—"You *are* one arrogant S.O.B! You think I'd kill my kin to get at you! No! *You* killed Laura and the kids! They weren't supposed to be anywhere near that house!

"What did you do, Witherspoon? Call Laura back and tell her to stay put and not go to your mother's place? Did you tell her you'd be coming home after all to play the part of the loving husband?"

"My God...Dan...Even with all I suspected, I never thought you had actually set the fire..."

Dan watched as Jake's hand lowered slightly. He threw the lamp on the floor. Flames spread like wildfire as Jake shot and missed. Dan lunged for the door, but Jake grabbed his arm, turned him around and hit him on the jaw. Dan swung at Jake, catching him on the right cheek.

Jake knew he had to stop Dan before he got to the door. He grabbed at his coat, heard it tear. Jake jumped on Dan's back, knocking him to the floor.

"I'll kill you, Jake!" Dan screamed in a voice unlike his, rolling over and grabbing Jake's neck with both hands.

"Like *hell* you will!" Jake yelled, rage giving him the strength to break Dan's grip on his neck. His knuckles smashed against Dan's nose. Blood was everywhere. Dan's eyes seemed to glow in fury. Jake heard the crack as Dan's fist connected with his jawbone.

The men grappled together on the burning floor, knocking into chairs, table legs, while the fire climbed the curtains, spread into the cafe, up the stairs to Jenny's apartment....

On Main Street lights were coming on, someone was ringing the fire alarm bell, people were shouting, trying to form a bucket brigade—

"Billy! Is that you?" Ben Hawley grabbed at the young man running past him in the street.

"Mr. Hawley! We've got to get in there! Mr. Witherspoon's in that fire!" Billy pulled at the older man's coat sleeves, trying to drag him toward the cafe that was now engulfed in flames.

Suddenly glass flew into the street and rained on the crowd as the windows blew out with the force of an explosion. The cafe darkened for a split second, and then flames roared back, sounding like some wild animal.

"Are you hurt?" Ben asked, seeing blood on the boy's forearm.

"I'm all right. Come *on*! He's in there, I tell you!"

Ben tried to grab the boy, but it was useless. All he could do was follow, as Billy ran toward the cafe. There was no way to get through the front of the building, so they ran around to the back. Ben noticed the remains of a barrel as he ran past the burning staircase in the alley. *This was no accident!* he thought.

"Billy! Wait up!" Ben shouted, but Billy had disappeared around the corner of the building. He followed.

Billy ran back and forth, looking for something. "I can see him! He's on the floor. We can get to him, if we can just get in. Gotta find something to help!"

"Are you *sure*, Billy? Are you *sure* Jake's in there?"

"Look for yourself. I don't have time to talk. I've got to get him out!"

Ben moved to a broken window, dodged flames trying to see into the smoke-filled kitchen. Billy smashed a bench through the window beside him. The frame and the boards below gave way. Billy rushed through the opening.

"Come on!" Billy yelled from inside the inferno, "I need your help!"

Ben stepped through the rubble, shielding his eyes from the smoke and flames. He grabbed his handkerchief, held it over his nose. Then he saw the boy. Billy held a man under the arms and was dragging him towards Ben.

Ben rushed towards Billy, and grabbed the man's feet. Together they carried him out into the alley and away from the building.

"Get this man some help!" Ben shouted, as someone ran toward them, and they laid the man down on the ground.

Billy ran back toward the cafe—

"Billy? Where are you going?"

"He's still in there, don't you *see*?" Billy ran toward the flames.

Another explosion ripped through the building, blowing Billy backwards onto the ground. The roof collapsed, and the building fell inward onto itself.

Ben ran to help Billy. The boy sat on the ground, hugging his knees to his chest, sobbing. Ben put his arms around him and tried to console him.

"You did everything you could," Ben said, patting the boy's back. "You got one of them out. That's all anyone could've done."

"But I couldn't get to him! I tried—" Billy voice cracked with sobs that jerked his body with each ragged breath.

Ben sat on the ground, holding the boy, watching while others tended to the man on the ground. The man's face had been battered and was covered with blood and soot. He hadn't thought to look hard. He'd just assumed it was Jake. *My Lord, if Jake was in there, where was Jenny?*

One of the people around the injured man ran toward Ben and Billy. It was Silas.

"Ben! Thank God, you're here. We're going to need your help in a minute to move him." Silas addressed Billy, who was hurriedly wiping the tears from his face, "Billy, he's asking for you. Come on now." Silas held out his hand.

Billy grabbed on and stood up. Silas put his arm around his shoulder, as they hurried toward the man on the ground. Someone was covering him with a blanket.

"That was a mighty brave thing you did, Billy," Silas said, "A mighty brave thing. You're a hero, young man. You can be proud of this day for the rest of your life."

Billy drew closer to the injured man, put his ear nearer his mouth, so he could hear him better.

"Did you get him out?"

Tears welled up in Billy's eyes, and spilled over, "No sir. I tried, but—"

"It's all right, son. Maybe it's better this way."

"He really *was* trying to hurt Jenny, wasn't he?" Billy asked.

Jake's eyes answered him before he uttered the words: "Yes, Billy, I'm afraid he was."

CHAPTER THIRTY

J enny ran to the telephone and grabbed the receiver, suddenly grateful that she hadn't dressed for bed.

"Hello?"

"Jenny? I'm sorry. Mrs. Witherspoon. It's Doc Livsey. I'm sorry to wake you."

"Is Jake all right?" she interrupted, trying to control the rising panic in her chest.

"He'll *be* all right, but for now, I think you'd better come down to my office."

"Wait! What's happened?"

"I think we should discuss all that when you get to town," Doc said. "Jake will be fine until you get here."

"I'll leave as soon as we hang up."

"Then we'd best do that. I'll see you when you arrive, Mrs. Witherspoon."

She heard the click of the disconnect, but the line did not go completely dead. She slammed the receiver back on its hook.

Five minutes later, Jenny was driving Jake's Duesenberg and heading toward town. She shivered, but it wasn't the cold. She tried to keep her mind from creating scenarios that grew worse as something new occurred to her. *He's alive, so stop making things worse than they are,* she told herself, but it didn't stop the images in her brain. It didn't stop her teeth from chattering either.

The lights were on in the doctor's office as she pulled in front and turned off the engine. Her hands were numb, and she nearly stumbled on the running board as she got out of the car. The air smelled of acrid smoke, but she didn't bother to find out why. She ran to the office and knocked on the door.

"Come on. Come on," she muttered under her breath.

Ben Hawley opened the door.

"He's all right, Jenny," Ben said.

Beyond Ben stood Billy, looking like a chimney sweep. He ran toward her.

For a moment, Jenny just stared. Tear tracks stained Billy's face through the grime. She felt as if she might faint...

"Jenny! Get a chair, Billy."

The voice sounded familiar. Some foul-smelling stuff cleared her head, but her stomach threatened to rebel.

"Jenny, it's Ben. Just sit still for a moment. I'll get the Doc."

"Where's Jake?" She managed to look up. Billy stood beside her, obviously ill at ease. "Billy?"

"Jenny, he's OK, really. Just a bit banged up, and Doc said something about breathing in too much smoke—"

"That'll do, Billy," Doc said, appearing out of thin air at Jenny's other side. "I'll take over from here. You go wash that face of yours. You'd scare *me* to death, if I didn't know what you'd been up to." He smiled up at Billy, who acted stunned for a moment before he ran to the washroom in back.

Doc turned back toward Jenny. "Now, young lady, let's see about you."

"I'm fine, Doc," she lied, "I'm just worried about Jake."

He cocked his head to one side, "Let's say for the moment that I believe you,"—he smiled and suddenly looked the part of the wise country doctor, which, now that she thought about it, he probably was— "and let's get Jake out of the way."

"I'd just as soon you didn't put it quite that way," Jenny said, not trying to be at all amusing. Doc and Ben laughed just the same.

"Jenny," Ben said, "we weren't lying. Jake really is all right."

"For the most part," Doc cut in. "I don't mean to worry you, but you want the truth, right?"

Jenny took a deep breath. "Right."

"He and Dan had quite a brawl in your place—"

"Dan?" she interrupted.

"We'll get to him in a moment. For now, I'm talking about Jake." (She leaned forward.) "When there's a fight like that, things get broken, and the men who are responsible end up looking like they've been in a fight."

"Just get to the point, Doc, please? Are you trying to tell me that Jake has broken something?"

"A couple of bones in his hand needed setting. I had to sedate him, so he'll seem a bit groggy—"

"And?"

"And he's inhaled too much smoke from the fire—"

"What fire?"

"I thought you wanted to hear about Jake?"

Jenny fought her growing irritation and the sudden desire to slap this kindly, old country doctor. "I'm sorry; please continue."

Ben interrupted. "Doc, all she wants to know is how Jake is, and whether he'll be all right."

"Is that all? Well, we've already told her he's all right, but that didn't seem to answer her questions, now, did it?"

Jenny stood up quickly and grabbed for the chair back. "Look. I realize I'm just his wife, but I'd like to see Jake, and I mean now. I can't sit here any longer; I want to see my husband!" She wasn't exactly yelling, but she was close, so the men parted.

Doc opened the door to his treatment area, and Jenny went in. The room was dark, and Doc started to turn on the light, but Jenny stopped him.

"Just leave the door open, Doc. I can see," she said, and moved to a chair beside the examining couch.

Jake lay there, his body covered up to his upper chest with a white sheet, which nearly matched his complexion. His head had a gauze patch near his left temple, and a nasty cut high on his left cheekbone had been stitched up. His badly swollen jaw distorted his face. His left hand was in a partial cast—probably his broken fingers.

His face bore traces of grime and soot, much like she'd seen on Billy. *The fire.* She wondered briefly if there was anything left of her cafe. She didn't care. He coughed, but it wasn't like any coughing she'd heard before; he sounded terrible. He kept coughing, but before she could do anything, Doc Livsey was there, followed closely by Ben. They lifted him so that they could insert another pillow behind his head. That seemed to help some. She looked up at the two men in front of her.

"Smoke inhalation," Doc said. "He'll cough for awhile, until his lungs get rid of it."

"But no permanent damage?" she asked.

He shook his head. "He looks a lot worse than he really is. His jaw was hit pretty hard, and that might bother him, but it wasn't broken. The swelling will go down before too long; he'll be out of that cast in about six weeks, and then he'll be as good as new."

"Thank you."

"He should sleep for a good long time. You can go home, if you want to, and I'll call you in the morning."

"But I thought you said I needed to come here?"

"That was my idea," Ben said. "I knew you'd never rest until you saw that Jake was OK, but there was another reason."

"Which was?"

"Let's go into the other room, where there's no chance of bothering Jake."

The three of them left the room, but Jenny insisted that the door be left ajar, so she could hear if he needed anything.

Billy sat in one of the waiting room chairs, looking much better with a scrubbed face. Jenny walked over to him and sat down beside him on an old sofa. She reached over and took his hand.

"All right, I want to hear what happened. In detail. Don't leave anything out."

Ben drove Jake out to the house after noon the next day. Jenny had barely had any sleep, but she had put on a fresh dress, along with a fresh face, and stood on the porch, holding the door open for the men. She noticed how heavily Jake leaned on Ben for support.

Jake started to grin, but his face crinkled into the stitches, so he winced instead. His jaw, still badly swollen and bruised, now displayed varying shades of purple blotches.

"Hi, honey," he said in a croaky voice. "Bet I feel worse than I look."

"Maybe, maybe not," she said, trying to keep a straight face. "You look pretty bad."

Ben grinned at her. "Shall I take him into your bedroom?"

"Hey, there! I'm fine. Let's all go into the parlor. I think I could use a drink."

Jenny frowned. "I'll bet you could, but you will have it in bed. Ben, just get him undressed and into the bed, will you? I'll bring him some soup in a few minutes."

"Soup?" Jake protested.

"Soup," Jenny said. "And if you can keep that down and your jaw doesn't give you too much trouble, then I'll give you something more, until you have enough on your stomach to have a drink."

Jake groaned as he and Ben made their way down the hall.

Jenny went into the kitchen and took a large gulp of her Scotch and water. Her hands shook so that ladling soup seemed like an insurmountable task. After a few minutes, the tremors subsided.

Ben walked in just as she took another sip.

"Caught cha."

Jenny shrugged. "Would you like a drink?"

"Absolutely."

"We've got Scotch—"

"That'll do just fine. Just don't let Jake know."

Jenny's eyebrows lifted. "I have no intention of telling my husband any-thing regarding what goes on in my kitchen." She paused. "I'll make you a deal; will you dip out some soup for Jake and put it on this tray? I don't think it's safe with me."

Ben smiled. "I can do that. Why don't you make my drink, while I take this to our invalid."

"Thank you, Ben."

"Nothing to it, Mrs. Witherspoon," Ben grinned. "Just wanted to say it once before I go back to Jenny."

Jenny smiled and started to get ice from the box.

"Oh, no ice and no water, either. I'm not shaking, but after last night, I really need that drink, too."—Ben ladled the soup—"Chicken?"

Jenny sighed. "What else? I don't know if it really helps with healing, but Bertha and my mother always said it did."

While Ben took the tray into Jake, Jenny poured Ben's Scotch into a regu-lar water glass. She was too tired to mess with the crystal whiskey glasses Jake was so fond of. She had barely poured the Scotch before Ben was back with the tray and the soup. He put the tray on the butcher-block worktable and poured the soup back into the pot, before joining Jenny at the smaller table Annie and Bill usually used.

"He didn't want anything?" she asked.

"He was asleep."

"Big drinker, that man."

"He would be, if he could just stay awake long enough," Ben downed his Scotch in one gulp.

Jenny held up the bottle. "More?"

"Sure."

After his second Scotch, Ben reached over and squeezed Jenny's hand. "It's over, you know."

"Is it?"

"Your part, at least. You and Jake are safe; Billy's safe—heck, I even think Fanny Runyon is safe, wherever she is."

"You don't know?"

Ben shook his head. "Jake never told me— or Larry, or Mike, for that matter. It's probably for the best. Look what happened the last time her whereabouts got out. Say, Jenny, could I trouble you for some of that soup?"

Jenny started to rise, but Ben stopped her. "I can get it. You want some?"

"As a matter of fact, I think I do. There's some bread, too, if you'd like a sandwich. I've got some leftover—"

"Chicken?" he chuckled.

"Actually, I roasted some beef the other night, and there's still some in the icebox."

"Do you have any cheese?"

"Of course. Toasted cheese sandwiches and soup. Why didn't I think of that?"

"You've had enough on your mind, lately," Ben said, looking into the breadbox and pulling out a loaf of white bread. He placed it on the wooden cutting board and sliced off four slices, while Jenny retrieved the cheese from the larder.

He took it from her, waved the knife towards the chairs where they'd been sitting, and started slicing.

"You know, Jenny. You've cooked for me nearly every day since you came to town. Why don't you let me do this?"

"Since you put it that way, I shall."

Jake woke up about an hour later. Ben had gone. Jenny sat next to their bed, watching him.

"How long have I been out?"

"Not long enough."

Jake tried to sit up but quickly decided against it.

"Is there a lot of pain, honey?" Jenny started to help him.

"Let's just say that the fight left me more battered than I remember. Funny. Nothing much hurt during the darned thing, except my jaw. It isn't broken, though."

"Well, it and your muscles are bound to be sore for a few days, you know," Jenny said, "and it can't help that you broke some fingers."

"I don't like lying here," he said. "I'm not an invalid."

"Doc said you'd be up and around tomorrow, so just rest and let me play nurse for today, OK?"

Jake attempted and failed to smile. "The swelling and these doggoned stitches!"

"They make you look like a man of mystery."

"Some mystery. I got the wrong end of a few punches."

Jenny laughed. "Is there a right end?"

"Guess not. Say, didn't you mention something about food before I conked out?"

While Jenny left to get his food, Jake relived the events that left him with a bit of discomfort but that had taken Dan's life. He tried, but he found no remorse at his late brother-in-law's demise. Dan's mind—at least the part that should have been a conscience—had been damaged or something. *How does someone with so much talent become so warped?* Jake lay there thinking of what Dan's actions had cost: Laura and his children, in the first fire set by him. Joe Runyon—thank God, Fanny had escaped with her life, but would she ever forget the terror and horror Dan had brought into her life? Jake hoped so, but thought not. Jesse Smith? Probably. Clarence Morgan. Certainly. And Slo-Joe Freeman, who had hanged for Dan's crime. How many others? When had Dan decided that human life had no value? Thank God, Jenny's name had not made Dan's killed list. And why had *his* life been spared? Sadness overwhelmed him as memories of Laura, Sarah, and Teddy filled the room.

"Jake?" Jenny stood in the doorway of the bedroom. "Honey, what is it?"

Jake jerked at the sudden return to the present, and realized tears were running down his face. He brushed at them with his good hand. "Oh, memories," he said, his forehead creasing as he tried to compose himself. "Sometimes

I wonder whether or not everyone would have been better off if I'd never re-gained them."

"If you hadn't, the killing would have kept on."

"You think it won't now?"

"I think that Dan was the murderer—how foolish of me to think he was something fine, even for a minute!"

"Yes, he was...a murderer. I need to keep reminding myself of that."

"No, you don't. Dan's dead. He can't hurt anyone anymore. *You* did that! If you still had amnesia—Oh Jake!—if you still had amnesia, I would have never known you! Dan would have kept on doing—whatever he did for whomever he did it—wrecking or ending more lives, and I'd have ended up a bitter old maid, or worse."

"Worse than an old maid?"

Jenny nodded as the narrow escape she'd had filled her consciousness: "I could have married Dan. I came so close!"

"You wouldn't have really married him, would you?" Jake considered the horror of the possibility.

Jenny shook her head. "I honestly don't know. If you hadn't been there; if you hadn't loved me...I don't know."

"So something good did come from all of this misery?"

"I think so. Unless you are regretting our marriage?"

Jake laughed, which caused him to start choking. Jenny pounded on his back. "Hey, watch it, woman! I'm fragile."

Jenny stopped pounding and looked at him as his coughing bout subsided.

"Fragile, my eye, husband."

Jake's jaw and fingers healed quickly, and Doc released him from patient status. It took a week or so more to work out the stiffness in his fingers, but the day arrived when nothing hurt, his lungs were clear, and he felt like a change of scene.

"Jenny," he said, as they walked toward the river where he used to skinny-dip as a boy, "how would you like to meet my friend Max?"

"Isn't he in Washington, D.C., or something?" she said, turning to look up at his face. The stitches had left a scar, but it added character rather than disfigurement to her husband's face.

"So he is. I'd thought we'd stop in Virginia first, where I'll have the pleasure of meeting your family, then up to D.C., where you'll have the pleasure of meeting Max, and then take that honeymoon trip we planned—"

"Really? I decided the trip was a fiction you'd cooked up to sweeten your plot."

"Partly, but I always intended to treat you to a real honeymoon."

"Oh, yes? And where and when did you think this might occur?"— Jenny looked around as she asked. This was *their* land. She'd never owned land before—"Jake, this countryside seeps into your soul, you know?"

He pulled her closer and put his arm around her waist. "I'm glad you like it," he paused. "Does this mean you don't want to have a honeymoon trip?"

"No, and I won't be cheated out of it, now that I know it's real. I really didn't know I'd said that aloud, about our land."

"So you're happy, Mrs. Witherspoon?"

Jake leaned down and kissed his wife. They stood holding each other for a while, until Jenny grew restless.

"Just where did you plan to take me on this trip?"

"You mean after our stop in D.C.?"

"Yes. And are we going to be gone long?"

"I'd thought about taking a steamship across to England, then crossing the Channel to France and meandering down the coast to Italy—"

"Could we go to Ireland? Scotland, even?"

"I don't see why not, but don't you want the Grand Tour?"

"Not particularly. I want to see where Bertha's from in Ireland. I've always thought Scotland would be romantic—"

"And cold."

"I don't care! I want to see the places I've read about, including London and Paris and Rome and Venice and—"

"You *do* want to come back here sometime in this half of the century?" Jake looked down at her with an expression Jenny hadn't seen before.

"Oh, is it too much? I didn't mean to carry on so!"

"No, it's not too much, but perhaps we could save some of it for another trip?"

Jenny smiled up at him, "Then you're not upset?"

"Heaven's no, woman! I plan on making the most of your newly found penchant for travel!"

Jenny laughed. She could see the bright silver thread of the river glinting below them. Winter was ending. The air smelled like spring.

"Jake."

"Hum?"

"I wanted to ask you something."

"Ask away."

"If I can, and there's a chance I cannot, you know...Do you want to have more children?"

Jake halted and looked down at her.

"Of course...As many as you want...But if the Lord decides not to give us any, I don't want you to worry. I love you. I loved you from the moment you entered our house after Mother died. So don't worry about children. They will come or not as God wills—you and my mother taught me that."

They stood together, looking down at the river.

"I think you should call Annie and Bill," Jake continued, "and see if they're up to taking care of things while we're away. And while you're at it, you need to plan a week when we can start shopping for more items to add to your trousseau, Madam. We'll pick up more along the way, but I don't want Max to think I'm not showering you with the lovely things you deserve."

"Jake! Really?"

"Really. I'll call Max and the steamship lines, and we'll be on our way before you know it!"

"Jake?"

"Yes?"

"If Annie and Bill need some help or can't do this, would you mind if I asked Bertha and her tribe to help us out? Since the cafe burned down——"

"Of course! I don't know why I hadn't thought of that myself. Annie and Bertha would have a fine time together, and their coffers will not be empty on our account."

They were nearly at the river's edge. Jenny had no idea how far they'd walked, but she felt invigorated instead of tired.

"Race you to the river! Last one there's an old man!" And Jenny took off.

Jake stood there watching her for a second, then started after her.

EPILOGUE

Jake and Max Howe, both in formal evening wear, sat in Max's parlor waiting for Jenny while she changed for dinner.

"I shall have to hand it to you, Jacob," Max said, saluting Jake with his drink. "Jenny lives up to everything you said about her."

"I had a feeling you two would get along," Jake said, raising his own drink in reply.

They drank for a moment in silence.

"It is quite unfortunate about Dan Johnson dying in the fire," Max said.

"Um," Jake nodded in agreement. "We'll never be able to get Harry Daugherty without his testimony. But even if Fanny had been able to identify Dan, her testimony against anyone other than him would have been useless. She really didn't know that much."

"Still, it is too bad that she could not identify him—confront the man who did her so much harm."

"Perhaps, but it's better for her, don't you think? Now she can go on with her life without having to look over her shoulder all the time." (A vision came to him of the woman he'd come to think of as a friend.) "And," he continued, "I have the satisfaction of knowing that the man responsible for so many deaths is dead. The courts couldn't have exacted a higher penalty." Jake sipped his bourbon, thinking.

"Did he admit to killing them?" Max asked.

"Not in so many words," Jake said, "but he admitted setting the fire that killed Laura and the children. I know that. I can lay them to rest at last—"

"The bride, I presume," Max said, getting to his feet as Jenny entered the parlor.

She wore an emerald green satin evening gown, with a stunningly uneven hemline that showed the curve of her leg. Her auburn hair was piled on top of her head in a becoming style. A striking diamond and emerald necklace—Jake's wedding gift to her—graced her neck. A matching dinner ring on her right hand did not detract from the simple but elegant wedding ring on her left. She took Jake's breath away as she walked toward him, a brilliant smile lighting her eyes, and placed her hand in his.

"Well, gentlemen," she said, "I'm ready to enjoy the evening."

Max bowed in a courtly manner. "Your wish is our command, Madame."

Jenny laughed, "For the moment anyway."

Max glanced at Jake, "I believe, dear friend, that your wife doubts our sincerity."

"You mistake me, Max!" Jenny said, sitting down so the men could do the same. "It's just that I've grown all too used to things not working out exactly as, and when, Jake plans."

Jake smiled and recaptured his wife's hand as he sat down beside her. "Guilty."

"Forgiven," Jenny said.

"Well, Max," Jake said, "now that we've been so gauche as to speak only of what we've been doing, you must fill us in about you. What have you been up to?"

Max started to speak, but Smithers interrupted. "Dinner is served."

Max rose and gave Jenny his hand to help her up. "May I escort you into dinner, Mrs. Witherspoon?"

"You may, Mr. Howe."

"Fine thing, taking possession of my bride like that," Jake said, as he followed them into the lavishly appointed dining room, filled with freshly cut flowers, gleaming crystal and silver, and fine Sèvres china.

"Privileges of the host, my friend," Max said, not bothering to turn around.

Max pulled Jenny's chair out for her and took his place at the head of the table. Jake took his seat to Max's right.

"Max, I'm serious about hearing about your life and recent exploits. I know you too well not to understand that there must be a lot going on that you're not telling."

"I'd love to know more about you, too, Max. You and Jake have been such friends for so many years! I'm a bit jealous, I confess, and I'd like to catch up a bit. I'd like to be able to say you are my friend, too."

"You should know, Jenny, that I considered you a friend the moment you walked into my home with this reprobate husband of yours. Are you looking forward to the opera tonight?

"Definitely," Jenny said, "It will be the first time I've had the opportunity, but now we *do* want to hear about your exploits. Jake won't tell me much of anything."

"I'll tell you all about them soon, I promise," Max said. "But tonight, we'll talk only of you, and, of course, the opera." Then he signaled for the wine to be poured.

THE END

AUTHOR'S NOTE

This novel is entirely a work of fiction. However, there really was a man named Gaston Bullock Means (1879-1938), who worked as a detective in the Pinkerton Detective Agency, and then as a Justice Department investigator for Harry M. Daugherty, the actual Attorney General under President Warren G. Harding (1865-1923). The claims attributed to Means came from his book, *The Strange Death of President Harding*, (as told to May Dixon Thacker), originally published in New York in 1930 by the Guild Publishing Corporation. Later editions (1931) were published by Gold Label Books, Inc. I happened upon an original 1930 copy in a rare bookstore about 1992 or so.

Means wrote that Daugherty had engineered the deaths of Jesse W. Smith and Thomas B. Felder, and also accuses Daugherty of much more than his role in the Teapot Dome scandal.

Means's theories offered an interesting path to explore, but Clarence Morgan, Slo-Joe Freeman, and Joe Runyon, a.k.a. Josef Andersen, are all creations of my imagination, as is the character of Dan Johnson. Means's allegations against Daugherty provided a plausible subplot for my novel and nothing more. My use of these should in no way be construed as my actual beliefs regarding the late Mr. Daugherty or events surrounding the Harding administration.

I should also point out that most of Means's theories, allegations, etc., are now regarded as wholesale imaginings of a gifted conman. If you should get the opportunity to read his book, you can decide for yourself.

The towns of Hulet and Mill Creek, Arkansas, and their citizens are completely products of my imagination.

ACKNOWLEDGMENTS

No one really writes a book without help from numerous people; I am no exception.

The seed for the book was sown when my father, now deceased, told me this strange story about a man he knew when he was a boy, visiting relatives in Arkansas. The man whom he called "crazy" turned into Jake Witherspoon: Jake's calendar tending, the businesses who waited to open until the dates were changed, the library "consultant" to lawyers—all were true of this strange man.

So many kindhearted people read the many incarnations of this story that I truly can't remember all their names, but I am grateful to them all. Jan Lee, Ed Hawkins, Jonathan Broughton, Lydia Payton, Rebekah Gamble (who not only read the manuscript, but retyped the entire thing into a new format), Pat Gamble, and Tina Bennett were particularly helpful. Many thanks, too, for the many prayers offered! Without them, this book would never have been available.

My thanks to the design and editorial team who helped give shape to this book; and many thanks to Posey Gaines, my web designer and fellow watercolorist.

My sons and their families, and, of course, my husband, have put up with me, encouraged me, and been helpful critics when I most needed them. And to my grandchildren, whose talents surprise and delight me daily, and teach me to keep honing my own, thank you.